LOSING IT

CRYSTAL KASWELL

Copyright

This is a work of fiction. Similarities to real people, places, or events are entirely coincidental.

Also by Crystal Kaswell

Sign up for the Crystal Kaswell mailing list

Chapter One

QUINN

I don't want to go to med school a virgin.

I don't want to screw a stranger.

I don't want to find a boyfriend.

Westley Keating, will you please do me the honor of taking my virginity?

I swallow another sip of gin and tonic. Fail to find liquid courage.

Wes is right there. On the couch. A mere ten feet away.

But he might as well be on another planet.

Dear Wes, I'll cut to the chase. Will you please take my virginity?

It's two sentences.

It's easy.

In theory.

I mean, if I were a completely different person.

If I were Wes, maybe.

He laughs at something. The pretty blonde sitting next to him.

She smiles and paws at his forearm.

He shrugs her off. Runs a hand through his sandy hair.

His blue eyes scan the room. Catch mine.

He holds up his drink. *Come here* or *hey* or *I hope you're having fun.*

Hell, knowing Wes, it could very well be *what are you doing after this? Want to help me celebrate my birthday in style? And by "in style" I mean in my bedroom naked?*

He's not shy.

Whereas I…

Fuck, my cheeks are burning. My chest is burning. My everything is burning. Anyplace capable of blushing —it's red.

The curse of auburn hair and fair skin.

God, he's still looking at me.

I hold up my drink. Nod… something.

I must get the point across, because he nods back.

Then he turns to his friends and launches into a story.

The women laugh.

I…

I need another drink.

Then I'll be able to do this.

Totally.

I move to the counter. Refill my glass. Add another ice cube. More gin. More tonic water. Even more gin.

The room spins with my next step. But that must be my imagination. Alcohol doesn't absorb this quickly.

I turn back to Wes. Plaster on my best *woohoo, let's party* smile (it's not great).

He doesn't see it.

He's moving. To the balcony. With a friend.

No, that's his brother, Chase. He's equally tall and broad, but he's dark in all the places Wes is light.

They're having a private conversation.

I shouldn't interrupt.

I should think up another twenty excuses for why I can put this off.

I swallow another sip. Recite my request. Follow Wes and his brother across the crowded room.

The speakers boom with a song from high school. It's good, catchy, jazz inspired. But way too familiar.

It threatens to drag me back to prom night. To my date's awkward dancing and the stuffy hotel ballroom and a kiss with too much tongue.

He wasn't sexy.

Prom sure as hell wasn't sexy.

But Wes?

Wes is the hottest guy on the planet.

God, just watching him lean over the balcony—

Ahem.

I'm doing this.

I can do this.

Deep breath. Steady exhale. Long sip.

I step onto the balcony.

Wes's head turns. His lips curl into a smile as his eyes meet mine. "Hey Quinn."

"Hey." My fingers curl into my drink. The glass is too slick. I can't get a grip.

Wes's brother Chase nods a hello. "Can you give us a minute?"

Wes shoots him a dirty look. "Not doing it. Stop asking."

"I, uh…" I'm interrupting. I think.

"Chase was just leaving." Wes motions something to his brother.

His brother shakes his head *your funeral*, but he still steps away from the balcony.

"It's nice to see you." Chase nods a goodbye as he passes. "Have a good night."

Wes waves his own goodbye. There's something in it. A friction. But I can't quite place the nuance.

I take another step toward Wes.

Until I'm next to him.

My hands find the smooth metal railing.

It's a beautiful night. Clear. Warm. Dark.

The sky smells of salt. And Wes's sandalwood shampoo.

Fuck, he smells good.

"Sorry about Chase." He turns so his body is facing mine. "He always has a problem."

"Did I interrupt?" I ask.

He shakes his head. "Just work stuff." Frustration flares in his bright eyes. Then he blinks, and it's gone. "I like your dress." He gives me a long, slow once-over.

"Thank you." My blush deepens. This is the sexiest thing I own—a black swing dress and red wedges—but it doesn't feel like enough. Not for this.

"How have you been?" He takes a long sip.

God, what a question. I don't have time to answer. I don't want to think about the answer.

I need to cut to the point.

I'm not usually this nervous. I mean, I'm usually nervous. But not this nervous. It's just that I'm working up the courage to ask you to screw me.

That's improvement.

Sorta.

"Quinn?" he asks.

"Yeah?"

"Must be a lot, starting med school next year," he says.

"Yeah." I swallow another sip, but it does nothing to dissolve the tension in my shoulders. "Next month."

"Fuck. What's that like?"

Uh… No comment.

"You okay?" His bangs fall over his bright eyes as he tilts his head to one side. "You need more alcohol or less?"

"What if I needed less?"

"Then I'm shit out of luck." He moves closer. Brings his fingers to my wrist.

My heart thuds.

My stomach flutters.

My limbs get light.

Wes is touching me.

Wes. Is. Touching. Me.

"If you want more—" He turns to the patio chair, pulls back the Kelly-green fabric to reveal a bottle of brown liquor.

I try to finish what's left of my gin and tonic, but an ice cube invades my mouth. Makes it too hard to swallow.

I gag.

Cough.

Just barely manage to avoid spitting on the balcony.

The perfect display of my sexual prowess really.

I can't swallow a cocktail.

How can I…

God, I can't even think that.

I can't possibly say *dear, Wes, please, please, please teach me how to suck cock. It's clearly going to take a while because I'm choking on an ice cube. But I promise I'm an excellent student.*

Wes just laughs. "You can slow down."

I can't. That's the thing. I have to do this. Tonight.

I only have four weeks left in California.

I need to seize the day.

Night.

Whatever.

"You sure you're okay?" he asks again.

I nod, but that doesn't sell it.

He tilts his head to the other side.

His blue eyes fill with concern. Then he blinks, and it's gone.

It's strange.

Unlike him.

Or maybe I'm imagining things.

Wes uncaps the bottle, refills his glass, offers it to me.

I swallow my last sip. "Yes, please."

He pours.

"I, um…" I take a long sip. I think that's rum. Or maybe whiskey. What the hell is the difference anyway? "I want to ask you something."

"Oh?" His lips part.

God, those lips look soft.

Kissable.

He's handsome.

And pretty too.

"Yeah, um." I swallow another sip. It's not as smooth as the gin. It burns more. "I've been thinking about this for a while."

His blue eyes fix on mine.

I look up at him. Try to hold eye contact.

It's too much.

My eyes go right to his chest.

To the tattoo peeking out from his t-shirt. Black lines. Words. Or maybe shapes.

It's hard to tell in the dark.

What do they say?

What do they say about Wes?

Is he more than the cocky party animal he pretends to be?

The thought makes my stomach flutter.

But getting to know him is out of the question.

This is all wham, bam, thank you ma'am.

I want you to take my virginity.

One sentence. That's it.

I take another step toward him.

My knees knock together.

The ground is weird. Floaty.

"Hey." He wraps his arms around my waist. Catches me.

God, he's so close.

And he smells good.

There's something earthy in his shampoo.

Something I need more of.

"The thing is..." I force myself to look into his eyes, but it's like staring into the sun. His baby blues are that pretty.

"Yeah?" He stares back at me.

I buckle.

He pulls me closer. "Come on, I'll put you in a cab."

"Right. Sure." That's a good idea. A car. To take me home. And far away from this embarrassing scene.

Far away from my only chance.

I can't let that happen.

I just have to blurt it out. It's one sentence. It's no problem. "Wes—"

"Yeah?" He pulls me closer.

"Will you take my virginity?"

Chapter Two

WES

Will you take my virginity?

Blood flees my brain at an alarming rate.

My balls tighten.

My cock stirs.

Fuck, I'm too close.

The innocent look in Quinn's hazel eyes is doing shit to me.

Shit she's going to feel.

Usually, that means *go time*.

Usually, I pull a woman close, whisper something dirty in her ear—*baby, you're making me so fucking hard*—pin her to the wall, and...

Well, go.

I want to tease Quinn. Touch her. Taste her. Rub her until she's screaming my name.

But she's not ready for that.

Not even close.

"Oh my God." Her cheeks flame. "I'm sorry. I should go—"

"I'll walk you down."

"No, I..." She takes a step backward. Stumbles. Reaches for the railing.

I grab her wrist harder than I mean to. "Slow down."

She looks up at me. Nods. "I..."

"I'm putting you in a cab or driving you home."

Her gaze shifts to the glass in my hand. "You've been drinking too."

That's a good point. "Putting you in a car. Come on."

She looks at me funny, like she's not sure when I got so bossy, but she still follows me.

I cut through the crowd.

A few people nod hello. Cheer *Happy Birthday*. Hold up their glasses and drink in my honor.

It's flattering.

But it's empty too.

I don't know these fucking people.

I'm not sure what they're doing here.

Or why they care I'm turning twenty-four.

Quinn holds me a little tighter.

Or maybe I pull her a little closer.

It's hard to say.

I lead her out the door, down the stairs, all the way to the curb.

She slips her purse off her shoulder. Pulls out her phone. Fumbles over the buttons.

"Let me," I say.

Her eyes stay on the ground as she nods.

I take the cell.

She clears her throat. "Wes, I—"

Hell yes.

Let's go now.

I'll get in this car with you.

Whisk you to your bedroom.

Fuck you senseless.

10

"You working tomorrow?" I ask.

"In the afternoon."

"Come by the shop. I have an hour free at noon."

"Are you sure?" she asks.

Hell yes. "We'll talk tomorrow." I call a ride share. Thank God for technology. It already knows her address.

It's close. About a mile east, just past the line that divides Santa Monica and West LA.

Ding.

Your driver arrives in one minute.

Fuck. There isn't much time.

"I think maybe…" She brushes her red hair behind her ear. "Maybe I should actually…"

I want to pull her close and whisper *hell yes, baby, I'm dying to be your first* in her ear.

But she's already terrified.

I need to take this slow.

It's impossible.

I've dreamed about fucking Quinn since we were teenagers. Our parents were college friends. They got together every year to catch up. They always brought us along.

I thought she was too smart for me.

That there was no way prim, proper Quinn Thorn would give me the time of day.

Now she's asking me to take her virginity.

Fuck, I'm already losing touch with conscious thought.

My body is raring to go.

The phone dings as a Prius pulls up to the curb.

"Noon to one." I pull the door open for her. "You know the address?"

She nods. "Everyone knows where Inked Hearts is."

I shoot her an incredulous look.

She returns a sheepish smile. "I can't consider a tattoo?"

"You have to make me a promise, Quinn."

"Yeah?"

"You'll go to me first."

"Of course."

I offer my hand.

She shakes.

She's talking about that tattoo.

But that's not where my head goes.

———

Happy fucking birthday.

I pound another shot.

Griffin pats my back. "Drinking your way to alcoholism."

I flip him off. The guy is my best friend, but he's not exactly possessing tact. He says whatever flits through his mind. No matter how rude.

I mean, he's rarely wrong.

But he could watch the phrasing.

Yeah, my brother Hunter is celebrating one year sober while I drink myself stupid.

But hey, Hunter isn't here.

Griffin takes a swig of his beer. "You enjoying any of this?"

There are a dozen people downing shots. I like three of them. Barely know the rest.

It's normal party shit.

But after Quinn's request—

This isn't fun.

Or thrilling.

Or intoxicating.

No, that's on point.

I lost track a few drinks ago, but I know enough to know I'm drunk.

Despite my family history (Mom has a problem too, but she's far from admitting it), I'm not a lush.

I drink a lot, sure, but only at parties or when I'm enjoying the taste.

I don't need it to numb some deep-seated pain.

Or cure some emptiness.

There's no fucking emptiness.

Just—

There isn't a fullness either.

Fuck, I sound like Griffin.

I'm not going there.

It's my birthday.

Quinn Thorn wants me to pop her cherry.

This is a cause for celebration.

I motion to the guy with the bottle of bourbon. Jim Beam. The shit Hunter used to drink.

It doesn't taste like a good time anymore.

It tastes like disappointment and bitterness and everything getting fucked-up.

"Fuck, you're in a mood." Griffin brushes a dark strand behind his hair.

"Fuck, you're an asshole." I swallow the rest of my drink. Which makes the room spin faster.

Too fucking fast.

This is my limit. Past my limit.

I need to slow down.

But there's no way in hell I'm admitting that to Griffin.

"That's why you love me?" he asks.

"In your dreams."

"I know you do." He reaches out and musses my hair. "I love you too."

I slap his hand away.

He chuckles. "You're too easy."

"I try."

He motions to the no longer occupied couch. It's late—well past midnight—but the room is still packed.

Griffin plops on the couch. Folds one leg over the other. "You're thinking about something."

"I am not."

"Yeah." He holds up his beer. "Saw you talking to Quinn."

"And?"

"And you've fucked yourself to her since you were a teenager."

"You didn't know me when I was a teenager."

"I've heard things," he says.

I flip him off.

He laughs, not at all bothered. "She's cute."

I study his expression. Try to see what he's getting at.

But there's no getting at with Griffin.

He says what he thinks.

"She's fucking gorgeous," I say.

"Maybe I'll give her a call." He takes a swig of his beer. "Since you're not thinking about her."

"Over my dead body."

"What did she say?" he asks.

"Go fuck yourself."

"I will. Later."

"Jesus."

He shrugs. "Got a girl begging for a video."

I don't need to know that.

"Think I'll shoot it tonight."

I really don't need to know that.

His laugh gets louder. Heartier. "You can admit you have feelings."

"Can we not do this?"

"What is this?" he asks.

"The thing where you make something dirty and beautiful into something sweet and disgusting."

"Dirty how?" His interest perks. It's hard to tell with Griffin—the guy is as steady as they come—but it's there.

"None of your business, that's how."

"She wants to fuck you?"

"Who wouldn't?"

His chuckle spills through the room. "You're usually jumping to brag about a woman that hot wanting to fuck you."

I shrug like I don't care.

"You're so full of shit."

"Maybe I want to enjoy the thoughts in my head."

"Maybe you actually like her."

"Maybe you should go fuck yourself."

"I can shoot the video here if you want."

Gross.

"I hate to do it in the bathroom mirror, but she's getting desperate." He pulls out his cell and taps a text to his paramour.

I only catch a flash.

Fuck, sweetheart, you're making me so hard. I'm gonna split you in half.

That's too much information.

Way too much information.

"Put that thing away." I motion to his phone.

"Funny, she's asking me to take it out," he says.

God dammit, I don't need to hear this.

"How about we make a deal?"

"How about—"

"I go fuck myself? You're really into that."

I can't help but laugh. And flip him off.

He lets out that low, hearty chuckle. "I put *it* away. You tell these assholes to leave."

"I don't care if they stay."

"I don't want to shout over this shit." He motions to the speakers, which are currently blasting one of Chase's playlists.

A guy groans about wanting his ex to die miserable and alone as a guitar screeches.

It's not hard to see why this music appeals to Chase—my brother is the picture of unforgiving—but why does anyone else like this shit?

All that bitterness isn't healthy.

That level of attachment isn't healthy, period.

I don't need that kind of passion or heartbreak or hurt.

I have enough from—

Well, I'm not getting into that tonight.

"Put something else on," I say.

He nods. "Then I ask everyone to leave and you give me every detail on the hot redhead."

I nod. "Deal."

Chapter Three

QUINN

For a split second, my eyes flutter open.

Bright light floods my senses.

It's too much light. Way too much.

I press my eyelids together. Shuffle to the counter.

My fingers brush slick tile. Then plastic.

It curls softly on one side. Loops on the other.

That's the electric kettle.

But I can't fill it with my eyes closed.

I take a deep breath.

Let out a steady exhale.

On three.

One, two—

Fuck, it's bright.

My eyes squint shut again.

My head throbs.

The brightness makes it worse.

Or maybe it's that I made it to twenty-two without learning how to cure a hangover.

They're caused by dehydration.

Maybe I can get to work early and beg Doctor Lee to hook me to an IV. Owen swears by that. Or he did. Before he settled down with the coolest, smartest, sweetest boyfriend ever.

Lucky bastard.

Don't get me wrong. I love my brother. I love my brother-in-law. I just hate how easily everything comes for Owen.

Excellent MCAT scores. First choice med school. Residency at a great hospital.

He works nonstop.

He loves it.

I'm supposed to feel the same.

I'm supposed to be thrilled to start school.

Four weeks of summer.

Then four years of med school. Residency. Actually being a doctor.

Working every waking minute.

Slaving to medicine.

Never, ever stopping to breathe.

I try to inhale deeply, but the nausea in my throat makes it impossible.

Fuck. What time is it?

I promised Wes I'd—

Oh God.

That happened.

I keep my eyes open for long enough to grab a glass and fill it with water.

I go to swallow my first gulp, but my throat is too sore.

I choke on the fucking water.

Like last night.

It takes five minutes, but I drink the entire glass of water.

Then I fill another. Fix a simple breakfast of bacon and eggs. With extra salt.

It's too much—it tastes like I'm eating the ocean—but it should help.

After another glass of water and a cup of English Breakfast (caffeine won't help with dehydration but skipping it will lead to an equally horrible headache), I pull out my cell.

There's only an hour until I need to head to Inked Hearts.

The shop where Wes works as a tattoo artist is a Venice Beach institution. It's incredibly cool. Visiting is a treat.

Usually.

When it's to beg him to take my virginity?

Uh…

I need to say something.

To figure out where we stand.

To figure out if I'll die of embarrassment.

I put my thumb to the digital keyboard.

Dear Wes,

I'm sorry for rambling about my virginity. I'm sure it was a memorable event at your birthday party, but I wasn't at my best. I really need to learn to watch my limits.

Sincerely,

Quinn

No.

That's way too weird.

This needs to be normal.

Well, normalish.

Hey Wes,

Sorry I was rambling last night. Hope things aren't weird. Happy Birthday again.

- Quinn

Hey Wes,

Your party was fun. Thanks for the invite! Sorry I got so drunk. Please forget everything I said.

I've realized I'm going to die a virgin.

But that's better than dying of embarrassment right now.

I'm sure you're already sleeping with some other woman.

Enjoy!

- Quinn

Hey Wes,

Let's skip these pleasantries and get down to business. I'm not going to med school a virgin. I want to learn everything. I want you to teach me. You're hot and fun and funny. You make me laugh and I'm pretty sure you'll be able to make me come too.

There's no way in hell I'm ever sending this. I can't believe I'm even writing it.

But, God, I really, really do want to study under you.

Is that too formal?

How am I supposed to phrase this?

Wes, please, teach me how to touch and suck and fuck?

I promise I'll study hard.

And, well, I'm pretty sure I don't need to spell out why this is win-win.

- Quinn.

My blush spreads from my cheeks to my chest.

The heat builds in my belly.

Then below it.

It's an appealing thought, his eyes wide as he reads this, that wicked smile pointed in my direction.

But he didn't say yes.

His rejection is going to be painful enough without adding a desperate text message plea.

I keep it simple and to the point.

Quinn: Are we still on for noon?

He texts back right away.

Wes: I'll be here.

And that's it.
I have to do this face-to-face.
Which is possible.
Totally possible.
Totally.

Chapter Four

WES

For the third time in ten minutes, I glance at my cell.

Same lock screen—the view from that hike Griff and I took last winter.

Same lack of notifications.

Same text from Quinn.

She's coming here.

It's still incomprehensible.

Quinn Thorn asking me to take her virginity is too far out of the realm of possibility.

She must be coming to say *oh my God, I'm so sorry, but I can't do this*.

But, fuck, if she's isn't—

If she's here to demand I fuck her—

My cock stirs.

Not good.

Not right now.

I have a lot of shit to do in the next fifteen minutes.

I shrug my shoulders. Focus my attention on my mock-up.

It's a his and hers piece inspired by a popular sci-fi show. The nuance is lacking, but the details are badass.

A guy with long hair and a huge gun.

A woman with big eyes and an *I'm going to kill you* stare.

I'm not sure why this set of love birds wants to celebrate their relationship by plastering their skin with fictional characters.

But if it makes them happy, who am I to judge?

I didn't get into tattoos for the love of them. Or the art.

It started as a way to show up my brothers.

But the first time I actually put the needle to something —a banana, of course—I fell in love.

It's the coolest feeling in the world.

The only thing that satisfies all the way to my bones.

My gaze flits to my phone.

Eleven forty-five.

Fifteen minutes until Quinn arrives.

"Fuck, you're in love with that thing." Hunter pushes himself onto the counter. He spins, turns to his girlfriend, motions *come here*.

She giggles as she leans in to kiss him.

His hand knots in her long hair.

Hers knots in his.

They move closer.

Make out like horny teenagers.

If he wasn't a blood relative, it might be hot. His girlfriend, Emma, is a total babe.

As it is—

Fuck, it's weird seeing him so happy.

Hunter was a miserable screwup for my entire life.

Until last year. Chase confronted him about his drinking problem. He lied about his desire to get sober.

But, somehow, we got him into rehab.

He dried out. Got his shit together. Fell in love.

He got me, Griffin, and Chase jobs here.

I owe him a lot.

And I don't have any way to repay him.

Hunter breaks the kiss and turns to me. "You can admit you're nervous."

I shrug. I'm not nervous. I'm interested. And I'm not falling for Hunter's *let's talk about feelings so we're not emotionally constipated and in need of the bottle* bullshit. "You can admit you don't stack up to me."

"Yeah." He turns to his girlfriend. "What do you think, Em. Is Wes packing heat?"

"Honestly…" She taps her finger against her chin, pretending to mull it over. Which is ridiculous. We banter like this every day. Hell, we go through this exchange every day. "Yeah."

"Obviously," I say.

"Why else would any woman screw him twice? With that personality?" she teases.

I press my hands to my gut like I'm trying to stop the bleeding. "Baby, you know I love it when you hurt me."

"Oooh, he's being all cute. He's got something to hide." Emma crosses the room to my suite. Gets close enough to study my mock-up. "You're here early."

"And?" I never manage to get work done at home. There's something about the vibe of my apartment. Something not at all conducive to concentration.

"And you're staring at your cell every three seconds." She reaches for my phone. "Who are you talking to?"

"None of your business," I say.

Her red lips curl into a wide smile. "It's a secret?"

"Or he's fucking with you," Hunter says.

She shakes her head. "No, look. He's flustered."

"Fuck off. I am not." I shrug. Smooth my t-shirt. My jeans.

This is what I always wear.

I'm usually comfortable in it.

But not right now.

It's too casual for Quinn.

She dresses like she's about to audition for *Mad Men*.

Or maybe a *Mad Men* inspired porno.

Okay, that's my depraved imagination. But now that I'm conjuring images of Quinn in some pinup lingerie set—

Fuck.

I need to get ahold of myself or I'm going to scare her.

And I'm not scaring her.

I'm not fucking this up.

My gaze shifts to my brother and his girlfriend. "What the hell are you two doing here anyway?" In theory, they're both here to work. He's a tattoo artist. She mans the front desk.

But the work they're doing is the type that pays in orgasms, not cash.

He raises a brow.

She blushes.

"Really?" I guess it's sweet they're still desperate to tear each other's clothes off after nearly a year, but enough already. They don't have to rub their happiness in our faces.

"Maybe." She reaches for my phone again. "Wouldn't you like to know?"

"Would like you to leave," I say.

"Tell me what you're hiding." Her fingers brush my cell. Emma is five eleven. In her four-inch wedges, she's taller than I am.

I put my phone behind my back.

"The more you hide it, the more she wants to know," Hunter says.

She looks back to him. "And you don't?"

He shrugs. "It's Wes."

He doesn't have to spell it out. *It's Wes. He lives for bragging. He'll tell us eventually.*

Usually, that's true.

With Quinn, it's different. Personal.

Emma and Hunter exchange a look. Then another.

I have no idea what it means, but it's clearly communicating something. That secret language couples have.

My brothers and I used to have that.

A long time ago.

Now…

We work in the same shop, but we barely communicate.

It's not my beef. It's Hunter and Chase. Chase hasn't forgiven Hunter for lying about getting sober.

Neither one of them has an issue with me.

In theory, everything should be normal between me and Hunter.

But it's not.

It's too close to the shit I keep locked up.

I'm not finding the key.

I'm not opening my heart.

I'm not getting hurt.

Quinn and I are going to have fun.

Period.

The end.

"Okay, Wes, I respect your privacy." Emma's smile is serene. "If you'd like to keep it to yourself, do that."

I shoot her a *really?*

She shrugs *who me?*

Hunter chuckles. "Baby, that's not the most plausible."

"When have I ever got into anyone's business?" she asks.

"When has anyone at Inked Hearts ever minded their own business?" he asks.

"Me. Every day," she says.

"Don't you have work to do?" I motion to the computer behind the counter. It makes my position a little too obvious, but I'm running out of patience here. Quinn is arriving in less than ten minutes. I need them disinterested now.

"Yeah, but I can do it when Hunter's appointment gets here." She takes a seat at my station. "You can entertain me until then."

I drop to one knee. "Baby, if you want entertainment, I'm happy to oblige." I take Emma's hand. "But I'm not sure your boy toy is going to like it."

Her smile widens. "This is juicy, huh."

I nod. "You know I'll make you—"

"You won't. And ew. 'Juicy'? That is not hot." She turns to Hunter. "Right?"

He nods. "Not at all."

"You're usually better," she says.

"You want me to go?" I offer.

She shrugs. "If you're even capable."

My heart thuds as the door swings open.

But those aren't Quinn's dainty footsteps.

They're sure, steady ones.

Griffin spots me and shakes his head. "This guy giving you a hard time?"

"I'm trying," I say.

Emma laughs. "Oh my God. That was terrible." She presses her knees together. Stands. Smooths her dark jeans. "You're really obsessed with—" Her eyes flit to my cell, even as I slide it into my pocket. "A girl, right?"

Griffin chuckles. "She didn't cancel?"

Emma's eyes light up. "Westley Keating, you're holding out on me."

"You're the one begging for dirty talk." I shrug like I'm completely disinterested in the subject at hand.

"Oh?" Griffin raises a brow. "You not getting enough at home?"

"Jesus, Griff. Wording." I motion to Hunter. "He's right there."

"He should know," Griffin says.

Emma laughs. "No, I get plenty. I think Wes was more… trying to prove something about how hot he is."

I pat my stomach. "No need to prove shit."

"Keep your shirt on, Romeo." Emma crosses to the counter.

Hunter pulls her into his arms. Leans in to whisper something in her ear.

She whispers back.

Yeah, they're adorable and happy and in love.

Enough with that already.

"You know Griffin won't tell you," Hunter says.

Emma makes a show of pouting. "Wes, I'm counting on you to deliver here."

"Baby, if you want me to satisfy you—" I motion for her to spread her legs.

She sticks out her tongue *gross*.

Hunter's eyes flit to me.

He's not bothered by me flirting with his girlfriend.

He's amused.

He knows I'm trying desperately to shake their interest.

Griffin lets out his typical hearty chuckle. He pats me on the shoulder as he makes his way to his suite.

Then he sits in his chair, the picture of contentment. And mystery.

The guy has been my best friend for half a dozen years

and I barely know anything about what he's hiding behind his dark eyes.

He talks about his trysts, sure. He has a hell of a dirty mouth. He doesn't realize he has a thing for his friend Juliette. (His very engaged, very unavailable friend).

But he never dives into what really makes him tick.

Not that I can talk.

No one knows how bad shit is with Mom.

I try to find a comeback. Something to convince the entire room to leave me the fuck alone.

The ringing door stops me.

It's not another tattoo artist.

Or a customer.

It's Quinn.

And, fuck, she looks good enough to eat.

White dress. Demure smile. Thick glasses.

"Hey." I keep my voice even. "You want to talk here or somewhere else?"

Her hazel eyes go wide as she takes in the room. "Maybe somewhere… more private."

My balls tighten.

But I keep my poker face. "There's a coffee shop down the street."

"Sure." She hugs her purse to her chest.

"First cup's on me," I say.

She offers me a nervous smile. Nods.

"After you." I hold the door open for her.

She nods a *thank you* and steps outside.

And I'm walking quiet, prim Quinn Thorn to a coffee date.

I'm trying to figure out exactly how to word my yes.

Chapter Five

QUINN

Wes holds his hands over his eyes. "Your head okay?"

"Huh?"

"After the party."

"Oh. Right." I copy his gesture. It's a beautiful summer day, but the big lemon sun is far too bright. My eyes are still screaming. "It's felt better."

"You want anything for it?"

"No. I took an ibuprofen earlier." I press my palms together. "But thanks."

"Sure thing." He smiles as he slides on his dark sunglasses.

They're classic black things that make him look like a movie star.

He really is cute.

No, cute doesn't cut it. Even with the oodles of boyish charm, Wes is hot, plain and simple.

He has his pick of women.

Experienced, skilled women.

God, I hope everything I hear about men and virgins is true.

If he says no…

"After you." He motions to the coffee shop on our right then pulls the door open for me.

"Thanks."

It's a hip place. Black line art. Modern chairs. Chalkboard menu with five items.

I order—iced tea for me, cold brew for him—and sit at the table in the corner.

He sits next to me.

His jeans brush my bare skin.

The soft touch makes my stomach flutter.

I'm not exactly calm and collected most of the time, but with Wes, I'm always tripping over my tongue.

He's just so…

Hot.

Experienced.

Funny.

Cool.

Sexy.

God, I'm so out of my league here.

"So…" His eyes meet mine.

"So…" I guess I have to come out and say it. Again. "I, uh…"

"People say things when they're drunk sometimes."

I nod.

"If that's what happened, I get it. I'm not going to like it, but I will get it."

"You mean—"

"Yeah."

I swallow hard. Is he saying what I think he's saying? I study his expression, but it doesn't offer a clue.

I guess there's no beating around the bush here.

I said it once.

I can say it again. "You want to?"

His blue eyes light up. "I want to what?"

Deep breath.

Steady exhale.

Here goes nothing. "Well, Wes, the thing is, it's not just one time. I mean, if that's all you want, that's okay. But I don't just want to check that box. I want to learn how to do this. I want you to teach me."

Chapter Six

WES

Thank fuck for elastic or these jeans would be torture.

As it is, they're awfully tight.

I blink twice.

Pinch myself.

There's no way this is real life.

I fell asleep in my chair.

I'm currently having a sex dream.

We're about to tear off our clothes and go right *here*.

God damn, what's she wearing under that adorable outfit?

Something as white and innocent as her dress?

Or something as sexy as those red sandals?

"Wes?" Her voice is soft. Nervous.

"Say that again?" I take a long sip of my coffee. It's ice cold, but it doesn't lower my temperature.

It fills my head—this big, beautiful image of Quinn spread out on my bed.

There isn't room for anything else.

Certainly nothing coherent.

My brain is screaming *Quinn Thorn naked*.

"I, um, it's not just that I want to lose my virginity." Her throat quivers as she swallows. "I want to learn how to do this."

"This?"

"Sex." Her cheeks flush. "All of it."

"How much all of it?"

"Well…" She twirls an auburn strand around her finger. "However much you're willing to teach me."

"Fucking?"

Her nod is nervous.

"Hand jobs?"

Her cheeks flush.

"Sucking cock?"

"Yeah." Her blush deepens.

Fuck, that blush is adorable.

I want to tease her until she's beet red.

I want to tease her all day, every day forever.

"Wes?" Her fingers curl around her iced tea. Her eyes stay big and surprised.

"Yeah?" Fuck, I know we're talking about something, but it's hard to grasp words at the moment.

I'm not lacking female attention. Or sexual partners. Or virgins, even.

But there's a big difference between a random woman who wants to screw the hot tattoo artist and Quinn.

Yeah, this might not be about me.

It might be the muscles and the tattoos and the manwhore reputation.

But she's Quinn.

"Is that okay?" she asks.

"Is it okay that you want me to teach you how to suck cock?"

The guy sitting at the table across from ours shoots us a dirty look.

Quinn clears her throat.

"Do I have your question right?" I ask.

"Yes." She folds her hands in her lap. "You can say no."

Jesus Christ. Why in the world would I say no?

My head tries to jump in. To tell me this is a bad idea. That it will be too hard keeping things casual with Quinn.

My cock pushes it out of the driver's seat.

It won't forgive me if I say no.

Still.

I need to find some hint of sense. "Anal?"

Her eyes go wide. "Um… maybe."

"Bondage?"

She clears her throat. "Is that something you're into?"

"I'm not against it."

"Which way?"

"Either way."

"No, um, I don't think so." She takes another sip of her iced tea. Swallows hard.

"Sixty-nine?"

Her eyes bulge out of her head. "Are you going to keep listing things?"

"Yeah."

"Why?"

"You're into school, right?"

"I guess you could say that." She adjusts her glasses. Then adjusts them more. "It's more that it takes a lot of studying to become a doctor."

"But you're into it?"

"It's my plan."

So, she's not into it?

That's hard to believe.

We're not exactly best friends, but every time we talk, she's in study mode.

"We need a lesson plan," I say.

"Oh." She pushes her glasses up her nose. "That's really smart."

"You sound surprised."

"Not surprised. More…"

"You think I'm an idiot?"

Her laugh is more nervous than anything. "No, I just… That's a great idea. What do you have in mind?"

"You leave in four weeks, right?"

Her eyes turn down for a split second. Then she blinks, and the hurt is gone. "Yeah."

"How much do you want to learn?"

"The basics, I guess."

"You want to learn to fuck and suck cock?"

Her eyes dart around the room. Fix on a guy in the corner, working on his laptop, earbuds on. Then on the barista who's texting on her phone, glancing in our direction. "She's listening, isn't she?"

"I'll use my inside voice."

"Is that your inside voice?"

I can't help but laugh. Yeah, I'm not so good at shutting up. "Yeah. But at least now you know I'm loud."

"Oh my God." She blushes. Hides behind her hands as she adjusts her glasses. "You… uh… how do you say stuff like that?"

"You want to learn that too?"

She nods.

"Dirty talk?"

"Yeah. But not just that. The confidence. The boldness."

"It's mostly experience and practice."

"Practice?"

"Yeah." My balls tighten. It's very fucking difficult hashing this out without picturing her naked.

"You mean in bed or—"

"Everything. Try it."

She leans in closer. Close enough to whisper. "Try it how?"

"Tell me what you want to do."

"Now?"

"At our first lesson," I say.

"Oh, well..." She looks around the bright room. Checks that no one is listening. Then she scoots toward me. Brings her lips to my ear. "I want to start slow. But, eventually, I want to... to have sex with you."

Her voice is low and shaky.

Her breath is warm and fast.

Fuck, she's doing shit to me.

Shit my jeans are failing to hide.

She pulls back. Settles into her seat. Wraps her lips around her straw.

If I didn't know better, I'd swear she was driving me wild on purpose.

But this is Quinn.

She's this innocent.

She wipes her hands on her dress. "So. Four weeks. I work Thursday to Sunday."

"You free tomorrow?"

She nods. "All day."

"Good."

"Should we meet at your place? Or mine? Or maybe some third location?"

"You want to spring for hotel rooms?" I ask.

"No, I just... I've never done this before."

"Me either."

"Yeah, but you—"

"I'm a slut."

"I was going to say you're experienced."

I can't help but laugh. "You don't have to sugar coat it. I'm used to Griffin."

"He's a little—"

"He's a tactless asshole."

Her lips curl into a smile. "He's experienced too?"

Yeah. And I'm not letting her linger on that thought.

I'm sure Griffin would be happy to teach Quinn.

He'd do a good job.

But there's no way in hell I'm letting another guy fill this position.

"My place is fine for our first meeting," I say.

"Our first meeting?"

"Tomorrow."

"Oh."

"We'll do one lesson a week."

"Is that enough?"

No. There's no way I'll ever get enough of fucking Quinn.

But I have to be smart here. I have to lay ground rules.

So neither of us get attached.

"On Mondays?" she asks.

"Yeah." Fuck, what a way to start the week.

"Okay." Her fingers tap her glass. She looks down at her drink. Watches the amber liquid swirl as she stirs with her straw. "What if, um… what if… well, I've always heard that sex makes people feel stuff."

"I'd hope so."

"I mean, emotionally."

"Oh." I try to figure out what she's getting at, but her expression doesn't offer any clues.

She's still shaking with nerves.

It's flattering.

But it's not good.

I can't do this if she's clenched and scared.

"I don't want to fall for you." Her eyes meet mine. "No offense, Wes, but you're a player and I don't need my heart broken."

That makes two of us. "We'll see how it goes."

She stares at me like I'm crazy.

"You start to feel something, you tell me."

"What if you start to feel something?"

"Same deal." That's not going to happen. But there's no reason to tell her that. It isn't personal. I like Quinn. A lot. But I'm not interested in love. Love is heartbreak, pure and simple. I've had enough of that for one lifetime.

"So, we meet once a week until August?"

I nod.

"And you teach me..."

"Everything."

"Everything." She adjusts her glasses. "In four weeks?"

I nod. "I'll have to pack a lot into our sessions."

Her teeth sink into her bottom lip. "Four lessons. Then we part. No strings attached." She extends her hand.

I shake. "Deal."

Chapter Seven

QUINN

My iced tea and Wes buzz fades faster with every passing minute.

A dry medical practice is not the place to fantasize.

It's not sexy.

And it's not at all appropriate.

I'm supposed to be writing down Dr. Lee's notes. She's saying something to her patient about albuterol and sports and exercising outside.

I don't need to write this down.

But the actual prescription.

Shit. I tap her commands into the computer.

This is a good job. An incredibly in demand job. Every medical school hopeful wants to work as a scribe. And there's no one better than Dr. Lee. She's patient, attentive, detail oriented.

I tell myself I'm lucky to work here.

But I still curse every minute.

I hate this job.

Every day, I try to imagine myself in Dr. Lee's (stylish yet practical) shoes. I envision myself with a white coat over my A-line dress, my fingers curled into a clipboard, my attention on my patient.

Every day, I see this blah grey blob.

That's what medicine feels like.

A blah grey blob.

I try to talk to Owen about it, but he assures me it's temporary boredom. That I'll fall in love once I'm spending sixty hours a week studying medicine. (Supposedly, true passion will kick in once I'm spending eighty hours a week doing rounds).

My parents—it's a non-starter with them. If I so much as mention the slightest negative feeling toward medicine, they stare at me like I've got horns coming out of my skull.

I think they'd feel better about the horns.

At least that would be something they could study and understand.

Whereas a Thorn who finds doctorhood blah?

That's beyond comprehension.

I let my thoughts flit to Wes as we move onto the next patient.

There's something so earnest about his smile. And, God, those gorgeous blue eyes—

He's sexy as hell in his clothes.

How the hell am I going to survive him naked?

Touching me?

Fucking me?

The thought is enough to make me blush.

I barely make it through my shift. Doctor Lee notices something is off, but she doesn't call me on it.

She sends me home with her typical *great work today, Quinn, now go have fun. You're too young to study all the time.*

Maybe she's smarter than I am. Or better at retaining information.

When school is in session, I have exactly zero time for

44

fun. It's all work and studying and enough exercise to kill my lingering anxiety.

Right now...

This is my last month in California.

I'm making the most of it.

I drive home. Shower. Change.

Fix dinner from a recipe.

It's good—white fish with lemon, salad, and mashed cauliflower—but it's exactly like the current state of my summer.

The same thing, all the time.

A plan that works well enough but fails to appeal.

Sometimes, I try to listen to my instincts. To create a dish without guidelines. But it goes about as well as any other time I go off plan.

It's a total disaster.

Better to stick to the unappealing thing that works.

That gives me four weeks.

Four weeks to learn to fuck.

Four weeks with Wes.

Four weeks of freedom.

———

I'M FINISHED WITH DINNER AND HALFWAY THROUGH *Bringing Up Baby* when my phone buzzes.

Wes: I have something for you.

My phone flashes with a picture message.

A photo of an STD test. His STD test.

He's safe.

Quinn: Oh.

Wes: Oh?

Quinn: It's good you're proactive.

Wes: If you're scared, we can use a condom.

Quinn: No. I want to try it this way.

I try to think of a sexier way to phrase it. Something Wes would say.

Nothing comes.

This…

Well, it gets the point across.

Wes: Do you have something in mind? I'm partial to doggy style, but I'm pretty open.

There's a link. To a list of sex positions. With photos.

My chest flushes.

He's so cool and collected about sending me a list of sex positions.

I close my eyes.

Try to imagine it as our bodies instead of random models.

Him on top of me. My legs around his waist. My arms around his chest.

Him on the bed. Me climbing on top of him. Pressing my palms into that spot just below his tattoo.

Him flipping me over onto all fours, peeling my panties to mid-thigh—

I want him so badly.

I can't see him or hear him and he's already driving me mad.

How am I supposed to survive touching him?

Quinn: Do I really have to pick one?

Wes: Unless you want to go all day.

Quinn: You can't do it in one session?

Wes: Are you teasing me?

Quinn: Maybe.

Wes: You should know there's a penalty for teasing.

Quinn: Yeah?

Wes: I tease back.

My sex clenches.

His confidence is so fucking hot.

I need some of that.

I am teasing him.

A little.

And awkwardly.

But it's a start.

Quinn: What's that like?

Wes: I have to be honest with you, Quinn.

Quinn: Yeah?

Wes: You can't handle those details.

Quinn: Try me.

Wes: I don't want to scare you.

Quinn: You won't.

Wes: Can I get that in writing?

Quinn: Sure. I, Quinn Thorn, promise not to call off our arrangement on account of Wes Keating's mastery of dirty talk.

Wes: You have enough?

Quinn: Enough what?

Wes: Of a plan?

Quinn: Well, actually…

Wes: That's what I figured.

Quinn: Is there something wrong with planning?

Wes: No, it's smart. Fuck knows there are a lot of times I could have planned better.

Quinn: I'm sensing a but.

Wes: Sex isn't like that.

Quinn: How's that?

Wes: You can't go in thinking "today I'm going to peel Quinn's panties to her ankles. Then I'm going to drag my lips up her thighs. Suck on her clit until she's screaming my name."

Holy shit.

Wes: You can't come in with an itinerary.

Quinn: Why not?

Wes: You have to be there, in the moment.

Quinn: That's not my strong suit.
Wes: That's okay.
Quinn: What if it's not?
Wes: It will be. I promise.
Quinn: You'll be patient with me?
Wes: Yeah.
Quinn: You promise?
Wes: On my love of Mission Impossible movies.
Quinn: Really?
Wes: What's better than Tom Cruise saving the world?
Quinn: Literally anything.
Wes: That's where you're wrong.
Quinn: Do you want a list?
Wes: Yeah.
Quinn: Casablanca for starters.
Wes: It's still your favorite?
Quinn: It's the greatest movie of all time.
Wes: Can I let you in on a secret?

My lips curl into a smile. My heartbeat picks up.

He's teasing. It's not a real secret. But it still feels good.

My best friend moved to New York three days after graduation. Then promptly got too busy working to respond to my texts.

Owen is the only person who really talks to me. Or trusts me.

He's the only person I really trust.

I don't get secrets.

I want them.

I want more from Wes.

It's too much, already. This is a physical arrangement. It's about our bodies, not our minds or our hearts.

But, God, my heart is racing.

It's singing.

It's completely desperate to flirt.

Quinn: My lips are sealed.

Wes: I've never seen it.

Quinn: No!

Wes: Yes.

Quinn: You know the premise?

Wes: Something about black and white and Nazis and Paris.

Quinn: Oh my God, Wes Keating! You are so close to blowing this.

Wes: Go on…

Quinn: Not in a good way.

Wes: Still want to hear you talk about blowing.

Quinn: I've never done that.

Wes: I know.

Quinn: What if I'm bad at it?

Wes: You've had boyfriends?

Quinn: A few, but we always moved glacially.

Wes: Your choice or theirs?

Quinn: Combination.

Wes: You made out?

Quinn: And a lot of second base.

Wes: You liked that?

My body buzzes.

It's like he's here. Like he's pushing my tank top off my shoulders to play with my chest.

Quinn: Yes.

Wes: We'll start there.

Quinn: Then?

Wes: What did I tell you, angel? We have to play it by ear.

Quinn: Angel?

Wes: You like it?

Quinn: Maybe.

Wes: Will you like it when you're coming on my hand?

My sex clenches. I stare at my cell, trying and failing to type a coherent response.

Wes: I'll take that as a yes.

Quinn: Yes.

Wes: Good. You're free all day Monday?

Quinn: You want the whole day?

Wes: Yes. I want all your Mondays.

Quinn: For sex?

Wes: I'm not going to send you home hungry.

Quinn: So it's like a date?

Wes: No, it's like I'm going to make you come and feed you.

Jesus Christ. How does he talk like this?

Quinn: Oh.

Wes: That a problem?

Quinn: Not at all.

Wes: Good.

Quinn: Are we going somewhere?

Wes: You want to go somewhere?

Quinn: Maybe. I only have four weeks left in California. There's a lot I want to do.

Wes: Anything specific?

Quinn: Well…

Wes: Well?

Quinn: It's stupid.

Wes: Does it matter to you?

Quinn: Yeah.

Wes: Then it's not stupid.

Quinn: I have a summer bucket list.

Wes: What is it?

Quinn: Some stuff I want to do.

My teeth sink into my lip. Wes is fun. And he's a doer. He could help with my list.

Maybe he'll think I'm a weirdo for orchestrating my fun.

But if I want his help…

Learn to paddle board.

50

Learn to rollerblade.

Hike in Malibu.

See the Hollywood sign.

Visit Las Vegas

Lose my virginity.

I can't send it.

Not yet.

But I can tell him a little.

Quinn: Normal stuff. Like seeing the Hollywood sign and losing my virginity.

Wes: I like the last part especially.

Quinn: I thought you would.

Wes: I can help with this. If you want help.

Quinn: Maybe. One thing at a time. Like you tell me what we're doing tomorrow.

Wes: Don't know yet.

Quinn: I need to know the dress code.

Wes: You always look perfect.

Quinn: At least tell me the necessary footwear.

Wes: Comfortable.

Quinn: I can do that.

Wes: Good. Come to my place. At seven. Keep the rest of your Mondays free.

Quinn: All day?

Wes: All day, all summer.

Quinn: You drive a hard bargain.

Wes: You haven't seen anything yet, angel.

Chapter Eight

QUINN

For the third time, I smooth my dress.

The skirt still falls to just below my knees. The top still hugs me in all the right places. The adorable polka dot pattern still screams *innocent virgin*.

It's a cute dress. A thick cotton sateen. The perfect weight for a warm summer night.

But is it the dress?

Does this dress really say *hey, Wes, I'm ready to touch your penis?*

I reach for my turquoise cardigan and slide it over my shoulders. It's the perfect subtle contrast to the mint pattern.

It's candy-colored cute.

Too cute.

I don't want to stroll into Wes's apartment in a dress that screams *I have no idea what I'm doing.*

I don't.

But I need my dress to say *I'm going to figure this out.*

I strip. Hang the dress in its spot in the closet— between a teal dress and a Kelley-green one. (Everything is arranged by color, from red to orange to yellow to green to blue to purple, then white, grey, black).

This needs to be more. It needs to be sexy.

I'm capable of being sexy.

I scan my drawers for something that says *Quinn Thorn is a sexual being*, but none of my underwear does the trick. It's all nylon bras and cotton bikinis.

The closet is no better.

My sundresses are adorable and sweet and girly.

I suck a breath through my nose. Try to exhale the tension in my shoulders.

It's a dress.

That's all.

It's a garment that drapes over my body.

That Wes will take off my body.

I…

Fuck, this is really happening.

I reach for my only red dress. My hands shake so hard I barely manage to slide it off the hanger.

There. I pull the zipper. Check my reflection. Spin until the skirt is twirling.

It's a cute dress.

And it's red.

Sexy.

This is…

It's good.

I can see myself at his place.

I can see his eyes going wide as he pushes the straps off my shoulders and—

Fuck, I can't do this.

Deep breath.

Slow exhale.

In. Out. In. Out.

We're making out.

That's all.

It's not like he's going to ask me to strip then order me onto the bed right away.

Probably.

Maybe.

I mean, I don't really know.

We haven't said.

He hasn't—

Fuck.

My reflection stares back at me with wide eyes and flushed skin.

The dress isn't the problem.

I'm the problem.

I move into the bathroom. Focus on my hair and makeup.

By the time I apply my last coat of mascara, my hands are steady.

My breath is even.

My heart is beating at a normal clip.

I look good. Sweet with a hint of grown-up sex appeal.

Wes will like it.

He… he does find me attractive.

It's weird. I can't really fathom Wes finding me attractive—he's so hot and he has his pick of women—but he's been very, very explicit about how attractive he finds me.

And I…

Well, I'm not bad looking. I have a nice figure (the one thing nerves are good for is the exercise required to tame them) and pretty eyes.

I'm not naturally gifted in any of the feminine arts (hair, makeup, fashion), but I'm an excellent student.

I spent weeks studying clothing books and style guides as I curated my wardrobe. Then I did the same with my hair and makeup.

I know every fashion system. I know my seasonal palette. I know which colors say sweet and innocent and which say *fuck me now*.

Deep down, I know the truth.

There isn't a dress or hair style or lipstick that will make this easier.

My white sandals are right there. They're sitting on the hardwood floor. My purse is packed on the bed.

This is it.

I'm ready to go.

Only my feet refuse to get into my shoes.

My hands are shaking again.

My heart is thudding again.

My breath—

Fuck, my breath is a mess.

I find my cell. Read over my text exchange with Wes. Try to think up some plausible way to cancel.

Sorry, Wes, you're super hot and I really, really want to learn how to touch your dick, but I'm too terrified to even get out the door.

Sorry, Wes, but I can't make it tonight. I'm too rambling and awkward for human contact, much less sexual contact.

Sorry, Wes, but I'm calling this off. I can barely keep it together for this message. How am I supposed to take off my clothes?

No.

None of it works.

None of it is happening.

This is happening.

I just need… something. Some trick or secret or magic shot of confidence.

My fingers move before my head can stop them.

I call Owen.

He picks up on the second ring.

"What's up?" His voice is tired but happy.

It's late in Chicago. And he works today. I think. It's

hard to keep track of his ever-changing schedule, so I tend to assume he's working. It's usually the case.

"Hey." I try to keep my voice even. Get halfway there. "How are you?"

"Wiped. Just got out of the shower."

"Am I interrupting?"

His laugh is low and hearty. "Reggie, Quinn wants to know if she's interrupting," he calls to his husband.

"If I have my say, yeah," Reggie calls. "Tell her I say hi."

"I can put it on speaker," Owen says.

"No, if she's calling..." Reggie's voice drops to a whisper.

"She's not," Owen says.

"She is. Go."

"He's worried about you," Owen says.

"He's sweet," I say.

"Hey." Owen laughs. "And I'm what?"

"Lucky," I say.

"I know." His voice softens. "Are you okay?"

"Just a little nervous."

"You haven't called in forever, Q." He calls me by my old nickname.

"I've been busy."

"You graduated a month ago."

"It was nice seeing you. I know how hard it was getting time off." I start rambling about seeing Owen and Reggie at graduation. Then about the dinner we had with our parents after. The one where they gushed about my accomplishments and how proud they were I'd be attending med school in Chicago. The same city as my brother.

As them.

And maybe I can move back home.

Or at least come home early this summer.

"Q, stop." Owen's voice is knowing. "Have you been seeing your therapist?"

"Can we not?"

"I have to ask."

"Yeah, I… I'm good. I'm eating right. I'm working. I'm exercising every day and watching the caffeine." My nerves aren't bad enough to qualify as an anxiety disorder. More… nerves. I only check in with my therapist once a month now. It's enough to keep me steady. Ish.

Concern drips into his voice. "If you ever feel like it's too much—"

"I'm okay. Really." Sorta. My heart is thudding against my chest. But I am okay. "It's just, I have a date tonight."

"Oh?"

"And I'm out of practice."

"Q, you know I'm even more clueless about straight guys than you are."

"Yeah." I can't help but laugh. He always says the right thing. "But you're good at this."

"I got lucky with Reggie."

"He's good at it too."

"Yeah." My brother's voice gets dreamy. "The first time we met, he asked me if I believed in love at first sight. Because he hadn't. Until just then. It was cheesy and obviously bullshit—he was clearly trying to get laid, but—"

"He was hot, so you went with it?" I tease.

He just chuckles. "I might not believe in love at first site, Q, but I'm pretty sure I fell in love with him that night."

"He was that good?"

Again, he chuckles. "Since when are you dating?"

"I'm always dating."

"No." He calls to Reggie. "Q has a date."

"She hates when you call her that," Reggie says.

"I'm putting it on speaker." He does. "You love it, right, Q?"

"Uh..." I hated it, at first, but it's grown on me. It's our thing. Owen and I always fought a lot, yeah, but only because we spent so much time around each other. Mom and Dad were (are) always working. We had to entertain ourselves. "It's tolerable. Like you."

My brother laughs. "You're cute when you're trying to be mean."

"Am not," I say.

"Are too."

Reggie laughs. "You're such a brat around her. I'm sorry, Quinn. Who's your date? Is he hot? Is he huge?"

"Yes. And I don't know." Probably. With that confidence... how could he not be?

"Where are you going?" he asks.

"He's surprising me." I tap my toes together. "He wouldn't tell me the dress code either."

"Hmm," Owen says.

"But, um, he said what I normally wear is great." My eyes flit to my alarm clock. I have to go soon. Really soon. "He likes my dresses."

"Of course, he does," Reggie says. "You look adorable in them."

"She does," Owen agrees.

"And so sweet and innocent too. Guys love that." Reggie laughs as he whispers something to Owen.

Owen whispers back.

"We're all perverts. Want to think we're the first to stake our claim somewhere," Reggie says.

"You did not just use a metaphor for penetration to describe my little sister," Owen says.

"Your little sister is a babe. If I'd met her first, who knows?" Reggie teases.

"Oh yeah? Should we bet on that?" Owen's voice gets—

Let's just not.

It's sweet of Reggie to say he'd go for me. It's not impossible (he is bisexual, well, pansexual, meaning he's into everyone, male, female, trans, gender non-binary, whatever), but it's about as likely as snow in Los Angeles.

He's way into Owen's cockiness.

"Are you showing your boobs?" Reggie asks.

"Straight guys love boobs," Owen says.

"How can you not like them?" Reggie says.

Owen shrugs. I'm not sure how I can hear it, but I can.

"He's crazy," Reggie says. "But he's right. And yours—"

"You are not talking about my sister's boobs," Owen says.

"Sweetie, you know it drives me crazy when you get all protective." Reggie's voice drops to something low and breathy.

As soon as they hang up, they're going to pounce.

Gross.

Don't get me wrong. I'm happy they're happy. But I don't need to hear details about my brother's sex life.

"Show your boobs while you can. It will be freezing by October," Owen says. "Mom is talking nonstop about taking you coat shopping. She thinks you've lost your ability to handle winter after four years in California."

"I might have."

"You were here at Christmas. You were good."

I was freezing and miserable, but more from the constant talk of med school than the surroundings. "I'll survive."

"Does Romeo know you're leaving?" Owen asks.

"He's not really the commitment type."

He whispers something to Reggie then takes the phone

off speaker. His voice gets clearer. Closer. "You don't have a summer fling in your bones."

"I do too."

"You sure?"

"Yeah. Positive."

"Then why are you so nervous?"

"I like him." That's close to the truth. Owen and I are close. But not *hey, I'm trying to lose my virginity, any tips?* close.

"Just be yourself."

"Ramble incoherently about *Casablanca*?"

"Yeah. If he's the guy for you, he'll find it charming."

"Maybe."

"Trust me, Q. If he's worth your time, he'll like your weird."

"There's so much of it."

"Everyone is like that. Some of us just hide it better than others." There's a soft clank. "Shit, I gotta go. You gonna be okay?"

"I think so."

"Love you."

"Love you too."

I end the call, slide my cell into my purse, slide my purse onto my shoulder.

Owen is right.

I just have to be myself.

A slightly less awkward, fumbling version of myself.

I can do that.

I can totally do that.

Chapter Nine

WES

The doorbell rings at five minutes to seven.

Quinn is early.

Of course.

The girl is the picture of manners.

I shrug my shoulders to break up the tension in my back.

I'm not thinking about cleaning up after Mom last night.

I'm thinking about pinning Quinn to the wall and making her come.

There are no cracks in my smile.

Period.

"It's open." I try to make my voice even, but I don't get all the way there. Like it's obvious how much this tugs at the strings holding me together.

That isn't happing.

I'm not going there.

"So it is." Quinn steps inside. She pushes the door closed behind her. Clicks the lock. Smooths her red dress.

The soft fabric hugs her perfect tits and her narrow waist. It flows over her lush hips.

It begs for my hands.

I need that fabric against my skin.

I need that dress on the floor.

I need my thoughts gone.

Shit, I'm using sex the way my idiotic brother used alcohol.

But I guess that's nothing new.

"Shoes off?" She motions to the row of sneakers by the door.

"Up to you."

"You sure?" She turns. Bends to study the shoes. "Seems like you went to a lot of effort to not track dirt all over the place."

"Still up to you."

She nods and slips out of her cork sandals. Her bare feet pad the ground as she crosses the living room. "You're kinda ruining my outfit here."

"Am I?"

She motions from her head to her toes. "They pulled the whole thing together."

"You look fucking amazing."

"Yeah?" Her voice is soft. Insecure.

It's ridiculous. Quinn always looks polished. Like a magazine photo come to life. "You doubt it?"

"I guess I picture you with a different type of girl."

"What type is that?" I ask.

"Well…" Her expression gets sheepish. "More aggressively sexual."

"Fishnets and fuck me heels?"

"Yeah. Exactly."

"You think I like trashy chicks?"

She tries a coy shrug. Doesn't get all the way there.

"Brutal."

"Sorry. But it's the impression you give."

I shrug like I don't mind. Usually, I don't. Usually, I cultivate my careless playboy image.

I want to be that guy.

I don't want to care.

Caring hurts too fucking much.

Quinn's eyes flare with something, some realization, but she keeps her lips zipped. She turns to the kitchen. Surveys the pan currently sautéing garlic. "What are you making?"

"Not sure." I never really think about what I'm making. Or what I'm doing for that matter. I listen to my gut. It usually works out.

"It smells good."

"Garlic always does."

She crosses to the kitchen. Gets close enough to the pan to watch the bulbs sizzle. "How do you do that?"

"Do what?"

"Start cooking without any idea what you'll make?"

"I have some idea."

"Yeah?" Her eyes fill with curiosity. She's genuinely fascinated by my thought process.

It's weird feeling under scrutiny. But her attention is still flattering. "Something that's good with garlic."

Her laugh is soft. Honest. "But... how do you know it will be good?"

"I don't."

She stares at me like I'm crazy.

"Figuring it out is the part that's fun."

Her fingertips skim the counter. "But what if you can't figure it out?"

"I do."

Again, she stares at me like I'm crazy.

"You never cook without a plan?"

She shakes her head. "Last time I tried… have you ever combined garlic, cinnamon, and charred chicken breast?"

"Can't say I have."

"Don't. It's not good. And, no matter how many times you tell yourself 'all these ingredients are in curry,' it's still awful." Her eyelids flutter closed as she inhales the scent. "I wish I could do that."

"Go off plan?"

She nods. "It's just… it doesn't work."

"You've done okay."

Her brow knits with frustration. "I guess so."

"You're starting med school in four weeks."

"Three and a half."

"You're not happy about that?"

"No." She shakes her head. "I mean, I am. It's a good plan. I just wish…" She turns to the stove. "This is really sizzling."

It is.

"You should probably add to it."

I take a step toward her. "You have any requests?"

"No." Her fingertips skim the counter. "Whatever is fine. I'm not sure I'll eat much." She swallows hard. "I'm a little nervous."

"I'll send you home with the leftovers."

"You don't have to."

"I know."

"Oh."

"You're not used to people taking care of you?" I ask.

"Is that what you do?"

"Like this? Yeah." I take a spot in front of the stove. Next to her.

"You're taking care of me?"

"You prefer calling it something else?"

Her eyes flit to me. "Are you always like this?"

"Always?"

"With other women?"

I'm not sure exactly what she's getting at, but I might as well set the record straight. This is fun. I want both of us to have fun. But it has to end there. "I show women a good time."

"Is that all?"

"What else would there be?"

Her brow furrows as she turns over my words. She nods, accepting them, then she moves closer. Close enough her hip brushes mine. "Can I help?"

"I don't know. Can I trust you near cinnamon?"

Her lips curl into a half-smile. "Probably not."

"How about you pick out wine?"

"You have options?"

"A red and a white."

She laughs. "I have to know what we're making."

"Yeah?"

"There are rules for wine."

I arch a brow.

She blushes. "They're more of guidelines. Flavors that go together."

"Cooking is the same thing."

She presses her lips together. "That makes sense."

"But?"

"No, it makes sense."

"You don't look happy about it."

"I just don't get it," she says.

"The wine?"

"I follow the rules." She moves to the fridge. Finds the two bottles.

I open the drawer and take out the cork.

She picks up *may I?*

I nod. "You gonna drink both?"

"I have to sample them."

"That code?"

"Is that an accusation?" Humor slips into her voice.

It warms me everywhere. Fuck, I want to make her laugh. I want to make her laugh more than I want to make her come. "I have a theory about wine snobs."

"You think I'm a snob."

"You're particular."

"And you?" She points to the bag of coffee beans sitting on the counter. A local blend that costs twice as much as grocery store shit.

"I know what I like."

"What's that?"

"Gorgeous redheads."

Her cheeks flush. "You're trying to make me nervous."

"Trying to make you blush."

"Why?"

"It's hot."

"Oh." Her blush spreads to her chest. "Thank you."

"Pleasure's all mine."

She uncorks the bottle of red and motions to the cabinets.

I grab two glasses from the high shelf.

Her fingers brush mine as she takes a wine glass. "You seem more like a bourbon guy."

"That was rum the other night."

"I don't know the difference."

"Do you want to?"

She shakes her head. Pours a splash of red.

Her fingers wrap around the glass. Then her lips.

She tilts her head back. Swallows hard. "Not bad."

I arch a brow.

"Considering." She motions to the label. "You bought it

because of the name, right?"

"Maybe."

"You really expect me to believe you didn't buy the wine named after threesomes?"

I shrug.

She laughs. "Red is good for more savory dishes."

"Should I bust out the fish sauce?"

"Sure." She pours two glasses. Hands one to me. "But you have to let me help."

It's not a bad idea. Might get her used to taking orders. And I can't exactly complain about having her this close. "On one condition."

"Yeah?"

"You put away the cinnamon."

"Asshole."

I shrug like I don't care.

But, fuck, her smile feels good.

I move close enough I can smell her shampoo.

Roses.

Of course, she smells like roses.

It's her.

It's hot as hell.

I take a long sip. Wine isn't my preferred drink, but it's not bad. And the savory flavor would go perfectly with a beef stir fry. "You're on chopping duty."

She holds her hand to her head in salute. "Yes, sir."

My cock stirs. That sounds way too fucking good on her lips.

I pull out the cutting board. Then the ingredients.

Slowly, I take her through the process of fixing a traditional beef bowl.

She hangs close to me. Her eyes stay wide.

Our glasses stay full.

Once everything is simmering, I hand her the spoon.

She places her body in front of the burner. Watches vegetables and meat fold together as she stirs. "You're good at this. Did you teach yourself?"

"Yeah." I move next to her. So the back of my hand brushes her wrist.

She lets out a heavy sigh. An *I want more* sigh. "Owen and I learned together. Because our parents were always working."

"You cooked with your brother?"

"At first. Then he realized I was terrible and sent me to do my homework."

I chuckle. "You're all right."

"I follow directions, sure, but I don't have that sense you do. I have no idea what works together."

"You can learn."

"I don't know. It's kind of like life. When I try to go off script… it never works."

"What about this?"

"This?" Her eyes meet mine. "I scripted this whole thing."

"Yeah?"

She nods.

"How so?"

"Well, I kinda… it's going to sound stupid."

"It won't."

"I made a list of guys I knew." Her eyes go to the stove top. She stares at the green beans as she stirs. "I narrowed it down to the best dozen, then I made a list of pros and cons."

"Really?"

"Yeah." Her cheeks flame red. "You, um, you won."

"Based on what?"

"Oh my God." Her eyes flit to me, then they're back on the stove. "This is so embarrassing."

"No, it's interesting."

"Well, there was a portion that was… shallow." Her cheeks flush.

"I was the hottest?"

She nods. "That was a big factor."

"No shame in that."

"Isn't there?"

I shake my head.

She sets the spoon down. Turns to me. "You have criteria too?"

"Not exactly."

"Still, I share my weird, you share your weird."

"You first."

"Only if you promise you're going." She offers her hand.

I shake my head and hold out my pinkie.

"Really?" She holds out hers.

I nod.

Yeah, it's a little old-school, pinkie promising.

But it's perfect.

She smiles as our fingers wrap around each other. "There were a few common pros. Hot was one. Experienced. And, well… bed hopping."

"Being a hot slut finally paid off."

"You're also a great host."

"I throw great parties?" I ask.

"Yeah, you keep people's needs in mind. That's important."

That's a good point, actually.

"And you're always very punctual."

"Fair," I say.

"And you make me laugh."

"I try."

"You do. You're good at it. Even though I'm always

nervous around you. I, ummm." She pushes her glasses up her nose. "I used to have a crush on you. I always did. But you never paid attention."

"I did."

"You always… I don't know. It was hard to quantify, but there's something about you."

"The tattoos?"

Her cheeks flush. "It's not. I swear I don't have a thing for bad boys."

"Yeah?"

"Really. I do like them. The tattoos, I mean. But it's more than that. It's more you. I like you."

"Thanks."

"God, that's such a lame compliment, isn't it? I like you."

"You could do better, yeah."

Her laugh is soft. "How about: I find you incredibly attractive."

"Make it dirtier."

Her cheeks flush. "You're hot as hell."

"And…"

"And?"

"You want to tear my clothes off?" I ask.

Her nod is shy.

"Say it out loud."

"I can't."

"You can." I hold up my wine glass. "We'll toast to it."

"We're going to toast to my desire to tear your clothes off?"

"Can you think of a better toast?"

Her laugh is loud. Hearty. "No, actually." She picks up her glass and brings it to eye-level. "Westley Keating—" Her blush deepens, but she pushes through it. "I desperately want to tear your clothes off."

Chapter Ten

WES

My cock stirs.

It's incredibly impatient.

It doesn't have time for the flirting, the tease, the foreplay.

It wants her hands, her lips, her cunt.

Quinn brings her glass to her red lips. Her throat quivers as she swallows.

Fuck, her neck is beautiful.

Her lips are perfect.

Her tits—

Uh-uh. Not going there. Not yet.

"Your turn," she says.

"For?"

"A compliment."

"You sure you can handle that?"

She shakes her head. "Do it anyway."

I should probably ease her into this. Say something about her dress or her hair or her smile.

My hand goes to the small of her back.

I pull her body closer. Not all the way into mine. But close enough I can feel the heat of her.

Fuck, she's positively electric.

I can't remember the last time I wanted someone this badly.

I'm not sure I've ever wanted someone this badly.

"I want to pin you to that wall, slide your panties aside, and drive my fingers into your cunt until you're groaning my name," I breathe.

"Fuck." Her pupils dilate. Her cheeks flush. Her chest heaves.

"I want to throw you on my bed and bury myself in you."

Her eyes stay wide with interest.

"I really fucking want to taste your cunt."

Her tongue slides over her lips.

"And I will." I release her. "But not yet."

She stumbles as she steps backward. She's too lost in something.

In me, I guess.

It feels good.

Like everything I want.

This is where we should be.

This is where everything makes sense.

No baggage. No pretenses. No pretending.

Just me driving her out of her fucking mind.

"I, uh… is dinner ready?" She motions to the stove.

"Should be."

"Let's eat then."

Fuck, she's adorable nervous.

I nod.

Together, we scoop everything into bowls, and bring them to the table.

74

She refills our glasses then scoops vegetables with her fork. "What about you? Your criteria?"

"It's not complicated."

"Oh?" She bites a green bean in half. Chews. Swallows.

"It's a sense I get."

"Of?" She leans closer. Stares into my eyes.

"How much I want to make a woman come."

"Oh." Her blush spreads to her chest. Her pupils dilate. Her fingers dig into the table. "That's, um... Do... um... do you want to make me come?"

"Fuck yeah."

"Oh. Good." She eats the other half of her green bean. "I also... I want that too."

Fuck, she's trying to kill me.

I swear she is.

"You... um... you're very sexy," she says. "How do you do that?"

"Don't really think about it like that."

"Still. There must be something."

"Just practice."

"Right." She scoops meat and rice with her fork. "You said that."

I nod.

"Sorry. I'm kinda nervous."

"It's okay." It's cute. Sweet. Hot. Still. I need to set her at ease. "You waited awhile to have sex."

She nods.

"Any reason?"

"I don't know." She takes a bite of her dinner. Chews slowly. "I guess I never met anyone who really inspired me. I've had the desire. I've gone on dates. But I never felt like I could trust anyone enough."

"You trust me?"

"Well... not yet. But I want to."

That's fair.

"What do you do?"

"Hmm?" Her fingers curl around her wine glass.

"When you want to fuck?"

Her blush deepens. "You know..." She clears her throat.

I shake my head. I don't know. I can guess. But I want to know.

She shoots me a *really* look.

"Say it."

"I masturbate."

"How?"

Her blush spreads to her chest. "I just... do." She swallows a sip of wine. "How do you?"

"You want a play-by-play?"

Her eyes go wide.

"'Cause I can walk you through it step-by-step."

"Maybe... Um... I..."

"Sometimes, I replay a past fuck. Sometimes I watch porn. Sometimes I think about someone I desperately want."

"Have you thought about me?"

"Yeah."

She chokes on her wine. "I... Uh..."

"I want you bad, Quinn. I'm not doing this as a favor."

"Good." She sets her glass down. Wipes her hands on her dress. "I want you too. A lot. I... um... I thought about you too. That's what I normally do. Imagine stuff. I've watched porn, but I don't really like it."

My cock stirs. A beautiful mental image fills my head—Quinn spread out on my bed, her eyes glued to the TV screen, her hand between her legs, her face contorted with pleasure. "Go on..."

"It's just so..."

"Fake?"

She nods. "I prefer something more…"

"Artistic?"

"Yeah. That's a good way to put it. Makes me sound pretentious, but yeah."

"You aren't?"

"If this is about *Casablanca*—"

"It's not."

"Because it's a highly entertaining film."

"I believe you."

She finishes her wine. Stares at the empty glass like she's not sure where her drink went. "There's not much I can teach you, Wes, but I will teach you about *Casablanca*."

"Yeah?"

She nods. "I'll bring it next time. We can watch together."

"Shit, you sure I'm ready for that?"

"You're right. We don't start with the climax. We work up to it."

"So you're bringing—"

"I'll make a syllabus." She holds up her hands like she's drawing a marquee. "Classic Cinema 101." She takes another bite into her mouth. Chews. Swallows. "You're um, you really are good. I said that, huh?"

"Yeah, but I appreciate hearing it again."

"So… what types of movies do you watch?"

"Besides *Mission Impossible*?"

She sticks out her tongue. "No offense."

"You're the one missing out."

"I don't think so."

"Have you seen any?"

"No, but—"

"I won't create an entire lesson plan. Just one action packed spy movie."

Her nose scrunches in distaste. "I don't know."

"You trust me?"

"Yeah, but there's trusting you and *trusting you*."

"It's only two hours." I hold out my hand for a pinkie promise.

"Okay. Deal." She wraps her pinkie around mine.

Her shoulders ease as she settles into her seat.

I keep the conversation light. Talk about movies. About the ones she loves.

She relaxes enough to gush.

Until we finish dinner.

She goes to the bathroom.

Then straight to the bedroom.

She leaves the door open a crack.

For me.

She thinks she isn't skilled, but, fuck, that's the smoothest thing I've seen in ages.

———

"So." Quinn presses her palms into the soft red fabric of her dress. "This is your bedroom."

Her innocent expression is irresistible.

I want to push that dress to her waist and dive between her legs.

I want to taste every inch of her sweet cunt.

I want to make her come so hard she wakes the neighbors.

"You like it?" I slide my hands into the pockets of my jeans. I need to slow down.

She's new and nervous and she's trusting me to lead her.

I can't think with my cock.

No matter how much I want to bury myself inside her.

"I do." She takes in the powder blue walls. The sleek white desk and dresser. The framed art hanging on the walls.

I flick the switch. Turn the main lights off and the string lights on.

Quinn lets out a soft gasp. She looks around the room like it's something out of her favorite movie.

I felt the same way when I first moved in.

But after three years of empty sex—

It screams at me: *you think this is better than drowning yourself in booze?*

I swallow hard.

Yeah, I should sort out the shit that's been going through my head.

But not right now.

Not with Quinn ready and waiting.

She presses her palms into her thighs. "We haven't talked about exclusivity."

"I assumed that was part of the deal."

"Oh. Good." She turns to me. "What do you think we'll do tonight?"

"Come here." I pat the spot on the bed next to me.

She smooths her dress as she takes a seat.

"That doesn't work."

"What doesn't?"

Her fingers trace the hem of her dress.

"No planning here."

"But…" She catches herself playing with her dress. Presses her hands into the soft grey bedspread.

I brush her hair behind her ear. "No but, angel. We take this one moment at a time."

She nods *okay*, but that doesn't ease the apprehension in her eyes.

She's nervous.

I get that.

And I can fix it.

Her hand goes to my chest. She pulls my t-shirt down enough to reveal my tattoo. "Did you always want that?"

"Want what?"

"To be a tattoo artist?"

I study her expression. Is she trying to get to know me? To slow down? To prove a point?

I don't know.

But talking can't hurt.

I sure as hell like talking to her.

"No." My eyelids flutter closed as her fingers brush my skin. "When Chase got Hunter a job as an apprentice, they made it clear it was their thing. That I was supposed to stick with school."

"And you couldn't stand that?"

"Am I that obvious?"

"Sometimes." Her eyes meet mine. "You love them a lot, huh?"

"They're okay." I mean to make it playful, but there's something missing. I love my brothers. I'd do anything for them. But shit is strained. It's been strained a long time.

"You've worked with them your entire adult life."

"So I can give them shit."

"Maybe." Her fingers curl into my skin. "Or maybe you care more than you let on."

Not having this conversation now. "I do care."

"Yeah?"

"About making you come."

Her breath catches in her throat.

For a split second, she freezes.

Then she blinks. Moves. Nods. "Is that what we're—"

"I told you, Quinn. You can't plan this." I shift onto the bed. Behind her. Then I slide my legs around her.

She sighs as I wrap my arms around her waist.

"This okay?"

"Yes. Thank you."

Fuck, she's so polite.

It sends my blood racing to my cock.

There's something wrong with me.

Her manners shouldn't be this much of a turn on.

But they are.

They really are.

I inhale deeply. Replay yesterday's most irritating client. This guy who walked in wanting a back piece, with no prep time. I tried to tell him I couldn't design something that intricate in twenty minutes, but he wouldn't listen.

Probably should have told him to fuck off.

But I made it work well enough.

It was a fun challenge, actually.

Kinda like—

Fuck, this isn't working.

I'm not cooling down.

I'm drifting off.

I have to stay here. In this moment.

And I have to stay patient.

Somehow.

"You love your job?" she asks.

"I do." I pull her closer. Until her back is against my chest. It's nice talking to her. Easy. I almost want to spend the night with our clothes on.

No, I do want that.

Only I can't handle that kind of intimacy.

I understand sex.

I don't understand this.

Fuck, I don't even have a word for it.

Better to focus on what makes sense.

I hold her in place with one arm. Bring my other hand to her thigh. Play with the hem of her dress.

"Wes…" Her voice gets low. Nervous.

This is a lot for her.

I need to go slower.

"Yeah?" I brush her hair behind her head.

"You, um… I forgot."

"That's okay." I press my lips to her neck.

She lets out a soft murmur. "How did you start with tattoos?"

"Stole Chase's gun."

"Really?"

I nod.

"What happened?"

"Got into a lot of trouble."

"How?"

"Lean down."

"What?"

"Pull my jeans up." I pat my right leg. "This side."

She leans forward. Grabs the denim fabric and tugs.

Fuck, this view—

"Oh." She shifts off the bed. Between my legs.

She's exactly where she needs to be. This is exactly where I need her.

Her fingers curl around my ankle. She traces the lopsided skull and cross bones. "You did this?"

"Yeah."

"It's—"

"Terrible."

"Crooked." She looks up at me.

Fuck, she's right between my legs.

Those hazel eyes are big.

Those glasses—

"Oh." Her gaze settles on my crotch. "I didn't, I, um…"

"It's not gonna hurt you."

She stares at my hard-on like it's about to bust through my jeans and attack her.

At the moment, it feels like it might.

"I…" She stands. Stays between my legs. "I did that."

I nod.

"But… how."

I bring my hands to her hips. "You're positioned like you're about to blow me."

"Oh."

"Puts ideas in my head."

"Good ideas?"

"Fucking great ideas." I pull her into my lap.

She yelps as she wraps her arms around my shoulders.

We fall onto the bed.

It's far from smooth.

But, fuck, seeing Quinn sprawled out over my grey comforter—

I'm going to come in my jeans at this rate.

"Come here." I place my body next to hers.

She moves closer.

I wrap my fingers around her wrist. Bring her hand to my waist.

"We haven't kissed yet," she whispers.

"Yeah?"

"I can't touch your dick until we've kissed."

"Let's change that." I bring my hand to the small of her back. Pull her body into mine.

She groans as my hard-on brushes her stomach.

She looks up at me for a moment.

Then those big, hazel eyes close.

Her lips meet mine.

It's not like kissing other women.
It's just as hot.
Just as deep.
But it's a million times better.
It's fucking magic.

Chapter Eleven

QUINN

I'm kissing Wes Keating.

The neon sign flashes in bright, brilliant orange.

I'm kissing Wes Keating.

He tastes like wine.

And like Wes.

And, well, I can do this.

I have done this.

Only…

He sucks on my bottom lip. Softly. Then harder. Then he's scraping his teeth against my flesh.

It's hot as hell.

And so beyond my level.

He's a great kisser.

We're just starting and I can tell he's a great kisser.

Whereas I…

Is this enough tongue? Too soft? Too hard?

Is my breath okay?

Is…

His fingers curl into my hair.

His hips rock against my pelvis.

His hard-on brushes my stomach.

My dress and panties and his jeans are in the way, but I can still feel the pressure of him.

I'm doing that.

I'm making him hard.

It's not the first time it's happened—I've dated a little—but it's the first time it's made my sex clench.

With other guys, I was scared.

Terrified I'd do something wrong.

Or that it would be uncomfortable.

Now…

Well, I'm still scared. But I'm more okay with my fear.

I have to go for it. To kiss him back.

I part my lips.

His tongue slips into my mouth. Swirls around mine. It's just the right pace. Not too slow or too fast.

And it's just the right pressure.

He's really good at this.

I pull back with a heavy sigh.

His fingers brush my temples as he slides my glasses off my face.

He reaches backward, drops them on his bedside table, brings his hand back to my hip. "You okay?"

I nod. "Am I… am I doing it wrong?"

"Not wrong." His eyes fix on mine. Something spreads over his face. Something he wants to say.

"But not right either?"

He doesn't answer the question. "What are you thinking about?"

"Everything."

"Stop."

"Stop thinking?"

He nods.

I stare at him, but that does nothing to change his suggestion.

He stares back with those piercing blue eyes.

Stop thinking?

He might as well ask me to stop breathing.

I shake my head.

"Try," he says.

"If I try, I'm just going to think about how I'm not supposed to be thinking."

"Try anyway."

"But——"

"Focus on the sensations."

I shake my head.

"Try. If it's not working, it's not working."

"Okay." If this is really what I need to do... somehow, I'll have to learn.

It's eluded me for twenty-two years.

But maybe it's possible.

Maybe...

"Quinn." He drags his fingertips over my temple. Along my jawline. My chin.

"Yeah?"

"You're doing it again."

"I'm trying."

"Close your eyes."

I shoot him a *really* look.

He nods *really*.

Fine. I close my eyes.

"I'm going to kiss you."

"Okay."

"I want you to follow my movements. Try what I do."

"Okay."

His fingers curl into my hair.

He holds me in place as he brings his lips to mine.

Again, he sucks on my bottom lip. Softly. Then harder. Then the gentle scrape of his teeth.

Desire floods my body.

My sex whines for attention.

I'm empty.

It's not an entirely new sensation, but it's more intense than ever.

I want him to fill me.

I want to make him this crazy.

I bring my hand to the back of his head. Knot my fingers in his hair. Wrap my lips around his bottom lip.

Suck softly.

Then harder.

He yelps as I scrape my teeth against his flesh.

Shit.

I pull back. "Too hard?"

"A little." He rubs his lip with the back of his hand. "But good."

"Really?"

His nod is sure. Confident. "Try again."

"I'm sorry."

"Don't be. It's hot you got carried away."

It was more a lack of technique, but I don't argue. His compliment feels too good.

All of this feels too good.

My entire body is buzzing with the strangest mix of nerves and desire.

I want him.

And I'm terrified of screwing this up.

But I… I'm getting over it.

No thinking.

Just doing.

I close my eyes. Knot my hand in his hair. Bring my lips to his.

Suck softly. Then harder. Then it's my teeth—as gentle as I can.

He groans against my lips.

His hips buck against mine.

He's still hard.

Fuck, it's amazing.

His tongue slips into my mouth. Swirls around mine. Slowly. Then faster. Then slower again.

I copy the gesture. Vary my speed. My pressure.

It's close.

But not quite there.

Wes pulls back.

His eyelids flutter open.

His baby blues fix on me.

There's something in his expression. Some mix of affection and pride.

Maybe because I'm getting it right.

Or maybe because he likes me.

My stomach flutters.

My limbs get airy.

I need to draw that line. We're friends. He's teaching me. There's nothing romantic about this.

But he has such pretty eyes.

How can I say anything that will make him look away?

"Better." He brushes my hair behind my ear.

My eyelids press together.

Fuck, that's intense.

Tender.

Sweet.

Hot.

"Can we keep going?" I ask.

"Fuck yeah." He brings his hands to my waist.

I stare up into his eyes for a long moment. Then I bring my lips to his.

He kisses back right away.

His tongue slips into my mouth.

His fingers trail along my chin. Down my neck. Over my collarbones.

He traces the neckline of my dress. Back and forth and back again.

I arch my back, bringing our bodies closer.

His cock brushes my stomach.

It's thrilling and terrifying.

I try to copy his gestures. To run my fingers over his cheeks and chin and neck. But it's not quite right.

His fingers curl around my wrist.

He takes my hand. Brings it to his hip.

Then closer.

Closer.

Closer.

There.

My palm brushes his crotch.

I can feel him through his jeans.

Fuck, I'm twenty-two and this is the closest I've come to touching a guy.

I'm hopelessly behind schedule.

And I...

What do I do?

I apply a little more pressure with my palm, but it doesn't cause a reaction. He doesn't groan against my lips or tug at my hair or rock his hips.

It's not bad—he isn't stopping me—but it's not good either.

I ease up on the pressure.

Try rubbing him the way I rub myself.

It's not quite the same—there's a lot more, um, surface area, and it's over his jeans—but it's better.

I'm not sure how I can tell.

I just can.

Wes breaks our kiss to groan. His reaches for my hand. "Not yet, angel."

"But—"

"I don't want to come in my jeans."

My cheeks flush.

My sex clenches.

He's so good at making me feel this strange mix of desperate and nervous.

"Give me your hands," he says.

I do.

His fingers wrap around my wrists. He slips both under his t-shirt.

One palm presses against his stomach. The other against his chest. Soft skin covers hard muscle.

He's so warm.

So hard.

So... good.

There's no other way to describe it. He just feels good. Like he's supposed to be against my hands.

Like we're supposed to be touching each other.

His eyelids flutter closed.

His lips find mine.

I kiss him harder.

He brings his hand to my chest. Cups me over my dress.

Mmm.

He finds my zipper. Undoes it. Pushes my dress to my waist.

He cups my breast over my bra.

Then under it.

He drags his thumb over my nipple. Back and forth. Then up and down. Around and round.

My thoughts dissipate.

My body buzzes.

Every brush of his digit sends desire right to my core.

He toys with me until I'm panting, then he moves to my other breast, and he does it again.

I pull back to groan.

He reaches around my back.

In one swift motion, he unhooks my bra, slides it off my shoulders, tosses it aside.

He rolls onto his back and motions *come here*.

I do.

I'm out of my fucking mind.

I'm crawling on top of Wes Keating.

There.

I'm straddling Wes.

I'm topless and I'm straddling Wes.

I'm topless and I'm straddling Wes and I'm grinding against his hard-on.

What the hell happened to my life?

He stares up at me as he toys with my breasts.

I lean down to brush my lips to his.

At first, I focus on my technique. Sucking on his lip. Swirling my tongue around his. Hitting that perfect mix of aggressive and patient.

With every flick of his digits, I lose a little focus.

Stop thinking.

Feel.

Fuck, I feel everything.

He winds me tight.

He makes me so fucking achy.

Then he brings his hand to my thigh.

He looks up at me, asking for permission.

I nod.

He nods back. Pulls me into a kiss. Drags his fingers higher, higher, higher.

Over my panties.

Fuck.

Pleasure floods my body.

It's so much.

It's too much.

I...

I try to go back to technique. To kissing him right. To touching him right.

But it's so much.

He's so close to touching me.

And I...

I can't do this.

I pull back. Mumble something about the bathroom. Dart to said room.

It's bright and white and quiet.

I pee. Wash my hands. Pull my dress back on.

Deep breath.

Slow exhale.

I can handle Wes touching me.

It's not a big deal.

It's really not.

I just have to breathe.

In.

Out.

In.

Out.

"Quinn?" His footsteps move into the hallway. "You okay?"

"Yeah. Totally." I pull the bathroom door open. Step into the hall.

He's standing there, his jeans doing nothing to hide his hard-on.

It's still thrilling.

But the terrifying part?

Yeah, that part is winning.

"I just, um, I have work early and I... I should probably go." I don't wait for him to reply. I move to the main room. I grab my purse. I slide into my shoes. "Good night."

"You okay?"

"I'll see you next week."

He says something in response, but I don't hear it.

Only this voice in my head yelling *Quinn Thorn is going to die an awkward virgin.*

Chapter Twelve

WES

I stare at my closed door for way too fucking long.

It fails to illuminate Quinn's mental state.

I shoot her an *are you okay* text.

When she doesn't answer, I escalate.

Wes: Come by the shop tomorrow.

Quinn: I have work.

Wes: I have your glasses.

Quinn: Oh.

Wes: Oh? How'd you get home?

Quinn: I walked. I have backups in my apartment.

She does live close.

But still.

Was she really so nervous she'd rather walk home without glasses?

I need to change my approach here.

To go softer.

Or harder.

Or from a different angle.

Or—

Fuck, all these metaphors are sending my head straight to sex.

Wes: I'll be there all day. Ten to ten.

Quinn: I don't know.

Wes: You want me to teach you?

Quinn: Yeah.

Wes: Then be there sometime between ten and ten.

Quinn: There's nothing to say.

Wes: This isn't a negotiation, Quinn. Come by tomorrow if you want this to happen.

Quinn: When did you get all demanding?

It's not the carefree impression I cultivate.

But I'm getting worse and worse at pretending I'm that guy.

I toss my phone on the couch. Try to find solace in an action flick.

For a while, the explosions entertain enough.

Eventually, my mind starts wandering.

To my visit with Mom last weekend—she was drunk, of course. The lecture Hunter gave me about enabling bullshit. Then follow-up from Chase about boundaries.

For two people who barely communicate, my brothers are really on the same wavelength.

I give up on the movie. Brush my teeth. Wash my face. Strip to my boxers.

The sheets still smell like Quinn.

My body doesn't care that she ran away.

It's already raring to go.

I ditch the boxers. Close my eyes. Wrap my hand around my cock.

She fills my head.

Soft red lips. Perky tits. Hard nipples. Big hazel eyes.

That groan—

Fuck.

I come so fast it's embarrassing.

———

"YOU KNOW BRENDON HAS A LOT OF ADVICE ABOUT deflowering virgins." Dean slides onto the counter and pats the space between his legs. He looks to his girlfriend slash apprentice and motions *come here*.

Chloe gives him a long once-over. She brushes a short, dark strand behind her ear. Slides one hand into her black jeans.

She only wears black.

It suits her.

She's sixty inches of badass babe.

She's an aikido expert who could kick my ass like *that*.

Usually, that would be a turn on.

But Chloe is so... Chloe, I guess.

"Brendon has advice on deflowering virgins?" She shoots Dean a cutting look. "And you don't?"

"Go on, sunshine." His smile gets wicked.

Well, more wicked.

Dean's smile is always wicked.

Chloe shoots me a *can you believe this* look.

I shrug.

I've been working here for nearly a year and I've known Dean for longer —he and Hunter were friends back in high school.

His effortless party boy act—

Well, it's kinda getting in my grill.

Even worse, he pulls it off better than I do.

He's happy.

Everything is easy for him.

It's fucking annoying.

Don't get me wrong. I like the guy. I really like Chloe

(though I'd never tell her in such plain language). I wish them both the best.

But I'm only human.

I can't help but find their easy intimacy disgusting.

Yeah, they're in love, they want to bang each other, they know how to communicate.

They could stop rubbing our faces in it.

"You haven't told everyone here that story?" She stretches her hands.

"Keep some things to myself." Dean turns to me. "When's the virgin coming over?"

"When did I say she was a virgin?" Fucking Griffin. He's usually better at keeping secrets.

This place makes it impossible.

Inked Hearts is all gossip, no privacy.

The entire shop knows I'm planning on popping Quinn's cherry.

"Quinn is coming by today." I fold one leg over the other. Bring my attention to the sketchbook in my hands.

I'm here early for a reason and it's not bantering with Dean. It's figuring this out.

Design is my weakest spot.

My tattoo technique is perfect.

My bedside manner is on point.

But my actual artistic skills?

Not as much.

"She sounds hot." Dean looks to Chloe. "You think?"

"You told him," she says.

He shakes his head.

"No way," she says.

He nods.

She looks to me. "You don't know the details?"

They had sex in high school. I've heard that much.

Based on the tone of her voice, I'm going to say he deflowered her.

They're together now.

But there were a lot of years between their sex and their love. And she spent most of those years hating his guts. Well, I'm pretty sure Chloe always hated Dean. But in that *I hate you so much I want you* way.

"How'd he fuck it up?" I ask.

"He was really sweet when it happened," she says.

Dean blows her a kiss. "Made sure to warm her up."

She rolls her eyes. "You say everything in such a—"

"Visceral way," he finishes.

"Where did you learn the word visceral?" she teases.

"Where do you think, sunshine?" he asks.

"I don't say it," she says.

He nods *you do too*.

She shakes her head *I do not*.

Yeah, they're adorable.

But I need this intel.

"Were you scared?" I ask Chloe.

"Who wasn't?" Her eyes flit from Dean to me then back to Dean. "But I... God, there was a stupid part of me that trusted Dean."

"Hey." He tries to fake hurt, but the playfulness is missing.

"He eased me into it." She folds her arms over her chest. "It was... it was special. Intense. In a good way." She turns her back to him. "But after... Never mind."

"Chloe." He slides off the counter and moves toward her.

She shakes her head. "It was a long time ago."

He wraps his arms around her and whispers something in her ear.

Again, she shakes her head.

He whispers something else.

This time, she nods.

He leans down.

She rises to her tiptoes.

Their kiss is more sweet than carnal.

It would be adorable if I was in the mood to support a healthy relationship.

As it is—

I clear my throat. "You better be escalating to penetration."

She flips me the bird.

He pulls back. Shifts right into bullshit mode. "You're only giving him ideas, sunshine."

"You want penetration, watch porn," she says.

"Amateur stuff," Dean adds.

She shakes her head. "Every day."

"People have to know," he says.

"Did you know that Dean prefers amateur porn?" She laughs.

"You watch it with him?" I ask.

Her cheeks flush.

It's cute.

Hot.

Don't get me wrong. I'm not into Chloe.

She's hot yeah, but we're too close. I can't think about fucking a woman I really know.

It's probably a sign my head is messed up. I'm sure Griffin or Hunter would have a lot to say about it. As it is—

I'm not diving into that.

Besides, I'm getting to know Quinn.

And I'm still desperate to fuck her.

I'm desperate for advice.

I shrug like I don't care. "The booze was the secret?"

Something flares in her eyes. "You like her."

I shoot Chloe an *of course* look. "Wouldn't fuck her if I didn't like her."

"You've been walking around on a cloud all week," Dean says.

They exchange a knowing look. One at my expense.

"You need some tips?" she asks.

"No." Not like this.

The buzz of a tattoo gun ceases.

Brendon stands. Stretches his arms over his head. Whispers something to his client.

The client—a short guy with bulging biceps—sighs with relief. He pushes himself off the chair—he's face down, getting a back piece—and rushes to the bathroom.

Brendon steps into the main room and shakes his head.

He adopts his usual paternal expression.

I know best and it's not this. It's not anything you could come up with. Quite frankly, you're an idiot.

He raises a brow. "You guys here to work or…?"

"Fuck around." Dean slides his hand into the back pocket of Chloe's jeans. "Of course."

Brendon's dark hair falls over his eyes as he shakes his head.

For a guy who despises emo music, he has awfully long bangs.

It's a good look for him. He's handsome. Dark hair. Dark eyes. Dominant demeanor.

Great for his girlfriend, I'm sure.

Hell, decent for a boss.

Easier to handle his direct *do what you're told* thing than Dean's *I don't care what you do* shrugs.

"Sorry." Chloe shoots him an apologetic look. "I—"

"Wes is looking for tips on deflowering virgins," Dean says. "In alleys maybe."

Brendon shoots him a *don't* look.

There's some story I don't know.

That I'm not going to find out.

I love working at Inked Hearts, but it's hard being the perpetual new guy. The original owners have a secret language.

Brendon's eyes fix on me. "You need some advice?"

Yeah, but I can't admit it in such plain language. "Always good for *the tip*."

Dean laughs. "Sounds like you want his tip."

I flip him off.

He laughs.

Chloe nods. "I hate to admit it, but Dean is right."

"Don't you two have shit to do?" I ask.

Brendon shoots them a *go away* look.

Somehow, it works.

Dean pulls Chloe to the office.

Brendon moves into my suite.

His gaze shifts to my sketchbook. "Coming along?"

"Getting there." I hold up the current design. A half-sleeve inspired by Chinese dragons. It's beautiful. Sharp details. Bold colors. Complete lack of personality.

He nods. "This going on a shoulder?"

"Yeah."

"It's good. Enough curve. Strong lines." He stares at the paper. "It's a nice piece." Something drips into his voice. A hesitation.

"But?"

"It's not a Wes original. Anyone could design that."

"Not everything—"

"Yeah, but some things." He steps backward. Shrugs. "Not my place."

"You are my boss," I say.

"Only technically." He leans against the half wall. "You ever want help, let me know."

"Sure." I swallow hard. Brendon is too straight-forward. He's not as bad as Ryan—that guy wears his heart on both sleeves—but he's still a lot.

"Who's the virgin?" he asks.

"Dean's being an idiot."

"Dean's always an idiot."

I shrug *true enough.*

Which does nothing to fool him.

He moves a little closer. "There is a girl."

"Yeah."

"You like her?"

"She's sweet, yeah."

"Sweet or *sweet?*" he asks.

Somehow, he packs pounds of intention into the single word.

Is she a sweet person or the kind of sweet innocence that demands getting very, very dirty?

She's both.

And I want both.

I want to cook dinner with her. Talk to her. Hold her in my bed.

And I want to make her come until she passes out.

"You really like her." He smiles. "I know the feeling."

"How is your girl?" My gaze flits to the clock. I have an appointment at the top of the hour. Which is forever away. There's nowhere to hide. No escape from how real this is.

"Good. At a coffee shop, writing." His expression beams with pride. "She's halfway through her first novel."

"That's great." I only sorta know his girlfriend, Kaylee. But it's obvious they're madly in love.

"I wish I could tell you I was sweet and gentle the first time I fucked her," Brendon says. "But I wasn't."

"Oh?"

"It wasn't what she needed."

"What did she need?"

"That is none of your fucking business." His eyes flit to the door as the bell rings. "But I can tell you this."

"Yeah?" I ask.

"As long as you give her what she needs, you're golden," he says.

The bell rings as the door swings open. "Hello?" Quinn's voice echoes around the shop.

My body responds immediately.

My cock stirs.

My heart races.

My limbs get light.

I want to fuck her.

And I want to hold her.

I have no fucking idea how to deal with that.

Chapter Thirteen

WES

Quinn folds her hands together.

Her hazel eyes fix on me.

"Hey." Her voice is soft. Shy. Pure Quinn.

I'm flattered.

Endeared even.

But I need to push past this.

I need her comfortable.

"Hey." I motion to my suite. It's as private as it gets here.

She nods an *okay* and follows me.

The hum of Brendon's gun mixes with the grunge song pouring from the speakers. The singer mumbles about the agony of—well, knowing grunge, it's something about heroin addiction or homelessness or meds for bipolar disorder.

It's not an upbeat style.

Certainly not the appropriate soundtrack for this conversation.

I motion to my chair.

Quinn nods a *thank you* and takes a seat. She presses her knees together. Smooths her skirt.

It's a loose brown thing that falls over her legs.

Between her shiny shoes, her skirt, her ivory blouse, and her tortoiseshell glasses, she looks like an artist on her lunch break.

Nothing about her says *future doctor*.

Or *I want a tattoo*.

Or *I'm the kind of girl who ends up with a guy like Wes Keating*, for that matter.

I fish her glasses from my backpack.

Her fingers brush mine as I hand them over.

"Thank you." She slides them into her purse. Places said purse in her lap. Looks up at me with attentive posture.

I reach for some way to start. Find nothing.

She's still scared.

I don't know how to fix that.

Her gaze flits to the tile floor. "Listen, Wes—"

No, whatever she wants to say in that defeated tone of voice, I don't want to hear it.

"I get it." I roll my shoulders back. Suck a breath through my teeth. I need to reassure her here. I need to convince her I'm cool and collected.

"I—"

"It's overwhelming thinking about how you can handle such large equipment."

Her laugh breaks up the furrow in her brow. "You're really—"

"You felt it."

"That wasn't…"

"Not at all?"

Her cheeks flush. "I was… well… um."

"I'll show you what to do."

106

"Now?"

Fuck yeah. Take off your panties. You need to come on my hand. Now. "You that eager, angel?"

She forces a smile.

It's completely fake.

She's still scared.

I need to keep this light. To ease her into it.

"I have an idea," I say.

Her eyes go wide. "What kind of idea?"

"You have that list, right?"

Confusion spreads over her expression.

"The summer bucket list."

"Oh. Yeah. But it's silly."

"Sounds fun to me."

She brings her index finger to her lips. Gnaws on her nail. "I'm sure it's stuff you know."

"I know less than you'd think." I tap my head. "Nothing but tits and beer."

"And tattoos?"

"Only when I'm working."

She motions to the shop around us.

I nod *fair enough.* "You gonna get one?"

"A tattoo? One day. Maybe."

"Can I do it?"

"What?"

"If you get one."

"Okay. I guess. But I don't think I will."

"They're addictive."

Her gaze moves over my arm. "I can see that." She tries to look me in the eyes. Settles on my lips. "It's a sweet offer, Wes."

"Think about it."

She nods.

"Decide by midnight."

"I have work later."

I shrug *too bad*.

Maybe it's not the best idea, putting more pressure on Quinn.

But I need her to decide she's in.

I hold up my pinkie. "Tonight. Text me. You're in or you're out."

"If I'm out?"

"Fuck, I'd really hate if some other guy got all your firsts."

She holds up her hand. "You're kinda manipulative."

"Only when I want something."

We pinkie promise.

I walk her to her car.

Hug her goodbye.

She doesn't say anything about the offer, but it's there in her eyes.

She wants this.

All of it.

Chapter Fourteen

WES

There's no sense in denying it.

I'm sweating this.

It's eleven fifteen and my cell is silent.

There isn't a single word about Quinn's decision.

I give up on flipping channels. TV is great most nights. But right now?

It's the least interesting thing in the entire world.

I rise. Move to my bedroom. Toss my sketchbook on my desk.

Brendon was right.

My shit is generic as hell.

It's empty.

It pleases clients.

Earns enough to pay the rent.

But it doesn't fill that hole in my gut.

It barely makes sense to me, the whole idea of pouring myself onto the page.

How the fuck does anyone do that?

Guys like Brendon or Ryan—they lay their hearts bare for anyone to see.

For anyone to destroy.

I close my eyes. Let my thoughts blur. Pick up the pen.

Draw what comes.

A broken bottle.

A shard of glass.

A finger spilling blood.

One of those Mom tattoos, with the letters a blur.

It's different than my usual shit.

Rougher.

Rawer.

Scarier.

It's not like I'm suffering under some fantasy that I know my own mind.

But actually facing it?

Fuck that.

Running is underrated.

I turn the page. Focus on my latest mock-up. A pop-culture inspired design for a college girl. Some anime I've never heard of.

The shapes are perfect for a tattoo.

The style is already there.

I just transpose it.

It feels good, getting it done, sending her an image, getting an *awesome*! in response.

But it only tugs at the hole in my gut.

This time last month, work and booze and women were enough to satisfy.

Now—

Something is different.

Quinn.

Fuck, that sounds awful. Like she's making this shit worse.

It's not her, exactly.

More the possibilities she promises.

Seeing Quinn reminds me of the guy I wanted to be.

Who didn't have to pretend he was easy.

Who didn't keep handing his heart over to someone who wanted to tear it in half.

Who—

My phone sings with the text tone I set for her. *Girl, You'll Be a Woman Soon* (obvious, I know).

It's right there.

One little word.

Quinn: Yes.

My fingers skim the slick surface of my cell.

Quinn: I'm all in. But you have to promise not to mock my list.

Wes: I'd die first.

Quinn: Really?

Wes: Yeah.

Quinn: That's awfully dramatic, even for you.

Wes: There's no "even for me."

Quinn: True.

A picture image fills my screen.

A list scribbled on a piece of paper.

Learn to paddle board.

Learn to rollerblade.

Hike in Malibu.

See the Hollywood sign.

Visit Las Vegas

Lose my virginity.

My lips curl into a smile.

I want to show her things.

To show her everything.

Quinn: Where should we start?

Wes: Monday. Eight a.m. I'll come to your place.

Quinn: That's all I get?

Wes: Yeah.

Quinn: What do I wear?

Wes: You have all your clothes at your apartment?

Quinn: Well, yeah, of course.

Wes: Seems like it shouldn't be a problem.

Quinn: Wes, trust me, you don't want to wait for me to get dressed. It can take ages.

Wes: It's a free show.

Quinn: It's less exciting than it sounds.

Wes: Are you taking off your clothes during this show?

Quinn: Yeah.

Wes: Then it's fascinating.

Chapter Fifteen

QUINN

At eight on the dot, Wes knocks on my door. "Hey, you request the cop or the fireman stripper?"

My lips curl into a smile.

He's just so... Wes.

"Fireman." My cheeks flush. He's so fucking sexy. It's hard teasing back without melting into a pile of desire. "He knows his way around his hose."

"Shit, I forgot the uniform. Does it count as stripping if I start naked?"

"Technically, no."

"How about if I start with jeans?"

"Could work."

"Hmm... might have to put on a show for the neighbors if you don't open up."

Right.

I cross the room, unlock the door, pull it open.

He's standing there in a pair of turquoise shorts, a white muscle tank, and tan Rainbow sandals.

Ultimate California Boy.

For my last summer in California.

Could I really ask for more?

"Lots of clothes for a stripper." My cheeks flush. It's so much harder doing this with him here.

Though, well, he's kind of an essential part of the formula.

Hard to lose it alone.

Hard to lose it if I keep running away.

I'm facing my fears.

Trusting him.

We're doing something today.

I'm okay not knowing what it is.

Really.

He tugs his tank up his stomach as he steps inside. "You want a show?"

My eyes go straight to the sliver of tanned, tone skin on display. He's so fucking hot. It's wrong. "It would be rude to turn you down."

"Yeah?" A laugh spills from his lips. It's big. Hearty.

His laugh sometimes sounds fake. But never when it's the two of us alone.

He's real with me.

I… I don't get much of that in my life.

It should make this easier.

But it only underlines how important this is.

If I fuck this up and scare him off, I'll have to settle for someone completely inferior.

Or remain a virgin forever.

Honestly, I'm not sure which is worse.

Shit. He's still standing there. Waiting for me. For something.

Well, whatever the circumstance, I do have manners. "You want something to drink? Water? Tea? Coffee?"

"You have coffee?"

"Instant."

His nose scrunches in distaste. "Anything but that."

"Black tea?"

"Sure."

"Of course." I motion to the kitchen across the living room. My apartment isn't nearly as nice as his—apparently, being a tattoo artist pays better than being a part-time scribe. It's small. Company is rare.

Him being here...

It's a big deal.

His gaze shifts around the room. He takes in the neatly stacked dishes by the sink. The medium sized TV. The blanket folded over the couch.

Then the walls.

They're covered in posters from old movies.

It's a theme.

They're big movies everyone has heard of.

But there's still something intimate about it.

He's in my space. Seeing all these clues to who I am.

I turn my attention to the kitchen counter. Fill the kettle with water. Turn it on. Pull almond milk from the fridge.

He moves into the kitchen. Into my space.

His hip brushes mine.

The back of his hand brushes my arm.

My body buzzes.

That proximity again.

He smells good.

Clean. Like soap.

I never thought soap smelled good, but it does.

He does.

He's just...

Wes.

"It, um, it will be a minute." I press my hands together, so I won't fidget. "I have decaf English Breakfast too. I've been trying to cut back. When school is in session, I'm really bad about caffeine. I drink more and more to get through studying, then, all of a sudden I'm drinking five cups a day to no effect."

"It happens."

"Yeah." God, what do I say here? "Do you like yours with milk or…"

"However you make it."

I nod.

The water steams.

I grab two mugs. Place a bag of English Breakfast in each.

Pour.

He gives me a long once-over as he dunks his tea bag. "When's it done?"

"Four minutes."

"You wait that long?"

"Coffee takes longer." Owen and I never could agree on the appropriate morning drink. Coffee is too much. Pure bitterness in liquid form.

Tea, now, that's the perfect drink.

I dunk my bag a few times (it speeds the steeping process), pull it out, add almond milk.

Wes copies the gesture.

He sighs as he takes a sip of his drink.

"Fuck, that's good." He sets his mug on the counter. Brings his hand to my hip. His fingers brush my glasses. Then the neckline of my fit and flare dress. "You look gorgeous."

"Thank you."

"You could have stayed in your pajamas."

I shake my head. "No, I don't think we know each other well enough for that."

"You'll let me touch your tits, but I can't see you in pajamas?"

My blush deepens. He still makes me nervous. But in a good way. In a really good way. "How many boobs have you touched?"

"Uh…" He scratches his head. "No comment."

"How many women have you seen in pajamas?"

"A lot. But I respect your boundaries."

"You sound like a shrink."

He laughs. "Fuck, I do. Slap me next time that happens."

"I'm not going to slap you."

"On the ass?"

"Sounds more like a reward."

His fingers curl into my hips. They press the soft fabric of my dress into my skin.

He moves closer.

Brings his other hand to the back of my head.

Pulls me into a deep, slow kiss.

My eyes close.

My lips part.

My thoughts scatter.

It's not like before. I'm not worried about technique or what I can handle or impressing him.

I'm there.

My body screams *Wes Wes Wes*.

One hand goes to his hair.

The other goes to his hip.

His ass.

I dig my fingers into the soft fabric of his shorts.

"Fuck." He pulls back with a breathy sigh. "You gotta warn me if you're going to pounce."

"You kissed me."

He shakes his head. "Not like that."

"Yeah like that."

"I gotta give you something, angel."

"Yeah?"

"You sure as hell retain information well."

"I, um… I'm a great student…" It doesn't sound flirty out loud. More awkward. "I mean thanks. You… um… you're a good teacher."

"Getting there." He takes a step backward. Motions to the coffee. "Why you cutting back?"

"Is it not obvious?"

He shakes his head.

"I, um… caffeine isn't great for my anxiety."

"Everyone gets nervous sometimes."

"Yeah… I do. A lot. I, um, I see a therapist sometimes. Well, I did."

"Did it help?" There's no judgment in his voice. Just casual acceptance. Like I told him I prefer my coffee without sugar.

It eases the knot in my stomach.

But it does something else too.

Makes everything light and airy.

Him accepting my weird…

I really want that.

"For a while. I… I didn't handle my senior year so well. There was a lot. With work and studying and applying to med school. I guess…" I wanted to figure out my future. Then all that therapy and my shrink was sure I wanted to be a doctor. That it was just fear standing in the way of that. And when I tried to say *no, it's more,* she'd argue with me. Remind me of all the other times fear got in my way.

It happened a lot.

But this…

I don't know.

Maybe she's right.

Maybe it's cold feet.

Maybe I don't know myself enough to know what I want.

"You guess?" Wes takes another sip of tea.

"I had a lot to think about."

"What's the verdict?"

"I didn't like my therapist. I fired her." I sip my English Breakfast. Mmm, it's good. But my brain has connected the taste with the caffeine boost. My thoughts are already moving a little faster. "Don't tell Owen."

"You talk about that shit?"

"Sometimes. He cares. But, um, he can be a know it all. He's going into psychiatry."

"And you?"

"Well, I did promise to fix your head."

"That interest you?"

"Sure. People are fascinating. And the mind…" I reach for my prepared answer. The one I deliver to friends, family, teachers, coworkers. "It's… It's a great field."

His head cocks to one side.

He nods with acceptance, but it's written all over his face.

He knows I'm full of shit.

"It's just… I don't think I could actually do the shrink thing. It was exhausting scrutinizing myself, my thoughts, my patterns. Dealing with someone else this… neurotic all day—"

"You're too hard on yourself."

"No, I just—"

"You can't help the way your brain works."

"Well, sorta. You can't fix a chemical imbalance with positive thinking. But the entire basis of cognitive behavioral therapy is that you can help the way your brain works. It's all about making new habits and patterns. But that's, um, that's more a psychologist. Psychiatrists are in such high demand they rarely have time to see patients for therapy. They're usually there to prescribe medication."

"I get what you mean." He sets his mug on the counter. Moves closer. "We all have shit we could do better."

I nod. "You?"

"Fuck, how much time do you have?"

"You seem... well-adjusted."

"Do I really?"

"Yeah." I move closer. Close enough to touch him.

Then I do.

My fingers brush his chin. His jawline. His temple.

He stares down at me with those gorgeous blue eyes.

There's this pain in them.

It's barely there, but it is.

What the hell is it that hurts him?

He blinks, and it's gone. He's back to that devil-may-care playboy. "Your place is nice."

"Oh, thanks." I motion to the posters. "It's not too much?"

He shakes his head. "It's perfect."

"So, um..." I reach for a response. Something flirty. "What are we doing today?"

"It's a surprise."

"I have to get dressed."

"Yeah, but if I tell you what to wear, you might not invite me into your bedroom."

Chapter Sixteen

QUINN

Wes's eyes go wide as he steps into my bedroom.

I pull my arms over my chest. Let out a steady exhale.

The last time I had a guy here was... never.

"You okay?" Wes presses my door closed.

I do the same thing when I'm alone.

Why do I do the same thing?

This is *my* apartment. Why not leave the door open? Why not walk around naked for anyone to see?

Wait.

Sure, Wes has touched my boobs, but it's not like I stripped naked for his viewing pleasure.

Though...

My sex clenches. There's something hot about that thought. About imagining the low, demanding tone to his voice. The desire in his eyes. The hardness in his shorts.

I want that.

I don't want to check off my bucket list.

I want to fuck him.

No, I do want to check off my bucket list.

And I want to fuck him.

Later.

Eventually.

Once I'm ready.

Which is totally happening.

Totally.

"Quinn?" Wes tilts his head to one side.

"Oh. Yeah. I was just thinking."

"About?"

"When I got this place. I work at the hospital on Twentieth." I smooth my dress. "It's nice being close to work, but traffic was so awful when I went to school."

"Bet you won't miss that."

"Yeah." There's no enthusiasm in my voice. It's like I'm going to war. "I mean, Chicago is no picnic. But I'm going to get a place near school. My parents want me to stay at home. But they're so far out in the suburbs." And the thought of sleeping in my old bedroom for a single night is suffocating. For four years? No way.

"Mine are in Beverly Hills."

"I always forget you're rich."

"They're rich."

"They don't share?" I ask.

"Not even a little."

"That sucks."

"I thought so at first."

"But you'd rather be self-reliant?"

He nods. "It feels good, not needing anyone."

That's a funny way to word it. I study Wes's expression.

It's the same as usual.

Effortless. Teasing. Wicked.

There are no signs of hurt in his deep blue eyes.

No cracks in his smile.

Maybe he means it's nice being self-reliant. Not that he never wants to need anyone.

God knows I can't judge. I'm not exactly good at letting my guard down. Thus the whole virgin at twenty-two thing.

I move to the closet. Pull the door.

Wes lets out a hearty chuckle. "That is exactly what I imagined."

"What?" My cheeks flush. There's nothing funny about my closet. It's well organized, sure, but that's completely sensible.

"Nothing."

"You're laughing."

"With you." He moves closer. Until he's right there. His fingers brush the back of my hand. My wrist. "This is you. It's a rainbow of gorgeous dresses."

"Well, yeah, what else would I wear?"

"Pants?"

"Why would I wear pants?"

"They're practical."

"Yeah, but…" They're pants. They're so plain. And frumpy. And blah. "You have to be really cool to look good in pants."

"You don't think you're cool?"

I stare into his eyes for a sign he's teasing, but there's nothing. He's completely earnest. "What about me is cool?"

"You dress like a *Mad Men* extra."

"That isn't cool."

He shakes his head. "You're into the things you love. You embrace them." He motions to the living room. "Those posters. That's the picture of cool."

"Good to know."

"You don't believe me?"

"No… it's more. Well…" I should take the compliment. "Thank you."

"Sure thing." He moves closer. "Besides."

"Yeah?"

He places his body next to mine. "I like the dresses."

"Oh."

"They're fucking sexy." He slides his hand over my hip. Drags it down my thigh then over the hem of my dress. Then under it.

My stomach flutters.

My legs wobble.

My heart thuds.

"Sorry." He pulls his hand back. "Supposed to help you get dressed, not *undressed*."

"That is the first step." *Let's skip these plans. Get undressed. Get into my bed. I can handle that. Totally.*

Deep breath.

Slow exhale.

I try to imagine a dirty demand falling from my lips.

Keep going, Wes. Make me come. Please.

God…

That's so…

It's so…

So not happening.

"How's your balance?" he asks.

Balance. That could be rollerblading. Or the paddle boarding. Or hiking even. Or maybe the trek to the Holly-wood sign. It's on private property, so getting close means trespassing.

"Quinn?"

"Pretty good. I do yoga three times a week."

His voice drops an octave. "Yeah?"

I nod.

"Show me something."

"In this?" I tug at my skirt.

He nods *yeah*.

"Mmm… why should I?"

"Because I asked nicely."

A fair counter.

God, there's something about the look in his eyes.

Like he absolutely, positively needs me to show off a yoga pose.

But I really can't do one in my dress. Not without flashing him. And that—

I'm not there yet.

I take a step backward. Bring my left foot to the inside of my right thigh. Press my palms together in front of my chest then raise them over my head. "Tree pose."

He nods *sure*. "You got any with more bending?"

"Not in this outfit."

He shrugs. "Thought I'd try."

"What about you?"

He cocks a brow.

"Are you flexible?"

"I do all right."

"Let's see."

"I'm not a yogi."

"I bet you've been to a class."

He shrugs *maybe I have, maybe I haven't*.

"Show me your most advanced pose."

"Fair enough." He slides out of his sandals. Leans down. Presses his palms to the carpet.

Right in the middle of the room, he kicks up to a handstand.

And he holds it too.

One, two, three, four, five—

Damn, that's impressive.

I've been practicing for three years and I can do a handstand against the wall.

I know, I know, you can't be good or bad at yoga. If you show up and practice you're good.

But to be that good…

I swallow my jealousy.

"Show off," I tease.

He returns to his feet. Tugs at the fabric of his shorts. "Feel these."

I do. They're thin. Nylon. Board shorts. "We're going swimming?"

"Probably, yeah."

So it's the paddle boarding. As in, we're probably falling in. "What about these?" I tap my glasses.

"How much do you need them?"

"I can see okay without them." Okayish.

"We'll leave them in the car." He turns to the dresser on the right side of the room. "You have a swimsuit?"

"Of course." I have five swimsuits. Every time there's a sale, I get this idea in my head that I'm going to magically transform into a California girl who lounges on the beach in a bikini and Daisy Dukes. (I do not own any Daisy Dukes. Only a pair of work out shorts).

"Probably want that."

"On top?"

"Nothing."

I swallow hard. "You want me to walk around in my bikini?"

"I want you to walk around naked, angel. But you're gonna want to skip the clothes on the paddle-board, yeah. If you don't fall in, you aren't trying hard enough."

That's a good attitude. Falling isn't a failure of balance. It's a sign of effort.

That's the kind of thing my favorite yoga teacher always says.

Falling means your challenging yourself.

And that's important. I can do that. Totally.

I move to my dresser. Grab my favorite swimsuit—a bikini with a cute halter top and skirted bottoms, all in classic blue and white stripes.

Wes's eyes light up.

He looks at me the way a puppy looks at a bone.

I shake my head. Motion to the living room. "No show."

"Cruel."

"Good things come to those who wait."

Chapter Seventeen

QUINN

"Just hop on." The paddle board shop guy offers me his hand.

He has one foot on the board and the other on the dock.

He's holding the massive piece of plastic in place.

And he wants me to hop on.

"One leg at a time," he says.

Which is a completely different instruction.

"Come on, it's easy." Paddle board guy offers his hand again.

Maybe it is easy.

Maybe it's me.

Okay.

I take his hand.

Slowly, I set my foot on the board.

It wobbles back and forth. I have to squeeze paddle board shop guy's hand for balance.

"You need more help?" Wes asks.

Yes. So much help. But only from him. Or maybe from a professional, at this point.

I mean, I've only got four weeks left to enjoy California and I'm angsting about my head instead of enjoying the sunshine.

"Let me." He takes my other hand. "You're almost there, angel."

Right. I'm almost on the wobbly board.

I need to focus or I'm going to faceplant on the water. Or the plastic. Or the deck.

I squeeze Wes's hand. Let go of paddle board guy.

Somehow, I get my other foot onto the board.

Oh God.

It's swaying back and forth.

I drop his hand immediately. Drop to my knees. Press my palms into the board.

This is impossible.

Seriously, impossible.

"There, you got it." Paddle Board Guy smiles as he hands me the paddle. "You remember the stroke?"

I nod, even though I completely fail to recall his five-minute lesson.

"This is the back." He points to the flat side of Wes's paddle. "As long as you have that, you're golden."

"Thanks." Wes shakes his hand.

I lean back on my heels. Grip the paddle like he showed us. One hand at the top. Other about a foot and a half below that.

The thing slips into the deep blue water.

I pull.

The board glides forward.

Woah.

That's intense.

Good intense.

"You got it, angel." Wes hops—actually hops onto a

board. He kneels, grabs the paddle from the shop guy, starts stroking.

I mean he's not *stroking*.

He's paddling.

It's just, God, how many times per minute can I think *paddle*?

Stroke is a much more exciting word.

Watching him stroke—

My cheeks flush.

My blush spreads to my chest.

In my bikini, there's nowhere to hide.

It's nice, feeling the sun on my skin. Feeling his gaze on my body.

I'm not sure how I can tell he's staring, but I can.

Slowly, I navigate past the rows of docked boats.

We're in Marina Del Rey. In the marina belonging to Marina Del Rey. It's a nice spot. Quiet. Calm. Picturesque.

Condos behind us, shopping center to the right, marina in front, open ocean to the left.

"What do you think?" Wes glides next to me. "Stay in the harbor or head to the ocean?"

The waves from the ocean are a million times bigger than the ones from the boats. (Okay, that doesn't sound like accurate math, but they're noticeably rockier). "Harbor."

"You have a thing for boats?"

"God no." I cross my legs. Settle into my seat. Sure, I could try to stand. But then I might fall. Better to stay here. To stay comfortable and capable.

"Your parents don't sail around Lake Michigan?"

"You remembered the geography."

He chuckles. "Had to look it up."

"No, thankfully, they aren't boat people."

"You don't want to hop on one of those?" He points to

a giant yacht at the end of the dock. It's the size of my apartment and it's named *Alec's Talent*.

"Think that's more *Alec's Ego*."

Wes's laugh fills the air.

It makes me warm.

I mean, I'm already warm.

But his laugh certainly helps.

It is a beautiful day. The air is bright, sunny, salty.

I'm competently gliding around the harbor.

Sure, I'm sit down paddle boarding. It's not what I want to learn. But it's something.

"Alec is probably compensating for something," I say.

"I never got that."

"No?" I arch a brow. "Guys… they seem to like to talk about it."

"About their dicks?"

I nod.

Wes laughs. "Yeah. They do. But why compensate with a huge car or boat? Why not get fucking fantastic at eating pussy?"

My blush deepens.

His smile gets wicked.

He gives me this long, slow once-over. Like he's savoring every inch.

"Um… maybe they do." I swallow hard. "You?"

"You've sized up the equipment."

"Sort of."

"Not enough for you?"

"No." It was… a lot. "Just… It's different when it's…" God, how do I phrase this? Wes makes dirty talk seem so easy. Um. Something sexy. I can do sexy. "It's different when you're naked."

"You almost convinced me to stay in."

"I did not."

He nods *did too*. "You have no fucking idea what you do to me, Quinn."

He's kneeling on his paddle board, in only those turquoise board shorts, the picture of cool.

It's hard to believe I do anything to him.

"Fuck, you look good enough to eat." He drops his voice an octave. "I will. Later."

"I'm not sure." My heart beats so loud I hear it in my head. "I'm not sure I'm ready for that."

"Later doesn't have to mean today."

My breath hitches.

"But it can."

My sex clenches. Fuck, there's no way I'm balancing like this. I need to change the subject. To discuss... anything else. "So, um, why Venice?"

"Why West LA?"

"Cheap rent." Well, cheapish. "I lived in the dorms my first two years. Which was nice in a certain way. Life was on campus. It was easy to head to the dining halls or the frat parties." Or the library, my usual Friday and Saturday night hangout spot. "Then I got a job at the hospital over on Santa Monica Boulevard."

He nods. "I know that one."

I switch sides. Drag my paddle through the water. It's nice, gliding over the marina. Peaceful. "I figured it was time to spread my wings. It was near the freeway, so it wasn't too bad getting around when traffic was light."

"So never?"

My laugh is more awkward than anything. "Yeah. I... I won't miss that."

"What will you miss?"

"God, where do I start?" I motion to the sun. "This."

"Chicago summers are beautiful."

"Yeah. But the rest of the year?"

133

"You're not a fan of snowstorms?"

I shake my head. I hate cold. I hate rain. I hate wind. I hate snow. Winter completely fails to appeal. Seventy and sunny all December—that's perfect weather. "No, it's beautiful here. I love the steadiness of the sun. It can be oppressive sometimes. Especially with this situation." I motion to my incredibly pale stomach.

"It suits you."

"Thanks. Sometimes I feel like I'm the only person in California who isn't tan and blond."

He runs his hand through his hair. "You have a problem with this?"

"No. It's more… there's a certain look here."

"The size two blond with big fake tits?"

"Exactly." I set my paddle on the board. Let the water carry me. "Not that there's anything wrong with being blond or thin or busty, natural or unnatural."

"I know what you mean."

"Was that your type?"

"Don't have a type."

"But if you had to pick?"

His eyes find mine. His brow furrows. He works something out. "I don't care how big a woman's tits are."

"You don't appreciate big tits?"

"Appreciate, sure? But it's more about how good they feel in my hand."

My cheeks flush.

My sex clenches.

Even though I'm sitting, I wobble.

Fuck.

We're back to sex.

It's so easy to go back to sex with Wes.

It's impossible not to.

"I, um, I'm surprised my parents didn't have an ulcer

when I decided to go to USC," I say. "They aren't fans of California."

"I remember that."

"They wanted me to stay home. Or least somewhere with equally frigid winters and public transportation."

"You're going back to Chicago." His paddle glides through the water. "There must be something appealing about it."

"You want to know the truth?"

He nods.

"It was the best med school I got into. And... I probably only got in because Dad went there." I press my lips together. Suck a breath through my nose.

"Would you rather stay here?"

"I think so."

"You want to try standing?"

I shake my head. "Not yet." I'm nowhere near steady enough yet. And I...

I don't want to fail.

"Try," he says.

I shake my head.

His eyes fix on mine. "Try kneeling."

"You say that a lot?"

He chuckles. "Try."

"I..."

"What's the worst that could happen?"

I could look like an idiot. Fail. Fall on my face.

But I can't say any of that.

Those aren't real consequences.

Falling isn't a big deal.

In theory.

"If you fall, you land in the water." His voice is steady. Easy. "No big deal."

My teeth sink into my lip.

He's right.

I have no excuse.

I have to at least try.

Okay. Deep breath. Steady inhale.

I push myself onto my knees. Pick up my paddle. Slice through the water as quickly as possible.

My board glides through the marina.

I stay upright.

Well, upright ish.

It's happening. I'm doing it.

Wes keeps pace next to me.

A speed boat drives by on the other side of the marina. It sends tiny waves rippling through the water.

They rock us back and forth.

I have to lean back on my heels to keep my balance.

But I do.

"Why did you stay here?" I ask.

"Never thought about it that way. It never occurred to me to leave. How would I fuck with Hunter if I left?"

My lips curl into a smile. He's teasing.

It helps. It really does.

"You ever hear of text?" I ask.

"Text? Not enough. I can make his life miserable almost every day now." Wes pops to his feet. Drags his paddle through the water. "And Chase—well, you've met him. I don't have to do much. He stays miserable all on his own."

"Whatever happened to his girlfriend?" I ask.

Wes shakes his head. "Don't ask him that."

"Oh."

"He can't admit he's still in love with her."

"That must suck."

"Yeah. He's just—he's as asshole about his righteous indignation, honestly. He doesn't forgive anything. Still hates me for that time I wrote *Chase Keating Eats Boogers* on his door."

"How old were you?"

"Eight."

I laugh, even though there's something in Wes's voice. He's teasing, yeah, and he's serious.

He really does believe his brother is holding that against him.

Maybe he is.

The times I've spoken with Chase… he's always been… difficult.

"He hasn't forgiven her?" I ask.

Wes nods. "Idiot can't get over himself."

"What an idiot."

"Tell me about it." His eyes move to me. "You want to try now."

"How?"

"Get the board going as fast as you can."

"But…"

"But what?"

"It's hard," I say.

"So?"

I can't really argue with that logic.

"Just try."

"What do I get for it?"

"Pride of accomplishment."

"What if that's not enough?"

"Too bad."

That's another fair point.

Yes, I might fall.

I might make a fool of myself.

But I can do it.

I have to try.

I nod *okay*. "How?"

"Paddle faster."

I do.

"Then stand as quickly as you can. Hop up like a surf-board. Or push yourself. Either as long as it's fast."

Okay, fast.

I grab the paddle with one hand. Press the other to the board.

There.

With one movement, I push myself up.

I wobble.

Catch myself.

Wobble more.

Fuck—

I fall sideways.

Right into the water.

Shit.

It's cold.

But good cold.

Refreshing.

And, well…

It's not so bad.

Sure, I fell.

But so what?

I tried.

And I… I can get it. Eventually, I'll get it.

I surface with a gasp.

Wes's lips curl into a smile. "You look good wet."

"Thanks."

"You all right?" he asks.

I nod. "I am." Right now, I am. He does that to me.

"You want to try again?"

"Yeah, I do." I really do.

Chapter Eighteen

WES

"Why did you decide LA?" I ask.

Quinn rolls onto one side. Her eyes meet mine. Then they travel down my body and up it again. "You really want to talk at this moment?"

"You gonna climb over here and fuck me?"

It's peaceful, lying on our paddle boards after gliding around the marina.

I have to hand it to Quinn—she fucking went for it. She fell a few times, but she kept trying. She's not quite a pro, but she's getting there.

I'm ready to ask her to come back tomorrow. And the next day. And the day after that.

"I don't think I have the balance." She pushes herself up. Slides her legs into the water. Lets out a heavy sigh. "It's so beautiful here."

It is. But the ocean and the sun are a hell of a lot less interesting than her.

Fuck, I think I'd rather stare into those hazel eyes than stare at her tits.

And she's in a perfect bikini.

It's all adorable and feminine and pure Quinn.

She brushes her wet hair behind her ear. It's different wet. Casual. Loose. Like she just got out of the shower after a particularly athletic fuck.

"Honestly? I wanted to get as far away from home as possible," she says.

"Did it work?"

She nods. "California is different than anywhere else. There are the shallow things. But there's this easiness too. It's hard to explain."

She looks to the beach opposite us—we're hanging out in front of the buoys by Mother's Beach. It's usually a popular spot for kids to swim—it's a bay, so the waves are tame—but it's quiet today.

I guess kids aren't ready to brave the water.

It's not freezing but it's not exactly warm.

Her eyes meet mine. "More laid back, I guess."

"You have a thing for surfer boys?"

"Don't laugh."

"You do."

"No…" She bites her lips. "Just one."

"Oh?"

"You're laughing."

"Look at my face."

She does.

"You see any laughter?"

"I guess not." She scoots a little closer. Until she can slide her legs onto my board. "Can we stay here forever?"

"Sure. But you won't make it to school."

"Yeah." All the energy drops out of her voice at once.

It's crystal clear: Quinn doesn't want to go back to Chicago in August.

But I can't tell if it's the school or the place that disgusts her.

I want to know what she wants. I want to help her realize how little her plan appeals to her. But right now, I want to make her smile. "The surfer boy?"

"Dylan."

"Sounds nice."

"He was very nice. And very laid back. He had a loose idea of time. Would show up late or early. And he, well… he was just so chill."

"It was infuriating?"

She nods. "Yeah, everything was fine and whatever and he didn't have opinions about anything besides different strains of weed and *Anchorman*."

"Ah."

"What do you mean ah?"

"You don't seem like you could handle a stoner."

"We dated for a month. If that."

"Did he?" I motion to her chest.

Her cheeks flush. "Yeah, we made out a lot."

"He a good kisser?"

She makes that *kinda* motion.

"Have you been with anyone who really set you on fire?"

"No… I mean not counting last week."

My balls tighten. She's adorable. This time, I came prepared. I, well, came. I rubbed one out first thing this morning.

But, fuck, that was hours ago now.

I'm already raring to go.

Never thought I'd curse my quick refractory time, but here we are.

"Why'd you date him?" I ask.

"I don't know. He was cute. And it seemed like the

thing to do. Here I was, starting my new life in California, ready to spread my wings."

"You figured 'might as well spread my legs too'?"

Her laugh is big. Hearty. "Oh my God."

"You did."

"Kinda."

"Didn't work?"

She shakes her head. "He would try. But I was too scared. I... well, we didn't really have conversations. I kept telling myself I was too picky, that he was a nice enough guy, so what if he looked confused when I tried to discuss the movie we'd just watched?"

"How arty was it?"

"Not that much."

I arch a brow.

"Oh my God, Wes, if I hear one more thing about *Casablanca* not being a masterpiece—"

"Never seen it. How would I know?"

"Do not remind me."

"Or?"

"Or... um..." Her cheeks flush.

"You gonna replace me with a classic film buff?"

"Maybe." Her lips curl into a smile. For a moment, she holds that confidence. Then her poker face falters. She shakes her head. "When I'm done with you."

"You kicking me to the curb?"

"After I get mine, yeah."

"Harsh."

"Get used to it."

My smile spreads over my cheeks. "I'm hurt."

"You going to play dead again?"

"No, but if you want to make me stiff—"

Her tits shake as she laughs. "Not here."

"So..." I motion *go on*. "Dylan was a dolt."

"He loved the Red Hot Chili Peppers. He could talk about that all day."

My nose scrunches.

"I know. I, well, I thought maybe everyone liked them. They play them on the radio all the time. And half their songs are about California. I thought maybe all Californians like them."

"Hell no."

She laughs. "Thank God."

"What do you listen to?"

"I like big band stuff."

"Anything I would know?"

"Nothing that gets radio play. Well, Amy Winehouse kinda had that sound. Sorta."

"She was great."

"Yeah. She was. There's this doc about her struggle with addiction. It's brutal, but it's beautiful."

"A documentary?"

She nods.

"A movie that's non-fiction?" I scrunch my nose like my objection to the film is its entertainment value. Not its content. I'm sure it's a fantastic movie, but there's no way in hell I'm watching some painful portrayal of addiction. I know that all too well.

"Don't tell me you don't watch docs?"

I shrug like I could give or take the movie. "I guess I would."

"Wes—"

"I'm going to end up in Dylan tier at this rate, huh?" I try to make my voice teasing, but I don't quite get there.

Quinn doesn't notice. She nods. "I do have standards."

"You're really into movies."

"I guess so. I just… there's something about that feeling

when the lights go down. Like you're going to be taken on a journey. You can forget everything else."

"You forget everything else?"

"I'm not that bad."

I shrug *aren't you?*

She laughs, but it's not easy. She's insecure about her inability to turn off her thoughts.

"It's endearing."

"Thanks... I think."

"What else do you do for fun?"

"Fun?" She swings her legs back onto her board. Lays flat. Stares up at the sky. "I'm not sure I've had any time for fun since... I don't even know."

"School keeps you that busy?"

"It doesn't come easily to me."

"Fooled me."

She pokes her head up. "Really?"

I nod. Really. Quinn always seems pulled together. Like she has everything figured out. Well, maybe everything besides flirting and sex.

"I guess I'm like you. Good at keeping up appearances."

"There are no appearances here, angel." I tap my head. "This is as empty as it seems."

"We both know that's bullshit."

I shrug *maybe*, but she doesn't buy it.

"I guess... hmm... fun. Well, I watch movies. A lot of movies. I talk to Owen. And the yoga. Though that's more because I have to. Or else my thoughts get too cluttered."

"You actually slow down and breathe?"

"It's a process."

Fuck, it's impossible to do anything but picture her in downward dog.

It's not the time.

She's letting me in.

A little, but still.

"What about you?" she asks. "Is it all babes and booze?"

"A lot babes and booze."

"When it's not?"

"Griff and I do a lot."

"Despite his lack of tact?"

"Yeah." I laugh. "He gets on my last nerve, but he's a good guy to have around. Makes me seem smooth as silk."

"That's it. Not that you actually love him and appreciate his honesty."

"The honesty is harsh, but it's good to have."

"Mhmm."

"Mhmm?"

"You're still trying to convince me you're this easy breezy guy."

"And?"

"You know I'm a mess. Seems fair I know the truth."

The truth. Fuck, what the hell is the truth? "What do you want to know?"

"You can't possibly be this effortless."

"You got me. I put product in my hair." I slide off the board. Swim to hers. Place my hands outside her legs. "This is a nice view."

Her blush deepens, but she holds strong. "Interesting."

"Interesting."

"You're trying to distract me with sex."

"You gonna follow in your brother's footsteps?"

"Promised to fix your head."

Good luck with that. "You trying to crack it open?"

"If you're okay with that."

Fuck, I don't know.

Being with Quinn is different. Easier. And harder.

I want more.

But she's leaving in three weeks.

And my heart can't handle any more disappointment.

I dig my fingers into her thighs. "How about I handle making you come?"

Chapter Nineteen

WES

"So…" Quinn pulls her robe a little tighter. "Should we have a drink first?"

The silky fabric slides off her shoulder. Reveals the strap of a lacy bra.

Quinn in red.

Fuck me. I'm already hard.

I take a deep breath. Exhale through my nose. "It's barely noon."

"I resisted margaritas at lunch." She brushes a wet strand behind her ear.

"Is that a brag?"

She laughs. "No. Just… There's something about tequila and tacos. Don't you think?"

"You drink tequila?"

"Yeah. I, uh, I kinda love Mexican food."

"Really?" I ask.

She nods. "Since I moved here. And, um, this one time Owen and I went to Mexico for vacation. This place had the most amazing strawberry margaritas. I lost track at three."

"How was the hangover?"

"Uh… not great."

"You have fun?"

She makes that *kinda* motion. "He was supposed to be my wingman, but he ditched me to hook up with this guy."

"The slut."

"Right?" She swallows hard. "Not that I object to promiscuity. Whatever makes him happy. As long as he's safe. Just—"

"Dick move."

She nods. "Exactly. He… um… It was for my eighteenth birthday. It was supposed to be *the* trip."

"Where you punched your v-card?"

"Yeah."

"Your brother was cool with that?"

"Well… I let him believe I slept with my high school boyfriend."

"Yeah?"

She blushes. "He doesn't know about my scarlet V."

"Scarlet V?"

"Like *The Scarlet Letter*. How Hester wears an A for adulteress."

I stare back at her.

"You skipped that lecture in American Lit?"

"Sounds vaguely familiar."

"It's a good book. You should read it."

"Book?"

"There's a movie too. But it's not on our syllabus." She ties her robe again, but that doesn't stop it from sliding farther down her shoulder. "Did you, um… Did you want to put on clothes?"

Her eyes pass over me slowly, from the tips of my hair, to my bare chest and stomach, to the towel slung around my hips.

Her pupils dilate.

Her fingers dig into her thighs.

Her tongue slides over her lips.

She wants me naked.

But is she ready for that? "Do you want me to?"

"Well. No. But also… I think I'm going to have a glass of wine. So, um, you might be more comfortable in clothes."

That's a yes.

I step aside so she can pass.

She moves into the main room.

I scour my backpack for a clean pair of boxers.

"You want one?" she calls from the kitchen.

"Sure." I pull on my grey boxers. Check my reflection in the full-length mirror.

I'm not a humble guy. Never saw the point of that. I work hard to look this good. Why deny the fruits of my labor?

Between the tattoos, the broad shoulders, the built arms—I'm catnip to women who want a certain type of guy.

Usually, I play it up.

With Quinn…

That feels wrong. Like a pretense.

But it's not like I'm admitting the truth either.

I like her. I do.

That doesn't mean I can tell her how fucked-up my family is.

Or how much my easy, breezy attitude is bullshit.

This isn't about becoming besties.

It's certainly not about falling in love.

I'm teaching her to fuck.

That's it.

If Griffin were here, he'd say something about how I'm deluding myself.

Or maybe something about boundaries.

That's what I need. A wall between my feelings and Quinn.

With sex on the other side.

That's doable.

Easy.

I've fucked plenty of women without getting invested.

Sure, Quinn is different.

But nothing has to change.

This can stay casual.

"You want it in here?" Her footsteps move closer. "Or here." She steps into the bedroom, a glass of white wine in each hand, her hazel eyes wide with trust.

It's obvious immediately.

This is different.

Completely different.

I have no fucking idea how to keep that wall up. "The couch maybe."

That's how I'm doing it.

Going back to sex.

My head. Wall. Sex. Quinn.

Perfect.

"Sure," she says.

Her fingers brush mine as I take the glass.

She spins on her heels, saunters into the main room, her silky robe swishing against her hips.

Fuck, that thing is perfect on her. A gorgeous, bright floral print that falls just below her ass.

She pulls the sleeve up her shoulder. Sits cross-legged on the couch. Brings her glass to her lips. "Mmm. This is good." She swallows another sip. "There's something about a glass of wine on a hot day."

"People say that about beer." I taste my glass. It's not bad. Mild, fruity, light. It tastes like wine. There's really no other way to describe it.

"Does that make me a snob?"

I shake my head. Quinn doesn't have lowbrow tastes, but there's no snobbery about it.

"You don't like it?" She motions to my drink.

I take another sip. It's solid, for wine, but it's still wine. Even so—"It's perfect." It's her.

"Good." She swallows a mouthful. "I, um… I had a lot of fun today."

"Me too."

"I guess I'm dodging."

"That's all right."

"I do want to touch you."

"Yeah?" I arch a brow.

Her gaze travels down my neck, chest, stomach, crotch. "Yeah. But I'm not sure… What do I do?"

"You want to go right now?"

She shakes her head. Holds up her wine glass. "This first."

"Fair enough." I take a long sip. "But I have my own demands."

"Oh?"

"I want to strip you out of that thing."

Her nod is nervous.

"I want your tits in my mouth."

For a split second, her expression goes blank. She turns white. Then red.

I can't tell if she's nervous or terrified or turned on.

All three maybe.

"You mean… when I'm touching you?" She tilts her head back to swallow her last sip. Her fingers curl around her glass. Her gaze goes straight to the floor.

"What did I tell you about choreographing this?"

"You can't."

I nod. "Exactly."

"You um…" She sets her glass on the side table. "You're still drinking."

I down my wine in one gulp. "Not anymore."

"Right." Her fingers brush mine as she takes my glass. Carefully, she sets it next to hers. "I think… music." She stands. Moves to the kitchen table. Opens up her laptop. "Do you usually do music?"

"Sometimes."

"The walls are thin here. So, um… I think it's good." Her robe falls off her shoulders as she leans over her laptop. "Any requests?"

"Whatever inspires you."

"Right. That's, um, that's a good question. Maybe there's a playlist."

"Yeah?"

Her laugh fills the room. It's nervous, but only a little. "Babymaking jams. Or is that bad luck? I don't want a baby."

"I'm not gonna come inside you."

She clears her throat.

"Not today."

Her chest flames red. "Uh… I… Uh… That is how that happens." She stands. Pushes her glasses up her nose. Turns to me. "How's this?"

An electronic dance song fills the room.

It's moody, rhythmic, sexy as all hell.

Not what I imagine Quinn listening to.

But perfect all the same.

"Good." I turn my body toward hers.

She crosses the room with nervous steps. Her fingers trail over the straps of her robe.

I motion *come here.*

She does.

I untie her sash.

The silky fabric parts.

Reveals the red bra underneath.

How is it possible she doesn't realize how sexy she is?

It defies logic.

My hands go to her hips. I press the smooth fabric to her skin as I pull her into my lap.

Her knees plant outside my legs.

Her palms rest on my shoulders.

I pull her closer.

Until I can feel her cunt against me.

Her panties and my boxers are in the way, but I can still feel her.

Fuck, I want out of these boxers.

I want to be inside her.

I want her coming on my cock.

"You're hard." Confidence builds in her voice. "Because of me."

"Get used to it, angel."

"But I—"

"Are walking around your apartment in lingerie." I push the sides of her robe apart. Cup her breast over her bra. "Don't tell me you're surprised."

"No." Her eyes betray her. She is surprised. She has no idea how fucking sexy she is. Or maybe she's too scared to see it.

It's fucking ridiculous.

I need to make her see it.

"You're fucking gorgeous, angel," I murmur into her neck.

"Thank you."

I look up at her. Brush her wet hair behind her neck.

Run my thumb over the edge of her bra. "You drive me crazy."

She rocks her hips against me. "Right back at you."

Fuck.

I'm already raring to go.

Coming once this morning wasn't enough.

Next time—

I'm not sure five minutes will be enough.

She's too fucking irresistible.

"I have a request." I bring my hand to the back of her head.

She looks down at me. "Yeah?"

"Glasses on."

"Really?" Surprise spreads over her expression.

"Hell yes."

"Oh." She pushes her glasses up her nose. "Okay. Glasses on. Unless they get in the way."

Fair. I nod. Dig my fingers into the back of her head. Pull her into a kiss.

Her lips close around my bottom lip.

She sucks softly.

Then harder.

My lips part.

Her tongue slides into my mouth.

She's already good at this.

I bring my other hand to her chest. Trace the outline of her bra to tease her.

But it teases me more.

I need those tits in my hands.

In my mouth.

Around my cock.

I need every fucking inch of Quinn.

This whole slowly teaching her thing is torture.

Sweet torture.

But torture nonetheless.

My tongue swirls around hers.

My hand slips into her bra cup.

She groans against my lips as my thumb brushes her nipple.

Fuck, she feels good in my hand. And that groan—

That's the best thing I've ever heard.

I slide her robe off her shoulders.

She pulls back to toss it aside. Then she reaches behind her back. Unhooks her bra.

Her eyes find mine as she peels it off.

Fuck.

It's only been a week, but my memory didn't do her justice.

I try to find some response.

Completely fail.

She makes me tongue tied.

It's weird.

"You're so fucking beautiful." I cup her breast with my hand.

Her eyelids flutter closed.

She sighs as I toy with her nipple.

I try different strokes. Soft. Hard. Fast. Slow. Circles. Zigzags. Up and down. Left to right.

Find exactly what she needs.

Then I bring my other hand to her breast.

Toy with her mercilessly.

Her fingers dig into my shoulders.

Her hips buck against mine.

Her lips part with a groan.

"Is this… is this good?" She barely manages to push the words off her lips.

Is this good?

Good doesn't begin to describe it.

"Is what good, angel?" I ask.

"My reaction."

"That what you feel?"

She nods. "It seems so… loud."

"Loud is good."

"Yeah?" Her eyes blink open. Fix on mine. "Not too much?"

"There's no too much."

"Oh."

"Louder is better." I bring one hand to her back. Press my palm into the space between her shoulder blades. "Louder means more."

"More?"

I nod. "Louder means you feel so fucking good you can't contain yourself."

She nods, attentively, like she's making a mental note.

It's weird.

Hot.

I can't remember the last time anyone paid this much attention to me.

Or gave my word this much weight.

Or looked at me like I mattered.

Nobody has ever looked at me the way she does.

"You don't have to play it up," I say. "But don't hold back either."

"Noted." She brings her fingers back to my shoulders. Drags them over my skin with a soft touch. "I want to touch you too."

"Not yet."

"When?"

"I'll guide you."

"You promise?"

"Cross my heart and hope to die." I tilt my head up to kiss her. "Need to torture you more first."

Her pupils dilate.

It's tempting, making her come first.

But I'm not sure I can survive all her groaning.

I need some hint of stamina if I'm going to teach her actual technique.

Her lips part.

My tongue slips into her mouth.

My fingers curl into her skin.

She groans against me.

Rocks her hips.

Drives me out of my fucking mind.

I break our kiss. Bring my lips to her neck.

A soft kiss to start.

Then a harder one.

She moans as I suck on her tender skin.

"Fuck." Her nails dig into my shoulders. "Wes—"

"Yeah, angel?"

"Keep doing that."

"Harder?" I mumble into her neck.

"Try it."

I suck harder.

Her groan gets louder.

I scrape my teeth as gently as I can.

She claws at my chest. "Yes."

I try a little harder.

She groans.

Harder.

She yelps. "Too much."

"Like this?" I dial it back.

"Mmm. Yeah." She rocks her hips, rubbing her crotch against mine. "What if I come from this?"

Fuck, if she keeps doing that, I might. "You never dry humped in high school?"

She shakes her head.

"That's what you're doing."

"I am?"

"This—" I bring one hand to her hip. Pull her toward me so she's rubbing against my cock. "Fuck, angel. You're gonna make me come if you keep doing that."

"Oh. Sorry."

"Don't be sorry."

"No. I just… I want to touch you this time." Her voice is eager. In a sexual way. And a curious way. Like she just learned how to do her first tattoo and is dying to try again.

"Climb off my lap."

"Oh." She takes a seat on the cushion next to mine.

Fuck, I already miss the warmth of her. The weight. I always thought I preferred it on top, but there's something about Quinn's body over mine—

There's something about Quinn, period.

I need all of her.

Her eyes meet mine. "So…"

My balls tighten. Her nerves are adorable, but I have to use my fucking head here.

I have to find some scrap of conscious thought.

"Don't go straight to the cock." I wrap my hand around her wrist. Bring her palm to my chest. "Gotta make a guy feel like you want him, not his unit."

"That makes sense. I do want to touch you, everywhere. Not just your… cock." She stumbles over the word like it's the first time she's said it.

Even so, hearing *cock* spill from her lips.

My balls tighten.

Quinn drags her hand down my stomach.

Pleasure floods my senses.

"I like touching you. A lot." She leans in to press her lips to mine. Softly. Then harder.

My body takes over.

I kiss back. Slide my tongue into her mouth. Swirl it around hers.

Her hand glides down my torso.

To the waistband of my boxers.

"Put your palm flat against me," I say. "Over the boxers."

She does.

"Focus on the tip. Start with a little pressure."

She rubs her palm over my boxers, pressing the cotton against my cock.

It's featherlight. I can barely feel it.

But what I can feel—

Fuck, I can't remember the last time I was this ready.

"Harder." My eyelids flutter together.

She rubs me a little harder.

Harder.

There.

"Fuck." I reach for her. Find her leg.

My fingers trail over her inner thigh. I need to touch her. To make her come. To drive her out of her mind.

After.

I can't distract her.

"When do I..." Her eyes meet mine. "How do I know to go forward?"

"Depends how badly you want to torture me."

"Mmmm." Her breath gets soft. Needy. "I like the sound of that."

Me too. But I can't handle it today. "Or if I ask you for more."

"Begs me for more."

"Fuck, angel, I have to watch you."

She nods. "That, um, that could be interesting."

Hell yes. "After this."

"Oh?"

"I'm going to make you come after this. We can go to the bedroom. So you can watch."

Her breath catches in her throat. "Should we go now?"

"Fuck no." My fingers curl around her wrist. I move her hand enough to grab the waistband of my boxers.

"You need me to make you come?"

My balls tighten. "Yeah."

Her gaze travels down my torso. "Say it again."

"Make me come, Quinn."

Her tongue slides over her lips. Her chest heaves. Her fingers dig into her thighs.

She stares as I slide my boxers off my hips.

Her eyes go wide. Fill with surprise. "It's so——"

"You've never seen——"

"In movies, yeah. But this——" Her hand goes straight to my cock. "It's so… big."

"I'm——"

"Yeah." Her fingers brush my shaft. "What do I?"

"Start with your thumb and pointer finger."

She nods.

"Wrap them around me."

She does. She stares at my cock with wide eyes, like she can't believe she's actually touching me.

It's hard to blame her.

I can't believe it either.

"Slide your hand up and down," I say.

She nods.

"Start soft and go harder."

She holds me with a loose grip. Slides her hand over my tip, up my shaft, back again. Then she does it a little firmer. "How hard?"

"Pretty fucking hard. It can take a beating."

She lets out an awkward laugh. Then she nods. Gets that *I'm absorbing this information carefully* look.

She tightens her grip around me. Drags her hand up my cock, then back down. "How fast?"

"There's no rule. You can keep going until you find the spot."

"How do you know?"

"You know."

"Okay." She grips me a little tighter. Works a little faster.

Fuck, it feels good.

My body swells with pleasure.

It rushes through my pelvis, my torso, my limbs.

It's everywhere.

Then it's—

Ow.

"Too much." I grab her wrist reflexively.

"Sorry."

"It happens." I take her hand. Bring it back to my cock. "Try this. Wrap your entire hand around me."

"Oh?"

I nod.

She wraps her fingers around me. Hooks them with her thumb. "It feels good."

"Fuck yeah."

"Different than I expected."

"How?"

"I don't know. Just different. You're so hard, but your skin is soft. God, I'm usually more articulate."

"Yeah." Honestly, I'm barely managing conscious thought, much less articulate conversation.

"It's just… good."

"Fuck yeah."

"Sorry, I-"

"Stop apologizing."

"Okay." She grips me a little tighter. "I want to make

you come, Wes."

My cock quivers.

"Where do you want your hands?"

I bring my hands to her chest.

She groans as my fingers brush her nipples. "Fuck, you're good at that." She leans in to press her lips to mine.

She kisses me hard as she strokes me.

Firmer and firmer and—

There.

I roll her nipple between my thumb and forefinger. "Perfect."

"Faster or—"

"Exactly like that."

"Okay." Her voice gets low and breathy.

She arches her back, driving her tits into my hands.

I toy with her.

She groans against my mouth.

Works me with her hand.

It takes her a minute to get back to that pressure, but once she does—

Fuck.

Desire rushes through my veins.

My entire body buzzes.

Quinn Thorn is giving me a hand job.

My teenage fantasies come to life.

She pulls back with a sigh. Watches her hand glide over my cock.

I stare into her gorgeous hazel eyes. Watch her watch.

There's something so fucking hot about her curiosity.

It makes me—

Fuck.

With her next stroke, I unravel.

All that tension unwinds.

My cock pulses.

Pleasure spills through my pelvis and thighs. Up my torso. Down my lips. All the way to my fucking fingertips.

I spill onto her hand as I come.

"Woah." Her chest heaves then falls. "That's—"

"Yeah."

She waits until I'm finished. Then she kisses me. Stands. Goes straight to the sink to rinse her hands. "I never—"

"I know."

"It's always that messy?"

"Yeah."

"How do you… when you?"

Fuck, I'm barely absorbing anything. My brain is flashing *Quinn, Quinn, Quinn*.

"Wes?"

"Huh?"

"You need a tissue?"

"Yeah, sure."

"You can use the shower too."

"Yeah." I stand. Move into the bathroom. Wash up.

It takes a minute to find conscious thought.

And it dissolves immediately.

I'm about to drag her to her bedroom and make her come.

Conscious thought is fucking useless.

Chapter Twenty

WES

Quinn is sitting on her bed, back straight, legs together, palms on her thighs, gaze straight ahead.

"Hey." She plays with the hem of her robe. It's draped over her shoulders. Showing off that sliver of skin between her tits, down her stomach, all the way to her red panties.

I swear, I'm ready to go again.

I'm not.

But give me ten minutes...

"What, um... What's the lesson plan, exactly?" She presses her lips together.

They're red again.

When did she put on makeup?

Suddenly, I'm desperate for her to mark me somehow.

I need her lipstick staining my neck, chest, cock—

"You ever relax?" I move farther into the bedroom.

She shoots me a *that's a stupid question* look. Motions to her laptop, now sitting on her desk, currently silent. "Music or no music?"

"You decide."

"Okay." She moves to the computer. Scrolls for a minute. Starts a playlist of R&B slow jams.

Fuck, this is perfect.

Her cheeks flush. "Was… um… was it good?"

"Very good."

"Oh." She beams. "Thank you."

Fuck, I can't say something as cheesy as *the pleasure is mine*, but I can't exactly accept the gratitude either.

I should be thanking her.

I should be gushing about her skill.

But this first.

I take another step toward her. "Stand up."

"Why?"

"That will give both of us the best view."

"You're really—"

"I'm really what?"

Her gaze flits to the mirror then back to me. "I can't watch myself."

"Why not?"

Her brow furrows. She stares at me like I asked her the stupidest question in the world. "It's weird."

"And?"

Her stare continues.

"Glad we got that out of the way."

Her lips press together. She shakes her head. Shakes it off.

Her eyes meet mine again. Then they travel down my body. Take in my bare shoulders, chest, stomach.

The waistband of my jeans.

Her shoulders relax.

It soothes her, me being dressed.

Or maybe it's knowing where we stand.

I'm dressed.

She's coming.

This is for her.

To help her figure out what she likes.

Guess I should verbalize that.

Quinn is smart, but she's not a mind reader. She's as far from mind reader as it gets.

"Turn to the mirror," I say.

She shoots me that same *are you out of your mind* look, but she does as she's told.

She's good at following orders.

Never thought I was into that whole *thank you, sir* thing, but imagining ordering Quinn onto her knees—

Fuck, my blood is rushing south.

How is it she does that to me?

"How do you fuck yourself?" I ask.

"What?" She coughs. Pats her chest. Swallows hard.

"How do you fuck yourself?" I repeat it a little louder.

"I just do."

"If you're not going to tell me, I'm going to demand you show me."

"Bossy for a guy who just got a hand job." Her voice is confident, but her cheeks are bright red.

"Damn straight." I move closer. Until I'm close enough to touch her.

Through the mirror, her eyes meet mine.

Her chest heaves with her inhale.

Falls with her exhale.

She's nervous again.

She's nervous a lot.

"How do you fuck yourself?" I ask.

She pulls her robe over her chest. "I guess I rub myself."

"Show me."

"Here?"

"Yeah."

"Standing up?" Through the mirror, she shoots me that same look. *Are you out of your mind?*

Probably. But it's necessary. "Do you know what you like?"

"I liked that." She motions to the living room. "And the biting. And what you were doing with your hands. I... I liked all of it."

Okay, I need to be more specific. "Do you know how you like to be touched?"

"No one has ever touched me." Her eyes light up with epiphany. "Oh. Right."

"Not completely insane."

"Not completely." Her smile is shy.

Fuck, it's weird her reverting back to shy.

But I get it.

A raging sex drive does a lot to assuage nerves.

I just need to wind her up again.

"Come here." I don't give her a chance to move. I place my body behind hers. Wrap my arm around her waist. Bring my lips to her neck.

"Wes..."

I suck on her soft skin. "Yeah?"

"What are... you... uh... you asked something."

"You don't have to talk."

Her nod is eager.

"But you do have to show me."

Her cheeks flush. "Now?"

"Not yet." I suck a little harder.

She arches her back, rubbing her ass against my crotch. "Can you?"

"Get hard?"

"Yeah."

"Not sure." I drag my teeth against her skin.

She lets out a low, deep groan.

"Usually need twenty minutes between throws."

"Uh-huh."

"Got three or four in me," I say.

"Oh."

"All guys are different."

"So I'll have to figure it out on a case-by-case basis."

"You want to go again already, angel?"

Her blush deepens. "No... I don't know. Maybe. It felt good, making you come." Her gaze shifts to the ground. "God, how do you say this stuff so easily?"

"Try it again."

"It felt good making you come," she repeats the words without any extra enthusiasm.

"Did it? Can't tell."

"Oh my God."

"Look me in the eyes."

"I can't."

"Not with that attitude."

"Oh my God, what a teacher thing to say." Her laugh is nervous. "When did you get all wise?"

"Don't ask a guy to teach you something if you don't want a teacher."

She nods *I guess that's true.*

Quinn takes a deep breath. Lets out a slow, steady exhale.

Slowly, she brings her gaze to the mirror. Makes eye contact with my reflection. Presses her lips into a coy smile. "It felt good, making you come."

My balls tighten. "Better. Again."

Her confidence falters for a second. She shakes it off. Nods. "It felt good, making you come."

"Fuck, angel. You're gonna make it happen again at this rate."

"Yeah?" Her voice perks.

"Yeah. But this first." I tug at the sash holding her robe together.

It falls to her sides.

Her breasts spill forward.

Fuck, she has gorgeous tits.

They defy reason.

They really do.

I hold her in place with one hand. Bring the other to her chest. Brush my thumb against her nipple.

Her eyelids flutter together.

My lips go to her neck.

I suck softly.

Harder.

Harder.

"Wes…" She rubs her ass against me. "More."

I scrape my teeth against her skin.

She lets out a soft moan.

I do it again and until.

Until the entire room is humming with her moan.

She rocks her hips against mine.

I dig my fingers into her skin to pull her closer.

She gasps as her ass brushes my hard-on. "Oh."

"Oh?"

"I like it. That feeling."

"Yeah?"

She nods. Makes eye contact through the mirror. "You're good at this," she breathes.

"You too."

She shakes her head.

"You're getting there."

Her gaze flits to my hands. Her eyes go wide as she watches me play with her tits.

It's like it's her favorite movie.

She's nervous, yeah, but she's into this.

I can lead if she can follow.

I push her robe out of the way. Wrap my fingers around the side of her panties.

She gasps as I slide them off her hip.

My eyes meet hers through the mirror.

She nods, offering me permission.

I bring my hand to her other hip. Push her panties off her ass and down her thighs.

She kicks them off her feet.

Stares back at her reflection.

She's standing in front of me in nothing but her robe.

Fuck, it's hot as hell.

My fingers curl around her wrist. Slowly, I bring her hand to her stomach. "Show me, angel." I slide her hand down her torso.

"Will you touch me?"

"After."

Her nod is heavy. Needy.

She's too turned on for nerves.

Perfect.

I hold her in place as she slips her hand between her legs.

Her eyelids flutter closed.

Her chest heaves.

Her lips part.

She drags her fingertips up her inner thigh. Over her cunt.

My body buzzes.

This is a million times better than her getting me off.

Than any fucking thing I've felt in the last… forever.

I watch as Quinn presses her index finger to her clit.

She rubs herself with slow circles.

Again. Again. Again.

"Look at me, angel."

Her free hand tugs at her robe.

Her eyes blink open.

She blushes as she stares back at me.

But she does stare back at me.

"Watch yourself." My voice gets low. Demanding.

Her nod is heavy. Like she's barely absorbing my words.

I bring both hands to her tits.

Toy with her exactly how she needs me to.

"Fuck." A groan falls off her lips. "Don't stop." Her gaze shifts to her chest. Then it drifts down her body.

Pulls back so she can take in everything.

Her breath catches.

Her pupils dilate.

Her legs shake.

She drags her hand to her thigh. "I want you..." Her voice is breathy. Heavy. "Wes. Please."

"Please what, angel?"

"Make me come."

My body buzzes.

What else could I possibly want?

"Hands at your sides, angel," I say.

She nods as her hands fall to her sides.

I keep my body pressed to hers. Keep one hand toying with her chest. Bring the other to her stomach.

I should tease her.

Drag it out.

But I can't.

I need her bliss too badly.

My fingers dip below her belly button.

Between her legs.

I spread her lips then I press my index finger to her clit. Work her with those same slow circles.

"Wes…" She reaches back. Hooks two fingers through my belt loop. "Don't stop."

I bring my lips to her neck.

Suck on her tender skin as I rub her.

Softly.

Then harder.

Harder.

There—

Her lips part with a groan. Her eyelids flutter together. Her limbs relax.

I want to watch this, but I'm not sure she's got standing in her.

I wrap my arms around her to lead her to the bed.

She shifts onto my lap.

Her back sinks into my chest.

Her legs part.

She's offering herself to me.

Maybe she doesn't realize it, but she is.

It hits me someplace that's usually empty. Someplace that's never been full.

I want her.

Like this.

And like everything else too.

I bring one hand to her chest.

Slip the other between her legs.

Work my way back to the perfect pressure.

"Fuck." Her breathe catches in her throat. "I… Fuck."

Her head falls to one side.

Her eyes flutter open then close.

Her fingers dig into my thighs.

I bring her to the edge.

Then push her over it.

She groans as she comes.

Her legs shake.

Her teeth sink into her lip.

Her brow furrows then relaxes.

It's fucking beautiful watching pleasure spread over her face.

I know it before she says a word.

This isn't going to be enough.

Nothing is going to be enough.

Chapter Twenty-One

QUINN

Warm water runs down my fingers. I pump soap into my hand. Press my palms together. Rub.

I'm washing *myself* off my hands.

It's weird.

But hot too.

Wes is just...

He's so fucking sexy.

I already owe him a lot. Everything.

He's just...

Deep breath. Steady exhale.

Wes and I are having fun. Period. The end.

It's easy getting attached to an authority figure, but it's not happening.

There are only three weeks left of my summer.

I'm...

I'm just not going there.

I'm enjoying all of this.

Fun. Sex. Freedom. The end.

Well, the end is Chicago and med school and the complete opposite of fun and freedom, but, um—

Not the problem yet.

I finish rinsing my hands. Dry them on my cream towel.

Reapply lipstick. Blot. Pop.

Perfect.

I step into the main room.

He's leaning against the couch, his gaze on his cell, his brow furrowed.

"Hey." I try to keep my voice even, but my chill drains quickly. Something is wrong. It's not me. I'm pretty sure it's not me. Or us. Or whatever you call this. But it's hard to avoid jumping to conclusions.

"Hey. I, uh, I gotta go."

"Oh." I swallow hard. That's fine. No, it's good. He's making our boundaries clearer. I should thank him.

"Was hoping to make you something to eat, but there's a family thing I have to take care of." He slides his cell into his pocket. Returns to his usual effortless expression. "Fuck, angel, you look gorgeous."

"Yeah?"

He nods and takes a step closer. "How about I fix you something fast?"

"I'll be okay."

"Dunno." He motions to the cinnamon sitting on the kitchen counter. "Can I let you near that?"

I shake my head. "Too risky."

"See, I'm gonna have to stay."

"It's early. I'll manage dinner." I press my lips into a smile.

He closes the distance between us. Cups my hip with his hand. Pulls my body into his.

Kisses me.

Mmm. He tastes good.

This feels right.

Like it's where we're both supposed to be.

Wes pulls back with a heavy sigh. "What are you doing today?"

It's already late afternoon, but I don't bring that up. "Recovering." I try to make my smile flirty. Get most of the way there.

He returns a wicked smile. "You trying to drive me crazy?"

I motion *a little*.

He takes a step backward. "I'll text you."

"Sure. Yeah." I nod goodbye.

He spins on his heels. Moves out of the apartment. Presses the door into the frame.

I cross the room to lock it.

Rest my back against the steady surface.

He's leaving.

It's normal.

But it feels like he's taking some part of me with him.

And, God, I have no idea how to get it back.

———

I fix an extra strong cup of English Breakfast. Add lots of honey and almond milk. Drink with greedy sips.

It's delicious, sweet, creamy perfection.

But it's not comforting.

It's only bringing me back to this morning. To Wes at my kitchen counter. And the couch. And my bed.

He's all over the apartment.

And now I...

This is casual. It's no big deal. I can handle that.

No matter how many times I repeat the mantra to myself, it fails to stick.

I turn the TV to Turner Classic Movies. A gorgeous black and white beach scene from *Some Like it Hot* flashes on screen, but it fails to grab my attention.

I pull out my cell.

Which is up to my texts with Wes.

Of course.

Ugh.

Not looking at that.

Not thinking about him.

Thinking about—

That's it.

I call Owen.

He picks up on the third ring. "Hey, Q, you're needy all of a sudden. Unless—is someone dead? Are you pregnant?"

"No and God no."

"You and Mr. Fling haven't crossed that bridge?"

"You'd kill Reggie for asking me that."

He laughs. "No. I'd give him shit. But later I'd… Um. Never mind."

Gossip about me, of course.

Owen clears his throat. "How is Mr. Fling?"

"He's good."

"No, Q. *How* is he?"

"Oh." I swallow hard. "Same answer." I can't tell him I'm nervous about going further. Or that I'm getting attached. Or that I'm completely failing to think of something that isn't Wes or my impending doom. "He's different than other people I know."

"How?"

"He's fun. But he's more too. He tries to pretend like he's shallow, but there's more to him."

"Oh, Q."

"What?"

178

"Guys like that—there's not more there. There's nothing there."

Owen knows a lot about guys, but he's wrong about Wes. I know Wes. I see the hurt in his blue eyes. "There is."

"Don't let orgasms cloud your judgment."

"I'm not. We're just… it's casual. We both get that." Maybe this was a bad idea. I don't need someone else questioning my judgment. I do it enough myself. "How are you?"

"Tired. Just got home."

"Work good?"

"Fuck yeah." His voice softens. "Are you and Romeo having fun?"

"Yeah." My lips curl into a smile. My chest warms. Wes is just… Wes. "A lot."

"That's what counts."

That is what counts.

"You like him?" he asks.

"I do."

"Only three weeks left with him."

"Yeah." I bite my lip. I know that. I don't mind. It's okay. Really.

"You gonna miss him?"

"I'll miss *it*." I'll miss him too, but I don't need my brother giving me the third degree.

Owen laughs. "Fuck, cold as ice. I like it."

"Get used to it."

"You know, I met the cutest resident yesterday. He'd be perfect for you."

"Would he?"

"Yeah. I'll introduce you when you get back. You have two weeks before school starts, right?"

"Right." Ideally, I'll spend them finding an apartment. I

don't want to live with my parents. I love them, but they're maddening.

"I'll put something on the schedule."

"Sure." The thought of another guy makes my chest heavy, but planning a future date is smart. It's a good reminder this is temporary. Three more weeks. Then we're done.

"And, well… you have anything planned when you get back?"

"Why?"

"Well…" His voice perks. "I promised Reggie I wouldn't say anything."

"But?"

Owen laughs. "I can keep a secret."

He can't, but I won't argue. "Why are you asking?"

"I can't want to spend time with my sister?"

"What time?"

He laughs. "We have something to tell you."

"Something good?" I ask.

"Really good."

He told me about their engagement on the phone. It must be bigger than that. But what the hell is bigger than that? "I'll be happy?"

"If you're not a total bitch."

"Asshole."

He laughs. "I'll make a reservation for dinner."

"The three of us?"

"Yep."

"Mom and Dad know?"

"It's going to you first."

My chest warms. It's sweet, Owen announcing news to me first. But making plans for my life in Chicago… it sucks the heat from the room.

Owen continues, "shit, I gotta go or the El will be jammed. Is Romeo gonna come back with you?"

"No. We're casual."

"You said that."

"And it's still true."

"Hmmm…" He makes that noise that means *I don't believe you.*

I clear my throat. "I have to go too." I reach for an excuse. "*Some Like it Hot* is about to start on TCM."

"You own it on DVD."

Okay, that is true.

"And you always say it's overrated."

"I do not."

"Oh my God, you do. I have all your movie opinions memorized. Because I hear them every Christmas when you and Mom debate your favorite old stars."

That might be true.

"You're thinking something about him," Owen says.

"About his massive cock."

"Since when do you say cock?"

"Since now."

"Is it really massive?"

"Goodbye, Owen."

"Tease."

"Goodbye!"

"Do me one favor, Q."

"Yeah?"

"Don't fall in love with him."

Chapter Twenty-Two

WES

"How much will it hurt?" Shanon sinks her teeth into her lip. Her eyes get big. Nervous.

She's a lot like Quinn.

A goth version of Quinn. Jet-black hair. Sky-high boots. Low pain tolerance.

Ironic, a girl who looks like she's into whips and chains can't handle a needle.

But facades drop fast in the chair.

Hard to keep up the *I'm a badass* front when you're whimpering over ink.

Not that I'm judging.

I'm a wimp when it comes to a new tattoo. That shit fucking hurts.

"You have anything else pierced?" I motion to her ears.

She clears her throat. "Anything like—"

She does. Fuck. My mind goes straight to the gutter. Not sure which I see more for Shanon—nipples or clit.

Fuck, I can't even imagine how badly that would hurt.

Dean never tires of bringing up his Prince Albert.

But, God, why?

"Less than that." I slide tape over the stencil. Press it to her skin.

Her eyes go straight to her wrist. "I passed out."

"No."

"Yeah." Her cheeks flush. "The piercer said he almost tore off my nipple."

That answers that question.

My cock stirs at the thought of her metal stud.

But my head skips over the image of Shanon naked.

Goes straight to Quinn.

Gorgeous hazel eyes. Thick glasses. Soft lips.

Fuck, I'm not even thinking about her tits.

And they're perfect tits.

"A lot less." I shrug my shoulders. Remind myself I'm supposed to be setting my client at ease, not fantasizing about my... pupil. "I promise."

"What if it's too much?"

"You'll look like a fool with *memento* and no *mori*."

She laughs. "Can you imagine? Just remember?"

"You could write something different every day."

"Oh God." She shakes her head. "Horrible."

"Remember to brush."

She laughs. "Remember to eat your veggies."

"Remember to call your mom."

She laughs. "Lots of possibilities."

"You change your mind?" I tap the stencil with my gloved finger. "Want to lose the *mori*?"

Her lips curl into a smile as she shakes her head.

I check the tape on her wrist. It's there. We're ready. If she's ready. "You want me to start with the least or most painful part?"

Shanon bites her lip. She looks up at me, her dark eyes big and vulnerable. "Most. I think. That way, the worst is over."

"I'd do the same."

She nods with all the trust in the world.

"You survived your tits. You've got this."

"Okay. Sure. Yeah." She takes a deep breath and exhales slowly. "My friend was right."

"You have a friend?"

She nods and mentions a woman I tattooed last month. "She said you're really calming."

"Do what I can."

"And that you're cute."

I shoot her a *fuck me* smile.

Her anxiety fades to desire. Then her eyes go to the gun and her nerves return.

I know how to keep her mind occupied.

It just…

It feels weird now.

Like I'm betraying Quinn.

Which is silly. All the guys here flirt. Well, the ones who are the flirting type. Chase would never stoop so low.

Where the fuck is he anyway?

This morning's text—*You have to stop cleaning up after Mom or she's never going to get better. We'll talk today. Dad is stopping by the shop*—is still burning a hole in my pocket.

Sure, I bailed on Quinn to keep Mom from driving drunk.

I made sure Mom wasn't a fucking mess.

But what else could I do?

Being older doesn't make Chase wiser.

He's so unforgiving he's without a single close friend or lover.

He's the one with fucked-up priorities.

"Guilty as charged." I open the ink pad and dip the needle. "You ready?"

"No. But go anyway."

"On three?"

She nods. "Yeah. Sure."

I borrow Hunter's old trick. "One." I turn the gun on. "Two." I bring it to her skin.

She yelps. "Fuck." Her eyes go to mine. "Asshole."

"Not so bad, huh?"

She bites her lip. "It's uh…" Her breath is shallow. "Not as bad as the other thing."

"Deep inhale for me, Shanon."

She stares at me like I'm crazy.

The way Quinn does.

But it feels different.

It's hard to explain.

It's just so obvious she's not Quinn.

She's sexy, stylish, vulnerable.

And distinctly not Quinn.

"I want to hear it." I trace the *m*. "Like an entire yoga class."

"You do yoga?"

"Hell yeah. Chicks dig limber dudes."

Her laugh eases the tension in her brow. "I've never heard that."

"You've been missing out."

"Oh?" Her eyes trace a line down my body. Stop at the tattoo peeking out from my t-shirt.

That's always where they stop.

I'm not sure if I'm appreciative or irritated.

I mean, I did choose the chest piece.

I do love it.

But the way women stare—it's like there's a blinking sign on my head that reads *bad boy fling*.

It works well enough.

Gets me laid.

Keeps expectations of intimacy low.

Hell, for a long time it was accurate.

But now that Quinn—

I don't know where the hell we stand. Where the hell I stand. Only that something needs to change.

"You need strength too." I dial my flirting up. "Combination helps."

"Good to know." Her cheeks flush.

I move to the *e*.

Shanon curses as I trace the skin closer to her wrist.

"That's the worst part, I promise."

She nods.

I slip back into my role. Tease her about all the sex positions she and I could unlock.

It works. Keeps her breathing and calm.

Earns me a fat tip.

And a card with her phone number.

I'm not an asshole. I slip it into my pocket.

She beams as she bounces out the door.

She's happy.

I'm paid.

This is win-win.

Even if it makes my stomach turn.

"Why you all pissy?" Griffin sets his sketchbook on his chair. Steps into the lobby. "Wasn't your date yesterday?"

I motion to my face. "Happy as a clam."

His dark eyes fix on me. They dig for cracks. "Something is off."

"Why do I tell you anything?"

"'Cause you love me."

"You're okay."

"I'm your best friend."

"Eh." I shake my head *kinda*.

His chuckle fills the room. Drowns out the mellow jams —his pick.

They're solid enough, but they're so fucking chill. Like the lead singer is taking one too many Xanax.

Guess it's the right background for calming clients.

Even if I can't stand it.

Griffin smiles. "What happened with her?"

"None of your business."

"She still a virgin?"

"You still an asshole?" I flip him off.

"He's defensive, huh?" Walker steps out of his suite. "Hiding something?" He pushes his dark hair behind his ear.

You'd think he'd appreciate the whole effortless act—he does the same thing—but no.

He's on Team Terrorize Wes.

Everyone here is on Team Terrorize Wes.

Griffin launches into a discussion of my arrangement with Quinn.

Walker's expression gets knowing. "Tried that."

"Really?" I clear my throat. Swallow my curiosity.

"Not the education, not formally. Informally though." He presses his lips into a very dirty smile.

"Now?" I ask.

"You've seen the ring," he says.

Yeah, he's engaged now. "That started as a casual thing?"

"What else could we have in common?" he asks.

True. His girl is… well, she's kinda like Quinn. She's a prim and proper educated woman. Whereas he's a dirty, depraved motherfucker.

"What is it about smart chicks?" I ask.

He shrugs. "Best kind."

Even Griffin nods.

"You need some tips?" Walker offers.

"You've got nothing," I say.

Walker laughs. "Yeah, well. Beyond 'don't fuck it up.'"

"Thanks for the insight, Casanova," I say.

Griffin nods. "You have to be honest with her. And yourself."

Oh lord.

Walker nods. "Last part is the hardest."

"Too sober for this conversation," I say.

"You tease, Wes, but we both know—" Griffin starts.

I cut him off. "Yeah, I know."

Walker shoots him a look.

Griffin whispers something in his ear.

Something about me.

Fantastic.

I'm gossip.

Should be used to it—these guys are worse than any women I've ever met when it comes to gossip—but I'm not.

"You got special plans for the big event?" Walker asks.

"None of your fucking business," I say.

Walker chuckles. "He's so into her."

Griffin matches his laugh. Shrugs *I know, right*.

I flip them both off.

Grab my sketchbook. Check the clock to figure out how long I have until my next appointment.

But there's no time for concentration.

Not with the procession coming through the front door.

Hunter.

Chase.

And my father.

Chapter Twenty-Three

WES

I push my hands into my pockets. "I have an appointment."

Hunter and Chase exchange a look. A *we know best. You know nothing. You're an idiot* look.

Fucking assholes.

Hunter's eyes meet mine. "Em canceled your afternoon."

My fingers curl into fists. This is what I get, taking a job at the shop where my brother's girlfriend is the manager. "You ever hear of asking?"

"It was fucked-up, sorry." Hunter's eyes fill with honest vulnerability. "Really, Wes. I hate to deceive you. But we—"

"We need to have this conversation." Chase folds his arms over his chest. He's lacking Hunter's vulnerability. He's all steel and fire.

Same as always.

Dad stands behind them, hands in his pockets, hopelessly out of place in his slacks and tie.

The guy doesn't know how to dress down to save his life.

I try to find a joke, but it's impossible.

There's only one subject the four of us need to discuss.

And there's nothing funny about it.

I move into my suite. Grab my sketchbook. Keep my eyes on the leather cover. "We doing this here?"

"No." Chase's voice is demanding. Clear. The same tone he used when we were kids. "There's a coffee shop down the street."

"Whatever." I slide my sketchbook into my backpack. Sling that over my shoulders. Follow my brother out of the shop.

Chase walks with steady, determined steps.

Hunter too.

They keep their distance. There's still a frost between them. Chase is still completely unforgiving. But I guess he's willing to put it aside for the moment.

He can team up with an enemy to fight a greater enemy.

Or some shit like that.

Dad doesn't notice their animosity. (Though there's not really any animosity from Hunter. He gets why Chase is pissed. He accepts that they're making slow progress on the road to repairing their relationship).

He doesn't notice anything but the sunlight bouncing off the concrete.

His gaze shifts to his long, white sleeves. Then his dress shoes.

"You come from work?" I ask.

"Yes." His voice is soft.

Fuck, I haven't heard that tone in a long time.

He's always held it together.

Or at least pretended.

If he's really this frayed…

I swallow hard. Wrap my fingers around the nylon straps of my backpack.

Chase motions to the coffee shop on the right.

It's empty for a Tuesday at three. I go straight to the square table. Sit. Cross one leg over the other.

Hunter sits next to me. Reaches to pat my shoulder.

I slap his hand away. It's immature as hell, but what do I care?

This is bullshit.

Everything is bullshit.

"Where's your girlfriend?" I ask.

"I don't keep tabs on her." His eyes betray him. He knows exactly where she is. She's waiting to console him if this goes to shit. Or celebrate if it goes well.

But this kinda thing—

There's no well.

Only *not a total mess*.

Chase and Dad fix cold brews then hand them out.

My oldest brother helps Dad into his seat. Takes his own.

Fuck, there's all this tension in Dad's dark eyes.

He looks exactly like Chase, only with darker eyes and less steel in his expression. They're both tall, broad, handsome.

But Chase is the only one who looks imposing today.

Dad looks pale. Like he's about to faint.

Maybe he is.

I wrap my fingers around my glass. Take a long sip.

It's the same thing this place served yesterday—a rich, chocolaty cold brew with just enough milk to make it creamy.

But it's not good anymore.

It's bitter and ugly.

"We've been talking." Chase's steely eyes go right to me. So I know I'm the only one who isn't in the loop.

"And?" I swallow another sip. Fold my arms in a pointless show of defiance.

Chase holds my stare. "There's a program in Santa Barbara with an opening this summer."

"Fuck off," I say.

"You want to watch her drink herself to death?" Chase asks.

"She's not gonna go," I say.

"She might." Dad turns to me. "She's proud of Hunter."

"Based on what? Thanksgiving and Christmas?" I swallow hard.

This is bullshit.

Total bullshit.

"She's my wife," Dad says. "I know her."

"You care now?" I blink and see red.

How can he suddenly give a shit?

My entire life, nothing.

Now that Hunter is sober, he believes in some magical rehab fairy.

"I've always cared, Wes." Dad's voice gets stronger. "Why do you think I work so much?"

"Why do you think she drinks so much?" I suck a breath through my nose. Push an exhale through my teeth.

I'm not doing this.

I'm not listening to his claims of devotion.

She drinks because he's not there.

Because she's lonely.

Because it's the only thing she understands.

If he pushes her—

That's going to snip the last thread holding her together.

That's going to ruin everything.

Fuck Dad.

Fuck Chase.

Fuck Hunter.

Fuck everything.

I stand. Take a step toward the door.

My foot barely hits the ground.

The room is shaking.

I'm shaking.

"Sit down, Wes." Chase's voice is steady. Clear. Pissed. "This is happening whether you're on board or not."

"If she says no?" I press my palms into the wood. "Then what?"

For a second, his stone expression cracks.

It flashes in his eyes.

Then we abandon her.

Kick her out of the house.

Cut her off from her friends.

Leave her to drink herself to death.

My gaze shifts to Dad.

He nods. "I've been talking to a lawyer."

He's ready to get a fucking divorce.

Now that I'm twenty-four.

That we're all out of the house.

Couldn't do shit when it would have mattered.

But now that he's free, why not abandon his wife?

I try to think up some response that will get across how much I want my family to fuck off.

Come up with nothing.

Whatever.

These assholes don't deserve a response.

I suck my last sip of coffee. Move from the table. Drop the glass in the bus tray.

Chase and Hunter exchange one of those looks, one at my expense.

But I'm too pissed to care.

Fuck them.

Fuck everything.

I need something that makes sense.

I jog the dozen blocks to my apartment.

And I call Quinn.

Chapter Twenty-Four

QUINN

Wes brushes his hair behind his ear as he steps inside.

"Hey." He slides his hand into the front pocket of his jeans. Presses the door closed behind him. Clicks the lock. "You look gorgeous."

I smooth my dress reflexively. Swallow hard. Try to find some appropriate response. Or at least something besides *you look as freaked as you sounded on the phone. What the hell happened? Not that I can handle us having a conversation that honest.* Settle on—"Thanks."

Wes moves toward me with quick steps.

He's eager.

Shaky.

Anxious.

I try to think up a question that doesn't probe too much, but nothing comes.

He crosses the room to me. Curls his hand around my hip. Pulls my body into his.

Mmm. He tastes good. Like mint toothpaste and like Wes.

My lips part.

His tongue slips into my mouth. Dances with mine.

It's aggressive.

But not like before.

More than before.

I break the kiss. Take a step backward.

My body whines. It doesn't want to figure out what the look in his eyes means.

It wants him on the couch. In the bedroom. Against the wall.

Wherever, really.

Yesterday was a million years ago.

I need more.

I need him.

I need to know why he rushed over here.

"Uh…" I move to the counter. Fill the kettle with water. Turn it on. "I thought you had work?"

"Appointment was canceled."

"That's too bad."

"Yeah." His voice steadies. "But it means I can be here."

"True." I swallow hard. Turn back to him. Force myself to hold his gaze.

There's so much hurt in his eyes.

It's not like him.

I want to ask why.

To soothe him.

To fix this.

How the hell do I handle this?

I have friends, sure, but we're not close. We're study partners or coworkers or yoga buddies.

No one spills their guts.

Or keeps my secrets safe.

Am I even capable of that?

It's been so long since I've leaned on someone besides my brother.

And even then...

There are things I don't want Owen knowing.

"Are you okay?" It's not exactly poetic, but it's all I've got.

"Yeah."

I stare into his gorgeous blue eyes. I try to believe his words, but they're so obviously bullshit. "You want something to drink?"

"You have rum?"

I shake my head. Bite my lip so I won't blurt out *oh my God, Wes, it's so obvious something is wrong. Stop pretending.* That's above my paygrade. That's girlfriend paygrade.

His gaze shifts to the fridge. "Wine?"

"Tea."

"Sure."

Right. I motion to the table. "Why don't you sit?"

His voice drops to something low and demanding. "Was thinking I'd make you come first."

My sex clenches. God, that's a beautiful idea. His hands, mouth, cock...

Maybe I'm ready.

I want to be ready.

I want to know what it feels like to have someone inside me.

To have Wes inside me.

His eyes bore into mine.

But they're not filled with desire.

More... desperation.

Like he can't stand the thought of sitting here drinking tea.

And I'm pretty sure it's not a preference for coffee.

"Wes…"

"Yeah, angel?"

"Are you—"

"Let's talk after you come on my face."

Fuck. My cheeks flush. My knees knock together. My body sings. Screams. *Yes. Hell yes. All the yeses.*

It's tempting.

It's really, really tempting.

The water steams.

I grab two mugs.

Fill them with tea bags. Then hot water.

Wes places his body behind mine.

Right behind mine.

He wraps his arm around my waist. Brings his mouth to my ear.

Fuck, his breath is so warm. He's so hard. And safe.

I really do want to collapse in his arms.

But I have to stay strong.

"'Cause I want to hear my name on your lips." He nips at my neck. Softly. Then harder.

My fingers dig into the counter. "Wes—"

"Yeah, angel?"

"Stop."

He steps backward immediately.

"I'm not your distraction." I suck a deep breath through my nose. "If you—"

"That's not—"

"Isn't it?" I turn to face him.

"No." He runs his hand through his hair. "Maybe."

"What happened?"

"Shit."

Again, I motion to the table. "We can talk over tea or you can leave."

He shoots me *fuck me* eyes. "You sure about that?"

God no. "Yes."

"It's not—"

"Don't."

"I…"

"How do you want your tea?"

"Black."

I nod *sure*.

He moves to the table.

I fix our drinks and join him.

His eyes bore into mine.

They beg for something. For everything.

It's not happening.

I'm putting my foot down.

I'm capable of that.

"I like you, Wes," I say.

His brow furrows. "I like you too."

"A lot."

"That's a good thing."

I shake my head. "We've had one date and I'm already—"

"We're friends."

"Are we?"

He shrinks back, hurt.

Or pretending.

He is a player.

I… maybe I should expect this.

Maybe I'm wrong about his honesty.

Maybe I'm completely unable to read men.

"I want to be your friend." He wraps his fingers around his mug. "You're… I like hanging out with you."

"I do too. I just… I want to make sure we're on the same page."

"Sure." His gaze stays on the table.

"I, um, I know you're not doing this on purpose."

His eyes fill with confusion.

"You're not trying to use me. You're just…" God, I don't know him well enough to guess at this. "What happened?"

"I don't want to talk." His voice is soft. Hurt.

"Then maybe you should go."

"Quinn—"

"I…" I don't know what to say. Or what I want. I can't demand more if I can't handle more.

I want more of Wes.

But it's a hopeless situation.

I leave in three weeks.

I start med school next month.

There won't be any room in my life for him.

This summer—that's it.

Okay.

I can handle that.

If he's honest with me.

"What happened today?" I ask.

"Family shit." He presses his lips together. "It's fucked-up." His gaze shifts to his mug. "We can talk."

"Okay."

"Later. I… I need something light right now."

"I'm not taking my clothes off."

He chuckles. "Figured."

"Or taking your clothes off."

His laugh gets louder. Heartier. For a second, all that tension fades from his brow. Then he blinks and it's back. "I like you, Quinn."

"I like you too."

"You're… different."

"I prefer quirky," I say.

"It's a compliment."

"Even so." I fold my hands in my lap. This is… We're… God, I don't know. I want to push him. To ask him to open up. But only if there's a chance he's sticking around.

But he can't stick around. It's a logical impossibility. So there's really no reason to think about it happening.

Unfortunately, that impeccable reasoning does nothing to convince my heart to quiet.

It thuds like a war drum. *Need Wes. Need Wes. Need Wes.*

"I like that you're quirky." His lips curl into a half-smile. "And that you give me shit."

I don't, usually, but no reason to argue with a compliment. "I have an idea."

"Oh?" His voice drops back to that seductive tone. He catches himself. Shakes his head. "Sorry. Habit."

"You're kinda a player."

He holds up his thumb and forefinger *a little*.

"I… I need you to be honest with me."

"I am."

"So, um… I have an idea for what we could do. But later. First—"

"I have an idea too."

"Yeah?"

"You'll have to take your clothes off."

I shoot him a *get real* look.

He laughs. "And put on others." He gives me a long, slow once-over. "Not sure you'll want to wear that."

"You're pushing your luck."

"Good thing I'm handsome."

"It really is."

———

"Oh my God." I reach for something steady. Find only air. This is… I…

My legs wobble.

My feet splay.

I'm a v.

My feet refuse to straighten.

They keep sliding outward.

Until—

My inner thighs tug. That's too much stretch. That's—

"I got you." Wes laughs as he wraps his arm around me.

I try to pull my feet back together, but it's not happening.

"One at a time, angel."

Right. One at a time. "How are you so still?"

God, this place is weird. Like it's stuck in time. Lacquered hardwood floor. White walls. Blinking neon lights.

Older patrons in roller skates and leg warmers.

Teenagers in rollerblades.

A couple doing a partner's routine in the center of the rink.

Spinning.

God, they're moving so much and I—

I lean my back against his chest. Reach for the railing. Find air. Again.

In the last hour, our positions have switched.

I'm shaky.

He's steady.

But, God, it feels good leaning on him.

I mean, it's literal at the moment.

But there's this promise of more.

Of *really* leaning on him.

And letting him lean on me.

It's different. Thrilling. Good.

Oh God.

My right leg—"shit."

He hooks his arm under mine.

I lift my right foot and place it directly below my body.

Then I do the same with my left.

A kid on speed skates whizzes past us. Shoots me a flirty wink.

He's about fourteen. But points for confidence.

Wes laughs. "Bet he wishes you were his babysitter."

"Isn't he a little old?"

"Tutor." He shifts backward. "You want to try again?"

"No." I want his body pressed against mine. I feel steady with his arms around me. Without them—

This is impossible.

The movement pattern.

And the whole not getting attached thing.

"Try anyway." He releases me, chest first, then hips, then hands.

I'm on my own.

I have to skate on my own.

I lift my left leg.

Move it forward.

Attempt to glide as I place it on the slick surface.

It works. Ish.

The next is a little better.

I'm walking more than I'm rollerblading.

But I'm not falling.

Wes does a circle around me. He smiles as his eyes meet mine. "Fuck, if you were my tutor..."

"Yeah?"

"I'd have to fuck myself before our sessions every week."

Jesus.

My knees knock.

I go down.

Hard.

Land right on my ass.

Ow.

It's softer than concrete, but it's not exactly cushy.

"Shit. Sorry." Wes drops to his knees.

I look up at him. "You did that on purpose."

"Maybe."

"It's cruel."

"Testing your balance?"

I flip him off.

He grabs my hand and brings my finger to his mouth. His lips close around my finger.

He sucks on my skin.

Softly.

Then harder.

Then it's the scrape of his teeth.

Thank God I'm already on the ground.

My balance is gone.

He's so…

I'm so…

Totally and completely fucked.

God, he has a nice smile.

And those eyes.

They're so gorgeous.

He offers me his hand.

My stomach flutters as I take it.

Something is different.

Everything is different.

I just…

Really like him.

But uh… "How do I get up?"

"Don't think about it."

I shoot him that *you're ridiculous* look.

He nods. "You trust me?"

"Maybe."

"You got someone else here who will teach you how to rollerblade?"

I scan the rink until I see the teenage boy who winked at me. Motion to him.

Wes laughs. "Fuck, he's better than I am too."

"Exactly."

"But my lesson ends with something a lot more fun."

"Oh?"

His expression gets wicked.

Oh.

So much for getting up.

I'm just…

Sitting is good.

Maybe forever.

Or at least until the rink closes.

Or my heartbeat slows.

"On three," Wes says.

I shake my head.

He nods. "One, two, three—" He takes my hands and pulls me up.

I climb onto my knees. Then my right foot. Left. Okay, I have it. Sorta.

"Perfect." He slides his arm around my waist. Holds me close. To steady me. Or maybe just because he wants me close.

It doesn't mean anything.

Wes flirts.

He can't help himself.

It's fun, yes, but it's not about me.

It's just Wes.

His eyes shift to me. "Fuck, I ever tell you how much I like your glasses?"

"Yes." I push them up my nose reflexively. "But I like hearing it again."

"You look like a sexy librarian." His fingers glide over my hip. "And these leggings. Fuck, angel. You're driving me mad."

"Right back at you." My lips press together.

It's a habit, him deflecting with sex, but that doesn't make it go down easier. Not that anything or anyone is going down.

Well, maybe later. That is our relationship. Just sex. Doing the sex part might help with reminding me of our boundaries.

In theory.

It's not that I want to fuck him.

I mean I do.

But…

Uh…

He shoots me that classic Wes Keating smile. "You ready to go again?"

"Do I have to?"

He nods *yeah*.

Okay. I… I want to get this. I want to tease him. To be here. To find out what happened.

Later.

He asked for a distraction.

I'm honoring that.

No matter how badly I want to know.

He interlaces his fingers with mine. "You've got this."

Okay, I've got this. I take a small step. Then another.

I just barely glide, but I do.

We move around the curve of the rink.

The disco song switches to *Staying Alive*.

Wes laughs. "Fuck, they need a new soundtrack."

"You taking other women here?"

"Where do you think I went yesterday?"

"I, um—"

"I wouldn't," he says.

"Oh."

"We're exclusive."

"Right."

"Besides… Only one thing I do with other women. Well, did." He motions to a roller skater doing tricks in the curve ahead. Helps me move toward the center of the rink.

Ish.

My foot lands wrong.

I teeter.

But he catches me.

Holds my body against his.

My heart thuds against his chest.

God, he feels good.

This feels good.

Different.

More…

Just more.

"You're overthinking it," he says.

"I know you believe that's helpful—"

"Talk to me about something."

"Well, um…" I glide forward. (Okay, forwardish). It breaks our touch.

Air-conditioning beats over my head and neck. I'm in a sweater and leggings, but I'm freezing. It should be a nice reprieve—it's a million degrees outside—but it's not. I miss the warmth of him.

"Where did you go yesterday?" I ask.

"Fuck, that's a long story."

Small step. Glide. Repeat. That part is easy. Now, putting it together… "I have time."

His laugh is soft. Endeared. "You're closer than you think."

I shake my head.

He nods.

"How about I keep trying as long as you keep talking?" I suggest.

"You blackmailing me?"

"No." It's hard to explain. "I just… I want to know."

"Yeah." His fingers skim my hip. My shoulder. My forearm. He intertwines his fingers with mine. "How steady are you?"

My heart is skipping. But that's not what he's asking. "I think I've got it."

"Okay." He squeezes my hand with his. "It's just… Fucked, I guess."

"I get that."

His gaze shifts from me to the rink in front of us. The space is clear. There are only a dozen people here and they're all in the fast lane, so to speak.

His eyes meet mine.

His voice drops to a whisper. "My mom's an alcoholic."

"Oh." Shit. My legs wobble. I squeeze his hand. It's enough to keep me balanced. I suck a breath through my nose. Exhale slowly. One foot after the other. Baby steps. "I'm sorry."

"Don't think I've ever said it out loud before."

"I thought she just liked wine." Mrs. Keating always indulged when our families got together, but no more than my mom did. They were old friends having fun. It seemed normal.

He shakes his head. "She's good at pretending shit's okay."

"Is that where you get it?"

"Yeah." His voice is soft. Vulnerable. He's still staring straight ahead. Avoiding my gaze. "Guess I'm not as good as I used to be."

"You're pretty good."

He chuckles. "Is that a compliment?"

"I don't know. Do you want it to be?"

"Last week, I would have said yes. Today…" His voice drops again. "She's getting worse."

"I'm sorry."

"Chase wants to send her to rehab."

"That's a good thing, isn't it?"

"In theory." His gaze shifts to me. His blue eyes fill with hurt. Need. Trust. "But what if she says no?"

"Then what's changed?"

"Everything." He motions to the exit door. Then to the rink.

I nod. "I'm good for another round."

"You're getting it."

"Kinda."

"You are." He releases my hand. Moves behind me. Rests his palms on my hips. "Try faster."

"Wes, I—"

"Just try."

"No, I…" I fail to find the appropriate response. It's not like there are words to fix this. Or even soothe him. "I'm sorry about your mom."

"Thanks."

"Does anyone else know?"

"Just Hunter, Chase, and my dad."

"That sucks."

"Yeah." His fingers curl into my hips. "Faster."

I nod. Try to hold my glide. It's shaky, but it's getting there.

We move around the rink again.

The song switches to a family hit from the early 80s.

We do another lap.

My steps get steadier.

I actually glide.

For three seconds at a time.

But it's something.

The air between us changes.

Gets warmer.

Sweeter.

He moves closer.

It's only a few inches, but it's so obvious.

He slows to a stop at the door. Presses his palm to the railing. Looks to the ground. "Chase thinks I'm an enabler."

I swallow hard. I want to say something to help him, but how the hell can I help him?

"Maybe I am. But is what they're doing better? They're gonna cut her off. Let her drink herself to death."

"I'm sorry."

"Thanks.

"Really, Wes. That must be hard."

He nods. "Let's do another round."

"Maybe we should talk more."

He shakes his head. "Don't have anything else to say."

"Okay." That's fair. "How about we not talk together?"

His eyes meet mine. They look for something.

He must find it, because he nods and offers his hand.

I take it.

He helps me glide around the rink.

Then, we do it again.

Again.

Until I really do have it.

We don't stop until we're sweaty and exhausted.

I get out of my rollerblades and into my flats, but the ground isn't any steadier.

The closer we get to his car, the more everything spins.

He's letting me in.

He's offering more.

And I'm taking it.

God help me.

Chapter Twenty-Five

QUINN

My apartment looks exactly as I left it this afternoon, but it feels like a different universe.

It's in the air.

In my veins.

In my heart.

Which is screaming.

I should be used to the *Wes, Wes, Wes* chant, but that's different too.

It's not my body whining for his.

It's something deeper.

Something in my soul.

God, is that what people say?

My main reference point is *Casablanca*.

Maybe it's okay we only have the summer.

Look at Rick and Ilsa. They only have their short affair in Paris and they wouldn't trade that for anything.

A summer with Wes is better than no Wes.

Better to love and lose.

I have absorbed the message of my favorite movie.

And he…

Well… he knows where we stand too.

"So." He wraps his arm around my waist. "You thinking what I'm thinking?"

My thoughts immediately float away. The only thing in my brain is *Wes, Wes, Wes*. Somehow, I manage to murmur some kind of *hmm*.

He motions to the bathroom. "I should shower."

"Oh. Sure." I try to step forward, but he doesn't release me.

"You should shower with me."

"Oh." *Oh.* "And we…"

"You want to move up our next lesson?"

Hell yes. "Depends."

"Fuck, angel, my ego." He makes a noise like he's been stabbed in the gut.

"Your ego is fine."

"Could be better with a little stroking." His voice drops back to that low, seductive tone.

He wants to forget all this heavy stuff.

Or maybe he wants to connect physically.

Or maybe he's as confused as I am.

I close my eyes. Take a deep breath. Try to find clarity.

His fingers curl into my hips.

His lips brush my neck.

Softly.

Then harder.

Then it's the scrape of his teeth and—

Fuck.

My body responds with gusto.

Hell yes.

"Depends on what, angel?" He slips his hand under my sweater. Traces the waistband of my leggings.

"What's our lesson?"

"I seem to recall demanding you come on my face."

Fuck. My sex clenches. I try to make my nod coy, but I don't get there. "Will you…" Confidence. I can do that. "Will you teach me how to suck you off?" My cheeks flush, but he can't see that. He's behind me. This is confident. Ish.

"Not today."

My pout is pure reflex.

"I'm too wound up to teach you." He brushes my hair behind my ear.

"Maybe that's a good thing."

"Yeah?" His fingers skim my temple. "If I can't control myself and I come in your mouth in thirty fucking seconds? That's a good thing?"

"Yeah." I swallow hard. Which is hard. Because now I'm thinking about swallowing and if I can manage that. "It will build my confidence."

He laughs. "You're a good salesperson."

"Thank you." I arch my hips against his. My brain tries to jump in with something about clarity and what the hell am I doing and oh my God, I'm so fucking attached but it's all so fuzzy. So much less important than this. "What if I make a demand?"

"Come in your mouth or leave?"

My knees knock together.

Fuck, he's so good at this.

I'm so…

Fuck.

"We can do the shower first," I say.

"We can do it in the shower." He pulls me closer, so his hard-on presses against the flesh of my ass. "Fuck, you're distracting me."

"Yeah."

"Want to get you off first."

"What if I want to get you off first?" I rub my ass

against his cock. It's weird, him being that close to my, well my ass, even with all our clothes in the way.

But not a bad weird.

A good weird.

A very good.

God, maybe I'm into *that*.

But one thing at a time.

"Fuck," he breathes.

I'm not sure what I'm doing.

Only that I need it.

Him.

This.

"Is that a yes?" I rock my hips against him again.

"Fuck, Quinn." His fingers brush my sex, over my leggings. Softly. Then harder.

The smooth fabric glides over my skin with just enough friction.

That's—

Fuck is right.

"Yeah." He leans down to nip at my neck. "Think I'll be the one who needs the lesson at this rate."

I shake my head. Stop myself. He's wrong, but I'm taking the compliment, dammit. "Let's um—"

"Yeah." He guides me to the bathroom.

I pull the curtain. Run the shower until it's hot.

He tosses his t-shirt aside.

Then his jeans.

His boxers.

God, he's...

There isn't a single word strong enough to describe him.

Beautiful, handsome, hot as hell, inviting, tempting—

None do Wes justice.

He's just—

Fuck.

"Clothes off." His voice gets low. Needy. Demanding.

It makes my sex clench.

I nod as I pull my sweater over my head.

He watches with rapt attention as I roll my leggings off my hips.

I kick them aside. Reach for my glasses.

He shakes his head. "We're gonna have to renegotiate, Quinn."

"Oh?"

He nods. "Need your glasses on."

"You like them that much?"

"Yeah." His fingers brush my temples as he slides my frames off my face. "Shower. Then I come in your mouth."

My cheeks flame. It's impossible to hold his gaze. It really is.

"You sure you want that?" he asks.

"Yes."

"It's a lot."

"But the way you say it..." My blush spreads to my chest. "It's really hot."

He nods.

"You... is that what you like? Usually?"

"Yeah."

"Do you..." Deep breath. Steady exhale. Confidence. I can do confidence. "Do you want me to swallow?"

"One thing at a time, angel."

"You don't think I can—"

"Just keep a tissue handy."

"Oh. Okay." God, this is weird. Honest. Awkward. Hot. I... I have no idea what I'm doing. Not just technically. Emotionally.

But that's such a distant concern at the moment.

Paris.

This is our Paris.

We'll always have the summer before med school.

I'm enjoying it.

No matter how much I dread what comes after.

His eyes meet mine.

For a second, they fill with vulnerability.

Then he blinks, and it's gone.

Back to sex god.

Or sex crazed.

Or both.

His eyelids flutter closed.

His lips meet mine.

He kisses me softly.

Then harder.

His tongue dances with mine.

I push my panties off my hips. Kick them off my ankles. Break our kiss to step into the shower.

He follows me.

Water pounds my head, drips down my neck, back, ass, legs.

He wraps his arms around me.

Pushes me past the stream. All the way to the tile wall.

I'm slick. My back slips against the surface.

He's slippery too.

His skin glides over mine.

It's too little friction.

He's not close enough.

I bring my hand to his shoulder. Pull him close. Kiss him hard.

Fuck, he tastes good.

He always tastes good.

And this is so…

It's just right.

Does it always feel this right?

Or is it just him?

He pins me to the wall with the heel of one hand.

Brings the other to my chest.

Draws slow circles around my nipple.

"Wes." I knot my hand in his hair. Pull him closer.

"Yeah, angel?"

"Don't stop."

"Never." His cheek brushes mine as he brings his lips to my neck.

He sucks on my skin as he toys with me.

Harder. Faster. Rougher.

Fuck.

It's different with my skin wet.

With less friction.

With my heart unfolding for him.

Everything blurs together. The running water. The soft scrape of his teeth. The rough feel of his fingertips.

He has such strong hands.

They're calloused in all the right places.

Pleasure spreads through my body as he toys with me.

He winds me up until I'm dizzy.

Then he pulls back enough to bring me under the water.

He's impossibly patient about squeezing shampoo into his hands and running it through my hair.

I tilt my head backward to rinse.

He does the same with conditioner.

Then we switch places and I wash his hair.

It's weird.

Intimate.

He's really taking care of me.

And I'm really taking care of him.

We're so… naked.

I mean, we are naked.

But I feel it. The walls dropping. The space between us shrinking.

It's not sexy lingerie and dirty talk.

No, it is that.

But it's more.

It's… real.

I think.

It's hard to be sure.

Especially with my body whining for, well, for everything.

I reach for my body wash. Squeeze it into my hands. "You're going to smell like me."

"Perfect."

I rub the gel over his shoulders. Slowly. So I can feel every inch of him.

Soft skin. Hard muscles. The slight raise of ink.

It's so inviting.

I drag my palms over his chest until I'm out of gel.

Then I retrace my path with my fingertips.

He steps backward.

Rinses his skin.

I squeeze more gel into my hands.

Do it again.

I take my time exploring his arms, back, stomach.

I crouch to rub his feet, ankles, legs.

I get higher, higher, higher.

There.

My palm brushes his cock.

He's still hard.

And, God, it still feels so fucking good.

He offers me his hand. Helps me up. Kisses me hard.

Then he steps back enough to rinse, switches places with me, and soaps every inch of my skin.

By the time he's done, I'm shaking.

The pounding water sends me into overdrive.

My body buzzes.

My sex aches.

My nipples wine.

I need him.

All of him.

And I need to stay here, in this beautiful, warm space where everything makes sense.

No wonder he tries to dodge with sex.

It's fucking amazing.

I rinse my hair one last time then I turn the water off.

He steps out of the shower and offers me a towel.

I cinch it around my chest. Take his hand. Step onto the rug.

Again, he kisses me hard.

Again, my heart thuds against my chest.

My stomach flutters.

My veins buzz.

He slides my glasses on.

Takes a step backward. "You ready for this?"

"Are you?"

His lips curl into a wicked smile.

I melt.

I really do.

Chapter Twenty-Six

QUINN

The door clicks into its frame.

Wind ruffles the sheer curtains.

Light streams through the window. Casts the room in the orange glow of sunset.

It's such pretty light.

The end of the day.

The start of the night.

That's what this is.

The end of casual.

The start of…

I don't know.

Something good.

Something great.

Wes takes a step backward.

His eyes meet mine.

They fill with that fire. The one that screams *I need you*.

I want to know how deep it goes.

I want to do this.

I want to do everything.

Deep breath. Slow exhale.

The ground is spinning again.

But there's no hope for steadiness now.

"How much do you know?" Wes asks.

I cinch my towel a little tighter. I'm here to do this. I want to do this.

I really, really, really want to do this.

"Nothing, really." I've read books, sure (and who hasn't scoured *Cosmo* for tips?), but I don't have any firsthand knowledge.

"Drop your towel."

"Is that part of the lesson?"

"Yeah." He motions *take it off*.

Slowly, I unwrap the towel and toss it in the direction of my desk chair. It lands in a pile on the floor.

Usually, I'd rush to pick it up.

Right now, I don't care about the mess. I don't care about anything but driving him out of his mind.

"Fuck." Wes gives me a long, slow once-over. "You get better every time I see you, angel."

"Since yesterday?"

"Yeah." He motions *come here*.

I take a step toward him.

His fingers skim my hip. Then it's his palm.

He pulls me closer.

I rise to my tiptoes to press my lips to his.

My glasses are in the way, but it still feels so fucking good kissing him.

I wrap my arm around his waist.

He brings his hand to my chest. Toys with my nipple with his thumb.

I rock my hips against his.

I feel it.

Him.

He's hard.

God, why is that so appealing?

It's fucking intoxicating. It really is.

"Does it always happen that fast?" I ask.

"Depends on the guy."

"For you?"

"Depends."

"On?"

"How much I've been drinking." He cups my cheek with his palm. "How much I'm into it. Into someone."

"And you're—"

"Into you, yeah." He looks down at me with heavy eyes. "You don't have to wait until a guy is hard to start."

"Oh."

"You don't have to go straight to it either."

"Have to make him feel special?"

He runs his fingers through my hair. "Guess it depends on what you're going for."

"What if I want to make you feel special?"

"Special how?" He tries to hide the desire in his voice, to stay the calm, even teacher, but he doesn't get there.

"Like I can't get enough."

"You're doing pretty good without instruction."

"Oh." I guess my body is getting the message across loud and clear. "Specifically?"

"It's all how you do it. You can go hard." He grabs my ass and pulls me into a deep, fast kiss.

My sex clenches. "Fuck."

"Or more tender." He drags his fingertips over my spine with a featherlight touch.

His lips brush mine.

Softly.

Then a little harder.

My lips part.

His tongue slides between them.

Dances with mine.

I kiss him back.

Copy his touch. Bring my palm to his chest. Trace the lines of his shoulder down his arm.

He pulls me closer.

Kisses me harder.

His fingers dig into my skin.

His tongue swirls around mine.

He's demonstrating technique, yeah, but it's there.

He can't get enough.

Neither of us can.

I tug at his towel.

He stares down at me as he tosses it aside.

Fuck, he's close.

We're close.

We're still damp from the shower, but it's different being naked in the bedroom.

There's so much intention.

Like we're ready to jump into bed.

To connect completely.

I want that.

But this first.

This now.

I bring my lips to his as I wrap my hand around his cock. My thumb and middle finger.

I run my hand over his length with a soft grip.

Up and down and up again.

Until he's groaning against my mouth.

He pulls back with a heavy sigh. "Don't tease me today, angel. I'm already wound up."

"Oh." My body buzzes. He's so fucking sexy and I want him so badly. I can't believe it's possible to want anyone this badly. "What should I do?"

"You want a step-by-step?"

I nod.

His pupils dilate. "Fuck, Quinn." He gives me a quick once-over. Motions to the wall. "Here."

"Okay." I follow him to the wall.

He presses his back against the white surface. "Get on your knees." His voice is half demand, half instruction.

Both halves are so fucking hot.

I just.

I really need to do this.

To do it right.

To do it now.

To—

One thing at a time.

Sucking cock can't be as difficult as rollerblading.

And I managed that okay.

Oh my God, I'm comparing blow jobs to sports.

I…

I need a grip.

Well, I do need a grip. But, um, I…

"Relax, angel. You've got this." He cups my hip.

"How?"

"I want you."

"But I… I didn't do anything."

"Yeah, but I'm already keyed up. That's half the fucking battle."

Okay. I make a mental note, but it disappears. I want to remember these instructions, yeah. But I want to be in this moment more.

I want to make Wes feel good.

I want to make him come.

I…

I can do this.

Slowly, I lower myself onto my knees. It puts his cock right at, well, at mouth level.

He's good at this.

Because he's experienced.

Because he's used to looking at girls and knowing exactly the position he needs.

Because he's been with God knows how many women.

But then I don't care about before.

So what if I'm a virgin and he's a manwhore?

He's here, teaching me.

He wants me.

God, he really fucking wants me.

"Start with your hand," he says. "Get a grip."

I wrap my fingers around his smooth skin.

He lets out a low, deep groan. "Start with a little tease."

I nod.

His eyes meet mine. "Brush your lips against my tip."

Fuck, I'm really doing this.

I stare up at Wes as I bring my lips to his cock.

I brush my lips against him. Softly. Then a little harder.

It's different than kissing his lips or his neck.

Softer.

But harder too.

Fuck, I really like it.

I do it again, on his other side.

Then the top of his tip.

The bottom.

His fingers curl into my shoulder.

His other hand goes to the back of my head.

I brush my lips against him again.

He lets out a deep groan. "Try your tongue."

I pull back enough to… well, to talk. "How?"

"Like an ice cream cone."

God, that's a mental image.

I… Uh…

I nod.

Okay, like an ice cream cone.

I think. Um… Well…

He shudders as I tighten my grip.

I bring my lips to his cock.

Then my tongue.

I start with a soft lick. Just enough to taste him.

The sweet soap from my shower and something distinctly Wes.

It's different than tasting his lips.

More intense.

Just more.

I try softer.

Longer.

Shorter.

Harder.

His fingers knot in my hair. "Fuck, Quinn."

"Good?"

"Yeah," he breathes. "Take me into your mouth."

"Okay." I stare up at him as I wrap my lips around his tip.

Mmm.

There's something about having him in my mouth.

It just feels good.

I try to find a better word, but nothing comes.

I don't care about words.

Only about how much this thrills me.

His fingers curl into the back of my head. "You can keep teasing like this."

I mumble a yes against him.

His laugh is low. Hearty. "Not the time to expect responses, I guess." He looks down at me with a heavy smile. "Try using your tongue to tease me."

I swirl my tongue around his tip.

Softly.

Then harder.

"Fuck." His hand knots in my hair. His eyelids flutter together. His lips part with a sigh.

It's so fucking beautiful, seeing pleasure spread over his expression.

I want more of it.

I want all of it.

I switch directions and do it again.

Again.

Again.

His groan fills the room.

It makes my sex ache.

I want him inside me.

I want him filling me.

I've never been so acutely aware of how much I wanted that.

But I really, really do.

"Put your lips over your teeth," Wes says.

I do.

"Try taking me deeper."

My eyelids press together.

I move my mouth over his cock.

Deeper.

Deeper.

Fuck—

That's a lot.

I gag. Pull back. But it's not enough. I—

I pull back to cough. "Sorry."

"Happens."

"Because you're…" Okay, there's no sense in being shy now. I lean back on my heels. Take a deep breath. He's still there, but not *right there*. "Because of your size?"

"Yeah. But with smaller guys too. How often you shoving six inches into your mouth?"

"Much less—" I clear my throat. "I mean."

"You don't have to deep throat."

Oh. Of course. I mean, I knew what it meant, but now I *really* know. "What if I want to?"

"Swallow to relax your throat."

I nod.

"And don't think so hard about it."

I stare at him like he's crazy.

"I know. Just try."

"The more I try—"

"Then don't try." His fingers skim my temples. Then my frames. "You need something to drink?"

I'm past the point of drowning nerves. And my throat… It's okay. I want this to keep going.

I…

I'm going to say it.

Deep breath.

Slow exhale.

"No." I force myself to look him in the eyes. "I want you to come in my mouth."

"Fuck, Quinn." His throat quivers as he swallows. "You gotta warn me if you're gonna say shit like that."

"Only if you warn me too."

His lips curl into a wicked smile. "No deal." He offers me his hand.

I take it. Let my gaze travel down his body. Strong shoulders, broad chest, defined abs, trail of soft hairs.

God, I get it now.

The happy trail.

It's such a happy place.

This is just—

It's hot.

It really is.

"You want me to lead or you want to lead?" he asks.

My gaze flits to his eyes. "How would I?"

"Bring one hand to my ass."

I reach around his hip. Dig my fingers into his flesh.

"Keep me in place or pull me closer."

"You won't..." I try to find a word that I can actually say aloud. "Move, I guess?"

"I'll try not to. If it's too much, pull back."

"And if I want you to lead?"

"There's no secret code, angel. Just tell me."

"But I, um—"

"Your mouth is occupied?"

"Yeah."

"All right. If you want me to lead, bring your hand to your chest. Play with your tits."

My sex clenches.

"Or fuck yourself."

"I..." Uh... "I don't think I have the coordination."

He laughs. "Come here."

I dig my fingers into his flesh as I take him into my mouth.

God, he tastes good.

And it feels right.

It really does.

I take him deeper.

Deeper.

There.

I swallow to relax my throat.

It helps.

It's still a lot, but in a good way.

In a fucking great way.

This time, I press my palm into his ass. Pull him closer as I take him deeper.

Then again.

I get it the third try.

It must be working, because his eyes are closing.

His limbs are shaking.

He presses his palm into the back of my head. It's just hard enough to demand more.

Fuck, it's hot.

My body buzzes.

He brings his free hand to my shoulder.

Then my chest.

His fingers brush my nipple.

Then he's rolling my tender bud between his thumb and forefinger.

Fuck.

I pull back enough to suck on his tip.

He toys with me.

I drag my mouth over him.

When I take him as far as I can, I wrap my hand around him. Use it like an extension of my mouth.

It must be what he likes, because his groans get louder.

He toys harder.

Shifts his hips into my mouth.

Lets out a low, deep groan.

God, that's a beautiful sound.

I swallow to relax my throat.

Then I take him as deep as I can.

A few thrusts of his hips, and he's there.

His cock pulses.

"Fuck, Quinn." He tugs at my hair as he spills into my mouth.

He's salty. Warm. Sticky.

I wait until he's finished. Then I swallow hard.

He looks down at me with heavy lids. Offers his hand.

I take it. Let him pull me up.

He wraps his arms around me and pulls me into a tight embrace. "Fuck. You're amazing."

"It was okay?"

"Fucking amazing, angel."

"Really?" I ask.

"What did I tell you?"

"I… Thank you."

He kisses me hard.

God, *that's* everything.

When he pulls back, I'm shaking.

He brings his lips to my ear. "Don't think I forgot my plans."

"Oh?"

"You're still coming on my face."

Chapter Twenty-Seven

WES

"After." Her cheeks flush. "My plans aren't as explosive, but... Oh my God, did I just describe that as explosive?"

"Yeah." My chest warms. She's so fucking adorable. I'm not sure how it's possible for her to be this rambling after I came in her mouth, but she is. She's just... Quinn.

"That was terrible." She spins on her heels and moves to the closet. "I'm going to get dressed. Do you need something to wear?"

"You don't want me sitting around your place naked?"

"You're welcome to stay naked." She turns back to me with a coy smile. "But it will be distracting."

"I'm okay with that."

She shakes her head. "We have important plans."

"More important than tasting your cunt?"

Her blush spreads to her chest. Her tongue slides over her lips. "It's kind of hard to compare."

"That a no?"

"Would you like something to wear or not, Wes?"

"Am I getting obnoxious?"

"No." She pulls open a drawer. Slides on a pair of panties. A matching beige bra. "Not yet."

Mmm. Fuck. I want her coming on my face now. Not later.

I want us here.

This makes sense.

This is something I'm good at.

A way I can help her.

Out there—

Fuck, I don't know.

She moves to the closet. Picks out a red dress. Unzips it and slides it over her head.

It hugs her curves like it was made for them.

Which doesn't help with the whole wanting her to come on my face thing.

But I'm a gentleman.

All right, that's bullshit. I'm not a gentleman, but I do have manners. I'm not leaving her hungry.

Or worn.

Or—

What the hell is it we're doing?

"You have something I can wear?" I ask.

"I think Owen left something last time he stayed here." She moves to the dresser. Bends to pull open the bottom drawer. Her brow furrows as she rifles. "Ah. Here." She pulls out a black t-shirt. Laughs. "This is perfect for you." She tosses me a t-shirt and a matching pair of shorts.

They're both screen printed with *Cock Hungry* in a rainbow font.

"Exactly what I wanted. How'd you know?" I pull on the shorts. They're a little small for me, but they work.

She stares as I slide into the t-shirt. "God, you're really wearing that. Can I... No, I can't send that to Owen. He'll have opinions."

"He doesn't know?"

"You tell your brothers who you're fucking?"

"Usually, yeah." I open the door. Motion *after me*. "Hard to brag without telling them."

"Do you really?"

I arch a brow.

"Are you still trying to convince me you're this asshole with nothing in his heart."

"Is it working?"

Her laugh lights up her hazel eyes. "No. I think we're past that." She moves through the door. Leads me to the living room.

We are.

She actually knows me.

It's terrifying.

Thrilling.

I follow her into the kitchen. "You want me to cook something?"

"Mmm." Her hand goes to her stomach. "Yeah. I'm starving. But I don't really have enough for two."

"I'll work it out."

She shoots me an incredulous look.

"You don't trust me?"

"I do. I just…"

"Like being in control?"

"Not exactly."

I arch a brow.

"Only a little."

I arch my other brow.

She laughs. "I'm not that bad." She pulls the fridge open and steps aside. "See. You have free rein."

"I'm thinking cinnamon and charred chicken breast."

Her smile spreads over her cheeks. "You're cruel."

"You're…" My thoughts disappear as my eyes meet

hers. She's so fucking beautiful. She's always been beautiful, but it's hitting me differently today.

Being here, with her, is so easy.

I still know everything is wrong.

But it feels far away.

"Owen, um… he's kind of like you." She moves to the counter. Rests her ass against it. "He wants everyone to know how outrageous he is."

"The outrageous doctor?"

"Yeah." Her lips curl into a smile. "He didn't come out for a long time. Not because he was embarrassed. Because he knew Mom and Dad would have to pretend they cared that he always had guys over."

"Did they?"

"No, it's the usual parental bullshit. Protect the innocent daughter. Let the son do whatever he wants. Not that I needed help. I wasn't exactly going for it. And they weren't around to stop me anyway."

"Was that hard?" I ask.

"My parents working?"

"Yeah." I scan the fridge. It's sparse, but there's enough to make this work. I pull red peppers, green onions, and limes from the fridge. Shrimp from the freezer. "Put on a pot of boiling water."

"Am I still following orders?"

"Dunno, how good does *sir* sound on your lips?"

She slides off the counter with a coy smile. "I don't know, *sir*. What kind of kinky stuff are you holding back?"

My balls tighten. "Don't know, angel. Think you might have just awoken some part of me that's been sleeping."

She shoots me a *please* look. "Like there's anything you haven't tried."

"Haven't tried it with you."

"Uh-huh." She grabs a pan from the cabinet, fills it with water, places it on the stove, turns the burner to high.

"What if I'm desperate for you to drop to your knees and beg for my cock?"

"Then you're greedy."

A full-blown belly laugh spills from my lips. Fuck, she's so... She's just Quinn. "True."

"Maybe next time. If you're still into the idea." She gets out a cutting board and knife. Sets both on the counter. "I'm pretty sure you're fucking with me."

"Maybe."

"Definitely." She moves to the counter on the other side of the stove. Hoists herself onto it. "You're good at distracting me."

"You too."

"But, um, I like talking to you too. About things besides sex."

"Me too."

"It was hard. My parents not being around. I love Owen. He's a great brother. But he's not... soft. I mean, not like your t-shirt. Just... He expects a lot from me. Everyone does."

"Like what?"

"I was supposed to be good at school, sports, socializing, taking care of the house even. And I was decent at school, but I had to work so hard that I didn't have time for anything else. Not that I really liked sports." She taps her feet together. "I don't like balls flying in my face. I mean." Her cheeks flush. "You know what I mean."

"I do." I tap my t-shirt. "Despite appearances."

Her laugh is easy. Effortless. But it doesn't erase the furrow in her brow. "It took a while for them to give up on the Quinn the athlete dream. Even after three years of youth soccer."

"Yeah?"

"I was terrible." She presses her palms into her thighs. "I kicked the ball out of bounds every game."

"Isn't that normal?"

"Maybe. Didn't feel like it." Her voice softens. "They never said anything, but I knew. I knew it wasn't enough."

"I'm sorry."

"Thanks. I just… I don't mean to complain. I love my family. I really do. I just wish…" Her eyes get fuzzy. Like she's far off someplace. Then she blinks, and her gaze sharpens. "They expect me to be this perfect person. And I'm not."

"Nobody is." I heat a pan and coat it with oil.

"Owen is."

I motion to the *cock hungry* label on my t-shirt.

She nods. "He's funny. Social. Successful. And it comes easily. He doesn't get how hard it is for me." Her eyes fix on mine. "I killed myself studying all through high school and college. I couldn't handle pre-med. How could I possibly handle med school?"

"What's he say?"

"That it will be different. Easier. Because I'll be able to focus more. But—"

"You don't believe him?"

Her nod is soft but sure. "I know my limits."

"You're the smartest person I know."

She shakes her head. "You don't have to say that."

"You graduated college a year early, Quinn."

She bites her lip. "Yeah, but… I… It's all I do. All I did. Until… until now, basically. I have no idea how to have fun."

"You have fun today?"

She nods.

"And you watch movies."

"Yeah." Her eyes go to the cutting board. "But that's been it for the last three years."

"Movies and school?"

"Yeah." Her gaze shifts to the stove. "What are you making?"

"Garlic shrimp."

Her tongue slides over her lips. "That sounds good."

"Will be. You have a rice cooker?"

"Yeah. Hold on." She slides off the counter. Grabs it from a high shelf, fills it, turns it on. "Takes half an hour."

"I know." I chop a green onion into tiny pieces. Slice a red pepper.

"I... I have fun with you."

"Yeah?"

"It's easier. You don't expect me to be smart or polite or pretty."

My gaze shifts to her dress.

Her cheeks flush. "What?" She smooths the soft fabric. "This is just—"

"How you relax by yourself?"

"Yeah."

I shoot her a *really* look.

"Sometimes." She bites her lip. "I just..."

"You realize we were naked together?"

"Yeah, but..."

"You look fucking gorgeous, angel. I'm not complaining. Just—"

"You think I'm contributing to the problem?"

Yeah. But I need to phrase it delicately. "It's hard, getting past the way you see yourself."

She pushes her hair behind her ear. "That's perceptive."

"I do all right sometimes."

"You do." Her eyes meet mine. "You're different than I expected."

"What did you expect?"

"I guess... more fun. Not that you aren't fun. Just this is..."

"Real."

"Yeah. I've never seen you be real."

"Am I disappointing?"

"No, I like it. I like you. I um... I can put on pajamas if you want."

"I don't care."

Her eyes bore into mine. *Sure, you don't.*

I don't. Not the way she means. "I want you comfortable."

"I..." She pulls her arm over her chest. "I am. But you're right. I don't wear this when I'm alone."

"What do you wear?"

"You'll think it's silly."

"Is it you?"

"Yeah."

"Then I'll love it."

"Okay. Stay here. I'll try. But if you laugh, I'm changing back into the dress."

"You could skip the clothes too."

She shoots me a *get real* look and moves into the bedroom.

I get lost in the rhythm of chopping vegetables until she returns.

Fuck, that's pure Quinn.

A flowing white nightgown straight out of an old movie.

Gorgeous. Classic. Elegant.

"It's ridiculous, isn't it?" The dress twirls around her as she spins.

"No. It's perfect."

"Really?"

"Yeah. Come here."

She does.

I wrap my arms around her. Pull her into a slow, deep kiss.

She groans against my mouth. Digs her hands into my hair. Pulls me closer.

She wants this too.

This easy intimacy.

But, fuck, I have no idea how to maintain it.

The only person I talk to is Griffin. And he's... well, he's insufferable.

She pulls back with a sigh. "You taste good."

"Thanks."

Her eyes go to the TV. "I was thinking we'd watch something. That was my plan."

"*Casablanca*?"

"No. We have to work up to that. But maybe *The Philadelphia Story* or *The Maltese Falcon* or *Bringing Up Baby*. I mean, you really can't go wrong with any of them."

"You pick."

"Okay." She chews on her bottom lip. "I think... something light and easy. Yeah?" Need fills her hazel eyes.

I'm not sure what she's asking.

Only that I want to give it to her.

I want more.

Period.

"You okay?" I ask.

"Yeah." Her eyes go to the couch. "Just thinking about Owen. He has news. But he won't say what."

"That's weird."

"Right? I'm sure it's good. But..."

"You hate not knowing."

She holds up her thumb and forefinger *a little*. "I just…
I don't know what he's going to say." Her eyes find mine.
"About this."

"What do you want him to say?" Is there anything to
say? She won't see her brother until she's back in Chicago.
Our arrangement ends before she gets on the plane.

Her brother never has to know.

Unless…

Fuck, I can't contemplate that possibility. Not now.

"I don't know," she says. "He knows I'm seeing someone. But not who."

Oh. That makes more sense. "You don't have to
tell him."

"That wouldn't bother you?"

Yeah, but I can't tell her that. It's not what we're doing.
"We're casual right?"

Her eyes flare with hurt, but she shakes it off. "Yeah.
Of course."

"If you want something different—"

"Let's watch a movie." She sits on the couch. Picks up
the remote. "And eat whatever you're making. It already
smells amazing."

She wants more than that.

But I don't call her on it.

It's not like I can talk.

I slip into cooking.

She puts in *The Philadelphia Story*.

As promised, we eat dinner as we watch.

Then she crawls into my lap, cuddles up in my arms,
and falls asleep.

And, hell, I must have it bad.

Because this is just as good as making her come.

This is better than anything.

Chapter Twenty-Eight

QUINN

I wake up in my bed.

In Wes's arms.

Whole.

That's the only way to explain the feeling stirring in my gut.

All the sonnets I studied in British Literature finally make sense.

This is it.

The reason why people write love songs. Why they throw away their plans. And tattoo names on their skin.

I remind myself that this is our Paris.

We'll always have the summer before med school.

As Wes fixes breakfast and tea, when I kiss him good-bye, as we text about nothing, when my mind flips to him at work—

On our next date, hiking Los Liones Canyon until we're sweaty messes, showering together, stroking him until he comes, his hands between my legs, his name rolling off my lips—

Another week of sweet texts—

The morning of our next date—

I keep reminding myself.

Repeating my mantra.

We'll always have the summer before med school.

Better to have loved and lost.

Better to have some than none.

Somewhere between my first cup of tea and our kiss hello, I believe it.

I forget about caution. About protecting my heart. About August.

For the first time in my life, I embrace now.

And now is fucking amazing.

————

"YOU REALIZE THIS IS JAZZ?" WES TURNS TO ME AND raises a brow.

Between the sunglasses, the smile, and the light hair, he's every bit the picture of California.

Which is perfect.

We're on our way to the Hollywood sign.

We're driving around the hills, windows down, stereo blasting.

It doesn't get more *Los Angeles* than this.

"It's not jazz." I turn up the volume. Sure, this big band song has jazz influence. It's positively Amy Winehouse-esque in its jazzy vibe. But it's clearly not jazz.

Jazz is a bunch of random notes in a nonsense order.

A then B then C then G then who the fuck knows.

(And, no, I have no idea if those are actual music notes).

There's a stand-up bass and a sax and an old-school vibe, but there's a repeating melody too.

Maybe if I was cool and laid back and knowledgeable about music history, I'd love jazz.

But I'm not.

I hate jazz.

I hate the randomness. The inability to predict where it's going. The total lack of repetition.

"Should I consult Wikipedia?" Wes asks.

"Yeah, you should. Because you're dead wrong." This is big band music. It's the picture of big band music. And, sure, I got into it originally because it was all over my favorite film soundtracks. But it's past that now.

I love the bombastic sound.

And, yes, that little hint of jazz.

But only because it's a hint.

Only because the impulses are contained.

He chuckles. "What if Wikipedia agrees?"

"Should we put it to the test." I pull my cell from my backpack.

His gaze shifts back to the street. "Let's go."

I pull up my browser. Look up this particular song.

Luck Be a Lady Tonight.

Big Band.

Parent Genre Jazz.

Shit.

"What's it say?" He stops at a red light. "Something about how I'm brilliant?"

"No, it says Wes Keating is full of himself."

"Fuck, I'm important enough to be on Wikipedia? My ego."

"Oh no." I laugh. "It's already enormous. I can't handle it getting bigger."

"Go on."

"In your dreams."

His laugh fills the room. Competes with the smooth vocals and the horn section.

Which is clearly not jazz.

Jazz inspired, sure.

But that's a repeating melody.

That's something comprehensible.

Enjoyable.

Not the utter nonsense that is jazz.

"Should I take you to a jazz club sometime?" he asks.

"Since when do you go to jazz clubs?"

"Since I got the idea of sneaking into a booth in the back, peeling off your panties, and making you come."

Holy shit.

My cheeks flush. My sex clenches. My nipples pang.

I need him touching me. It's been an entire week.

A week of flirt texting.

A week without his lips, hands, cock.

A week and I'm cock hungry.

I have no idea what happened to prim, proper Quinn Thorn and I really don't care.

This feels too good.

He feels too good.

Hell, if Wes is going to make me come while we listen to a Miles Davis—

I'm not going to object to that.

Even so—"Listen to this." I press my palms into my leggings. Focus on this moment. The trumpet. The hum of the engine. Wes's laugh. The electric charge to the air.

"Fuck, I'm supposed to listen to shit? Still imagining you coming on my hand."

"Sounds dangerous."

"It is."

"Should we pull over?"

"Only if you're going to push those leggings to your knees."

My sex clenches. God, that's a good idea.

A big, beautiful idea.

I want to come on his hand.

I want to tear off his shorts and wrap my fingers around him.

I want to hear my name roll off his lips.

But not here.

The car doesn't offer nearly enough privacy. Not with dozens of million-dollar mansions within view.

When we go home, sure.

Now…

Not so much.

Though then again…

Ahem.

"Um… the melody." I motion to the stereo. "There is a melody. So not jazz."

He nods. "Not what?"

"The song."

He cocks his head to one side. "The what?"

I can't help but laugh. "Are you okay to drive?"

"Just need to think about baseball for a minute." He turns to the right.

There's a sweeping canyon to the right.

Another row of mansions to our left.

This place is beautiful.

But still less appealing than him.

God, his smile.

It makes my stomach flutter.

It makes my heart thud.

It makes my limbs light.

"What was I supposed to listen to?" He follows the winding road up the hill.

"This part. Here." I turn the volume up.

Wes taps his fingers in time with the beat.

"See. There's a rhythm. A melody. Not jazz."

He chuckles. "What's wrong with listening to jazz?"

"Nothing. I just… don't."

"You don't like it?"

I nod.

"You want to know where things are going?"

"Is that wrong?"

"No. It's Quinn."

"Do you really… what do you know about jazz?" I turn the volume down. Lean into my seat. He's right. I don't like the way jazz skips around. I need to know where a song is going. But I do like this. The tease of uncertainty. It's not quite jazz, but there's still a mystery.

"Nothing, really. Looked up big band music after you said you liked it."

"Really?"

"Yeah." His gaze shifts from the road to me. "Must have listened to a dozen playlists."

"Yeah?"

He nods. "Drove Chase out of his mind playing it at work."

"He's not a fan?"

He shakes his head. "You ever notice his bangs?"

"What about them?"

"Emo bangs."

I laugh. "So?"

"He's got a hard-on for that shit. Something about the way the guys despise their exes. And their ex friends. It speaks to him."

"And his inability to forgive?"

"Yeah. And he likes the sound too." Wes's nose

scrunches in distaste. "It's not terrible. Emma plays it all the time at work."

Jealousy flares in my chest. "Emma?"

"Yeah. Hunter's girlfriend. She's manager at Inked Hearts."

"Oh."

"You jealous, angel?"

"No." I swallow hard.

"I think so."

"I just…"

"Yeah?" he asks.

"I don't like the thought of you caring about someone else."

"I don't."

"Good." The song switches to the next. It's something I don't recognize. The beat skips around. Up. Down. Down. Way down. Up.

"This is jazz."

"A little." There. The rhythm repeats. It's the same erratic nonsense, but it's repeating erratic nonsense. Which isn't that bad.

There's something compelling about it.

Don't get me wrong. I love the idea of jazz. Of a dark club, strong gin, a handsome guy with a massive instru-ment between his legs—

Uh, I mean.

Uh…

Music.

I wish I loved jazz. Honestly, I do. I wish I was smart and knowledgeable enough to appreciate it.

But it grates on me in thirty seconds flat.

I always try to guess where it's going.

And when I can't…

I hate it.

"This is good." Wes points to the stereo as the saxo-phonist launches into a solo.

And, well, yeah, I can't really argue.

The song is jazz.

And this trip, this entire relationship, is jazz.

It was supposed to be a pop song. Something with a clear ending. That would make me smile then disappear into the ether.

Now…

I have no idea where this is going.

His gaze flits to me. His lips curl into a soft smile.

"What?" I cross my legs again.

"Nothing."

"You're giving me a look."

"I like that you're jealous."

"Yeah?" I bite my lip. I like it too. And I hate it. I'm invested. I don't want to be invested. Not if this is ending in two weeks.

"Yeah. Never liked it before. Always pissed me off. Like women didn't get our arrangement. But I don't know… It's kinda sweet."

"What if I show up at work threatening to kill her?"

"Would you?" he asks.

"No." I try to imagine the scene playing out. What if there was another woman who had Wes's heart? What if that was the reason for his inability to commit?

My stomach churns.

My heart aches.

I hate her.

She doesn't exist, and I already hate her.

Which isn't healthy.

At all.

But here we are.

"Angel?"

"Yeah?" I ask.

"You got murder in your veins?"

"I don't think so." What would I do? Nothing, probably. That's been my entire life. I'm the good girl. The one who follows the rules and sticks to the plan.

It's worked well enough so far. I'm on track for a hell of a future. For all the success in the world.

The plan is good.

Why step away from the plan?

We have a plan here.

I need to stick to the plan.

The easy pop song.

Not the... fuck, I'm bad at metaphors.

"The heart wants what it wants," I say. "If you want to be with someone else, I won't be able to change your mind."

"Mature take."

"It's a hypothetical."

"Still." His eyes flit to me for a split second then they're on the road.

"What if I was into another guy?"

"I'd hit him."

"What's that solve?" I ask.

"Nothing. But it feels good."

"Don't you need your hands?"

He raises a brow. "Do I?"

My cheeks flush. "For work."

"Yeah, but you're worth it."

Chapter Twenty-Nine

QUINN

"You've got this, angel." Wes presses his palms into my ass as he hoists me to the top of the fence.

I grab onto the metal railing with both hands. Swing one leg over. Then the other.

I drop down.

He jumps on top of the fence in two moves. Drops to the ground in one. Smiles as he wipes the dust from his tank top.

He looks good today.

He looks good every day.

But he looks especially good today.

Wes holds out his hand, offering it to me.

I take it and follow him up the beaten path.

This time of year, everything in the Hollywood Hills is dry and dusty. Taupe and grey-green brush blend into the sand. They surround the multi-million-dollar mansions in something halfway between grey and beige.

It's beautiful. Big glass houses looking out on miles and miles of earth.

The signs of money.

And the dirt everything returns to.

Wes squeezes my hand. "I gotta tell you something, Quinn."

"Oh yeah?"

"I hate the sunglasses."

"Oh?"

"They ruin something beautiful." He turns back to me with a wicked smile. One that screams *I'm going to take you home and fuck you senseless.*

My body responds with gusto. We haven't done that. We've barely moved toward it. I get that he's trying to ease me into this whole sex thing, but I'm tired of waiting. I want his body against mine. I want him inside me. I want...

I want everything.

I push my sunglasses up my nose. Fix my pony tail. Smooth my leggings. "They're prescription."

"Still."

"I need them to see."

"You can see in your glasses."

"If I want to squint in agony because it's so bright." I motion to the big lemon sun. It's late morning now, but it could easily pass for afternoon. The sun is oppressive. It's bright. Hot. Cloudless.

Shadeless.

"You ever think you should get dressed according to what my dick wants?" He slides his arm around my waist.

"Gee. I didn't. I wonder why." I shoot him a *you're ridiculous* smile.

"Smart people can miss obvious truths."

"Uh-huh."

"I've got your backups in the car."

"In your dreams."

"Hmm." He pulls me closer, so my hip bumps his.

"You're wearing glasses in that one. But you're *only* wearing glasses."

"You're obsessed." Truth be told, I like his obsession. No, I love his obsession. I always felt awkward and dorky in my glasses. His gushing makes me feel like a sex goddess.

"I know what I like."

"You always have a thing for glasses?"

He shakes his head. "Just yours."

"Oh." My cheeks flush. My gaze shifts to the dusty path. I'm getting better at flirting, but I'm nowhere near Wes's confidence level.

"How about we negotiate?"

"You have no bargaining power here."

"Yeah, that could be a problem." He makes a show of scratching his head. "You gonna wear them when we get home?"

"I'm not going to wear sunglasses inside."

"Thank fuck." He turns to me. Leans in to press his lips to mine.

It's a quick kiss.

But, God, I feel it everywhere.

He tastes like tea and honey.

And Wes.

And, God, I do have it bad.

Sure, this ends in two weeks. I can still enjoy the now.

I don't have to think about the expiration date.

In theory.

"Here's a deal. You skip the sunglasses, I skip the sunglasses," I say.

"Quinn, you can negotiate better than that."

"Oh."

He nods as he leads me around the bend.

The path is quiet. It's a particularly hot weekday, but it's still strange seeing the landmark quiet.

I guess we've got a ways to go until we're actually there.

I can just barely see the Hollywood sign, a few hills away.

Thank God for my usual workouts. Wes is fast, and he has near infinite endurance. And not just when we're naked.

Whatever it is, he can go all day.

Or all night.

"How about, I skip the sunglasses, you skip the pants," he suggests.

My blush deepens. "How about I'm not going to manipulate you into taking your clothes off."

"You could just ask."

"Yeah." I swallow hard. "Of course."

"So…" He raises a brow.

"Here?" I want to. But it's even less private than the car and the exhibitionism is more awkward than sexy.

He nods. Motions to the empty trail. *Why not?*

"I hear people." Sorta. It's mostly the wind. But there's the faintest sound of conversation. It might be one of the giant houses on the other side of the hill. But it's something.

"Probably a movie star sunbathing naked."

"Where do you get this stuff?"

He laughs. "They'll probably get off on our show. Start fucking themselves."

"Probably." I shake my head. Wes is so… Wes.

"That would be hot, but I gotta be honest with you, Quinn."

"Yeah?"

"I'm not willing to share."

Desire spreads to my chest. And something else too. This warmth. He likes me too. He wants more too. I just…

have to articulate that at some point. "I have bad news for you."

"Yeah?"

"I have self-control."

"No."

"Yeah." I nod. "And patience. I can wait until we're home."

His fingers brush my hip. "You daring me?"

No. Yes. Maybe. Honestly, my patience is… not great. Not when it comes to Wes. I try a coy shrug. "Maybe."

"You know I have a strict policy of taking dares."

"I can only assume."

"Gonna have to wind you up and leave you wanting now."

I shrug like I don't care, but I completely fail to sell it.

Wes chuckles. He pulls back enough to take my hand.

Then he gets closer. Too close for a hike, but I don't care.

I walk in time with him. It's a hot day. I'm already sweating bullets.

The breeze helps, but only so much.

Still, I want him closer.

It's pretty much my motto at this point.

Besides the *we'll always have the summer before med school* thing.

My gaze shifts to the rolling hills. "It's beautiful here." I hold my hand over my eyes to block the glare.

We're not up that high, but I can see so much. The skyscrapers downtown. Century City to the west. The Pacific Ocean past that.

The mansions.

They're gorgeous.

And way out of my price range.

I guess, one day, if I'm some sort of high earning

doctor—a plastic surgeon or a radiologist—I'll be able to afford a place like this.

Hell, I could work in a free clinic and marry a plastic surgeon who will keep us afloat. (Going into medical school single seals my fate. I'm either marrying a doctor or staying single forever).

I try to imagine that future. Coming home from a long day of work to my giant all glass house. Stripping out of my lab coat and shoes and sitting by the pool.

It's not beautiful and free.

It's ugly and suffocating.

I just…

There's no reason to focus on August.

Not when I have now.

"You okay?" Wes's voice is soft. Caring.

I nod *sure* and pick up my speed. I need to keep my mind occupied. So it won't go back to those awful subjects.

"Quinn?"

"Imagining buying one of those giant houses."

"Fuck, think I'd need to own three tattoo shops."

"Or you could be a reality TV star. What was that show called? With the woman who launched a makeup line?" Some kind of animal. Foxie. Or Rex. Or Kat maybe.

"You think I know makeup lines?"

"It's very reputable."

"Even so." He catches up to me. Stays close, but not as close as he was earlier.

"Maybe you had a thing for eyeliner in high school."

"You think I could pull it off?"

"A charcoal pencil on your top lid? Definitely." I try to make my voice teasing, but I don't get there. August is already weighing on me.

"Good to know." He laughs, but there's something missing in it.

He knows I'm drifting off.

I try to bring myself back to the moment.

It's a beautiful blue day. We're in paradise. I'm with the hottest guy I've ever seen.

But, God, med school is weeks away.

In August, I leave.

I return to Chicago.

I go to med school.

I...

Ugh.

I round the curve.

Another set of houses come into view. A backyard with a massive pool. One covered in sculptures. An overflowing garden. "You could be the next reality TV star."

"Not sure anyone at the shop would go for it."

"Would you?"

"No." His fingers brush mine. "Where are you going, Quinn?"

"Nowhere."

"Somewhere."

"It's nothing." I walk faster, but that doesn't really accomplish anything. It's still there. It's everywhere.

"It would be nice. Owning a place like this." He motions to the backyard with the giant pool. "Could skinny dip every night."

"Or all day."

"Wouldn't get much done."

"Would you care?"

He shoots me a curious look.

"Do you really need work to fill your soul. Or is it just... work?"

"Fuck, my soul? We're really escalating." His voice is

teasing. But it's not too. There's something in it. He knows I'm getting at something.

I nod.

He moves closer. Interlocks his fingers with mine.

It steadies me.

But not enough.

There's no denying it.

I leave in two weeks.

He's being all sweet and caring and loving, but what does that matter?

This ends in two weeks.

I can't have him acting like this.

Not if I lose it in two weeks.

His voice is soft. Honest. "The other day, Brendon told me my work was generic."

"Yeah?"

He nods. "I've been thinking about it for a while. I do a good job with my shit. I make clients happy. I can earn a living like this forever. But my soul?"

"You're not pouring your heart out?" I bite my lip. I want to pull back the walls around his heart. I want to know everything.

But I can't have that.

We can't have that.

He nods. "Maybe that's good."

"Less painful."

"Yeah. But there's something missing too." His gaze shifts to the sky. "I don't know. I always figured it was better to keep things light. That's the only thing that kept everyone laughing. But I guess you can't run forever."

I swallow hard. He's talking about himself. Not me. But it feels so... accurate.

His gaze shifts to me. He lifts his sunglasses. Then mine. "What's wrong?"

"Nothing."

"Don't bullshit me."

"I'm just… thinking."

"About?"

I lower my sunglasses. Motion to the path ahead.

He follows me down the dirt.

He stays right next to me.

He stays tuned to me.

I try to walk faster, but it's not like there's an escape nearby. Just the sun, the dirt, and the two of us.

He keeps pace with me with ease. "You love California."

"Yeah." The awkward conversation doesn't detract from the beauty of the scenery. "I love the look of the desert." I motion to the scraggly bushes. "And the beach too. You have everything here."

"You complimented the mall at Hollywood and Highland."

"It's not the least touristy spot, but—"

"Why are you going back to Chicago?"

I stop dead in my tracks. I… He… "I told you. That's the best med school I got into."

"You sound excited about it."

"Fuck off." I drop his hand. Fuck this. He doesn't do this. We're having a nice day. We're avoiding the subject of August. Of this ending.

"Quinn." He runs to meet me. "I'm not trying to push."

"Right."

"Just tell me why."

"Why what?" I fold my arms over my chest, but it feels too pissy. I'm not a child throwing a tantrum. I'm an adult in an adult relationship with an equal.

"Why are you going to med school?"

I unpeel my arms. Press them to my sides. "That's the plan."

"So?"

"So?" I stare back at him, but it does nothing to convey my feelings. Just gets me lost in his gorgeous blue eyes.

"Yeah, so? Maybe you need a new plan."

A new plan... "Are you insane?"

"Maybe, yeah."

"I... That's what I'm going to do."

"What if you did something else."

He... I... What?

"What if you weren't a doctor?"

"I..."

"Is it that hard to imagine?"

"Yeah." I turn away from him. It's the only way I can manage a proper inhale. This... I... He... "I don't think you get it, Wes. You know Harry Potter, how he's the only one who can defeat Voldemort, how it's his destiny?"

"You watch *Harry Potter*?"

"Not really the point."

"Yeah, but—"

"Do you know?" I ask.

"Of course."

"That's what it's like being a Thorn. I've known since I was old enough to understand. I'm going to be a doctor."

"But do you want to be a doctor?"

"That doesn't matter."

"Of course it does."

"If I wasn't..." I swallow hard. God, it's so hot. And dry. And the air is suffocating.

I swing my backpack off my shoulder. Reach for my bottle. But it's under something.

I set it on the ground.

Paw through makeup, sweaters, books.

There.

I pull out my water bottle and suck down a sip.

It's not refreshing.

Or soothing.

Or comforting.

"What if you did something else?" he asks.

"I… what would I do?"

"Whatever you want."

That's ridiculous. "This is what I'm doing."

"But is it what you want?"

"That doesn't matter," I say.

"Yeah it does."

I shake my head.

"There's not a genocidal maniac who's going to kill every human in the world if you fail to become a doctor."

"But…"

"Quinn, I—"

"You think you know what's best for me?"

"No," he says.

"Then what?"

"Every time you bring up medicine, you cringe."

"I do not." I fight a frown.

"You just did."

I shake my head.

He nods. "If it's what you want, then I want it for you. But is it? Do you actually want to be a doctor?"

Chapter Thirty

WES

"Fuck you." Quinn's eyes narrow. "You don't get to do this."

I step backward. My heels make contact with the dirt, but the ground isn't steady.

"You don't get to ask me what I'm doing with my life."

"I'm not."

"You are." Her chest heaves with her inhale. "My future is mine. Not yours."

"I know."

"Have you changed your mind?"

"What?"

She presses her sunglasses up her nose. "Have you changed your mind about this being casual?"

Fuck, there's a long answer for that. But if I have to narrow it down to yes or no? "I know where we stand."

"No, Wes, you don't. You're acting like my boyfriend."

"I care."

"Exactly." She steps backward. Turns in the direction of the car. "You know what, I'm going to catch a ride."

"We're in the hills."

"I can call a ride share."

"Quinn—"

"Don't."

What the fuck?

She stops in her tracks. Turns back to face me. "Do you want to be my boyfriend?"

Yeah, but I can't offer her that.

"Then stop acting like one."

"But—"

"No. No fucking buts. If you don't want more, if you don't want this to become something, then stop acting like my fucking boyfriend."

"Quinn."

"Maybe this is easy for you. But it's not easy for me. I'm falling for you. I don't want to fall for you. I leave in two weeks. So unless you're ready to ask me to stay or offer to go to Chicago with me, stop."

I swallow hard. "Okay." I motion to the Hollywood sign in front of us. "Are you really going to leave?"

"I don't know." She takes off her sunglasses. Rubs her temples with her thumbs. "Can we... Maybe we need a few days."

No. I only have ten days with her. "I'll be good."

Her lips curl into a frown. "No... I need to... I need to go."

"I'll drive you home."

Her gaze shifts to me for a second. She studies my expression. She must decide I'm worth trusting, because she nods *okay*.

I turn back toward the car.

She follows two paces behind me.

We're quiet the entire walk.

I know where we are, but I'm still fucking lost.

ON THE DRIVE HOME, I CHANGE THE SUBJECT TO OUR most recent classic film, *Bringing Up Baby*.

But it lingers in the air.

Our awkward inability to manage our feelings.

She turns the music up. Leans into her seat. Loses herself in a catchy melody.

For half an hour, everything is okay.

Until it's not.

It's really fucking not.

Chapter Thirty-One

WES

I pull the car up to Quinn's apartment.

The stereo cuts off.

A familiar melody fills the car.

Chase.

"Wes, I..." Quinn presses her lips together. "I'll call you later, okay?"

"Yeah." I nod as I pick up my cell.

She nods back, but she doesn't move.

She stays in the passenger seat.

I look at her for a split second. There's all this concern in her hazel eyes.

She cares.

More than she should.

And so do I.

This is it.

Where we cut and run.

Where I lay down the law. *You're right. I'm not your boyfriend. I can't keep acting like your boyfriend. I can't do this, period.*

But I can't say shit.
The only thing I can do is answer my brother's call.
I know before the words are out of his mouth.
I know this is completely fucked.

Chapter Thirty-Two

QUINN

Bright light streams through the window.

Afternoon light.

Beach light.

It's beautiful.

But not with Wes sitting in the driver's seat, phone pressed to his ear, back to me, shoulders slumped.

Even though he's two feet away, I can't make out his reaction.

Only that it's bad.

Really bad.

Which isn't my problem.

I'm not a heartless bitch.

But he's not my boyfriend.

He's not even my friend really.

I need space.

We both need space.

I can't help him here.

I have to pull back.

I suck a breath though my teeth. Force an exhale through my nose.

I like him too much.

I want more.

I want to comfort him in whatever this is.

He turns back to me.

His eyes find mine.

His lip corners turn down.

It's all over his expression.

This isn't okay.

Whatever is happening, it's not okay.

I don't ask.

I get out of the car. Sling my backpack over my shoulder. Adjust my leggings.

He sits there on his cell.

Not talking.

Listening.

It's not like Wes.

He's a good listener, sure, but he's loud. Vibrant. Demanding.

Right now...

All the life is fleeing his body at once.

I shift my weight between my legs. Fish my keys from my front pocket.

My apartment is ten feet away.

I don't have to stay there. I can hide inside the cool air-conditioning. I can shower away today. Seek comfort in my favorite movie.

But I don't.

I watch until he hangs up the phone.

He gets out of the car. Stays pressed against the door.

"Hey." I pull my arm over my chest reflexively. "Are you..."

"I have to go."

"Oh." I force myself to unpeel my arms. To press my hands to my sides. "What happened?"

"My mom got in an accident."

"I'm sorry."

"She was… it doesn't matter."

"But…"

His blue eyes are filled with hurt.

And apology.

This is it.

He's going to say something about how we're over.

About how he'll never be my boyfriend.

About how I'm delusional thinking someone like Wes would ever want to be my boyfriend.

"Wes, I…" I don't know what to say. Only that I want to hold him. To fix whatever this is. I hate that he's hurting. I hate that I hate that he's hurting. I'm too fucking invested.

It hurts.

It aches.

It's like when Owen hurts.

His pain is my pain.

"You were right." His voice is flat. Lifeless. "We need a few days."

"Yeah. Sure. Will you…" What the hell do I offer here? "Will you be okay?"

"Sure." He offers me a smile, but it's empty.

He needs someone.

Maybe he needs me.

But if he can't admit that, if he doesn't see it—

Owen was right.

I can't fall in love with him unless I have a safe place to land.

Chapter Thirty-Three

WES

Chase is sitting in a hospital chair, arms folded, eyes closed, head resting against the blue-grey wall.

He looks hurt and helpless.

It's weird.

Completely unlike him.

Chase has always been the strong one. He's steady. Ice cold.

He doesn't give into bait. When someone pushes, he holds his ground.

Right now...

Fuck, it's bad.

It's so fucking bad.

He stirs as I approach.

His eyes blink open. His gaze shifts to the shiny tile floor. The muted wall. The fluorescent lights shining from the ceiling.

To me.

For a second, vulnerability streaks his expression.

Then he nods, and it's gone.

He's back to the icy brother I know so well.

"What time is it?" he asks.

"Four." I slide my hands into my pockets. Try to think up something to say. Find nothing.

Well, nothing worth verbalizing.

Our mom is a piece of shit sometimes goes without saying.

"How's Quinn?" His voice is flat. Even. That usual *nothing will ever rattle me* tone.

I shrug like I don't care.

His eyes narrow. He stares at me, looking for cracks. "Don't you do dates on Mondays?"

"Yeah." God dammit, I need to stop telling Griffin shit. He's not keeping his mouth shut the way he usually does.

"And…" Chase looks me up and down, assessing my outfit, my posture, my expression. "You two go on a hike or something?"

"Yeah."

"And…"

"We got into a fight."

He nods *oh, of course*. "You do something stupid?"

"Not really the time to talk about this."

He shakes his head *of course it is*. "You like her, don't you?"

Fuck, I'm not having this conversation.

He stares back at me, waiting for a response.

Not happening.

Not going there.

Not with him.

New topic. It's a horrible topic, but it's not like I can avoid it. "Where's Mom?"

He shakes his head *if that's how you want to do it, fine* then he motions to the room down the hall. "She's asleep."

"Is she okay?" My chest gets heavy. I want her to be okay. But there's this other part of me. One that just wants it to be over.

"Yeah. The drunk one always is."

"The other driver?"

"Looks like it." His gaze shifts to the room. "Too soon to say."

I swallow hard. I should be happy.

She's alive.

She didn't crash into a tree and die in a fiery explosion.

She didn't drink herself to death.

Today.

At the moment, it's so fucking obvious.

Maybe she isn't dead today, but she might be tomorrow, or next week, or next month.

Chase gave me this lecture when it was Hunter, but I never saw it.

I thought Hunter liked to party.

That he neglected his limits.

That he could stop anytime he wanted.

And why would he want to stop?

Why would anyone want to stop for long enough for their thoughts to catch up with them?

Even after Hunter got through rehab and came out the other end better, wise, stronger, I didn't see it.

Hell, yesterday morning I didn't see it.

But something changed.

I can't do this anymore.

I can't survive another disappointment.

I can't give my heart to someone who will tear it to shreds.

"The lawyer thinks she might get a deal. Rehab for dropped charges. But her blood alcohol was over twice the legal limit. That's the kind of thing—"

"I know."

"Not how I wanted this to go."

For once we agree.

I try to think up some response that will articulate how much this sucks, but I don't have anything.

Somehow, Chase gets it.

He explains about the lawyer, and the deal, and the details of the accident.

It was Mom's fault.

She could have killed herself.

She could have killed someone else.

She could have killed someone, and she didn't fucking care.

This is what happens when I'm not around to clean up her mess.

I can't be around every time.

Not if I want to live my life.

Fuck, even if I'm willing to drop everything whenever she calls, I'll miss things. Be in an appointment or asleep or with Quinn.

Or…

Fuck, I have no idea if that's happening.

If we're happening.

I listen to Chase for a while.

Eventually, Hunter shows up with coffee from the chain across the street. He and Chase discuss Mom's possible rehab with their usual awkwardness.

Chase is still pissed at Hunter.

Hunter is still waiting for forgiveness.

It would be pathetic if it wasn't so necessary.

I focus on my coffee, but it doesn't have any taste.

I let them talk. Watch them struggle to form a plan. There's too much neither of them is saying.

But that's the Keating way at this point.

Never mention Mom's problem.

Never mention Chase's unwillingness to forgive.

Or Hunter's past.

Or my inability to face the fucking truth.

This is where I got it.

But I can't do it anymore.

After a while, they turn to me. Invite me to join their pow-wow.

"Dad's in the room," Chase says. "We've talked."

"Wes, I know you want the best for Mom," Hunter says.

"We're doing this with or without you," Chase says.

Hunter shoots him a look. *You have to pull that card now?*

Chase nods *obviously, I do. I thought you'd understand that after all the shit you pulled.* "This is it, Wes. If she can't clean up her shit after this…"

He's right.

I hate it, but he's right.

"Okay." I swallow hard.

Hunter's eyes go wide.

Chase's fix on mine. "You sure, Wes?"

"Yeah." My gaze goes to the tile floor. "I can't do this anymore."

"You don't have to." Hunter pulls me into a hug. Pats my back.

It should feel better.

Like this is going to be okay.

But it doesn't.

It feels like everything is fucked.

Chapter Thirty-Four

QUINN

Roman Holiday fails to fill the hole in my gut.

I give up after half an hour. Go straight to the big guns. English breakfast with extra honey. Toast and strawberry jam. *Casablanca*.

It helps.

But not enough.

My thoughts stay on Wes. On the hurt in his blue eyes, the frustration in his brow, the frown on his soft lips.

I want to fix this. To soothe him. To help him.

His mom…

I can't even imagine.

I try to ignore my cell. To convince myself to stay far, far away. To keep my hands busy by packing things I won't need for the next week and a half.

I'm leaving in ten days.

This is a time to pull back, not to move forward.

But my heart won't listen to reason.

Around the time the TV sings with *As Time Goes By*, I pick up my cell and I text Wes.

Quinn: Are you okay?
He doesn't respond, but I still feel better.
I want him to know I care.
And I do care.
I care way too fucking much.

Chapter Thirty-Five

WES

After dinner, the doctor gives us the clear to visit Mom.

She looks up from her hospital bed with a fuzzy gaze.

She's high.

What fucking irony.

Land yourself in the hospital for driving drunk and they pump you with morphine.

The sad thing is, her out of it expression is the most familiar thing about her.

She's not wearing makeup or designer garb.

She's in a light blue hospital gown far too big for her small frame.

She's pale.

Frail.

Tiny.

It's so clear right now.

She doesn't give a fuck.

Did she ever give a fuck?

I can't remember a time when my mom was sober.

Only an always full glass of wine between her fingers.

Dad goes right to her. He holds her hand. Stares into

her eyes the way only married people can.

More rich irony.

A few weeks ago, he was consulting with a divorce attorney. Now, he's holding her hand.

It's bullshit. He's still going to pull the trigger.

But I guess I get the logic. Why kick a woman when she's down?

"Mom, we have to talk." Chase's voice is calm. Steady.

Usually, that annoys me.

Right now, it helps.

It really fucking helps.

She looks up at him like she can't believe he's here. "This is a misunderstanding."

His eyes narrow.

Hunter tries to jump in.

But I stop him. "It's not."

Mom turns to me.

"Don't bother, Mom. We know better. I know better. For so fucking long, I've known better. Chase tried to tell me. Hunter tried to tell me. Hell, even Dad tried to tell me. I should have listened."

Surprise streaks her expression.

Of course it does.

Hell, I can't believe it.

I can't believe I'm putting my foot down.

"I knew. I always knew. I just couldn't admit it." My voice breaks. This is hard. Fucking impossible. But I have to say it. I have to be done. "I love you, Mom. I thought, maybe, if I kept helping, you'd see that. I thought, maybe, if I helped for long enough, you'd stop twisting the knife in my chest."

"Wes—"

"But you don't care. I don't blame you for being an alcoholic. I blame you for staying an alcoholic." I take a step backward. "I'm done. This is it. If you don't get help, you're on your own."

"Wes," she says it again, a little louder.

But I can't hear it.

I can't hear any of this.

"I love you, Mom. I hope you get better. But if you don't... I can't watch this anymore." I turn and leave.

I keep walking, even after I hear footsteps.

"Wes." Chase catches up to me.

I ignore him.

But he's too fucking fast.

He grabs my forearm. "It's gonna be okay."

I shake him off. "If she says no?"

"You feel better?"

Yeah, actually. I nod.

"Free?"

Fuck, I hate how perceptive he is. "How'd you know?"

"I've been there awhile." He walks in step with me. "Let me take you home."

"I'm okay."

"Are you?"

I try to muster up a shrug, but I don't have it in me.

"You will be." He leads me to the hospital entrance. The parking garage. His car.

Right now, I don't care about practicalities.

I don't care that I'll have to come back for my car.

Only that I need a lot of sleep.

And, well, a strong drink would be too much irony to take.

But I need something.

Chase slides into the driver's seat and turns the car on.

I take the passenger's seat. Focus my attention on the stereo. But I can't bring myself to change the album.

It's the one where the guy keeps wishing his ex would

die in a fiery car crash.

One of Chase's favorites.

Fitting as hell.

It fills the car as he pulls onto the street.

He waits until he's cruising to turn to me. "What the hell happened with Quinn?"

"It was casual."

He shoots me a *get real* look. "You're crazy about her."

"Yeah."

"So?"

"So you're giving me relationship advice?" I ask.

"Yeah."

"How's your love life going?"

"Exactly how I want it to go."

I return his *get real*.

He nods, sure.

"Really?" I motion to the speakers as the singer croons about wishing his ex would drive off a bridge. (It's always a bridge with this guy).

"I know where I stand."

"I know where I stand."

He shakes his head. *You haven't got a clue. You're hopeless. Honestly, I'm not sure why I'm bothering to help. That's how far gone you are.*

"All right, I don't get off on righteous indignation." It's not much of a delaying tactic, but it's something. I'd rather talk about his issues. Like his inability to forgive Mom or Hunter or the ex who broke his heart.

"Dodging, huh?"

"Fuck off."

"What happened with her?"

"Nothing."

"Where is she?"

My gaze flits to the clock. She's probably home. Or

maybe she's out. Maybe she's finding some other guy to do the job. "We're taking a break."

"From fucking?"

"Yeah."

He stares at me like I'm crazy.

Not the way Quinn does, like she can't believe I expect something of her.

More like...

Like he thinks I'm an idiot.

Maybe I am.

But he is too.

Chase doesn't have anyone besides me and Hunter.

He barely has me and Hunter.

"What, she tired of your pump and dump shit?" he teases.

I flip him off. It's rare Chase teases. I should appreciate it. But I don't.

"She dump you because you ask too many stupid questions?" he asks.

"She doesn't want me acting like her boyfriend."

"Seems fair."

"Yeah." It is. I don't like it, but it is.

"You do realize there's a reason why you were acting like her boyfriend?"

I shrug like I don't know.

"You're in love with her."

"I barely know her."

"Okay, maybe it's not love yet. But it's something."

I shrug, but I don't sell it.

He shakes his head *you're so full of shit.* "Are you really gonna walk away from that?"

"I don't want anyone to get hurt."

He stops at a red light. "Are you fucking kidding me?"

Uh...

"Got news for you, Westley Keating."

"Fuck off—"

"You are hurt."

I can't deny that.

"She is hurt."

"But—"

"But this is nothing compared to what it will be later."

"Are you trying to encourage me or discourage me?"

"Trying to get you to be less of an idiot," he says.

"Good luck with that."

"Tell me about it." He chuckles. "You can't live your life afraid of getting hurt."

What the fuck?

Chase is giving me advice?

Chase is telling me to go for it?

"That's your MO," I say.

"And?"

"And fuck off telling me what to do."

"You want to be like me?" he asks.

"Hell no."

"So why you following in my footsteps?"

"If I was following in your footsteps I'd be praying she died in an explosion."

"I don't pray for anyone's death," he says.

"Uh-huh." I motion to the speakers. It's a new song, but it's also about the ex. The singer is still claiming he doesn't care about her. He cares so little he wrote another song about her. He's as full of shit as Chase is.

"Stop deflecting."

"But it's fun."

"You want to be her boyfriend?"

I flip him off.

He chuckles. "That's as good as a yes."

"She's leaving in ten days."

"So?"

"So, what the hell am I going to do with her two thousand miles away?" I ask.

"They don't have tattoo shops in Chicago?"

"I can't handle winter."

"They don't have med schools in California?"

Fuck, these are valid points. I hate that he's making valid points. I can't tell him to fuck off. Well, I can. But his stupid suggestions will still infect my brain. "I can't ask her that."

"Why not?"

"Because…" It's asking way too fucking much.

"Because you're an idiot?"

"You're an asshole."

"Not news." He leans in to turn up the stereo right as the singer belts out something about his ex sleeping with a new guy. And how dare she. Even though they're broken up and he has no claim to her.

Though, well, I kinda see the singer's point.

Quinn has every right to tell me to fuck off and find a new guy, but the thought still makes me sick.

Chase continues, "I'm an asshole. You're an idiot. She's way too good for you."

"Obviously."

"Where do you want to go right now?"

"Besides for a drink?"

He chuckles. "You got a strong sense of irony, kid."

"Thanks."

"Where?"

"Loving hanging out with you."

His laugh gets louder. "Say I insist on dropping you off somewhere. Who would you want to see?"

"Her, but that doesn't mean anything."

"Doesn't it?"

Chapter Thirty-Six

QUINN

The doorbell rings.

"Hey." Wes's voice flows through the wood. "Can we talk?"

Maybe.

I want to listen, but there's so much going through my head.

I want him here. I want him gone. I want to stop falling for him if I don't have a safe place to land.

But I really do want him here.

"Sure." I pull the door open.

Wes is standing there in his usual jeans and t-shirt outfit, but he's not his bright self. His expression is worn. Tired.

"Is your mom okay?"

"Depends on your definition."

"You want to talk about it?"

"Later." He steps inside. Moves closer. Close enough to wrap his arms around me.

Then he does.

He pulls my body into his.

Kisses me hard.

Fuck, he tastes good.

Like coffee and sugar.

I want to kiss him forever.

I want to stay here forever.

But the taste of his lips doesn't change anything. "Wes, I'm sorry about your mom, but—"

"I don't know if I want to be your boyfriend."

"Okay…"

"No, I do."

"Oh."

"But this is a big deal."

It is.

"One of us will have to uproot our life."

Either he asks me to stay here, or I ask him to come to Chicago. There's no compromise. Not really.

"It's a big ask."

"Yeah."

"For you too."

Yeah, I want him to commit.

But I'm as fuzzy as he is.

I can't fault him for his lack of clarity.

His palm cups my cheek.

I lean into the tender touch.

My eyelids flutter closed.

God, I want to soak him in all day.

But I can't.

Not when everything is so… what the hell is it?

His voice is soft. "I can't ask unless I'm sure."

"Me either."

"I guess we have ten days to figure it out."

I nod.

"And, well, I was thinking about your bucket list."

"Yeah?"

"We have a lot to fit in." He pulls me closer. "Can you give me this weekend?"

"I have to pack."

He nods. "I'll help."

"Okay." I don't know what to say. I want to spend this time with him. I want to hold him as close as I can. And I want to pull back to protect my heart. "What about Vegas?"

"We can go next week."

"I'm supposed to leave Thursday."

"I know. You'd have to fly out of MacCarran."

There's no reason why I can't.

Hell, it will be easier.

I can pack up my life. Send it to Chicago. Escape the dread in Sin City. At least for a few days.

A last hurrah before I kiss freedom goodbye.

Before I kiss Wes goodbye.

Or maybe…

God, if he asks me to stay.

What would I say?

"Okay." I nod. "I'll make the arrangements."

"You sure you're okay with this?"

No, but I'm not okay with giving him up either. "Yeah."

"You know what this means?"

"What?"

"You need to come on my face now."

My heart thuds against my chest.

Yes, I want that.

I want to make him come.

To connect.

To be here, in this moment.

No more talk about all these new possibilities.

They're exciting, yeah, but they're terrifying too.

I...

Fuck, I can't think about it now.

I can't think at all now.

"Angel?" Wes cups my hip with his palm.

"Yeah."

"That okay with you?"

"Absolutely."

I float off the fucking ground.

Our connection charging the air between us.

Making it more electric.

This could be more.

This could be everything.

Do I want it to be everything?

Do I—

His fingers curl into my side.

He pulls my body into his. Brings one hand to the back of my head.

I rise to my tiptoes to kiss him.

He still tastes so fucking good.

My lips part. His tongue slips into my mouth. It dances with mine, leading just enough.

I follow his steps.

We tumble to my bedroom.

He scoops me into his arms, carries me to the bed, lays me flat on the clean sheets.

He pulls his t-shirt over his head and drops it on the ground.

I reach around my back to undo the zipper of my dress.

There.

I lift my hips. Push the dress all the way to the floor.

Wes drops to the ground between my legs. "I've been

waiting too fucking long for this." He presses his lips to my inner thigh.

My sex clenches. My breath catches. My body screams *Wes, Wes, Wes.*

"Fuck, Quinn." He mumbles a groan into my skin. Like he can't get enough. Like this is everything he wants. Like he's obsessed with making me come.

Maybe he is.

God, I...

I pinch myself.

Nothing.

I'm not dreaming.

I'm really here.

Wes is about to eat me out.

We might be more.

We might be—

Fuck.

It's as terrifying as it's exhilarating.

I try to push it aside. To focus on this moment. His fingertips on my skin. His breath on my thigh. His lips on my—

Fuck.

He tugs my panties to my knees then rolls them to my ankles.

I kick them off my feet. Reach around my back to unhook my bra. Fling it aside.

I'm wearing nothing but my wedges.

He's between my legs. Staring up at me like I'm everything he wants.

I've died and gone to heaven.

I really have.

Wes pries my knees apart.

He pulls me to the edge of the bed. "Lie on your back, angel."

"I want to look at you."

He motions to the mirror opposite my bed.

Oh. It's the perfect view. Him, in only his jeans, between my legs.

I lie back.

Let my arms fall to my sides.

Let my legs splay.

Wes presses his lips to my knees. "Might be intense." He drags his lips up my thigh. "If it's too much or if you don't like something—"

"Okay."

"Fuck, Quinn." His fingers curl into my knees. He holds me in place. Pins me to the bed.

It's different than usual.

Needier.

More possessive.

I never thought I'd like that.

But I do.

I really fucking do.

"You smell good." He drags his lips higher. Higher. Higher.

I reach for something.

Find his shoulder.

His head.

My fingers curl into his hair.

He nips at the skin of my inner thigh. "You have no fucking idea how much I've been thinking about this."

"Yeah?"

"Yeah."

"You touch yourself to it?" I ask.

"All the time."

"You fuck yourself to me?"

"Every fucking day."

My body buzzes. He's too sexy. It's wrong, but it's so right too.

"Do you?" He plants a kiss on my thigh.

"Do I?"

"Fuck yourself to me?" Need drips into his voice.

It's hard to believe he wants me that badly.

But he does.

I look down at him. Run my fingers through his hair. "Yeah."

"What do you think about?"

"Everything."

"This?" he asks.

"Sometimes. But it's... it's more fuzzy. I don't know what to imagine."

His fingers brush my sex. It's so soft I can barely feel it. Then it's harder.

He teases me with one finger.

Then two.

"You fuck yourself like this?" He pushes his fingers deeper.

My eyelids press together.

God, that's a lot.

It's good.

But it's still a hell of a lot.

"No." My lips part with a groan. "Wes. Please."

"Please, what?"

"Please make me come."

"Fuck, you're always so polite."

"You like it?"

He takes my hand. Stands enough to bring my fingers to his cock.

He's hard.

Those God damn jeans are in the way again.

But it's still so fucking beautiful.

"May I make you come? After this? Please?" I ask.

"Fuck, Quinn."

"Or we could... I want to fuck you."

"Soon."

My body whines. Not soon. Today. Now. I want everything, and I want it now. He makes me greedy, bossy, petulant even.

"Yeah." He lowers himself to his knees. Looks up at me as he brings his lips to my inner thigh. "But not until I'm done with you."

Holy shit.

His fingers dig into my tender skin.

Again, he pins my legs to the bed.

He plants a kiss on my inner thigh.

The top of my pelvis.

The spot just below my belly button.

My other inner thigh.

Slowly, he brings his mouth to me.

His tongue flits against my clit.

It's so much.

He's warm, wet, soft.

And he—

He does it again.

This soft, long stroke.

He holds me against the bed as he teases with those long, soft strokes.

His movements get harder.

Shorter.

He tries fast. Slow.

Back and forth.

Circles.

Zigzags.

He licks me up and down.

Tastes every fucking inch.

My eyelids press together.

My legs go slack.

My fingers dig into his hair.

I pull him closer.

He teases me with soft flicks of his tongue.

He moves up.

Down.

Right.

There—

"Don't stop." I hold his head in place.

My hips buck of their own accord.

I need more.

I need everything.

He's so warm and wet and perfect.

And I need him working me like this.

I need him driving me to the edge.

He scrapes his nails against my inner thighs. This tiny, perfect hint of pain. Enough to wake up my nerves. To remind me he's in control.

To remind me I'm his.

I mean, I'm not.

Not yet.

But, God, I want to be.

Wes winds me up with every flick of his tongue.

Pleasure collects in my core.

It gets tighter and tighter.

Until it's almost too much to take.

Until it *is* too much to take.

With the next flick of his tongue, I unfurl.

My world goes white.

Nothing but this soft, beautiful, blissful light.

Like his t-shirt.

And my walls.

And the sky on a cloudy morning.

I groan his name as I come.

He licks me through my orgasm, then he pulls back, and he looks up at me like I'm everything he wants.

And for the first time, I believe it.

This is possible.

We're possible.

Chapter Thirty-Seven

QUINN

Wes stretches his arms over his head. His t-shirt slides up his torso.

My gaze goes straight to his taut stomach.

He's beautiful.

He really is.

He yawns. Blinks twice. Looks straight to me. "Good morning, angel."

"Good morning." My lips curl into a smile. My heartbeat picks up. My skin buzzes. He's half-naked in my apartment. Mornings don't get better than this. "You want coffee?"

"You have coffee?"

"Instant."

His nose scrunches in distaste.

"We can go out and get something."

"Out?" He raises a brow.

I nod.

He gives me a long, slow once-over. "You gonna change into something else?"

I smooth my short nightgown. "I can't wear this."

"Then we can't go out."

"You're choosing me over coffee?"

"You're better than coffee."

My cheeks flush. It's flirting, not a declaration of love, but after last night…

Everything is different.

We're possible.

This is possible.

Maybe it's a remote possibility—can I really walk away from my life or ask him to walk away from his—but it's there.

"How about I make you tea?" I offer.

He nods *sure* then moves straight to me.

His hands brush my palms. My wrists.

He pulls me into a tight hug.

One hand goes to the back of my head. The other goes to my waist.

His lips connect with mine.

It's a soft, slow kiss.

Then it's deeper. Harder. Hotter.

My chest warms.

My sex aches.

I need more of him.

All of him.

Nine days.

I have nine days to decide to jump.

Or nine days left with him.

No pressure.

My thoughts dissolve as his tongue slips into my mouth.

When he releases me, I'm shaking.

"Fuck, angel, you're too good at that." He keeps one arm around my waist as he leads me into the kitchen. "This tea stuff—"

"This tea stuff?"

"That a problem?"

"You need to show a little respect."

I nod. "Oh?"

I nod. Fill the electric kettle with water. Turn it on. "What if I referred to your twenty-dollar-a-pound beans as 'this coffee stuff'?"

"Dunno. Maybe you should try."

"Maybe you respect quality." I rise to my tiptoes to reach the high shelf. This is it. The good stuff. The rich, malty Assam I can barely afford.

His fingers brush mine as he takes the tin. "This is the good stuff?"

"The best."

"Any booze in it."

"You need a drink this early?" I tease.

He smiles, but there's something in his eyes. This frustration. From last night. His mom.

We still haven't talked about that.

Should we talk about that?

I want to help him.

I just don't know how.

Is it better to give him space or demand a discussion?

If it was me…

I don't know.

Maybe I should just ask him what I should ask him.

"How do we make this good stuff?" His voice bounces back to his usual teasing tone, but there's still something in his eyes.

Or maybe I'm getting better at reading him.

"It's much easier than coffee." Okay, it's more that I'm incapable of making halfway decent coffee. I pull the teaspoon from the drawer. Then the tea strainer. "One teaspoon per six ounces."

His fingers brush mine as he takes the metal utensil.

"Steep for five minutes."

"That's it?"

"There are subtleties."

"Yeah?"

I nod.

He places his body behind mine. Wraps his arms around my waist. Rests his head in the crook of my shoulder. "What kind of subtleties?"

Mmm. What are we talking about again?

"Quinn?"

"Yeah?"

"Sorry, am I distracting you," he teases.

"Mhmm."

"That a no or a yes?"

"Uh…"

"Or maybe a *don't stop*?"

"That one." It flits through my brain. He's deflecting with sex because he doesn't want to deal with this. But maybe that's not such a bad thing. I like sex. He likes sex. There's no urgency to this issue. We can… Uh…

His fingers skim the hem of my nightgown. "I have an idea."

"The water temperature."

"Huh?"

"It needs to be boiling for black tea. That's, the, uh—"

He slips his hand beneath my nightgown.

"The subtlety."

"Oh." He drags his fingertips up my inner thigh. "I like subtlety."

"Wes," I breathe.

"Yeah?"

"Do we need to talk?"

"Do you need to talk?"

"No." I'm losing interest in conversation quickly. "But if you do—"

"Not right now."

"Okay." My eyelids flutter closed. "But soon."

"That a demand or a request?"

"The first one."

"I like you demanding, angel."

"Thank you."

He draws circles on my skin as he scoops tea into the strainer. Then as he pours the boiling water.

"You only have five minutes," I say.

"Five minutes to make you come?"

I think I say yes, but, honestly, I'm not sure.

"Sounds like a challenge." His fingers brush my sex, over my panties.

"Uh-uh."

"Is that a hell yes?"

I nod.

He brings his lips to my ear. "Need to hear the hell yes, angel."

"Hell yes."

———

AFTER, WE TAKE OUR DRINKS TO THE COUCH. TALK about nothing until our stomachs are rumbling.

My apartment is tragically out of food.

And he has an appointment in the afternoon.

"Let's go out." He slides his arm around my waist. "I'll buy you breakfast."

"Anything I want?"

"You ordering lobster and steak for breakfast?"

"That a problem?"

"Fuck no." He laughs. "I want some lobster and steak. You know a joint where I can get some?"

I shake my head. "How about tacos?"

"How about them?"

"That a yes?"

His bangs fall over his eyes as he tilts his head to one side.

It feels good seeing his bright blue eyes lit up with joy.

But what the hell is that look?

"Yes?" I ask.

"Nothing."

"You're giving me a look."

"Admiring your beauty."

"Hmm... I appreciate that. But it's bullshit."

He shrugs *who me?*

I nod *hell yeah, you.*

"Angel, if you keep delaying, we're gonna be late."

"Late to what?"

"Well, I'll be late," he says.

"Then maybe you should admit it."

"That I love your tits? Fuck yeah, I'll shout that from the rooftops."

I shake my head with mock outrage. He's ridiculous. But I kind of love it. No I really love it. I really...

Am I already there?

I don't know.

I've never loved anyone before.

"I'm getting dressed," I say. "You can... What are you going to wear?"

"You have any more cock hungry t-shirts for me?"

"I might."

He chuckles. "We can stop by my place on the way."

I nod. We can stop by his place. But—"Maybe you should leave some stuff here."

His expression screws with confusion.

Which is weird.

But, um, well I'm not going to read into it.

I move into the bedroom. Scan my closet for the perfect dress. Not that it needs to be perfect. It's just breakfast. But it might be my last breakfast with Wes. So maybe it does need to be perfect.

No, it's a dress.

The dress doesn't matter.

This matters.

"What are you doing with your apartment?" he asks.

"Oh, well… I already let go of the lease." I swallow hard. I don't want to face the reality of our situation. But I have to. "I talked to the landlord. He's okay with me leaving the furniture."

"Yeah?"

I nod. "He rents to a lot of college students who don't have anything. I guess this one needs stuff. So, um, I have to pack everything else."

"Everything else is a lot."

"True." My clothes and makeup will probably take up four boxes on their own. Then there are DVDs, cooking appliances, books. God, I should really sell some of those old text books. Especially if I'm ditching med school. Even if I'm not. I'm never going to return to my biology 201 text. And, well, I really can't think about that right now. One thing at a time. I figure out what I'm doing with Wes. Then I figure out school. "I have some boxes coming this weekend."

"You want me to bring friends to help?"

Yes. But I want him all to myself too. "Depends who the friends are."

"Griff maybe."

I nod *sure*.

He nods *of course*. "What happens if you decide to stay?" He doesn't add *if I ask you to stay and you say yes.*

"I guess I'd have to bring my boxes to a new apartment."

"You can keep them at my place."

"Wes, I—"

"I'm not asking you to move in."

"Good." I think. Maybe.

"But if you need a place to stay for a while, you can stay with me."

"Oh." I go to smooth my dress. Hit my skin instead. This nightgown is short. I have nothing to grab onto. "Thank you. I'll think about that. If I decide to stay." *If you ask me to stay.* I mean, I can ask him to come with me. But I don't know… It's not like I want to be in Chicago. I'd rather be here. I just don't know how much I can really handle here if he doesn't ask me to stay.

There will be too many memories.

There are already too many memories.

"Quinn?"

Please ask me to stay. Right now. Give me the week to decide. Tell me I'll have someplace soft to land if I jump. "Yeah?"

"Mind if I check for a t-shirt?"

"Oh, no. Go for it."

"Thanks." He turns to the dresser.

I focus on my closet. Nothing feels right. It's not nice enough for this occasion.

I know, intellectually, that the dress doesn't matter. But, God, it really feels like it does.

I settle on a comfortable white sun dress. A red purse. My favorite cork sandals.

Somehow, Wes finds a fresh t-shirt. It must be Owen's, but I have no idea when he left it here.

312

It's a simple white thing, but, God, it looks good on him.

White t-shirt. Blue eyes. Sandy hair. Light jeans. Tattooed arms.

Picture perfect California boy.

It's intoxicating. It really is.

He offers me his hand. When I take it, he leads me to the main room.

Wes steps into his shoes.

I scoop my keys into my hand.

"You still want tacos?" he asks.

"Are you gonna tell me what's funny about that?"

"Depends."

"On?"

"What I get out of it?"

I swat him playfully.

He smiles.

My heart jumps. He's just so…

God, I really like him.

"Look in the mirror," he says.

"The mirror is in the bedroom."

"Damn, angel, if you want a second round, you can just ask."

I flip him off.

"Now? Well, if you really insist."

I push him.

He wraps his arms around me. "I tell you how much I like you?"

"Not in the last few minutes."

"I do." He presses his lips to mine. And it's there. That he means more than like.

But how much more?

Chapter Thirty-Eight

WES

Quinn gathers her skirt as she slides into the booth. She crosses one leg over the other. Shoots me that same *what is this about* look.

God, it's an adorable look.

And those thick frames of hers make it ten times cuter.

"Yeah?" I ask.

She arches a brow *really*.

I nod *really* and slide into the both next to her.

The hostess giggles. "Your server will be right with you." She hands us two menus, then takes her leave.

Quinn scoots to the end of the booth, giving me room.

But I don't want room.

I want to stay pressed against her.

I want to fill every minute of the next nine days with her.

I want her to stay.

But there's no way I can ask. Not now. Not with my heart torn in half.

Yeah, I'm moving on from that.

In theory.

Eventually.

Right now, it's too fucking fresh.

"Are you going to torture me with this all day?" Quinn asks.

"Are you going to come to work with me and observe?"

"Why would I do that?"

"Maybe you're thinking about learning to apprentice."

Quinn's eyes light up as she laughs. "Am I?"

"You could do it."

"I can't draw a stick figure."

"Let's test that." I hail a passing server.

He stops by our table with a friendly smile. "Do you need something?"

"Coffee," I say.

"Water please," Quinn adds.

"And kids menus. With crayons," I say.

He looks at me like I'm crazy, but he still nods. "Of course."

After the server leaves, Quinn turns to me and shakes her head. "You have a sudden desire for mac and cheese?"

"They serve mac and cheese at a Mexican restaurant?"

"A quesadilla?" Her brow furrows with concentration.

Which is also fucking adorable.

"Oh my God, Westley Keating, if you don't explain that look, I'll leave." She unwraps her napkin.

"Grabbing the knife to stab me?"

"If that's what it takes."

"Shit, everything you know about medicine—you could probably kill me with a single gesture."

"Not yet. But I'll get there. I mean, if I stay on the path —" She lays her napkin in her lap. "You're not distracting me."

"I think I am."

She shakes her head.

I slide my arm around her shoulders. "How about now?"

She looks up at me with a coy smile. "Still not."

"Damn, I've lost the magic."

"Just tell me."

"You gonna beg for it?"

"No." Her eyes meet mine. "You can handle begging for it."

She's right about that. But my cock isn't interested in practicalities. "Go on…"

"If you tell me."

"Dirty trick."

"Learned from the best." She smiles as she rests her hand on my thigh. "Tell me."

"Look." I motion to the mirrored wall across from us.

Her brow furrows *huh*. She takes in our reflection slowly.

We look good together. Hell, we match.

But—"You're a little overdressed, angel."

"So?"

"You don't seem like the type of girl who gets her hands dirty."

"We both know I do." She nods to my crotch.

My cock stirs. Where the fuck did this confidence come from? How can I convince her to talk like this every fucking day forever? "What was that, angel?"

"Doesn't seem fair, does it?" She drags her fingertips up my thigh. "You torture me nonstop, but I don't get a chance to torture you."

I nod.

"You got me off this morning, but I don't—"

"Your coffee, sir." The server drops off our drinks. His eyes dart to the action, but he says nothing. "Do you need another minute to order?"

317

"I'm ready." Quinn pulls her hand into her lap. She blushes as she scoots away from me. "Huevos rancheros."

"Steak and eggs," I say. "Medium rare."

"Anything to drink for you, miss?" the server asks.

"Iced tea if you have it." She collects our menus and hands them to him. "And salsa with the food. Thanks."

"Sure." He takes his leave.

She turns to me. "I'm overdressed?"

I nod.

"You didn't even order carne asada."

I can't help but laugh. "And?"

"And, that's what it is."

"It's steak, isn't it?"

"Carne asada is more specific."

I intertwine my fingers with hers. "When did you get all picky about labels?"

She squeezes my hand. "Not picky. Just think it's odd the guy who's lived in southern California his whole life doesn't call Mexican dishes by their proper names."

"Oh?"

She nods.

"You're the defender of this fine cuisine?"

"Hell yes."

"Really?"

She nods.

I rub the space between her thumb and forefinger with my thumb. It feels right. Intimate. Loving. "You really do love it."

A sigh falls off her lips. "Is that a problem?"

"No, just… curious."

"Because I'm from Chicago?"

I nod. I've been to Chicago once. A long time ago. I don't remember much about the food, but I'm pretty sure I didn't see a Mexican restaurant the entire trip.

"The first day I moved into my dorm, my roommate was already there. God, she was so cool. Like someone who belonged on MTV. She was wearing a cropped t-shirt, ripped jeans, and Converse. She asked if I wanted to go for tacos. When she took me to the place, I was shocked. Did people really eat at places like that? But I played cool. It was the best meal I'd ever had. And it became our tradition. Every Friday. We'd get greasy tacos. She wanted to coat her stomach before partying. I... well, I went to a party with her once."

"But you hated it?"

Quinn nods. "Is it that obvious?"

"There's no shame in preferring movies to booze."

"You've never had wine with a movie?"

I shake my head.

She studies my expression. Looking for cracks. Trying to figure out if I'm ready to talk about my mom, I guess.

I'm not. Not yet. "Should I try it?"

"Yeah. It's amazing."

"Makes shit like *Mission Impossible* entertaining?"

"No." Quinn's eyes light up with her smile. "There's not enough wine in the world."

"Cruel."

"True."

Fuck, I love her smile. I want to admire it all day.

She's just so fucking Quinn.

I get lost in her hazel eyes for a minute.

Try to find the thread of our conversation. "Your roommate introduced you to Mexican food?"

"Yeah. She's amazing. Funny, smart, completely apathetic to what other people thought of her."

"You admired that?"

She nods. "We got really close. But, um, she moved to New York after graduation. And I..."

"Miss her?"

"Yeah. It still feels like home." She motions to the decorations on the walls. "Like love. You know?"

I do.

"God, I probably sound crazy."

"No. I get it."

"You have anything like that?"

I hold up my mug.

"Really?"

"Yeah." I've never thought about it. But it's true. "Hunter got me into it. He was dating this girl who scoffed at the mention of Starbucks and he wanted to impress her. So he went out and learned all this shit about French press and pour over. After about a week, the thing with the girl ended. But he was hooked."

"You too?"

"Yeah." I stir half-and-half into my coffee. Take a sip. It's not great—restaurant coffee never is—but it's still comforting. "He fixed me a cup every morning. Without fail. Even after he started drinking more than doing anything else."

"You two still go for coffee?"

My guts churn. Fuck, the last few times we've had reason to be together—"No."

"Maybe you should."

"We work together."

"But do you really hang out?"

"Things have been different since he got sober," I say.

"Yeah?"

"Yeah." I can't hide behind jokes or booze. It's like with my tattoos. I don't know how to pour myself into them. It's too fucking painful.

I try to find a way to elaborate, but nothing comes.

I pick up a set of crayons. Pop it open. Hand the red one to Quinn. "Stick figure."

"Explain first."

"At the same time."

She nods. "Fair."

I turn the kid's menu over. There's a square for kids to draw their favorite animal. Good enough.

For a second, I close my eyes.

Let my subconscious take over.

If I had to design something from the heart right now...

The crayon glides over the page.

"Fuck." Quinn sighs. "Wes, that's amazing."

My eyes blink open. It's like last time. It's dark shit. A shard of glass pressed to skin. A vein bleeding bourbon.

"Do you usually design stuff that—"

"No."

"I... I check your social media, but I haven't really seen anything."

"You want something?" I ask.

"No. I... we've been over this."

"Yeah, we agree I'm doing the work."

"I can't get a tattoo." Her fingers brush my wrist. "My parents would die."

"So?"

"I..."

"If you were going to get something, what would it be?"

Her eyes find mine. "I don't know. That's like asking 'what defines you as a person?'"

"What defines you as a person?"

"Besides love of *Casablanca*?"

"Why besides?"

"You've never seen it. How are you going to think up a design?"

"Never seen a lot of things I design." My gaze shifts to my drawing. It's good. Real. Raw.

A hell of a lot better than my usual stuff.

I'm not ready to show it to the world. Not yet.

But I want to get there.

I want to do more shit from the heart.

I want to stop running away from getting hurt.

Fuck, Chase was right.

That's terrifying.

"Well… the thing I've been thinking about a lot… No, I can't say it. It's too much of a spoiler." Her eyes find mine. "You really don't know the ending?"

"It's a romance, isn't it?"

"Yeah."

"Don't they end up together?"

"You know I can't tell you." Her fingers curl around my wrist. "God, you really are a tease."

"You're the one delaying my education."

She laughs. "Okay. Come over tonight."

"We ready to do the deed?"

"Not even close. We still have to work up to it."

I laugh. "How much?"

"So much."

"Until then, what can I design for you?"

"I guess I have to think about it."

I stare into her hazel eyes. "First impulse."

She answers without blinking. "A pinup."

"Yeah?"

She nods. "With movies. Somehow. Maybe a film projector. Or… I don't know. Something."

"You really love movies?"

"I do."

"You ever think about doing that?"

She looks at me like I'm crazy. "Doing what? Watching movies isn't a job."

"No, but I'm sure there's something you could do."

"Well, I'd love to be the host of *Turner Classic Movies*, but I think that job is taken."

"Still."

"I… I don't know Wes. It's a nice idea, but—"

"There's a lot of shit out there."

"Like tattoo apprentice." She looks at me like I'm crazy.

All right. Maybe Quinn shouldn't be an apprentice. But there are plenty of other possibilities. "Like a million things."

"Why do you care so much?"

I brush a stray hair behind her ear. "I hate seeing you hurt."

"I… I'll think about it."

"You promise?"

"I do."

I hold up my pinkie.

She laughs as she takes it.

But, fuck, it still feels like everything.

Chapter Thirty-Nine

WES

After I walk Quinn home, I float to work.

It's a beautiful day. Blue sky. Bright sun. Ocean for miles.

The shop hums with conversation, the buzz of tattoo guns, the steady mumble of one of Griffin's favorite bands.

"Fuck, that guy needs a cup of coffee." As do I. I move to the Keurig. Fix a medium roast. Pod coffee is never great, but this cup tastes like heaven.

After the last twelve hours with Quinn—

Life is good.

It's capable of being good.

After yesterday—

I didn't think that was possible.

Sure, I'm not ready to dive into it yet.

But I will get there.

I really will.

"Fuck." Griffin's deep voice fills the room. It's not steady and even the way it normally is.

Which is scary.

He's usually as calm as, well, as the guy singing about

325

his lust. Is this really supposed to be lust? The singer couldn't possibly sound more bored.

Whereas Griffin is wearing his frustration.

He's sitting at his suite, his brow furrowed, his eyes glued to his cell.

"Griff? You okay?" Fuck, it's weird hearing his name in that tone. I never worry about him. Or pry. "Your play-thing dump you?"

"No." He doesn't look up from his phone.

"Then what's with the face?" He never looks this worried.

He shrugs like it's nothing, but he's missing his usual casualness. His gaze goes straight to his cell. His eyes fill with concern.

"Griff? You there?"

He tries another shrug, but it's even more strained. "She called off the wedding."

Isn't that a good thing? "You two finally fucked?"

He stares at me like I'm crazy. "No."

"She finally realize she's in love with you?"

He shoots me a *come on, offer me a real answer* look. He's either bullshitting me or in deep, deep denial about his true feelings for his best friend.

Griffin doesn't bullshit, so it must be the latter.

I need to push him. To force him to see it. "You real-ized you're in love with her? She wanted time to process that, so she called off things with Mr. Boring?"

"Seriously?" Irritation drips into his voice. He has no time for my stupidity.

But he's the one being stupid. "You're gonna realize it one day."

"Uh-huh." He shakes his head again—*really, how can you be such an idiot?*—then he turns to his phone. Stares at his text chain with his no longer engaged best friend.

It's obvious. It couldn't be more obvious. "Explain something to me, Griff."

"Yeah?" His eyes stay on his cell.

"Mr. Boring was a snooze."

"What do you need explained?" He taps something into his cell. "Seems like you have it figured out."

All right, I'm going to have to spell it out. "Your best friend is free of the weight around her neck."

He nods *obviously*.

"How is that a bad thing?"

He looks up at me. Shakes his head. *How can you be so oblivious?* "She might not see it that way."

"You're worried about her?"

"No shit, Sherlock."

That's fair. But it doesn't explain his concern. This is more than *my friend is hurting*. It's a whole other level.

I move closer. So I can whisper. "This shop is full of nosy assholes."

"Yourself included." His voice lifts to a teasing tone.

I flip him off.

He chuckles. For a moment, his mood is free and clear, then his gaze shifts to his cell and his brow furrows.

"Maybe you should get out of here. Go to her place."

"She doesn't have a place." He bites his tongue. "Fuck, I'm not telling you shit."

"Invite her to stay with you."

He shoots me an *obviously*.

"If it's so obvious why are you freaking out?"

"I'm not—" His cell buzzes in his lap. He picks it up. Stares at the screen like it's a picture of his paramour naked.

I guess this is just as good.

It's a response from her.

I can tell by the way his eyes light up.

Fuck. He's so into her.

And so oblivious to it.

I guess I need to handle him more delicately.

Not my strong suit. But I can try.

"Where is she?" I ask.

"At her mom's place."

"Head over there. Talk to her."

"Maybe." He runs his fingers through his hair. "She just told me."

"So how'd you know?"

"Her mom sent texts to the wedding party."

Shit, he was supposed to be one of the groomsmen. That's how little he realized his feelings.

He was willing to stand there, next to her future husband, while she married someone else.

Griffin is usually the one making everyone else face obvious truths.

I don't know how the hell I can force him to do it.

I barely know Juliette.

She's a lot like him in her complete unwillingness to bullshit people. But, otherwise, they're opposites.

She's a studious good girl from a rich family.

Whereas he…

Well, he's a slutty tattoo artist.

I understand it's a tough job that requires years of dedication.

But the kind of people Juliette hangs with—they don't always get that.

"Fuck." His voice gets louder. Stronger. "I hate that asshole."

"Jackson?"

"He—fuck, I can't tell you shit."

"Hey."

"You can't keep your mouth shut."

That might be true. "And you like her more than you like me."

The tension in his brow eases. His lips curl into a half-smile. His shoulders drop. "You just figure that out?"

"I barely know her, and I like her better than I like you."

He flips me off, but it's good-natured this time.

"You want to give me a hint?"

"You know her," he says.

I nod.

"Why do you figure she called it off?"

Because she finally realized she's into Griffin. But, well, I can't say that. I'm not as tactless as he is. "Something he did?"

"Yeah." He taps a text. His phone buzzes. He taps another. "She says she's okay, but Jules is always like that."

"Yeah." I know that feeling well.

His phone buzzes. His eyes go straight to the screen. Go wide. "She wants to get out of here."

"That's a good idea."

"Blow off steam for the weekend." He looks up at me. "I told her about Vegas."

"What about it?"

"How you're going with Quinn."

"Since when am I going with Quinn?"

"Aren't you?"

Yeah, but how the hell does he knows that? "It's on her summer to do list, yeah."

"And she's leaving next weekend. You waiting for a red carpet or something?"

I can't help but chuckle. *That* is the Griffin I know. "Waiting for you, obviously."

"Well, get your shit together, Romeo. It needs to happen now."

"If I'm Romeo, shouldn't I be with Juliette?"

He rolls his eyes like I'm the stupidest person on the planet. "Good luck with that."

My laugh gets louder. Heartier.

"You know she finds you obnoxious."

"Fuck, you ever hear of letting someone down gently?"

He stands. Reaches out to muss my hair. "You ever hear of narcissism?"

"No. But it sounds like it might be about me, so I'm listening."

He smiles. Full on smiles. "I should take her. To Vegas."

"You should."

"It's perfect. An easy drive. And—"

"Plenty of alcohol," I say.

He tilts his head to one side to assess me. He must decide it's bad, because he shakes his head *Wes is an idiot*. "There are other ways to let your hair down—"

"One in particular." Dean's voice bounces around the shop. He stands. Moves into the main area.

Chloe follows. She shakes her head *Dean is ridiculous* then looks to Griffin. "I'm sorry about your friend."

"Don't be sorry. Make plans." Dean wraps his arm around her waist. "Next week. Vegas. All six of us."

She leans into his gesture. "Aren't we here to work?"

"Got half an hour until our appointment." He motions to something in their suite. "Do another mock-up or stay and talk."

"You inviting me as my boss or my boyfriend?" she asks.

"Depends." He leans in to whisper in her ear. Though he doesn't whisper. At all. "Which will be a hotter fuck?"

Her cheeks flame. "Umm…"

"The boss," Griffin says. "Obviously."

Her cheeks burn redder.

"You two do that kind of shit?" Griffin raises a brow. "You order her around? Ask her to call you sir? Punish her if she's bad?"

Dean's smile gets wicked. He looks down at his apprentice slash girlfriend. "Dunno, sunshine, should we fill them in?"

"Oh my God, if you say one thing about who you really want to fill..." She shoots Griffin a *mind your own business* look. "Get your free porn elsewhere."

"You can't blame him for trying, sunshine. The amateur stuff is the best," he says.

Chloe rolls her eyes. "Every fucking day."

I laugh.

Griffin does too. "He is right."

Chloe clears her throat. "I don't need to know that."

"But it is the best," I say.

She looks around the room with horror. Then she turns to her boyfriend. "Look what you've done."

"Sunshine, you know it is," he says.

She shakes her head, but it doesn't hide her smile.

"We do have half an hour—" He motions to the back room.

"Are you going to bring your laptop?" she asks.

"If you want me to," he says.

"No laptop," Griffin says. "Just leave the door open. You can find out if you get off on exhibitionism."

"Go fuck yourself," she says.

"That's what I'm trying to do," he teases.

"You only encourage him telling him that," I say.

She ignores us. "Do I know Griffin's friend?"

"Yeah." Dean nods. "She was at his birthday party."

"Oh. Her. She was cool. Way too cool for you," Chloe says.

Griffin nods *obviously*. "And you're too good for Dean but look where we are."

"Maybe she has a thing for cock piercings," I say.

"Maybe you should shut up," she says.

"Definitely." Dean turns to us. "What do you say? The six of us go to Vegas together. I know a guy with a minivan."

"Who?" I ask.

"My secret," Dean says.

"It's supposed to be special," I say.

"You want to deflower your virgin in private?" Dean asks.

"You haven't done it yet?" Griffin shakes his head *sad*.

Jesus Christ, this is why it's a bad idea.

"Why don't you ask her?" Chloe suggests. "Let her decide."

That's fair.

"Maybe… maybe she'd actually enjoying hanging with these idiots?" She motions to Dean then to Griffin. "You too, Griff. Invite Juliette. If Wes and Quinn say no, it can be the four of us."

"When did I invite you?" Griffin asks.

Dean chuckles. "Ice cold."

"Suit yourself." Chloe shrugs.

I turn to my best friend. "You don't want her coming?"

"No, I do. I just don't want her assuming," he says.

"You're an asshole," I say.

He shrugs *obviously*.

It's a smart idea inviting people. Makes it seem more like a fun trip with friends rather than a getaway that screams *I'm in love with you. Isn't that a lot of pressure*?

Even if he is.

And it is.

Maybe that's what Quinn wants too.

Or maybe…

Maybe this will convince her she wants to stay.

If it's not just me, but a whole fucking army of people who want her around.

I'll take all the help I can get.

Chapter Forty

WES

After work, I head to the gym with Griffin. It's not our usual routine, and I'm desperate to be at Quinn's place, but, fuck, I'm worried about him.

I pry through a dozen sets, but he doesn't offer much intel.

He keeps insisting he and Juliette are only friends. That he's only worried as a friend. That he only wants to help her as a friend.

He wears out the word *friend*.

Turns it back to me and Quinn and what the hell I'm doing about her leaving.

I don't know.

Not yet.

But I'm going to figure it out.

Eight days.

I have eight more days with her.

Or eight days to ask her to be mine.

"Six people?" Quinn's eyes go wide. She pulls her long red cardigan over her shoulders. Covers her sheer white nightgown.

"Yeah." It's a crazy idea, I know, but it's perfect too. "You know Juliette?"

She nods *of course*. "How is she?"

"Just called off her engagement."

"Oh." Quinn's expression fills with sympathy. She doesn't know Juliette well—they met at one of my parties a year or so ago—but she still cares. She's a good person. Empathetic. Caring. Sweet. "I should call her. Say… something."

"Yeah." After we nail this down. "If you think it will help."

She bites her lip. "I don't know. We're not really friends. I mean, I like her, but I don't know her."

I get that. And I'm sympathetic. Hell, I like Juliette. Yeah, she finds me obnoxious, but so does everyone else at the shop. "You can always text."

"Yeah." She nods. "Maybe just like 'I heard about your engagement. I'm sorry.'"

"Or 'I hear we're heading to Vegas together next week.'"

Quinn shifts her weight to her other foot. "Maybe."

"It's up to you, angel." I scoop stir fry onto her plate—we've been making dinner for the last half an hour. Fuck, it feels good being with her like this. Doing nothing. "I didn't invite Griff."

"He invited himself?"

"It was more Dean inviting everyone."

"Dean?"

Fuck, she doesn't know Dean. How the hell do I explain his incredibly annoying personality? "Guy at the shop. He's kinda obnoxious?"

"The same way you are?"

"Watch it, angel."

Her laugh is soft. "Sorry. You know what I mean. You're kinda…"

"Involved?"

She nods. Scoops rice and stir fry onto her plate. Grabs chopsticks. Moves to the table. "This looks so good."

"'Cause it is."

She shoots me a *you're ridiculous* look as she slides into her seat. She folds one leg over the other. Scoops food with her chopsticks. Brings it to her mouth.

Her eyelids flutter together.

A sigh falls off her lips.

"Fuck, Wes—"

My balls tighten. That's music. It really is.

"You're too good at this," she says.

"I've heard that before."

She swallows. Then shakes her head. "I'm sure you have, but—"

But I should stop teasing her. Get to the point.

We only have eight days.

I want to soak up every minute.

"It was a joint effort, angel," I say.

Her gaze shifts to the counter. To the cutting board filled with bits and pieces of chopped vegetables.

"You helped. Trust me."

Her eyes find mine. "Why does that sound like a line?"

"Would I lie to you?"

"No. I don't think so. Not on purpose." She takes another bite. Chews. Swallows. Sighs. "Can you pour me a red?"

"Can you trust me to pick?"

She shakes her head and names a bottle of wine.

I grab it from the cabinet. Pour two glasses. Bring both, and my plate, to the table.

"Thank you." Her fingers brush mine as she takes the glass. "And thank you for dinner."

"Thank you for dinner." I take a sip of my wine. It's not my usual drink, but it's good. Rich and dry with this hint of raspberry.

"You—"

"Say you're welcome."

She shoots me a *really* look.

I shoot it back.

"Okay, it was a joint effort. And you're welcome."

"Good." I bring a scoop of beef and veggies to my lips. It's fucking great. I was steering sure, but I couldn't have done it without her. "And you're welcome."

Her smile spreads over her cheeks. "You're ridiculous."

I shrug *am I* and take another sip of wine.

She nods *you are* and holds up her glass. "To team work."

I toast. "To team work."

She brings her glass to her lips. "Is that what you want?"

"Huh?"

"Your friends joining us in Vegas?"

I don't want to give up our alone time, but if this might convince her to stay—"They're not going to be around the entire time."

"Oh?"

I nod. "Still going to drag you to our hotel room and fuck you senseless."

Her cheeks flush. "You promise?"

"Cross my heart and hope to die."

She motions to the couch. "Could do it now."

I could. But it's going to change things. And they're so

good right now. "Could torture you for, well, how long do you want to spend in Vegas?"

"You're waiting until Vegas?" Her voice drops to a whine.

I shrug *maybe I am, maybe I'm not.*

Her throat quivers as she swallows. "You're cruel."

"Definitely."

"We could go tomorrow," she says. "You know, in theory."

"Don't you have work?"

"Yeah, but I'm quitting. If I leave early—"

"You're not capable."

She shrugs *sure I am.*

I shake my head. "Quinn, you don't have an impulsive bone in your body."

"What if you fuck me?"

"Huh?"

"Then I'll have an impulsive bone in my—"

"Fuck, angel, that was terrible."

"I know." A laugh spills from her lips. "I can't think. I'm too distracted."

"Go on…"

She shakes her head. "I'm making you wait."

"It will be more painful if you keep talking."

"True." She takes another sip. Sets her glass down. "I'm flying out Thursday."

I nod like I don't have the date and time memorized. "We could leave Tuesday."

"Two nights and a day?"

"Yeah."

"Would you rather they come?"

"Angel, it's up to you."

"Oh." She bites her lip. "It might be fun. Like a going away party. Or a—"

"Staying here party."

"Yeah. Right." She leans back in her chair. Pulls her sweater a little tighter. "I guess… I only know Griffin, really."

That's true.

"So I guess I need your judgment. Do you think I'll have fun with them?"

"I do." I hate to admit it (their egos are already enormous), but my friends are fucking amazing.

"Okay. Then I'm in. But our last night—"

"Wouldn't give it up for the world."

"Good." Her smile is soft. Bittersweet. "And, um, after this, um… well, we're going to watch *An Affair to Remember*."

"We're working our way to the money shot?"

She laughs. "Yeah."

"How many to go?"

"Three."

"Including this one?"

She nods.

"Almost there?"

"Yeah. We are." She says it like she's talking about the movie, but we both know she's talking about us.

Chapter Forty-One

QUINN

After, we watch movies until we fall asleep on the couch.

He cooks me breakfast.

I pack. Research Vegas. Head to work.

When I get home, he's at my front door. Waiting for me. For more.

He shows off the design he's made for me—a raven haired pinup sitting on a stack of film canisters.

Then he flips the page to show off the stuff he's been working on for him.

I don't understand half the drawings. I certainly don't know anything about color or composition.

But I can see something in them.

Something he usually keeps buried.

We watch old movies until I fall asleep on the couch.

I wake up in his arms with that same feeling of wholeness.

We fix tea and breakfast, part for work, do it again and again.

Everything goes so fast. Packing and shipping my apartment consumes the weekend. Then Monday.

Then all of a sudden, I'm waking up at the break of dawn, meeting Wes's friends in front of a Santa Monica apartment building, next to a massive SUV.

It's good.

Like this is a party, not a sendoff.

But, God, it's still so obvious.

This is either the end.

Or the beginning.

———

"I'M NOT SURE WE'VE MET." A TALL GUY WITH LIGHT hair and broad shoulders offers his hand.

"We haven't." I take it. Shake.

He flashes a million-dollar smile. "Dean."

"Quinn."

"Oh I know." Dean winks at Wes. "I've heard a lot about you."

"Anything I should know?" I ask.

Wes jumps in. "Angel, don't listen to a word he says."

"Oh?" I ask.

Wes wraps his arms around my waist. Pulls my body into his. "He lives to start shit."

"But he wouldn't repeat lies." I look to Dean. "Would you?"

"Me? Never." He feigns innocence.

"My bullshit meter is going off." A short woman shakes her head. With disgust. No, feigned disgust. She's already smiling.

"Sunshine, the only word I heard there is *off*." He motions *come here*.

She squeals as he lifts her into his arms. "How are you making that dirty?"

"Me getting you off? Hmm, how could I make that dirty?" He leans down to kiss her.

It's not some chaste, PDA avoiding kiss.

They're full-on making out. Tongue. Grinding. Touching over the clothes.

It's hot.

And cute too.

They're opposites. She's barely five feet tall and dressed entirely in black. He's tall, tan, and dressed like an Abercrombie model.

"You're supposed to introduce your girlfriend," Wes says. "But if you guys want to give us a show…" He nudges me. "You want a show, angel?"

My cheeks flush. "Depends where it ends."

"You guys escalating to penetration this time?" Wes calls.

The woman flips him off.

Dean pulls back with a smile. "What do you think, sunshine? We could do it right here."

"Get real, dick face," she says.

The nickname makes him smile. "You trying to turn me on?"

"Why is it the word dick—"

"Oh, fuck, Chloe. You said it again." He brings his hands to her ass. Keeps her body against his. "We keep doing this—"

"Down boy." She laughs.

He leans in to whisper in her ear, but he doesn't lower his volume. At all. "That to me or my—"

Her laugh gets louder. "Both of you."

He sets her down.

She turns to us with a sheepish expression. "Sorry, I, uh… I'm Chloe. I've heard a lot about you, Quinn." She shakes with a strong grip.

"There's gossip, isn't there?" I ask.

She pulls two fingers over her mouth *my lips are sealed*.

"Sunshine, don't tell me that's true," Dean says.

She swats him.

He laughs. "I remember hearing something about Wes wanting that sweet virgin pussy."

"Oh yeah?" I turn to Wes.

"No." He shoots Dean a *get real* look.

Wait. "Oh. So everyone knows I'm—"

"Now, we do." Dean chuckles. "That's the oldest trick in the book, Quinn."

Shit, it is.

"You look smarter than that," he says.

"Glasses don't make someone smart." I tap my frames.

Dean shakes his head. "Maybe. But they make you look pretty fucking hot."

"Watch it." Wes pulls me closer. "Or I'll have to kill you."

"Oh?" Dean raises a brow.

Wes nods.

"You think I'm afraid of you?" He turns to his girl-friend. "Chloe could kill me like *that*." He snaps his fingers. "You want to show them something?"

"Mmm… hurting you… might be fun. But not right now." She reaches for the door.

He jumps in front of her. Opens it for her.

She shoots him a *you're ridiculous* look as she slips inside. "You make me wait another five minutes, I'm going to demand tea."

"There's a London Fog in the thermos in my back-pack." He smiles.

"Sometimes, I really love you," she says.

"Only sometimes?" he asks.

She nods, and motions *come here*.

He does.

They kiss like the ship is going down.

Dean turns to us. "Wes introduce you to everyone else on this expedition?"

"I know Griffin and Juliette," I say.

"Shit, you're hanging out without me?" Dean shakes his head. "Cruel."

"Yeah, can't imagine why we'd skip your invite," Wes says. "It's not like you're obnoxious or something."

Dean blows him a kiss.

He makes a show of dodging it.

I pretend to catch it.

Dean chuckles. "I like her." He slides into the car. Takes the seat next to his girlfriend.

Wes motions *after you*.

Our stuff is packed in the trunk.

This is it.

First stop Vegas.

Then the rest of my fucking life.

———

WE PICK UP GRIFFIN AND JULIETTE AT HIS APARTMENT.

He looks the same as always—all tall, tattooed, and handsome.

She looks different.

Don't get me wrong. I don't know Juliette that well. We've only met a few times. But she always seemed calm and together.

Right now...

There's something about her expression. Like she's fraying at the seams.

I get that.

I'm there.

I can't even imagine calling off an engagement.

Or having a sexy as sin best friend there to console me.

God, Griffin really is hot.

Don't get me wrong. My heart beats only for Wes. But I can certainly see the appeal of the dark-haired tattoo artist.

"Have you been to Vegas before?" I take the seat next to Juliette. Well, sorta. She and Griffin are on the bench in the back. Wes and I are in the single seats in front.

This car is ridiculously huge.

"Only as a kid." She smooths her denim shorts. "It's freezing in here."

"It's already ninety outside," Dean calls from the front seat. "If I turn the air down, we'll melt."

"There's a blanket behind you," Chloe says.

"Oh yeah?" Griffin chuckles. "Is it used?"

Chloe clears her throat.

Juliette blushes. Just barely, but she does. "I'll pass."

"Here." Griffin shrugs his hoodie off his shoulders. Slides it over hers.

She smiles wide and looks up at him with puppy eyes. "I'm not sure I can stomach advertising your shitty taste in music." She points to the band logo on the front.

One of those bluesy bands where the singer mumbles every line.

I know Wes hates this particular band, but they're kinda awesome.

Griffin taps her shoulder with his. "Thank fuck Chase isn't here."

Wes nods. "Truer words have never been spoken."

"Those are fighting words, Wes." She turns to me. "You've heard Chase's stuff?"

"Vaguely." I hear a lot about Chase's taste in music. But not the music so much. "I'm not super familiar with the genre."

"Play her something." Juliette pulls out her cell.

"Sorry, driver picks," Dean calls.

She shakes her head. "That's injustice."

"My car, my rules," he says.

"I thought it was driver picks?" she asks.

Chloe laughs. "She has a point."

"There's a reason people wish their exes would die in car crashes," Juliette says.

"Yeah, toxic masculinity." Griffin shakes his head.

She interrupts. "I'm the one that taught you—"

"You should be proud you taught me well," he says.

She shakes her head *no way* then offers me her cell. "Put on the playlist called *Fuck Jackson*."

"Damn, Jules, could you be more childish?" Griffin teases.

She shakes her head. "I don't know. Could you be more annoying?"

"I could try." He leans in to whisper something in her ear.

She laughs.

His eyes fix on mine. He studies my reaction, looking for something. "You gonna put the music on, Quinn?"

"I thought you hated it?" I ask.

He nods. "I hate this shit more than these fucking singers hate their exes."

"You certainly whine more than any of them do," Juliette says.

He chuckles. "Why'd I invite you anyway?"

"Masochism." Juliette brushes a dark strand behind her ear. Her long, wavy hair is in a messy ponytail. Stray strands fall in front of her face, framing her eyes in coffee brown.

She's pretty. Really pretty.

In a laid back way.

Like she doesn't really care if she's pretty or not.

She probably doesn't.

Which is so unfair.

But then...

Well, I like doing my hair and makeup. I like curating my wardrobe. I like cultivating my sexy librarian look.

A few months ago, I wouldn't have been able to think of myself as sexy.

But now...

Wes has done so much.

He really has.

I really like him.

So fucking much.

Ahem.

"You can think about Wes's dick after you start the music," Griffin says.

"Oh my God, Griff." Juliette shakes her head. "I'm sorry. He's an idiot."

Griffin shakes his head. "We all know what she's thinking."

"You don't have to say it," she says.

"No, I do." He leans in to whisper.

She laughs.

He scoots a little closer.

Neither of them realizes it, but it's obvious.

Or maybe I'm reading into stuff too much. Going on Wes's word. He thinks Griffin and Juliette are madly in love. But he doesn't know.

It's better to take people at their word.

If they say there's nothing there...

Well, it's really none of my business.

Even if other people's problems are so much easier than mine.

Ahem.

"Pretty please." I offer Chloe my best smile. I don't really know her, but she seems sweet. Well, helpful.

She nods and passes me the aux cable.

"What happened to driver picks?" Dean teases.

She flips him off.

He grabs her hand, brings it to his mouth, sucks on her fingertip.

She giggles as he sucks on her digit. "Hands on the wheel."

"You're better than the wheel," he says.

"And if we die in a car crash?" she asks.

"Then we'll die together." He tries to make it teasing, but there's something in his voice. He means it.

Griffin shakes his head. "You'll make this guy proud." He motions to the stereo. A peppy guitar riff fades into energetic vocals.

Sure enough, the singer is cursing his ex's name.

I don't have any exes of note, certainly none I hate, but I get the impulse to scream about lost love.

The thought of this being the end...

I can't go there.

"Fuck, I must like you a lot." Griffin shakes his head. "This is such awful shit."

"Jesus, Griff." Wes shakes his head. "Tact."

"You hate it too," Griffin says.

Wes motions *kinda*. "I'm coming around."

"Since when?" Griffin asked.

"Since I learned to expand my horizons beyond my narrow point of view," Wes says.

"There's no fucking way you've done that." Griffin laughs.

"Which of us is bitching about music we didn't like in high school?" Wes asks.

"I suggested it," Griffin says.

"Fuck, you both realize I have to deal with shit at the shop all the time?" Dean shakes his head. "You seem nice, Juliette, but I can't take this shit lying down."

She laughs. "I'm always up for a challenge."

"I have a suggestion," Dean says. "A way to decide what we play after this."

He's acting all tough, but he is letting her finish the playlist.

It's sweet.

He's kinda like Wes. Playing the shit starter when he's really—

Well, I don't know, but Chloe seems like the kind of woman who doesn't put up with that.

"Oh God." Chloe shakes her head. "Don't say it."

"Ten fingers," Dean says.

Chloe bursts into laughter.

Juliette too.

Then Griffin.

And Wes.

I do too.

Dean really is ridiculous.

"Who wins?" I ask. "Who gets to pick the music?"

"Last one standing, of course," Dean says.

"You do realize I'm a virgin," I say.

"Yeah, but if you want to go on about those details, I'm all ears," Dean says.

"I will kill you," Wes says.

"Not if I kill him first," Chloe says.

Chapter Forty-Two

QUINN

"I'll start," Dean says. "Never have I ever lusted after a virgin." He makes a show of dropping a finger.

"Can he do that?" Wes asks.

Dean nods. Motions for Wes to drop his finger.

Chloe nudges Dean. "Dick face, shouldn't you keep your attention on the road?"

"You want to take over?" he asks.

She nods *sure*.

He motions to the wheel *take it then*.

"I'm not climbing into your lap," she says.

"Then why bother?" he teases.

She shakes her head *you're ridiculous*, but it does nothing to hide her smile.

"See." He motions to the windshield. Keeps his back to us. "Eyes on the road."

"Good boy," she says.

"Sunshine, you keep talking like that and I'll—"

"Down boy."

He laughs. "I'll think about it."

They're cute, but she has a point.

Sure, we're stuck in traffic on the ten, but we're still in a several thousand pound killing machine.

Car accidents are incredibly dangerous.

Sure, I didn't see many working as a scribe for an allergist, but I've heard horror stories from Owen.

And, well, if I go into medicine… who knows? Maybe I'll become an ER doctor. Maybe I'll spend my entire life glued to my stethoscope.

No family. No friends. No lovers.

Just medicine.

I… Uh…

Next question. "How are we doing this?" I ask. "I mean, is it clockwise, or—"

"Clockwise is good." Wes reaches over the space between our seats. Offers his hand.

I take it. Squeeze tightly.

His skin is soft in some places. Calloused in others.

This is good.

Hanging with Wes.

With his friends. With people who are practically my friends. Almost. Kinda.

We're getting there.

"Who dropped a finger?" Dean asks.

"I'm not narrating this for you," Chloe says.

"All right. How about you have to say when you're out?" Dean suggests.

"That's actually a good idea," she says.

"I have my moments," he says.

"Not that many." Griffin's chuckle fills the car.

He's still pressed up against Juliette. She's still hugging his hoodie to her chest.

They make a really cute couple.

Sickeningly cute.

I mean, they're not a couple.

And I'm totally minding my own business about that. Totally.

"It's fair." Juliette holds up her hand. Nine fingers. "We were all teenagers once. We've all lusted after virgins."

"Don't think that's what Dean means." Griffin brushes a wavy hair behind his ear. "He means getting off on conquering uncharted territory." He winks at Wes.

Juliette scrunches her nose in distaste. "But where's the line? How do you say if your lust was because of the person or because of their inexperience?"

"You know." Griffin nudges Wes. "Right?"

Wes shoots him a *what the fuck* look.

My cheeks flush. God, we're so... I...

Ahem. "This isn't... You're not... It's not about that." Right? "It's about me. Us. I mean, um—"

"Angel, you know I don't have that kind of capacity for self-reflection." He shrugs like he doesn't give a fuck.

It's convincing.

But I know better.

I stare into his eyes. "Is it?"

He stares back at me. "Quinn, you could have fucked a thousand guys before me. I would have said yes."

Griffin claps. "This is a beautiful moment."

"Oh my God." Juliette shakes her head. "Let them have it."

"Proud of Wes for facing his shit. It's not like him," Griffin says.

She presses her palm to her forehead. "You do realize you don't have to verbalize every single thought you have?"

"Where's the fun in that?" he asks.

"Gotta agree there," Dean calls. "It's any virgin, ever, for any reason."

Everyone groans.

Even me.

"Your turn, sunshine." Dean nudges his girlfriend.

She nods. "Never have I ever harassed a subordinate."

He chuckles. "I'm out. Probably need to lose two for that."

"Probably." She laughs.

Wes holds up his nine fingers. "Never had a subordinate. Emma is technically management."

"Not at first," Griffin says. "And you were really fucking obnoxious."

"She liked it. She was begging me to sub in for Hunter," Wes says.

Griffin chuckles. "Keep telling yourself that."

"I did," Wes says.

"Fucking yourself to it maybe?" Griffin raises an eyebrow.

"Oh my God." Juliette shakes her head again. "You have to—"

"I won't," Griffin says.

"All right. You got me," Wes says.

Griffin, Juliette, Chloe, and I hold up our nine fingers. We've all lusted after virgins. (Who didn't lust after a fellow virgin in high school?) But we've never harassed subordinates.

The game moves to me. "Never have I ever gotten a tattoo."

The entire car groans. Everyone else loses a finger.

"Gonna have to change that," Wes says.

"Until then." I tap his index finger, the one curled into his palm. "That's mine."

"Already was." His smile gets dirty. Very dirty.

I... Oh...

Yes. Good idea. But, I, um...

Ahem.

Griffin takes his turn. Says something about how he's never done a water color tattoo.

Juliette brings it back to sex. "Never have I ever sent a nude picture."

"Really?" Griffin raises a brow. "You're missing out."

Her blush deepens. "I don't need my pictures on some horrible website."

"You think someone would do that?" he asks.

"I don't know. It happens," she says.

"Jackson—"

"I thought I knew him."

"Yeah, but would he really—"

"Can we not?"

"I would never," he says. "No matter what happened."

"Okay. I... Um... Your turn, Wes." She swallows hard.

Griffin leans in to whisper.

She nods.

He turns to Wes. They trade a knowing glance. I haven't got a clue what it means, but I'm glad they're communicating.

Fuck, I've only been "dating" Wes for a month and the thought of walking away from him makes me sick.

I can't imagine calling off an engagement.

Wes nods. "Never have I ever gotten anything pierced."

Dean chuckles. "That for me, specifically?"

"How many times a day do you really need to bring it up?" Griffin teases.

"Until it stops being interesting." Dean laughs. "You gotta admit. You're curious."

"Don't like guys." Griffin's voice is completely even. He has no problem with the idea of liking guys. He's not all scared of being accused of being gay the way so many straight guys are. He's just not interested.

"Curious what it would be like if you did it," Dean says. "Admit it."

"Of course," Griffin says. "If it makes sex better—"

"Jesus Christ, Griff, don't invite him to talk about it." Wes shakes his head. "He'll never stop."

"Does it make it better?" I ask.

"E tu, brute?" Wes mimes being stabbed in the gut.

"Where did you learn Shakespeare?" I ask.

"I know things," he says.

I shake my head *you don't*.

He laughs. "Know how to make you come."

"The piercing helps with that," Dean says.

"Helps you make Chloe come?" Griffin asks.

Chloe clears her throat.

"Yeah." Dean laughs. "Makes it more fun for me too."

Chloe clears her throat louder.

"It's really win-win," Dean says.

"Jesus Christ," Wes mutters.

"It was your question," I say.

"'Cause of these." His fingertip brushes my earring. My earlobe. The line of my jaw.

Fuck, his touch is soft. Tender. Hot.

I want to be alone with him.

I want to be out of this car.

I want to fuck him senseless.

We're doing that.

Maybe not tonight.

But really fucking soon.

And, I, uh…

"Drop a finger, angel," Wes says.

I do.

It moves back to Dean.

We go in circles forever.

The guys make a point of knocking each other out.

Well, the tattoo artists make a point of knocking each other out.

It comes down to me and Juliette.

I play the *I've never had sex* card.

Then I let her win.

She's heartbroken.

She deserved to pick the music.

————

I CAN'T LIE.

I kinda love Juliette's taste in music.

I kinda love Juliette.

We stop at Barstow to pee, get coffee and tea, trade seats.

Wes takes over driving duty. I sit with Juliette. Talk about undergrad. She went to USC too.

We never shared a class—it's a school of tens of thousands, it would be weirder if we did share a class—but there's still plenty of gossip.

When we hit Baker, we head to some shop known for its jerky, hot sauce, dried fruit, and alien theme.

There's a fake spaceship in the parking lot. And all sorts of Area 51 signs inside the shop.

I'm not really a jerky fan, but I do appreciate the atmosphere.

I get an iced tea, pee, join Wes in the car.

This time, we're in the back.

We talk, but not about anything important. About the last few movies we watched, and his intention to show me *Mission Impossible*, and the tattoo designs he's been working on.

He's perfected my pinup.

And he's designed something for himself too. A heart

made of glass with this intricate, rose adorned lock.

Because roses make him think of me.

And I…

Well, he doesn't say it, but it's obvious.

He wants to give me the key to his heart.

Or maybe he's sure it's completely closed to anyone and anything, including me.

I… Uh…

I mean, it's obvious it has something to do with me.

Just not what exactly it has to do with me.

I talk about Chicago and Owen and med school. The latter still feels like a prison, but I want to be home. Not forever. Not even for a while.

For long enough to see my brother and my parents.

To tell them…

Well, I'm not sure yet. I'm not ready to say it out loud. But I'm getting there.

I'm pretty sure I don't want to go to med school.

I don't have any idea what else I'm doing with my life.

But there's something about cruising down the highway with friends—

My life feels full of possibilities.

After a while, I rest my head on Wes's shoulder. Watch the desert pass us by.

It's beautiful. Bright blue sky, long stretches of sand, thorny cacti, burnt orange rocks.

I relax until we come up on the city.

It's there, in front of us, an actual oasis in the middle of nothing.

The city looks different in the day. Well, different than the pictures I've seen.

It's so strange. A giant pyramid, a fake castle, the New York City skyline, all this modern steel and glass.

Wes brushes my hair behind my neck. Brings his lips to my ear. "First thing I do when I get to our hotel room—"

"Pee?"

He chuckles. "Fuck, angel. You're taking this literally."

"Always."

"Sure. After I pee, and wash my hands, then—"

"Then?"

"I'm gonna make you come."

Chapter Forty-Three

WES

Quinn stretches her arms over her head.

A yawn falls off her lips.

Her dress hikes up her thighs.

Fuck, she has gorgeous legs.

"Why does sitting in a car make you so tired?" She lets out another yawn. Looks around the hotel room.

It's nice enough. A king bed with purple sheets. Too hard carpet. Framed stock art on the walls.

A wide window that looks out on Las Vegas Boulevard.

Fuck, The Strip really is beautiful. It's faded and gold in the bright sunlight, but that's stunning in its own way.

The afternoon light flows through the windows.

Surrounds Quinn in a soft glow.

My angel with Sin City behind her.

Fuck, why is that so hot?

I push my suitcase out of the way. Cross the room toward Quinn.

She yelps as I wrap my arm around her waist.

"That a *what are you doing* or *God, please don't stop*?" I ask.

Her hazel eyes fix on mine. "I'm not sure."

"You're not?"

She nods. "Depends what you do next."

"You baiting me, angel?"

"Maybe."

Fuck, she is.

My cock stirs.

My fingers curl into the soft fabric of her dress.

God dammit, I love this confident, in control side of her.

I...

Maybe I do love her.

I don't know.

I have to figure it out in the next thirty-six hours.

And I will.

But right now—

"Take off your panties." I slide my hand to her ass. Pull her body against mine.

She lets out a soft groan as my cock brushes her stomach. "Fuck, Wes—"

"Yeah?"

"I... Uh..."

"Go on..."

"In this position. I, um... How do you get hard so fast?"

"You."

Her cheeks flush. Her eyelids flutter closed.

She rises to her tiptoes.

Presses her lips to mine.

Fuck, she tastes good. Like tea and honey.

She always tastes like tea and honey.

I can't go near a bag of Lipton's without thinking about her lips.

I slip my tongue into her mouth.

She digs her fingers into my shoulders, pressing the cotton of my t-shirt into my skin.

I need this shirt gone.

I need her dress gone.

I need her naked on that bed.

Trying to figure out how I can give her my heart is impossible.

This is easy.

This is everything.

"Panties off." I slip my hands under her dress.

She groans as my fingertips skim her hips.

I push her panties off her ass. Bend to pull them to her knees. Ankles.

She kicks them off her feet.

"Bed." I stand. Wrap my arms around her. Pull her into my chest.

She squeals as I carry her to the bed.

Groans as I lay her flat on her back.

Fuck, this is a beautiful sight. Quinn splayed out on the purple sheets, her red hair falling over her flushed cheeks, her sundress falling over her light limbs, afternoon light surrounding her in a soft glow.

She really is an angel.

She saved me from—

Fuck, I don't even know how to describe it. I never would have found the strength to stand up to my mom without her.

I wouldn't be trying to pour my heart into my work.

Or trying to communicate with my brothers.

And—

No, I'm not getting lost in that shit now.

No more thinking.

More making her come.

"Spread your legs, baby." I pull my t-shirt over my head and toss it aside.

Her eyes travel down my body slowly. My chin, shoulders, chest, stomach, hips, cock.

I'm already so fucking hard.

These jeans are torture.

But I don't fucking care.

I only care about making her come.

Now.

She nods as she pushes her legs apart.

"Pull your dress to your waist." I slide onto the bed, on my knees. "I want to look at you."

"Wes—"

"Don't make me ask twice."

Her pupils dilate at the dirty demand. Her fingers dig into her skin.

Slowly, she pulls the dress up her thighs.

Fuck, she's beautiful.

For a long moment, I savor the sight of her.

Then I place my body between her legs.

Lower myself onto the bed.

My fingers curl around her ankles.

My lips brush the inside of her knee.

I move closer, closer, closer—

She reaches for me. Finds my shoulder.

Her nails dig into my skin. "Wes, please—"

"Please what, angel?" I nip at her inner thigh.

She lets out a mumbled moan. "Please."

My balls tighten.

I fucking love the way she says that.

That she's always so polite.

And under my spell.

That I know exactly what she means.

Please make me come.

Fuck, I can't think of anything better. I really can't.

I bring my hands to her thighs.

In one swift motion, I pin her legs to the bed.

I drag my lips up her thigh. Closer, closer, closer—

There.

She groans as my lips brush her cunt.

She tastes so fucking good. I want to lick her up and down. To savor every drop of her.

But I have to tease her first.

I have to drive her out of her fucking mind.

I press my lips to the apex of her thigh.

As softly as I can, I drag my lips down her thigh. All the way to the inside of her knee.

"Wes." Her nails are sharp against my skin. "Please—"

"Please?" I murmur into her thigh.

"Please."

I work my way back up her skin.

"Fuck." She tugs at me a little harder.

But, still, I tease her.

Up one thigh, over her sweet cunt, down the other thigh.

Again and again.

Until her nails are digging enough to draw blood.

And her groans are bouncing around the room.

And her pleas are so loud and needy that *I* can't take it.

Finally, I bring my mouth to Quinn's cunt.

I lick her up and down.

Slowly.

So fucking slowly.

I savor her sweet taste for a long moment.

I scrape my teeth against her lips. Plunge my tongue inside her. Suck on her clit.

"Fuck." She bucks against my mouth. "Wes. Fuck."

I bring my hands to her ass. Dig my fingers into her flesh to hold her in place.

Then I work her exactly how she needs me to.

Long flicks of my tongue.

Then shorter ones.

Faster.

Harder.

Until it's exactly what she likes.

She tugs at my hair. Claws at my skin. Groans my name like it's a curse.

I keep the same pressure.

Same speed.

"Wes. Oh my God. Fuck." Her hand knots in my hair.

She groans my name as she comes.

Her toes curl into the sheets.

Her thighs fight my hands.

I lick her through her orgasm. When she's finished, I plant a soft kiss on her pelvis. Her stomach. Her hip bone.

Her inner thigh.

I give her a moment to catch her breath.

Then I dive back between her legs.

I don't tease.

I suck on her clit until she's groaning.

I push her to the edge again.

She comes quickly this time.

Her breathe catches. Her limbs shake. Her nails scrape my skin.

She gets wetter. Sweeter.

I pull back enough to look up at her.

Fuck, it's so beautiful watching pleasure spread over her face.

I'll never get tired of it.

Ever.

She looks down at me with hazy eyes, her expression equal parts satisfaction and need.

"Wes..." She pushes herself onto her elbows. "You need to fuck me."

Yeah, but not yet. "Later."

Her eyes fix on mine. "Now." She sits up. Reaches for my jeans. Gets my stomach.

Her fingers brush my skin.

She looks up at me with hazy eyes.

With affection. Desire. Pure, unbridled need. "Please."

My cock pulses.

Fuck, I really love the way she says that.

I want to fuck her. Badly.

At the moment, I can't exactly remember why I'm waiting. Something about things being perfect like this. About fear of change. Of her getting what she wants from me then leaving.

She's not like that.

But I can't shake the idea.

"Quinn—" I slide my arm around her waist. "Later."

"Tonight?"

I nod. "Tonight."

She brings both hands to my shoulders. "I'm not waiting for tonight—"

"Angel—"

"I need to make you come now."

Fuck.

"On your back."

God dammit, she's hot bossy. "Take off your dress."

"You first."

Fair enough. I climb up the bed. Lower myself onto my back.

She reaches around. Unzips her dress. Pulls it over her head.

Her eyes fix on mine as she does away with her bra.

She straddles me.

Her hands plant on my hips.

Slowly, she lowers her body onto mine. Grinds against me, rubbing her cunt against my hard-on.

My stupid fucking jeans are in the way.

But she still feels so fucking good.

I reach for her. Get her hip.

It's not enough.

I bring my hand to her chest. Toy with her nipple with my thumb and forefinger.

Her eyelids flutter together. Her head falls to one side. Her hair curtains her gorgeous face.

She groans with equal parts agony and ecstasy.

Still, she grinds against me.

She teases me until I'm aching, then she slides down my thighs, brings her hands to my waist, undoes my jeans.

She pushes the fabric off my hips.

The denim.

Then the cotton of my boxers.

Her eyes go wide as she wraps her hand around my cock.

She looks at it like it's her favorite thing in the world.

She teases me with her thumb. Then it's long strokes of her index finger and thumb.

Just the right pressure.

Just the right speed.

Fuck.

Quinn's eyes meet mine for a second. They fill with determination. Need. Lust.

My cock quivers in her hand.

She's too fucking good at this.

I wish I could take credit, but it's all her.

Her hair falls over her eyes as she brings her mouth to me.

She brushes her lips against my tip.

Then it's her soft, flat tongue.

I let my eyelids flutter closed.

Let my body sink into the bed.

She wraps her hand around me as she takes me into her mouth.

She starts soft.

Then gets harder.

Deeper.

Fuck, her mouth feels good.

Soft. Wet. Mine.

I want every part of her to be mine.

I really fucking do.

I reach for her. Bring one hand to the back of her head. The other to her chest.

My fingers brush her nipples.

She groans against my cock.

I play with her tits as she sucks me off.

The harder I toy, the deeper she takes me.

We fall into a perfect rhythm.

She works me.

I toy with her.

Again and again.

Until I'm there.

"Fuck, Quinn." I dig my fingers into the back of her head. "I'm gonna come."

She keeps her mouth glued to my cock.

She works me through my orgasm.

I groan her name as I come.

My cock pulses as I fill her sweet mouth.

She waits until I've spilled every drop, then she swallows hard.

She pushes herself up. Brushes her hair from her eyes. Looks down at me like she has me exactly where she wants me.

She does.

But then there's nowhere else I'd rather be.

I push myself up. Wrap my arms around her. Kiss her hard.

She isn't shy about tasting herself on my lips.

She kisses back, hard and hungry.

"I need to make you come again, angel." I brush her hair behind her ear.

She stares back at me. "Then fuck me."

God dammit, maybe I need to reconsider.

I want to be inside her.

To be one with her.

To feel her come on my cock.

God dammit, I really want her coming on my cock.

"Give me a minute." I pull her close for a moment, then I climb out of bed, move to the bathroom, pee, wash my hands.

A knock interrupts. "Get dressed. You're coming to dinner with us." Griffin's voice flows through the door.

"Go away," I call back.

His friend laughs.

Quinn does too.

I step out of the bathroom.

She wraps the blanket around her chest. Shoots me a *should we* look.

I shake my head. We should stay here. In this room. Forever.

"I'm kinda starving." She presses her hand to her stomach. "Let's eat. Then after—" she motions to the bed.

"Have after dinner plans for us already," I say.

Her lips curl into a frown.

"But after that."

"Okay." She smiles. "After that."

"You have twenty minutes," Griffin says. "The place downstairs."

"Sorry," his friend says. "We, um, didn't want to interrupt."

"Speak for yourself, Jules. I wanted the free audio porn," he says.

She laughs. "Okay… Um… see you then."

Quinn slides off the bed. "Until then."

Chapter Forty-Four

WES

The six of us cram into the hotel's nicest restaurant, a sushi place with insane prices and strong drinks.

The food is decent at best. But with my friends here, and Quinn by my side, it's perfect.

Everyone makes a point of including her. And Juliette.

The girls go over the plans for tomorrow. Museums. Or the pool. Or gambling. Or the fake Venetian canals. Or the sweet air-conditioning of our respective hotel rooms.

Okay, maybe I'm the one lobbying for that.

But I can't help myself.

Quinn is too fucking irresistible.

———

"Oh my God." Quinn cringes as she steps onto the walkway. "Is this really the temperature at night?"

I nod. I'm not exactly a Vegas regular, but I've been enough to know this is a normal summer evening.

She looks at me like I'm crazy. "And people come here by choice?"

"Why you here?"

"You dragged me."

"You want to go home?"

Her lips curl into a coy smile. She wants to be here. She wants to be here forever.

I do too.

"'Cause we can hop in the car and head home right now," I say.

"It's not our car," she says.

That's true. But—"We can take a taxi to the airport."

Her gaze shifts to the hotel across the way—the New York, New York. "Well…"

"Well…"

"We did drive all this way." She moves onto the concrete walkway. It's crowded with people. Tourists taking in the kitsch of a fake castle next to a fake skyline, gamblers looking to win big, drunk or soon to be drunk twenty-somethings looking to *connect*—

Fuck, why are we here instead of our hotel room?

Quinn looks so fucking delicious in her snug white dress. Fuck, the way that thing hugs her curvy hips.

I have to stop staring or I'm going to get hard.

And I'm pretty sure security is serious about kicking out miscreants.

I need to focus on something besides her perfect body.

Like teasing back. "It's just about the long drive?"

She nods. "It would be a shame to miss out on the glory of New York City."

"Or you're full of shit."

"Hmm… seems more likely I want to take in the skyline."

"It's so realistic."

"You've been?"

I nod. "A long time ago."

"It's been a while for me too." Her eyes meet mine. "I can see you there."

"You too."

"Really?"

"Yeah. You never considered New York?" I ask.

She shakes her head. "No. It's always been Chicago. I've always assumed I'd end up there. Even when I came to USC trying to escape. It still felt like Chicago was my fate." She clears her throat. "But it's not special enough for a casino."

"So it's clearly inferior."

"Though…"

"Yeah?"

"I don't see a Los Angeles casino." She interlocks her fingers with mine and leads me across the bridge.

"This whole place is a Los Angeles casino."

"Is that so?" Quinn sighs as she steps into the air-conditioned casino.

"We're a desert, this is a desert."

"I'm just saying. A tiny Hollywood sign and a fake pier would go far."

"I could see it."

"Me too." She inhales deeply as we pass a pretzel stand. Her lips part with a giggle. "Just like New York."

"You look like you belong in New York, angel."

"You mean this?" She smooths her dress. Shoots me an impossibly coy smile.

I nod.

"Or maybe these?" She taps her red heels together.

Fuck me.

"Wes?"

"Yeah."

"You okay?"

I shake my head. Wrap my arms around her. Pull her into a slow, deep kiss.

Her lips close around mine. She sucks softly. Then harder. Then it's her tongue swirling around mine.

Fuck, she tastes good.

Like the chocolate mousse she had for dessert.

I need to have her now.

I need to have her always.

Quinn pulls back with a needy sigh. "Tease."

"You started it."

"How?"

My fingers skim the hem of her dress.

Her lips curl into a coy smile. She shrugs and turns back to the path. "You didn't tell me where we're going."

"Thought you wanted to take in the skyline."

She laughs. "You can't see it inside."

"It's still a hundred and four outside."

Quinn groans in agony. "It is, isn't it?"

"Yeah."

"You're evil."

I slide my arm around her waist.

She looks up at me with a wide smile.

Fuck, this is addicting.

I want to stay here with her forever.

I want this to be forever.

I want fucking everything.

"Evil and incredibly vague," she says.

"We're doing something you'll like."

"That's all I get?"

"Yeah."

We stop at the escalator. It heads down to the casino floor. It's a wall of sensation. Bright lights, vivid colors, conversation, clinking glasses, the ding of slot machines.

Quinn's eyes go wide. "God, it's so…"

"Much."

She nods. "How much time do we have before our—what are we doing?"

"Nice try."

She shrugs *who me?*

"About an hour."

"Well." She motions to the casino floor. "Shall we?"

I offer my hand.

She giggles as she takes it.

I lead her onto the escalator. We hug the right side to leave room for people to pass, but no one does.

For a place modeled after New York, the attitude is strangely laid back.

I stay close to Quinn, explaining the games of chance as we survey the floor.

She shakes her head at slots. Dismisses craps. Stops at the roulette table.

Her fingers skim the wood. "Do people really do it?" Her gaze shifts to the table. To the dozen bets scattered over felt.

"They're not here for the free cigarettes."

"Maybe it's the free booze."

Right on cue, a cocktail waitress stops by. "What can I get for you?"

She shoots me a *should we?*

I nod *hell yes.* "Jack and coke."

"Gin and tonic." Quinn leans in close enough to whisper. "Are we really gambling?"

"Why the hell not?"

"It's just so…"

"Why'd you want to come to Vegas?"

"It always seemed so…"

"Like the place where you wanted to lose your virginity?"

Her cheeks flush. "Fun."

"That won't be?"

Her blush deepens.

"You two in for this round?" the dealer asks.

"Yeah. Can I cash this in?" I pull out my wallet. Hand him five twenties.

He hands back ten chips.

I give half to Quinn.

She runs her fingers over the edge of the stack. "How do I know what to bet?"

"What's your heart say?"

Her blush deepens. "I think I'm more in touch with my libido at the moment."

"There's no sixty-nine on the board."

"Oh my God."

The dealer shoots us a look. "Last call."

Quinn bites her lip.

"You can wait, angel."

"But it's happening now."

He waves his hand over the table *that's it* then spins the wheel.

The ball bounces along the slotted edges.

Quinn leans over the table. "I have to decide what I want before the next round."

"There's no rush."

"There is." Her fingers curl into the table. "There isn't much time left."

"What's your heart say?"

"I don't know." She presses her lips together. "I'm trying to listen, but I'm not sure."

Story of my fucking life.

"Thirty-two," the dealer calls. He settles bets with quiet professionalism.

"I want to be in this round." Quinn squeezes the chips

in her palm.

"Go with your gut," I say.

She looks at me like I'm crazy.

"First instinct, red or black," I say.

"Red," she replies.

"There you go."

She shoots me that same look.

"Try it."

"But…"

"It's ten bucks. Try it."

She turns back to the table. Leans over enough to place a single chip on red.

The dealer spins the wheel.

Quinn turns to me. "What if it's not red?"

"Then it's not."

She stares up at me like I'm not understanding.

Maybe I'm not.

But, at this point, it's really all I can say.

———

RED WINS.

Quinn shrieks and jumps into my arms.

We hang at the roulette table, placing ten-dollar bet after ten-dollar bet, until we bust.

Seeing her excitement fills me in this way nothing else does.

It takes all my attention.

I barely make our show time.

Quinn's eyes go wide as soon as she sees the sign.

It's one of those contortionist shows.

One about sex and love.

It's a trip.

Topless performers swim around a martini glass with

symmetrical movements, meeting to kiss, touch, dry hump.

A lean guy glides down a silk hanging from the ceiling.

A woman in a thong contorts herself into a tiny box.

We laugh.

Drink.

Kiss.

When the show ends, Quinn brings her lips to my ear. "You made a promise."

"What's that?" I play dumb.

"You know what it is, Wes." Her fingers brush my thighs, over my jeans. "Tonight, you're taking my virginity."

Chapter Forty-Five

QUINN

Click, click.

The door beeps as Wes pulls the key from the lock. He turns the handle, pushes the door open, motions *after me*.

It's the same hotel room from this afternoon.

But it's a completely different universe.

This is really happening.

We're really...

Fuck.

His fingers brush my lower back. Then it's the soft pressure of his palm.

He leads me into the suite. Past the couch, the wet bar, the bed. All the way to the window.

Wes draws the curtains. Lets in the light of the strip.

It's gorgeous.

Bright.

Gaudy.

Perfect.

He turns his body toward mine. Cups my hip with his palm. "You want the city to see this?"

"Can they see all the way up here?"

His voice drops to something low and demanding. "I dunno, angel. You want them to see?"

"Maybe." There is something hot about the idea of being watched. One day. "But not today."

He nods *fair* and pulls my body into his.

I melt into him, one part at a time. Thighs, crotch, stomach, chest, lips.

Fuck, he tastes good.

Like rum and sugar and Wes.

This might be it.

We have tomorrow.

My flight leaves first thing the next morning.

That's barely thirty-six hours to figure this out.

I hope it's not our only night together.

But if it is…

I'm enjoying the hell out of it.

He brushes my hair behind my ear. "I tell you how fucking fantastic you look tonight?"

"Yeah." I lean into his touch. "But I still want to hear it again."

"You look gorgeous."

"Thank you."

His fingers skim my jawline.

"You do too."

Gently, he slides my glasses off my face.

I stare up at him. Even in my heels, I'm a little shorter than Wes. There's something right about that. Our bodies fit together. "You're not insisting?"

"Don't want to break them."

"You're gonna get that—"

"I might."

"But you…" I suck a breath through my teeth. Exhale slowly. Yeah, I want this to be perfect, like something out of a movie. But the reality of awkwardness and pain and—

"You're scared?"

"A little."

"That's okay."

"It is?"

"Yeah." He sets my glasses on the side table. He takes a step backward. Motions *come here*. "I just need you to breathe."

"Breathe?"

He nods. "Can you do that?"

"I think so."

"Good."

Again, he motions *come here*.

I follow him to the bed.

One hand goes to the strap of my dress. The other goes to my ass.

Wes pulls me into a slow, deep kiss.

I rise to my tiptoes.

Knot my fingers in his hair.

Arch my hips to meet his.

I can feel his kiss all the way in my bones.

It's hard to explain.

It's deeper, fuller, harder.

Better.

So much better.

He pushes my straps off my shoulder.

The right.

Then the left.

Slowly, Wes traces the neckline of my dress with his fingertips. Right to left. Left to right.

He dips a little lower the next time.

Lower.

Beneath the stiff fabric of my dress.

His fingertips brush my skin.

The outline of my breath.

Beneath that.

Fuck.

The friction of his digit against my nipple—

It's feather light.

So soft I can barely feel it.

But, fuck, how I feel it.

I pull him closer.

Kiss him deeper.

He teases with those same feather light touches. Right to left, left to right, lower, again, again.

Then back up.

He's slow.

So fucking slow.

Too fucking slow.

Just slow enough.

When his fingertips hit my collarbones, he brings one hand to my back. Right to my dress's zipper.

Drags his lips to my ear. "Turn around."

I do.

He bends as he pulls my zipper down my spine.

Stands as he traces its path.

His fingers are light against my skin.

It's not enough.

It's too much.

I'm already buzzing.

I'm already pent up.

I'm already desperate.

"Please," I breathe.

"Please what, angel?"

"Please fuck me."

"I will." He brings his lips to my neck. "Soon."

"Now."

"No, angel." His lips brush my neck. Softly. Then harder. "I'm not even close to done with you yet."

My sex clenches.

My knees knock.

My legs shake.

He's so fucking sexy.

It's wrong.

It really is.

"Remember." He scrapes his teeth against my skin. "Breathe."

I nod, like I've got it under control.

But I don't.

There's so much whirling inside me.

I want him.

I need him.

I really, really fucking need this.

Deep breath.

Slow exhale.

Maybe I don't know about tomorrow.

Or med school.

Or the rest of my life.

But right now, I have absolutely no doubts.

I want Wes.

I push my dress to my waist.

He bends to pull it all the way to my ankles. His fingertips skim the backs of my calves.

Slowly, he traces a line up my body. Along the crook of my knee, up my thighs, over my ass.

He stops at the straps of my thong. "You wear this for me, angel?"

"Yeah," I breathe.

"You like teasing me?"

I nod.

"You like driving me out of my fucking mind?"

Again, I nod. But it's hard to grasp that possibility. It's hard to believe I affect him at all.

I arch my back until my ass is against his crotch.

There's no denying it.

He's hard.

For me.

He wants me.

Needs me.

Maybe as badly as I need him.

God, I need him so fucking badly.

"Please." I rub my ass against him, over his jeans. "Wes, please."

"Yeah, angel?"

"Make me come."

"Fuck." He traces the outline of my thong. "Quinn."

"Please."

He drags one hand up my back, all the way to my bra. With one flick of his fingers, he unhooks it.

The strapless thing tumbles to the floor.

With his other hand, he pushes my thong off my hips.

There.

Except for my heels, I'm naked.

It's far from the first time I've been naked with Wes.

But it's the first time we're doing this.

It's the first time, period.

My heart thuds against my chest. It's so loud. It's the only thing in my head.

"Breathe, angel." He rubs my shoulder with one hand. Slides his other arm around my waist.

My body melts into his.

His lips find my neck.

He winds me up with those soft scrapes of his teeth. Just enough to hurt. Just enough I feel it everywhere.

He works his way to my shoulder, then he moves to the other side and does it again.

Every brush of his mouth winds me tighter.

I'm so fucking close.

So fucking empty.

I've never been so acutely aware of how much I need to be full.

How much I need *him* inside me.

His fingers trail up my thigh.

Closer.

Closer.

There.

His hand brushes my sex.

Softly.

Then harder.

He teases me with one finger.

Then two.

Fuck, I need that.

"Please," I breathe.

He doesn't ask what I mean.

He knows exactly what I mean.

He toys with my neck as he slides a finger inside me.

The pressure is intense.

Almost too much.

It hurts.

In a good way.

But it really fucking hurts.

Breathe.

Slow inhale.

Slow exhale.

"You okay, angel?" His breath warms my ear.

I nod. I am. I really am.

He holds me close with one arm.

Then he drives his finger deeper.

Deeper.

Fuck.

My eyelids flutter closed.

My senses tune to Wes.

The pressure of his finger.

His hand against my hip.

His teeth against my neck.

He pulls his finger back.

Adds a second.

Slowly, he drives inside me.

It's not *him,* but it's close.

It makes me fuller.

And emptier.

I need this.

But I need him more.

"Please," I breath, though I'm not sure exactly what it is I'm demanding. "Fuck me."

"Soon." He pulls his fingers back then drives them into me a little harder.

I reach for something to steady myself. Find his jeans.

My fingers curl into the denim.

My back melts into his chest.

He drives his fingers into me again.

Again.

Again.

His rhythm steadies.

I can feel him stretching me.

It doesn't hurt exactly.

It's more a pressure.

A hell of a lot of pressure.

He pulls back. "You okay?"

"Yeah?"

"Too much."

"No."

"You're wincing." He nods to the mirror in front of us.

Oh. My cheeks flush. I'm still shy about watching. About him watching.

"Look at your reflection, angel."

My gaze stays on my shoes.

"Quinn, look."

"I can't."

"See how fucking gorgeous you are." He releases his grip of my waist. Brings his hands to my chin.

Slowly, he tilts my chin.

My gaze travels up my calves.

My thighs.

Fuck, that's his hand between my legs.

It's so fucking sexy.

Desire spreads through my chest, torso, limbs. All the way to my fingers and toes.

Every molecule of my body needs him.

How is it possible to need someone this much?

To need anything this much?

"Please." I make eye contact through the mirror. "I need you inside me."

His pupils dilate.

"Please, Wes." I rock my hips to drive his fingers deeper. "Please fuck me."

"Sit on the bed." He pulls his hand back.

My body wines from the loss of pressure. Then proximity.

But I still follow his orders.

I like his dirty demands.

I really fucking like them.

I take a seat on the bed.

Spread my legs.

Stare up into his eyes.

"Back against the headboard," he says.

I scoot up the bed.

He gives me a long, slow once-over.

Then he strips.

He takes his sweet, sweet time doing away with his shoes, socks, t-shirt, jeans, boxers.

It's just us now.

Just our bodies.

No bullshit, no pretenses, no promises.

Just a perfect, pure connection.

Wes climbs into the bed.

He places himself between my legs.

"Angel, you should know something." His lips brush my lips. Chin. Neck.

"Yeah?"

"You're coming on my face first."

My sex clenches.

He's not asking a question.

I nod anyway.

Slowly, Wes kisses a trail down my torso.

His lips brush my pelvis.

My inner thigh.

There.

He licks me up and down with long, slow strokes.

Then short, fast ones.

His sucks on my lips.

Then it's that same soft scrape of his teeth.

Fuck.

I reach for him.

Get his hair.

Hold him in place as he works me.

He winds me so fucking tight. Until the tension is too much to take.

Then he brings his tongue to my clit. And he licks me exactly how I need him.

I come quickly.

In spasms.

My sex pulses.

My heart races.

My limbs go slack.

I groan his name as I come.

It bounces around the room.

Echoes off the walls and into my ears.

Wes, Wes, Wes.

The perfect fucking soundtrack.

"Fuck me." I drop the politeness. "Now."

He climbs up the bed. Plants his hands outside my shoulders. Wraps his arm around me.

His eyes meet mine. "Deep breath, angel."

I suck an inhale through my nose.

"Exhale."

I sigh through my lips.

"If it's too much—"

"I know."

"Just breathe and feel, okay?"

Again, I nod.

"Legs around me."

I lift my legs. Wrap them around his waist. He's too far off the bed. I can't quite make it.

He lowers his body onto mine.

Mmm. There's something about the weight of him.

The hardness.

The pressure.

How is it possible to feel full and empty at the same time?

I do.

I really fucking do.

Wes's eyes meet mine. "Try again."

This time, I manage to hook my legs around his waist.

"You good?"

I nod.

His eyes fill with affection, concern, tenderness.

It's almost too much to take.

But, somehow, I manage to hold his gaze.

He cups my cheek with his palm. Rubs my temple with his thumb. "Take a deep breath."

I do.

"Exhale."

I do.

He shifts his hips, bringing our bodies together.

His cock brushes my sex.

Then it's one inch at a time.

My eyelids press together.

My fingers dig into the sheets.

My legs squeeze his back.

"Breathe, angel."

I can do that.

Inhale.

Exhale.

It's so much.

Too much.

And not enough.

He brings his lips to mine.

Kisses me softly.

Then harder.

It's weird, tasting myself on his lips.

But good weird.

He shifts deeper.

Deeper.

Fuck.

I have to break our kiss to groan.

He studies my reaction like I'm a painting he's trying to recreate. "Too much?"

"No. Just..." I take a deep breath. "A lot."

"You need a break?"

"God no."

His lips curl into a smile.

"What?"

He stares down at me with all the affection in the world. "Just thinking."

"Yeah?"

"I really fucking like you, Quinn." He presses his lips to mine.

It's all there.

In his kiss.

It's more than like.

Or maybe I'm already confusing love and sex.

But, fuck, I more than like him too.

Slowly, Wes shifts deeper.

Deeper.

Until he can't go any deeper.

Then he pulls back and does it again.

It's a lot.

Almost too much.

I have to tug at his hair to hold on. I have to pull back. I have to remind myself to breathe.

But I do.

He drives into me with those slow, steady strokes.

Again.

Again.

Again.

Bit by bit, the discomfort fades.

I'm still stretched and full.

But it's good.

Really fucking good.

I stare up into his eyes.

He stares back at me.

For a moment, it's crystal clear.

I understand everything.

Where I should be.

What I should do.

What the hell should become of us.

Then he drives into me and my body takes over.

I rock my hips to meet him.

He brings his hand to my ass. Guides my body over his as he drives into me.

A few more thrusts and he's there.

His brow furrows. His eyes close. His nails dig into my skin.

He groans my name as he comes.

His cock pulses as he spills inside me.

It pulls me right to the edge.

When he's finished, he untangles our bodies.

Then he pulls me into his chest, slips his hand between my legs, and pushes me over the edge.

I come two more times.

Then I dissolve in his arms.

Chapter Forty-Six

QUINN

"Oh my God." Hot air hits my face as I step through the doorway. The casino's freezing AC dissipates.

My goose bumps disappear.

My skin burns.

My hair sticks to my neck.

It's way too hot.

No one should live in a place this hot.

We're standing in the shade—under a wide awning— and it's still way too hot.

The hotel pool is every bit as lush as an actual desert oasis. Crystal blue water. Palm trees. Waterfalls dripping off fake rocks.

Wes's arm slides around my waist. He pulls me closer. It's too much with this temperature. The warmth of his body is threatening to overheat me.

But I don't ask him to stop.

I don't want him to stop.

This trip has been perfect. The drive, our afternoon activities, dinner with friends, gambling, that ridiculous show, and finally...

Finally having sex.

Hell, I even enjoyed watching *Mission Impossible* after.

I mean, it was terrible.

But with the overpriced room service wine and Wes's arms around me—

Even a bad movie is bliss under those circumstances.

I'm rested, fed, caffeinated, and ready to relax in the pool all freaking day. (Well, until I drag him back to the hotel room to have my way with him).

"Are we really meeting our friends here?" My sandals sink into the carpet as I walk the path to the pool. Fifty feet under the awning. Then concrete and bright, unadulterated sun.

"Yeah." Wes's fingers curl into my side. It's sweet, gentle, possessive.

Hot as hell.

Which I can't handle.

I'm already melting.

And I'm already crazy about him.

I think I know where I stand, but, for once, I'm giving myself time to be sure.

We have all day together.

I'm enjoying the hell out of it.

"Is that really the best use of our time?" I hold my hand over my eyes, but it does little to block out the sun. It's so bright.

This heat is unlike any summer day I've experienced.

Somehow, the air is both dry and saturated with warmth. It's not like a sticky New York summer or a breezy Santa Monica afternoon.

It's the kind of weather that makes Death Valley sound like a quaint name.

I find an empty chair, lay my towel down, do away with my glasses.

Wes gives me a long once-over as I pull my cover-up over my head and fold it neatly on my chair.

He watches as I bend to unfasten my sandals.

His attention makes me shudder.

But the concrete against my feet—

Fuck that.

"Pool. Now." I move toward the oasis as quickly as I can. It's tough—the patio and the pool are both crowded —but I still hurry.

Finally, I get to the beautiful water.

My body sings as I dip one foot into the water. Then the other.

I don't ease in. I rush down the steps. Let the water cover my legs, hips, stomach, chest, shoulders.

There.

I dunk my head.

Fuck, that feels good. Crisp. Cool. Refreshing as hell.

And there's Wes, standing on the steps, smiling like he just won the lottery.

He swims to me. Wraps his arms around me. Brings his lips to mine.

His tongue slips into my mouth.

My fingers dig into his hair. It's still dry. His top half is still dry.

I need to change that.

I step backward, pulling him with me.

He falls with me.

Dives under the water with his lips pressed to mine.

We surface, break, gasp for air.

"I'm going to get you back for that, angel." His fingers skim my lower back. Under the water, his touch is smooth. Slick. Frictionless.

It's not enough.

I want to feel more of him.

I want every sopping wet inch of him pressed against me.

But, God, I really need the reprieve of the pool.

Even with most of my body submerged, I'm melting. The sun is oppressive.

I motion *follow me*. Swim (well swim-walk) backward. Until I'm under the shade of a palm tree.

He stays a few strokes behind me.

Then comes closer.

Close enough to kiss me.

But he doesn't. He just keeps his body near.

His proximity makes me buzz. It always does, but it's different today. After last night. After being one with him.

My skin flushes at the memory.

"Where are you going, angel?" He brings his lips to my ear.

"Thinking about what I want to do to you after this."

"Yeah?"

I nod. There's so much. A lot is dirty, yeah, but it's more than that too. "You've done something to me."

"Go on…"

"I'm insatiable." I press my cheek against his, so I can whisper. The skin-on-skin contact makes me shudder. He makes me shudder. "I want you all day."

"We can go all day."

God, it's tempting. But this is nice too. Lounging in the cool water, desert in front of me, Sin City behind me. And Wes… just here.

I want all of him I can get.

His body, mind, heart, soul.

And, well, there's something we haven't discussed.

Maybe he wants to keep it to himself. But I want to help.

For once, I'm going to push instead of folding. That's what he needs. And I lo—

Well, I'm still not sure if I love him. But I do care enough to push.

"We will." I break our touch to swim to the far corner of the pool. It's distant enough to offer some privacy. Not as much as I'd like, but some.

Wes follows.

I press my back against the concrete wall.

He copies my posture. Places his body next to mine, his legs brushing mine, his arm around my waist. "You do look different."

"Like I'm finally a woman?"

He chuckles as he brushes a stray hair behind my ear. "Like you were properly fucked."

"Do I really?"

"Yeah." His lips curl into a smile. "But I'm a little biased."

My chest gets light. Then my limbs. He has such a beautiful smile. I want to stare all day. But I want to talk about this too. "I was thinking—"

"I'll go right here, but we'll probably get arrested."

"Probably."

"You'll get kicked out of med school," he says.

"Yeah." I mean, he's right. Getting arrested, especially for public indecency, will completely fuck up my life. But I still cringe at the thought of med school. The thought of quitting?

It's terrifying.

But in a freeing way.

Like zip lining or sky diving or some other extreme sport.

I don't want that life.

I'm not ready to say it out loud yet.

But in my head…

I don't want to go to med school.

My heart thuds against my chest. My breath catches. My shoulders tense.

At the moment, scary is winning.

But I'll get there.

I will.

"I… um… I was actually thinking about your mom." I press my lips together.

His gaze shifts to the pool. "Quinn, why—"

"Well, if you don't want to talk, that's okay. But if you do, I… uh… I want to be here… to listen. If that will help."

"You're sweet."

"Thank you." I mean it as a confident statement, but it comes out more like a question.

"But I—"

"It's an offer, not a demand."

"You sure?" He presses his palm against the wall, under the water. "I can do a lot of shit but diving into my head isn't on that list."

"I don't know. The sketches you've been showing me are amazing."

"Yeah." His cheeks flush. It's slight, but it's there.

Holy fuck.

I'm making Wes blush.

It's hard to believe.

He's a confident sex god, but I guess he's as nervous and inexperienced as I am when it comes to this kind of intimacy.

"It's such a fucking mess," he says.

"Your mom?"

"My head."

"That's okay."

His eyes meet mine. "Is it?"

He's asking more than that. Asking if I could love someone who was still a mess.

But that's a stupid question.

"We're all a mess." I turn so I'm facing him. "You think I have it together?"

"Well…"

"Hey."

His laugh is soft. Loving. "You wear it well. I don't."

"Yeah, but you still…" God, I don't know how to explain it. "I've been thinking about this a lot. About life. And plans. And knowing myself and what I want and what I'm doing. I'm not good at it. But I'm getting there. It's kind of like organizing your closet."

"Organizing your closet?" His brow knits. His fingers dig into the wall.

He's pulling away.

I have to keep him here.

"Yeah." It's a quick explanation. He can take it or not. But I have to say it. I have to explain how I feel about him. "When you organize your closet, you start by taking inventory. And that means dumping your clothes on your bed."

"You dump your clothes?"

"I lay them on the bed."

His lips curl into a half smile. "I'm not going to believe you make a mess."

"Well you should. Because I do." Okay, mess isn't the right word. But it's certainly disorganized. "I clear out every drawer, shelf, hanger. Until there's this huge pile of clothes. Stuff I love, stuff I hate, stuff I don't remember I have. It's overwhelming seeing everything there. But it's the first step to getting rid of anything that isn't serving you."

He presses his back into the wall.

But he doesn't say anything.

Is he going to say anything?

I...

Ahem.

"I've done it a few times. It's always scary. And messy. But it's good. There's something freeing about letting go," I say.

His eyes meet mine. "There is."

"Are you... um... you never really told me what happened?"

"It's the same shit she always does. She drank too many mimosas at brunch. Ran into another car on the way home. Got carted to the hospital in handcuffs. She was recovering for a few days. She broke a bone in her arm from the impact, but that was it. The other driver..." His gaze gets fuzzy. "They were in the ICU for a while. They're gonna be okay, but the damage might be permanent. We don't know."

"I'm sorry."

"I am too. But not for her." His voice wavers. "I told her I was done. That I wasn't going to hold her hand anymore."

"Did you mean it?"

"Yeah." His gaze shifts to the sky. "But it's easy to say."

I nod.

"I can't do it anymore. If she gets clean, I want to help. But I can't help her destroy herself anymore."

"It's what she needs."

"Yeah, but—"

"It's what you need."

He says nothing.

"It is, Wes. And, well, I like you better than I like her. I care about you. And I want the best for you. And I'll hurt anyone who hurts you. Including your mom."

His lips curl into a half-smile. "Really?"

"Really."

"You're sweet."

"I was going for scary."

"That too."

Under the water, my fingers brush his wrist. I place my palm over his hand. It's not the pinnacle of comfort, but, right now, it's all I have. "So you… you're okay?"

"I'm getting there."

"What do you think she'll do?"

"I don't know." He turns to me. Interlocks his fingers with mine. "But I'll be okay either way."

"You sure?"

"No." He presses his forehead to mine. "But I'm hopeful."

"Me too." I bring my hand to his shoulder. "Wes, I… I really like you."

"I really like you too."

Neither of us says it, but it's there.

It's more than like.

It's so much more than like.

Chapter Forty-Seven

QUINN

After half an hour of talking, swimming, kissing, we find Dean and Chloe. They're behaving as usual (as far as I can tell), giving each other hell, and making out like there's no tomorrow.

Whereas we...

Well, I'm done reminding myself there might not be a tomorrow.

I'm enjoying every minute of today. I'm figuring out what I want to say to Wes. If I still feel the same in the morning—

Well, that's a problem for tomorrow morning.

We join their teasing. Discuss shop gossip and Las Vegas and the whereabouts of our travel companions.

"Have you heard from Griff?" Wes asks.

Dean shakes his head. "Guy's gonna call you before he calls me."

Wes nods *yeah*. "Never thought I'd be the least obnoxious guy in the room, but here we are."

"You got a lot to live up to." Dean smiles wide. He turns to Chloe and motions *come here*.

"I'm not encouraging this behavior." She moves closer. Smiles just as wide.

He brings his hands to her ass. Lifts her into his arms.

He has to lift her out of the water to do it. He's that tall and she's that short.

It's adorable.

But dirty too.

They don't seem to care that we're watching.

At all.

"I like this show," Wes says. "But if you're gonna get started, I'm going to have to take my girl upstairs to finish."

My cheeks flush. He's so good at saying stuff like that. And—"I'm your girl?"

"Of course." Wes turns to me. "You have any doubt?"

Yeah, that whole I might be flying two thousand miles away tomorrow thing… that's a doubt. "I, uh—"

"Hey." A deep voice cuts through the air. It pushes away the laughter, small talk, clinking drinks, splashing water.

Griffin is standing at the edge of the pool in jeans and a t-shirt.

"Where the fuck have you been?" Wes asks.

Dean and Chloe are curious enough they stop making out.

"Where's your friend?" Dean asks.

Chloe shoots him a look, but I have no idea what it means.

"She's in her room." He brushes his wavy hair behind his ear.

He—

Oh my God.

"Where the fuck did you go last night?" Wes asks.

Griffin's left hand falls to his side. It's hard to see the shiny silver band around his ring finger.

But the thick black tattoo that reads *Juliette*—
That's clear as day.
It's right on his forearm.
Holy shit.
Griffin clears his throat. "We got married."

Chapter Forty-Eight

QUINN

"You what?" Wes stares up at his best friend.

"Yeah." Griffin tilts his hand to show off his ring. His brow knits with frustration. His lip corners turn down. "I gotta go."

"No fucking way." Wes turns to me. "Can you give me an hour?"

I'm not sure an hour is going to cut it. I nod anyway. I need him, yeah, but, right now, his best friend needs him more. "Go."

"Where's Jules?" Wes asks.

"Her room," Griffin says.

God, she must be freaking out.

Or ecstatic.

No, there's no way she's happy. Not with him this upset. But then is he upset because he wants to stay married and she doesn't? Or because he realizes he made a horrible mistake?

I want to know.

God, I want to know.

But it's so not the time to ask.

And, well, if this is the end for me and Wes...

I'm sure Chloe will fill me in on the dirt. Eventually. Maybe.

"Maybe I should talk to her." I swim to the edge of the pool. "See how she's doing?"

"You're not exactly friends," Griffin says.

"Jesus Christ, Griff. That's what you want to say right now?" Wes shakes his head. "Juliette liked you. She'll appreciate the uh—"

"Bring tea," Griffin says. "Matcha."

Shit, I don't know anything about matcha. Starting with where to get one. "I'll see what I can do."

Griffin nods *thanks*. "She's in room 2120."

"Sure." I follow Wes and Griffin to our stuff.

Wes hugs me goodbye.

The guys separate.

And I go in search of powdered green tea and clarity.

Chapter Forty-Nine

QUINN

"Hello?" Juliette's voice flows through the door.

"Hey." I shift my weight between my feet. Suck a breath through my teeth. Pep talks aren't my strong suit. Advice is worse. I'm barely in control of my life. But I want to help. "I couldn't find matcha. But I have jasmine green tea."

"Just you?"

"Yeah."

"Okay." She pulls the door open and motions *come in*.

I step into the hotel room. It's the same as our room, only with a view of the desert.

Juliette nods a *thank you* as she takes her tea. She sits on the unmade bed. Crosses one leg over the other.

She's wearing denim shorts and one of those t-shirts with rings of color around the neck and sleeves. It's royal blue and light with a *Dodgers* logo in the middle of the chest. Her hair is in a messy bun. Her face is bare.

She looks like she's heading to softball practice, not her first day of married life.

But I guess tomboys get married too.

I, uh… "Congratulations."

"Yeah." Her gaze shifts to the ring on her left hand. It's a twisting band with tiny stones. Vintage. Gorgeous. Expensive.

I hide behind my English Breakfast. There's a lot I want to say, but none of it is helpful. "What happened?"

She groans and falls onto her back. "Tequila." She reaches her arms over her head. Lets out a yawn that's equal parts frustration and exhaustion.

"Ah, tequila. I know it well."

"You don't seem like the type."

"Neither do you."

Her chuckle is more misery than anything.

It's a lot like Griffin's. Kind of removed. Like she's above all the usual bullshit.

"He's a good guy," I say.

"He is. The best guy in my life. But… We… this… it's crazy."

"You didn't… ahem?" I motion to the messy bed.

She shakes her head. "You're safe to sit."

I can't help but laugh. "Did you?"

She nods.

"How was it?"

Her sigh is dreamy. "Perfect." She takes a long sip of her tea. "Too perfect. It's wrong how perfect it was."

"He's good?"

"Yeah."

"Huge?"

She looks at me funny, like I'm crossing a line. "Is Wes?"

"Yeah." My cheeks flush. "But then I don't have a lot to compare to."

Her smile is soft. "So you finally…"

I nod.

"How was that?"

"It's wrong, how perfect it was," I steal her words.

"Good. My first time was… ugh. I'm glad someone's was good." She pushes herself up. Pulls the elastic holding her hair. Lets dark strands fall over her eyes. "Thanks for the tea, Quinn, but I…" She pulls her arm over her chest. "Fuck, I don't know."

"You mind?" I motion to the bed.

She shakes her head.

I sit next to her. It's weird, trying to dive into an intimate conversation with someone I barely know.

But it's good too.

Like I'm capable of connecting with normal human beings.

Well, normalish.

I don't think any of Wes's friends are really normal.

"I love Griffin," she says. "More than anyone. He's been there since I can remember. But it's always been…"

"You never thought about him that way?" I ask.

She nods *yeah*. "And he hasn't thought about me that way either."

"Are you sure?" I ask.

"Very sure."

I'm not, but I don't have the evidence to back it up. "You love him. He's the best guy you know. What's the rush to figure it out?"

She turns to the window. Stares at the bright blue sky. "I don't know. Maybe… I do have time."

"How much?"

"Not enough."

"Is it ever?"

She nods. "No, it's not." She presses her palms into her thighs. "I… uh… Wes is a good guy too. More obnoxious, but still sweet."

"He is."

"Are you guys?" She clears her throat. "Are you serious?"

"That's a good question." I bite my lip. "I don't have enough time to figure it out either."

"Yeah." She nods. "Just don't try to find the answer in tequila."

I laugh. "Good to know."

"Or wine or gin or vodka—"

"I get what you mean."

She stares at her to-go cup. "Thanks Quinn, but I think I need a little—"

"Sure. I hope I'll see you later."

"You too." Her smile is slight, but I still feel it.

I have friends. Yeah, they're as bad at sorting out their lives as I am, but that's kind of perfect too.

We're all a little dysfunctional.

We belong together.

———

I finish my English Breakfast on the elevator ride to our floor, but the caffeine does nothing to ease my exhaustion.

I'm ready to collapse.

To climb into our plush bed, nestle next to Wes, dissolve between his arms.

But he isn't in bed.

He's in the bathroom.

In the shower.

With the door wide open.

He pulls the glass door open and motions *come here*.

And, somehow, all my exhaustion slips away.

Chapter Fifty

WES

My thoughts dissolve the second Quinn presses the door shut.

Her eyes lock with mine as she steps out of her shoes, shimmies out of her sundress, does away with her bra.

She pushes her panties off her hips.

She's standing in the bathroom naked.

It's not the first time, but it's every bit as thrilling.

More.

It's obvious now.

I need her.

I really fucking need her.

Griffin marrying his childhood best friend, Quinn's plane leaving tomorrow, my plans for tonight—

None of that matters as much as this moment.

As her body against mine.

I hold out my hand.

Her fingers brush my skin. Then it's her palm against mine.

She holds on tightly as she steps into the shower.

415

Water pounds the back of her head. Drips down her hair, neck, shoulders, chest.

She laughs as she pushes her wet hair out of her eyes.

Fuck, she looks beautiful like this. She always looks beautiful, but there's something about the intimacy of this tiny space.

For once, I want that with no ifs, ands, or buts.

I want Quinn closer.

Period.

The end.

"Is Griffin okay?" She wraps one arm around my waist.

"He will be." His situation is a mess at the moment, but he'll figure it out. He always does.

I want to help. I do.

But, for once, I get that it's out of my hands.

He has to realize how he feels.

No one can do it for him.

"Is Juliette?" I bring my hand to Quinn's cheek. Rub her temple with my thumb.

She nods. "Yeah. Well, I think it's the same. She will be."

Will you? I want to ask her, but not now. Not yet. I need this moment with her.

I thought I liked fucking other women, but that was nothing compared to Quinn.

Being inside her is heaven.

"Wes." Her gasp dissolves in the water. She digs her fingers into my side as my hard-on brushes her stomach. "Already?"

"Yeah." I run my digit over her skin. She's already slick from the shower. There's something about that featherlight friction. Something that sets every one of my nerves on fire. "That's what you do to me, angel."

She looks up at me with those big, hazel eyes. "I'm not sure if I have the balance."

I can't help but laugh.

Her brow knits for a second, then it eases. Her lips curl into a smile. "You thought I'd stop being awkward now that I popped my cherry?"

I shake my head. "Didn't think you'd say 'popped my cherry.'"

"How should I describe it?"

"You tell me." I bring my hand to the back of her head. Press my lips to hers.

She kisses back hard.

Her lips part.

My tongue slips into her mouth.

We're both wet and slick. There's less friction than usual. But I can still feel all her lust.

I still don't understand everything she needs when we're dressed.

But this?

I've fucking got this.

"I think"—she digs her fingers into my skin—"I was thoroughly fucked."

"For the first time?"

She nods. "Are we focusing on that?"

"Yeah."

"Wes Keating took my virginity." She shifts her hips, pressing her body against mine.

My cock brushes her stomach.

Fuck, the feeling of her slick skin against my flesh—

"Wes Keating ruined me for other men." She brings her other hand to my hip. "How is that?"

Fucking amazing. "Is it true?"

"I don't know. Maybe." Her eyelids flutter closed.

Mine follow.

Our lips connect.

It's slow.

Then harder.

I lead.

She follows.

My tongue dances with hers. My hands go to her hips. My groans vibrate down her throat.

I pin her to the wall. Slip my hand between her legs. Stroke her with my thumb.

She moans against my lips.

She feels different under the water. Farther away.

But, fuck, the way her nails dig into my skin—

The way her groans bounce around the tiny space—

The way her chest heaves—

My balls tighten.

I need to be inside her.

Soon.

This first.

This always comes first.

I keep her steady with my free arm.

Then I stroke her exactly how she needs me.

Faster. Harder. Higher.

There—

Her breath hitches.

Her teeth sink into her lips.

Her knees buckle.

But I have her.

I always have her.

Well, for the next day, at least.

I watch pleasure spill over Quinn's expression as I rub her through her orgasm.

Her cunt pulses as she comes.

Her moans dissolve into the running water.

Her body melts into mine.

I bring my lips to her neck. Turn her around. Press her into the wall.

"You steady?" I dig my fingers into her hips.

She nods.

"We can move to the bed?"

"No." She presses her palm into the slick tile. "Here."

"Yeah?"

"Yeah." She arches her back. "Please, Wes."

My balls tighten.

"Please fuck me."

Hell yes.

I hold her hips in place as I bring my body onto hers.

My tip strains against her.

Then it's one delicious inch at a time.

Fuck, she feels good.

Soft. Wet. Warm.

I wrap my arm around her hips.

I hold her close as I drive into her.

"Fuck." Her fingers dig into the tile wall. Slip on the slick surface.

I bring her hands back to the wall, one at a time.

My lips brush her shoulder, neck, ear. "I've got you."

She nods. "I know." There's so much in it. Love. Trust. Need.

I need her body.

I need her sweet cunt enveloping me.

But I need so much more.

Her back against my chest.

Her racing heartbeat.

Her heavy breath.

Her soul.

God dammit, I'm buried inside the most gorgeous

woman I've ever seen and I'm thinking about how I want her soul.

I have it bad.

But I don't care.

I love her.

I really fucking do.

"Fuck." Quinn groans as I drive into her. She arches her back to meet me. "Don't stop."

"Say it again, angel."

Her voice drops to something low and demanding. "Don't stop."

"Again." I dig my fingers into her hips, holding her in place.

"Fuck me, Wes."

God dammit, I love that tone of her voice. I drive into her with a steady thrust.

A gasp falls off her lips.

Her fingers claw at the wall. Again, they slip. I help her back in place.

Thrust into her.

Her groans get low and deep.

I bring my lips to her neck. Suck on her tender skin. Softly. Then harder. Then the gentle scrape of my teeth.

"Fuck." She rocks her hips to meet me. "More."

Again, I fill her.

Again, her hands slip.

Her knees buckle.

I have to catch her to keep her upright.

I love being in this tiny space with her.

But I need more. I need the room to fuck her properly.

I reach behind us. Turn off the water. "Bed."

She nods.

I wrap my arms around her.

She squeals as I lift her to my chest.

I carry her into the bedroom and lay her on the bed. "On your stomach, angel."

Her eyes fill with pure desire.

She nods as she rolls onto her stomach. She arches her back, lifting her ass into the air, putting her cunt on full display.

She's so fucking beautiful.

She really is.

I climb into the bed. Position myself between her legs.

My fingers dig into her tender skin.

I lower my body onto hers, chest, stomach, pelvis, legs.

My cock brushes her thigh.

The flesh of her ass.

Her soft folds.

"Fuck, you feel good, angel." I hold her in place as I fill her.

Her groan bounces around the room.

I lower my body onto hers. Lock my fingers with hers. Bring my lips to her neck.

I scrape my teeth against her soft skin until my name falls off her lips.

She rocks her hips to meet me.

We stay locked together, moving, breathing, groaning together until she's there.

She groans my name as she comes.

Her cunt pulses around me.

It pushes me over the edge.

I nip at her neck. Groan her name into her skin. Fill her with everything I have.

When I'm finished, I untangle our bodies, collapse next to her, wrap my arms around her.

She looks up at me with those big hazel eyes.

She doesn't say it, but I can still feel it.

She loves me too.

And I…
I want to say those three little words.
After my plans for tonight.
Fuck. This might scare her off forever.
But it's necessary.
It's so fucking necessary.

Chapter Fifty-One

WES

After we dress, we get an early dinner at a place off the strip known for their authentic tacos.

It's not an accurate claim, but she's all smiles anyway.

She looks at me like I hung the moon. "So." She licks guacamole from her index finger. "What are the mystery plans?"

"If I tell you it's not a mystery."

Her eyes flit to the clock on the wall. "When do they start?"

"Six."

"You're running out of time."

I am. But, God, I'm terrified to ask.

"Wes?"

"Yeah?"

"You okay?"

I nod. Okay is the wrong word. But this is a good thing. It really is.

"You look cute nervous." She adjusts her glasses. "But, um, I do want to know."

"You might not like it."

"Is it *Mission Impossible Two*?"

I can't help but laugh. "Less bad than that."

"Well, obviously."

"You didn't hate the first one."

"I didn't like it."

"You kinda liked it."

She holds out her thumb and forefinger *a little*.

"You even really liked it."

"You're ridiculous."

"Maybe."

"Definitely." She wraps her lips around her straw. Sucks in a sip of water.

There's no booze here.

Which was a conscious thing.

I should probably tell her why.

I am running out of time.

I unzip my backpack, pull out my sketchbook, flip to the right page.

The design I've been working on all week. A locked heart, made out of bottle shards, filled halfway with bourbon.

"Wes." Her hand goes to her mouth. "That's gorgeous."

I nod. It's all I can do. Nod.

"You… what does that mean?"

"I'm gonna get it."

Her eyes go wide as she takes it in. "You should. It's perfect."

"Not too much?"

"Exactly enough."

"I was thinking." Fuck, this is a big ask. As big as asking her to stay. "I designed this too." I point to the ornate skeleton key on the other page.

It's a thick bronze thing with a curving, heart shaped

handle.

"It's a couples tattoo." My heart thuds against my chest. "It could be. If you're into it."

She blinks twice. "You want to get a tattoo with me?"

"Yeah." I swallow hard. "If you're into it. I have this too." I turn the page to show off her pinup. Which is just as perfect for her. Or even more. "It won't hurt my feelings if you'd rather get this. Or something else. Or nothing."

Her fingers trace the paper.

She studies the pinup, turns the page, studies the lock and key.

Her eyes meet mine. "I think I'm going crazy—" She swallows hard. "But yes. I want to."

"Are you sure?"

"I am. I really am."

———

QUINN HOLDS MY HAND THROUGH HER INK.

Then I take over for the artist. (I had to pull a lot of strings to make that happen). Outline her key in black. Fill it in bronze.

She's nervous as hell, but she takes it like a champ.

When we're finished, she stares at the design like it's the greatest thing she's ever seen.

It is.

My art on her body.

Our love on her body.

That's what it is.

It's so fucking obvious.

We go back to the hotel. Fuck. Order room service.

Watch *Casablanca*.

It's perfect because it's her.

I love it, but I don't agree with the message.

Yeah, it's beautiful that Rick and Ilsa reunited in Morocco. That they'll always have their time together in Paris.

But it's bullshit that he sends her to America with Victor Laszlo.

So what if Victor needs her?

Sometimes duty wins over love, but only if it comes from love.

I want what's best for Quinn, whatever that means.

Fuck, I hope I'm right about what it means.

Chapter Fifty-Two

QUINN

Sunlight streams through the curtains.

It falls over the Strip.

Las Vegas is faded in the day. The kitschiness is more obvious.

I mean, it's plenty kitschy at night, but there's something about watching the neon fight the bright sun.

I don't have time to take in the city. Or to reflect. Or to think, period.

My flight leaves in three hours.

That's it.

Three hours.

Not even. With security and early arrival, it's more like two.

It's…

I suck a breath through my teeth. Exhale slowly.

There's time. All I need to do is dress and finish packing.

I rise, move into the bathroom, go through my morning routine, empty the dressers.

There isn't much. I only packed for a few days. Everything else is in boxes on the way to my parents' house. No matter what I do, I have to stop in Chicago. I have to talk to them. To explain...

Well, to explain the rest of my life.

If Wes doesn't want me, I'll be lost.

But I need to face facts.

I'm not going to find myself in med school.

I don't want to go to med school.

I don't want to be a doctor.

No matter what, I go to Chicago and I tell them.

Deep breath.

Slow exhale.

The oxygen does nothing to clear my head. There's too much racing through my mind. His touch. His kiss. His smile. His laugh. His arms.

God, I love his arms.

They're so strong and safe and warm.

It feels good being next to him.

Being with him.

I pack my last pair of panties. Move to the bathroom. Go through my makeup as quickly as possible—concealer, lipstick, mascara (waterproof, of course), eyeshadow.

Owen might take this well, but my parents?

They're going to freak about me pulling out of med school.

It's still the right call.

But that doesn't make telling them any easier.

And, well... I'm not sure I'll have the strength to get through that if this is a sendoff.

If Wes says *it's been fun, enjoy Chicago*—

Ahem.

I'm not getting lost in that.

I'm getting ready.

I bring my makeup to my suitcase, arrange it in the bottom corner, pull the zipper.

There.

I'm ready to leave.

Practically speaking.

I go to wake Wes, but I can't bring myself to rouse him from his slumber. He looks so peaceful lying in bed, sandy hair falling over his closed eyes, sheets pressed against his bare chest.

His new tattoo is vivid. A locked heart right over his actual heart.

And I have the key, right here, on my ribs.

It's cheesy as hell. But it's perfect too.

I sit on the bed next to him. Watch his chest rise and fall.

He's so close.

So warm.

So mine.

It echoes through my head. Right now, he's mine. For another few hours, he's mine.

After that, I don't know.

But, fuck, it's good to have right now.

Chapter Fifty-Three

WES

There's no time for breakfast in bed. Or Quinn coming on my face. Or a romantic gesture.

I barely have time to brush my teeth and throw my shit into my suitcase.

Quinn looks at me funny. "You're packing?"

"Yeah." I want to explain. But I can't. Not yet. Not until I have all the words in order.

Her brow furrows with confusion. She presses her palms to her dress. Smooths the fabric. Plays with the hem.

I zip my suitcase, grab it, take her hand. "You need help with that?"

"No." Her fingers curl around the handle of her bright red suitcase. "I've got it."

"After you." I motion for her to lead.

She does.

I pull the door open.

She steps into the hall.

We're quiet the walk to the elevator. Through the lobby. To the valet.

I hand the guy my ticket.

He nods and tells me it will be ten minutes.

It isn't enough time.

But it's what we've got.

Quinn shifts her weight between her heels. She stares straight ahead. Like she can't bear to look at me.

Fuck, I'm not sure I can handle looking at her either.

I just can't look away.

She's so beautiful.

Smart. And sweet. And honest.

Right now, it's so obvious.

I open my mouth to articulate the feelings whirring in my gut, but words refuse to form.

I'm good at a lot of things.

This isn't one of them.

This is so far from one of them.

But I have to get there.

For her.

"Quinn." I reach out. Let my hand brush her wrist.

She turns to me. Looks up at me with those big, hazel eyes. "Yeah?"

"I…" I stumble over nothing. Over everything. This is everything. I didn't ask. I should have asked yesterday. I should have asked a week ago. It should have been obvious from the beginning.

"Are you okay?"

Hell no. But I will be. "Lacking coffee, but yeah."

"Me too." She presses her red lips together.

"When did you get up?"

She holds her hand over her eyes as she looks to the sky. "I'm not sure I really slept."

"Yeah." It's funny. I was lying awake half the night. I could tell she was up, but I couldn't sense her thoughts.

I should have turned around. Explained this.

Now, I'm running out of time.

I'm asking for too much.

But that isn't stopping me.

"Why didn't you make tea?" It's all I can think to say.

"With the coffee maker?" Her nose scrunches in distaste. "Wes, you know me better than that."

"It's caffeine."

She shakes her head. "Not worth it."

"The coffee shop downstairs?"

Again, she shakes her head.

She didn't want to leave.

She didn't want to give up a single minute between us.

Screeching tires grab my attention. A valet pulls the minivan into the driveway.

I find a five in my wallet. Hand it to the guy as he offers my keys.

He's a gentleman about taking our bags and opening the door for Quinn.

I should appreciate it.

But I don't.

I don't want anyone else taking care of her.

Not now.

Not ever.

Fuck, there isn't much time.

There isn't any time.

I need to come out with this.

But even as I buckle my seatbelt and pull onto the street, the words refuse to come.

The airport is right there.

Five minutes away.

The closest airport in the history of any city anywhere.

The one time I want the drive to the airport to take forever, it's five fucking minutes.

Quinn leans forward to change the radio station.

I'm still not sure what the hell I'm doing with the car.

But I know I can trust Griffin to figure it out. Even if he's got plenty of shit to figure out for himself.

Quinn leans back in her seat. She folds her hands in her lap. "Wes, um…"

"Yeah?"

"If, um… if this leaves with me getting on that plane alone, could you tell me now?"

My heart pounds so hard it drowns out the music. "Is that what you want?"

"Um…"

It's not. I know it's not. But I can't force this on her. I need her to be as excited as I am.

"I just… I guess there's no sense in beating around the bush now."

I nod.

Her eyes flit to the windshield. She watches as I turn onto the airport's street. "I… Um… fuck, we're really doing this?"

"Yeah."

"I… Uh… I really like you."

I turn toward the parking lot.

Her eyes go wide. "Wes, if you're… if I'm getting on that plane, I don't need you walking me in."

"I know."

"So…"

I take a ticket and pull into the garage. "Give me a minute, angel."

"But…"

"Sixty seconds."

"Okay. I just… What are you doing?"

"Let me park before I explain this."

Her brow furrows with confusion, but she still nods.

Fuck, I need to say something to reassure her. Something that will wipe the frown from her face. "It's good."

That doesn't help.

"Really good."

She presses her lips together. It's not a smile, but not a frown either.

Fuck, this garage is full.

I drive around the corner to the second level, but it's just as packed.

Quinn crosses and uncrosses her legs. She shifts to her right. Then her left.

Her eyes go everywhere.

"There." She points to a spot in the corner. "Then we... then we can talk."

"Yeah." I pull into the parking space. This car is a lumbering thing. It's a pain in the ass. A good reason to skip the suburban soccer dad thing.

Fuck. This is the first time I've ever entertained the idea of a wife, much less a family, much less a family in the suburbs.

I'm getting better at this.

I'm still not good at this, but I am getting better.

I turn the car off and set my keys in my lap.

Instantly, the temperature climbs.

"Fuck, I forgot." I open the door. "Let's do this outside."

"Oh... okay."

I rush to her side of the car, but she's too fast. She's already standing in the garage.

Quinn stares at me like I'm crazy. "Wes, will you please explain?"

Okay. I will. I don't have a choice now.

I pull my cell from my pocket, open the right app, show her the screen.

Her eyes go wide. "I... I don't understand."

I point to the name on the ticket.

"You're going to Chicago?"

"If you'll have me."

"But… you're here. Everything is here."

"I know."

Her brow knits with confusion. "So you—"

"You have to go back no matter what."

"Well, yeah."

"I want to go with you." I slide my cell into my back pocket. Take her hands into mine. "I want you to stay, Quinn. But I can't ask you to give up med school if it's what you really want."

She nods.

"I want you here. I want you in my bed, every fucking day, until we're too sore to move. But, more than that, I want to be where you are. If that's Chicago, I'm in Chicago."

"You have any idea how cold it gets?"

I shake my head. "I look great in a coat."

She laughs. "Probably true. But Wes… it's… it's not you."

"You gonna be there?"

"I don't know."

"Well, fuck, I didn't have a response planned for that."

Her lips curl into a smile. "You really want to come with me?"

I nod. "More than anything."

"That's…" Her smile gets wider. "Yes. Definitely."

Her smile gets wider. "But, Wes?"

"Yeah?"

"I hate Chicago."

I can't help but laugh. "We can still make it work."

"I mean, we do need to go now. I need to face Owen and my parents, and God, I have no idea what they'll say. But I don't want to be there long-term. Maybe I'll apply to another med school. Go somewhere else. But I want to be here. Well, not here—"

"In California?"

She nods. "With you."

"Yeah?"

"Hell yeah." She wraps her arms around me. "But, Wes?"

"Yeah?"

"We can't take this flight."

"No?"

"We need to celebrate this properly?"

My smile widens. "What do you mean, angel?"

"You know exactly what I mean."

Chapter Fifty-Four

QUINN

"Please prepare for our descent into O'Hare." The captain's voice booms from the speakers.

I press my palms together. Suck a breath through my teeth.

This is it.

Twenty minutes until I'm on the ground. An hour, maybe, until I explain this to my brother.

I'm dropping out of med school. By the way, my boyfriend is here too. He's not the reason. Well, not the way you think. He kinda is the reason. But I'm not dropping out for him. It's more that he helped me realize I hate medicine.

That might fly with Owen.

But my parents?

"Breathe, angel." Wes's fingers graze my wrist.

Breathe.

Yes.

It's good advice.

I focus on a slow inhale. A steady exhale. All the yoga teacher calmness I can handle.

It's not very much.

But it's something.

I can do this.

I think.

Probably.

"You want me to talk or shut up?" He unwraps my clenched fists—funny, I don't remember clenching them—and intertwines his fingers with mine.

"Talk." I think. Over the last few years, I've gotten better at handling my anxiety. I'm more nervous than anxious. But I'm still… well, I'm really fucking nervous.

"I gotta tell you something you're not going to like."

"Is it about *Mission Impossible*?" I stick my tongue out.

Wes laughs. "No, but I do have the DVDs for all the sequels."

"All of them?"

He nods. "Every single one."

"Why?"

"Quinn, do you really need me to go over this again?"

"I saw the movie. I know it's terrible."

"It's at least bad."

My laugh eases the tension in my shoulders. He's right. It's not terrible. It's even decent.

Or maybe all the wine and Wes confused me.

Yes. That's what I need.

Only—

Well, we can't exactly cuddle here.

We can't even sneak to the bathroom for—

Okay, I'd never actually consider joining the mile high club. Not in a commercial airline in the bathroom.

If I somehow win the lottery and buy a private jet, then sure. I'll pin Wes to a plush leather seat, climb on top of him, and ride him hard.

"Angel, you're thinking something dirty." He rubs the space between his thumb and forefinger with my thumb.

"Says who?"

"Me."

"Based on what?"

"Your blush."

God, my cheeks are burning. And the flirty tone of his voice is only making it worse.

"Fuck, I tell you how much I love it when you blush?"

I nod.

"It's fucking sexy."

The guy sitting in the window seat clears his throat.

Poor guy has had to contend with our conversation for nearly four hours.

I mean, mostly, we sat and listened to music—we actually shared Wes's headphones, like in high school—but there was enough flirting to make this experience... awkward.

Which is good practice for today.

This is going to be awkward as hell.

And painful.

And all around awful.

But, right now, with Wes here, I feel like I can do it.

God, I really hope I can do it.

———

OH MY GOD.

I can't do this.

I can't do this.

I really, really can't do this.

Ding-dong.

The doorbell echoes through the apartment.

It's so loud.

It's the loudest doorbell in the history of the world.

It's screaming *Quinn is here to disappoint you.*

"Breathe, angel." Wes squeezes my hand. "It's gonna be okay."

Right.

It's going to be okay.

Owen will accept this. In theory.

And if he doesn't…

I'll live with that. Whatever happens, I'll live with it.

Which requires breathing.

I squeeze Wes's hand.

The pressure of his palm is soothing.

So is the smell of his shampoo.

And his proximity.

It makes my body buzz.

Which is a bit too much at the moment. But it's nice all the same.

Hey Owen! Romeo is here. You know Wes. Sorta. He, uh, he really likes you. And he's a great guy. And he had the weekend free, so he thought he'd come help me… talk to you.

"Is that you, Q?" Owen calls. "It's open."

It's open.

There's no way to stall.

Awesome.

No, it is awesome.

I have to tell my brother. I want to tell my brother. I want to explain, to get his support, to hear his news.

This is good.

It's going to be good.

Eventually.

My fingers curl around my suitcase.

Wes looks to me and raises a brow. "You ready?"

No, but I need to do it now. Before I lose my nerve. I nod.

He turns the handle and pushes the door open. "Hey."

"Huh?" Owen's footsteps pad the tile floor. He rounds

the corner. Steps into the main room. "Oh." His lips curl into a smile as he spots Wes.

"Don't." I drag my suitcase into his apartment.

My brother laughs. "Don't what, Q?"

"Comment," I say.

He looks from me to Wes then back to me. "Comment on what?"

"Hey." Wes offers his hand. "It's nice to see you again."

Owen nods. Shakes. Then pulls Wes in for a big bear hug. He pats Wes's back. "You're the guy who's been fucking my sister?"

"Yeah." Wes takes a step backward. He looks to me. "Didn't realize you were talking about me."

Oh God.

"She's had a lot to say," Owen says.

"Good things?" Wes asks.

Owen holds out his hand and shakes it. *So-so.*

"Fuck, angel, you speaking ill of my abilities?" Wes asks.

My blush takes over my chest. My stomach. My shoulders.

I think my entire body is red.

This is horrifying.

"She didn't say much about them." Owen shakes his head. "Worst insult of all."

"It is." Wes's eyes meet mine. "You been faking it, angel?"

I clear my throat. "So, um, Wes is here."

"I can see that," Owen says.

"And we're done discussing my sex life." I push the door closed and click the lock. "Immediately."

"What was that about Quinn's sex life?" Reggie's deep voice booms through the apartment. He steps into the main room with a wide smile. "Hey."

"Please save me." I press my hands together like I'm praying to... well, to Reggie I guess.

Somehow, his smile gets wider. "You torturing your sister?"

Owen nods. "Think her boyfriend is helping." He turns to Wes. "Are you her boyfriend?"

"Of course." Wes motions to my suitcase. "You want me to take that for you?"

"Where are you taking it?" I ask.

"You're staying here," Owen says. "Both of you."

"Aren't you supposed to insist we sleep in separate beds?" I ask.

Reggie nods. "You know I love your protective side." He motions *come here* to Owen.

Owen does.

Their embrace is sweet.

Even though they're opposites, they look perfect together. Owen is a pale as the moon white kid from the suburbs. Reggie is a dark-skinned black guy from the wrong side of the tracks. He's a head taller than Owen, built like a football player, and completely and totally in love with sports.

Owen watches nothing but TV dramas.

Reggie is sweet and tender where Owen is... prickly.

Which is why I'm...

Fuck.

"Sorry, baby." Owen presses his lips to Reggie's cheek. "I don't want either of them on the couch."

Reggie laughs. "Where would you watch *Vampire Diaries*?"

"Don't mock because you don't understand Elena's pain," he says.

"Oh yes, deciding between two super-hot vampires. What horrible pain." Reggie shakes his head. "You look cute, Quinn. Cute coming from the airport is an accomplishment."

"Thanks." I smooth my sundress. "I, uh… do you have tea?"

Owen nods. "English Breakfast?"

"Thank you," I say.

"I'll make it." Reggie steps toward the kitchen. "You know he can't do it right."

"Hey!" Owen feigns offense.

Reggie blows him a kiss.

Owen catches it.

God, they really are adorable.

Which is good.

The happy, in love vibes will make this easier.

I think.

"I, um… I have to talk to you." I take a step toward the couch. Then another. Then I'm there. Their apartment is nice, but it's small. Two bedrooms, a tiny den, a smaller kitchen. "About some stuff."

"Sure." Owen turns to Reggie. They exchange one of those couple looks.

Reggie motions *one minute* then he fills the kettle with water and turns it on.

Right. He's making the tea.

And I… Uh…

"Wes, can you take your bags to the office?" Reggie asks. "The couch is a pull out. It's small for two, but—"

"I wouldn't dream of getting between Owen and *Vampire Diaries*," Wes says.

"My kind of man," Owen says.

"Should I be jealous?" Reggie teases.

Owen nods.

Reggie shakes his head *you're ridiculous*.

He is. My brother is ridiculous. And tough. And caring.

And I…

I just have to say it.

I open my mouth to start, but words refuse to form.

So I sit.

The leather couch is cool against my bare legs. It's a million degrees outside, but the air-conditioning is turned to high. It's freezing in here.

Too freezing.

I press my palms into my thighs. Smooth my dress.

Owen takes a seat next to me. "How was your flight?"

"Good. Long." I press my lips together. "I… um, I'm pretty used to it now."

He nods. "You're back and forth a lot."

Thanksgiving, Christmas, summers. Well, my first two. I've spent a lot of time in Chicago.

It's not as horrible as I remember.

But it's already clear it's not for me.

That this life isn't for me.

"Here we go." Reggie moves into the main room with a steaming mug of tea. He crosses to us, sets it on the side table, plants a kiss on my cheek. "I'll give you a minute."

"Thanks." I press my palms together. Watch my brother-in-law clear the room.

It's just me and my brother and my confession.

No time like the present.

I just have to say it.

In one go.

"Owen, I have to tell you something." I force the words off my lips.

Owen nods. "Sure."

"I…" Deep breath. Slow exhale. Fast. Like a Band-Aid. "I'm not going to med school."

"Oh." Concern fills his hazel eyes, but he stays silent.

"It's not because of Wes. I mean, it kind of is. But it's

not that I'm leaving school for him." Deep breath. "It's that he helped me realize I don't want to be a doctor."

Owen stares back at me, still and silent.

"I hated my biology classes. I hate scribing. I hate hospitals. When I catch a glimpse of *House*, or *ER*, or *Grey's Anatomy*, I feel sick. I don't want to be a doctor. I don't have any clue what I want to do, but I know it's not that."

My brother nods. An *I understand* nod.

It's not an *I accept this and also see how right you are and by the way I love and support you no matter what* nod, but it's a start.

"I've spent my entire life on this plan someone else laid out for me." I unfold my hands. Turn toward my brother. "It was a good plan, but it wasn't for me. I need to get off it. I need to figure out what I want."

"Okay."

"Okay?"

He nods. "You hated pre-med that much?"

"I did."

"Why didn't you say something?"

"I talked about it all the time."

He shakes his head. "You said it was hard. That you were stressed. That studying was a drag. But, Q, if I had any idea you were this unhappy—"

"You're not mad?"

"No." His voice is soft. Sweet. "Why would I be?"

"I don't know. I thought… I don't know."

"You know what I want for you, more than anything?"

"A hot boyfriend?"

He chuckles. "No, that comes in second." He turns toward me. "I want you to be happy."

"Oh."

"Oh?"

"I just… I really thought you'd be mad."

He shakes his head. "You're sure about this?"

"I really am."

"How do you feel?"

"Terrified. But in a good way."

"Then I'm happy for you." My brother pulls me into a tight hug.

"Thanks." I settle into my seat. Wrap my fingers around my cup. Take a sip.

It's good tea. Strong, malty, comforting.

But I don't need the comfort.

I… I'm okay.

I'm really going to be okay.

Well—"Mom and Dad are going to freak."

"Yeah, but they'll get over it?"

"You think so?"

"Yeah." He stands and looks to the bedroom. "They want you to be happy too."

"I'm the first Thorn to ditch med school… ever."

"They'll freak until you find a job. Then, they'll be happy."

"And Wes?"

He laughs. "They love the Keatings."

That is true.

"You know, Mom used to talk about how she wanted the two of you to get married."

"She did not."

He nods. "She thought you'd make an adorable couple."

"We do."

"Yeah, you do."

"Why are you standing?"

"I have news."

Maybe I should stand too. I push myself up. Press my hands to my sides. "You still swear it's good?"

"It's really fucking good." He slides a hand into his back pocket. "Reggie, you ready for this?"

The bedroom door opens. Footsteps move closer.

Reggie's gaze catches Owen's. "Are you?"

My brother smiles. "Yeah." He turns to me. Pulls something from his jeans. "Q, you're gonna be an aunt."

"What?"

He unfolds a photo of a baby girl. She's tiny, a few weeks old at most. "We're flying to Vietnam next month."

"Really?" God, she's beautiful. And small. I've never seen a baby this small.

I already want to protect her.

"Yeah." Reggie wraps his arm around Owen. "Her name is Ilsa."

"Like *Casablanca*?" I ask.

"I told you that would ruin the moment." Owen shakes his head.

"No." Reggie wipes a happy tear from his eye. "It's perfect.

It really is.

I hug my brother and his husband. Then I call Wes, tell him, insist we go out to celebrate.

We eat too much pasta and drink too much wine.

But it's perfect.

It's love.

My future is a blank page.

For the first time, I'm not scared of the unknown.

Well, I'm a little scared.

But I'm ready for it too.

Epilogue

WES

"I love her so much." Quinn smiles as Ilsa wraps her hand around Quinn's finger. "I love her so much I actually want to move to Chicago."

"Bullshit." It's beautiful here in June. But I remember Christmas. Even in the world's puffiest coat, I was freezing. Quinn took it even worse. "Do we need to come back in December?"

"Yeah." She leans in to press her lips to her niece's forehead. "Every month."

"You shouldn't bluff with me, angel."

"There's bluffing then there's love." She stares into Ilsa's big, dark eyes. "You're too sweet," she coos. "Much sweeter than Owen deserves."

It's hard to argue. I never got the fuss about babies, but Ilsa is awesome. The room lights up when she laughs. And she laughs at the drop of the hat.

She coos over her tiny stuffed giraffe and her favorite brand of baby food.

She's like a baby on TV. Always well-behaved.

At least, when we're here.

Owen and Reggie tell tales of sleepless nights and constant crying, but she's rarely grumpy around us.

"Don't get ideas, Q." Owen calls from the kitchen as he pours tea for three.

"What if she likes me more?" She makes faces at the baby. "If she'd be happier?"

"She's too young to like you more."

She shakes her head. "Look at her smile."

He enters the room with two steaming mugs. Sets both on the end table. Grabs the third. "When she's older, maybe. But everyone likes aunts more. You show up with gifts"—he motions to the stuffed rhino on the couch—"and praise."

"I'm sorry he's jealous." She offers Ilsa her finger. Lets the baby grab at that instead. "He's always been this way."

"You're lucky I love you, Q."

"I know." She turns to her brother. "I've always been lucky that way."

He shakes his head *you're so full of shit*, but he still smiles. He's sentimental as hell now that he has a kid.

He reaches over and bops her on the head.

She laughs.

I shoot him a look of faux aggression. "Watch yourself, Thorn."

"Or?" He takes a long sip of his tea. Raises his brow *come at me*.

"Don't threaten to kill my brother." She keeps her eyes on Ilsa.

"You know Owen wants to throw down," I say.

Owen chuckles.

"He can't stand a depraved bad boy taking his sister's honor," I say.

Quinn scoffs. "Have you been watching those CW shows with him?"

"Maybe." Okay, we were up all night watching TV. Ilsa was fussing. He needed company. We kept the volume low. Kept our conversation quiet.

Owen is a good guy and, well, I needed to clear some stuff with him. And to get some advice.

But, shit, I can't think about that yet.

I'm already nervous as hell.

"I'm not a surgeon." Owen holds up his free arm. Curls his fingers into a fist. "I can risk injury."

I motion *come at me.*

He chuckles. "You realize I could kill you with a single swipe?" He mimes slicing a knife through the air.

Quinn nods. "He could. But shut up about it or I'm taking Ilsa to another room." Her voice lifts. "You don't need to listen to silly boys and their lust for violence. Your honor is yours. And there's nothing dishonorable about sleeping with tattooed men. Or women. Or gender non-conforming people."

"You sound like Reggie," Owen says.

"He's the smart one," Quinn says.

"Yeah, but I married him. So who's really smart?" Owen teases.

Quinn's smile gets wider.

"You sure you're good to watch her?" Owen asks.

"Yeah. Go. Enjoy your date night." She shoos her brother away. "I know the drill. I've done this a lot now."

This is our third timing visiting Owen, Reggie, and Ilsa this year

We do know the drill.

Hell, by now, I know Chicago inside and out.

It's a nice city.

It's not home, but it could be. If that was what she really wanted.

I meant what I told her last year.

I want to be wherever she is.

I want to be with her.

And this—

Fuck, it's not happening yet.

No reason to think about it yet.

I wave a goodbye to Owen.

He stares at us for a long moment, assessing our babysitting abilities. He nods his okay, disappears into his room, reappears in a suit and tie.

Quinn gushes about how well he cleans up.

As soon as he leaves, she turns all her attention to Ilsa.

She lights up around the kid.

I thought it would terrify me, but it doesn't. I'm not scared of family anymore.

I'm not scared of my head.

I'm not Hunter. I'm not spilling my guts to anyone who asks. But I pour my heart into my work. I talk to Quinn. I let feelings into my head.

Yeah, I'm still afraid of getting hurt.

But not enough to keep my heart locked tight.

Missing out on love is a million times worse than losing it.

Casablanca was right about that.

———

QUINN RESTS HER HEAD ON MY SHOULDER. HER EYELIDS flutter closed. Her sigh echoes around the cab.

"That a happy sigh or a tired sigh?" It's a warm night, but the AC is turned up high. I wrap my arm around her waist. Pull her closer.

She murmurs something as she nestles into the crook of my neck.

"I'll take that as 'tired.'"

She just barely nods. "Happy too."

"Should I take you straight to the hotel?"

"Where else would we go?"

Somewhere scenic and romantic. A backdrop for this. "It's a beautiful night."

Her eyelids blink open. Her gaze shifts to the window.

The city whizzes by.

A yawn falls off her lips. She stretches her arms over her head, pulling her dress up her body.

Fuck, I never get tired of her lush legs.

I want them around my waist.

Against my hands.

Pressed to my cheeks.

I know how to make Quinn come.

This?

Fuck, I can't remember the last time I was this nervous.

"It is." She stares out the window, watching sky and steel bleed together. "I've never thought of Chicago as beautiful before."

"It's nothing compared to you."

Her laugh lights up her eyes. "I'm not that tired."

"Fuck, you don't like it?"

She shakes her head.

"It was smooth as silk."

She shakes her head harder. Hard enough her red hair falls over her eyes.

I brush her hair behind her ear. Let my fingertips skim her temple, cheek, chin. "I don't care if it's cheesy. You're more beautiful than any city I've ever seen."

"Yeah?"

"Yeah."

"What if I take these off?" She taps her glasses.

"Still beautiful."

"But?" She raises a brow.

"My dick won't like it."

"Aw, poor Wes's dick." She tries to keep a poker face, but it doesn't hold. "How will I make it up to you?"

"I can think of something."

"What if I get LASIK?"

I feign shock. Shudder. "Angel, don't talk like that." I motion to my crotch. "He might rebel."

"Oh yeah?"

I nod.

She shakes her head. "Aren't you the one in charge?"

"Sometimes." I slide my hand to the back of her head. Pull her into a soft, slow kiss.

She groans into my mouth as I scrape my teeth against her top lip.

Her hand goes to my chest.

Blood rushes south.

I need her.

I really fucking need her.

She pulls back with a sigh.

"Like that." I curl my fingers around her wrist. Bring her hand to my cock. It's over my jeans and boxers, but the pressure of her palm still feels fucking good.

"Wes." She clears her throat and nods to the driver. "You're evil." She pulls her hand into her lap. Makes a show of facing forward. Folding her legs.

Her blush spreads to her chest.

It's hot as hell.

But this isn't the time.

Quinn is far too shy to fuck in the backseat of a cab.

And, well, I'm out of excuses here.

This happens tonight.

"I, um, you were saying something about the night?"
She interlocks her fingers.

"That it's a perfect night to fuck you senseless."

Her blush deepens. "That wasn't it."

"That's it now."

"I'll consider that proposition."

"Consider it?"

She nods. "You think I'm a sure thing?"

"I think I know how to press every one of your buttons."

"Well..." She smooths her dress. Clears her throat. Presses her lips into a smile. "That may be true. But only if I let you, ahem, play with my buttons."

"Go on."

She shakes her head *not here*. "I... uh... Reggie and Owen seem happy."

They do.

"Ilsa is the sweetest thing, isn't she? I want to smoother her with love."

"Not sure smothering is the way to go."

"Ha-ha." She makes a show of rolling her eyes. "You're really bringing the dad jokes tonight."

"Who taught you about dad jokes?"

"People at the office."

"Which people?"

"All of them. It's the topic du jour. Well, it was." Her lips curl into a smile.

Joy overtakes her face.

She loves her job.

I swear, she loves it more than she loves me.

When we first got back to LA, Quinn was scared. She had no idea what she wanted to do. Or what she was even capable of doing. Her biology degree was great for med school applications, but it didn't help when it came to jobs outside of science.

It took her a while to find a gig at a new media company. It was a lucky break. A friend of a friend.

She wasn't sure if she'd be able to manage the work.

But she did.

She was fucking amazing.

Honestly, I don't understand half her job duties. Something about researching popular media to help the production team decide where to focus their efforts.

She writes long, detailed reports about TV shows, movies, albums. She can analyze the world's most inane pop song and come up with something brilliant.

She's really fucking good at her job.

Everyone there loves her.

They tell me how much they love her every time I visit.

I appreciate their praise, but I still remind them she's mine every fucking time.

And this.

Fuck, if this works—

"Can we steal her?" Quinn jumps right back to her favorite topic: Ilsa. "Just for a few months?"

"You'd never let her go."

She nods *true*. "Maybe we should have one." Her hand goes to her lips. "Did I just say that out loud?"

"Yeah."

"Pretend I didn't."

"Why?"

"Because…" She clears her throat. "You're scared of commitment."

"Says who?"

"Me."

That was true once, but not anymore. "No more than you are."

"Well… um… I'm not even close to ready for that."

458

Her gaze shifts to the driver, who is still incredibly uninterested in us. "I, um, I mean it would be fun. The part where we try."

"It would."

"But it's a lot of responsibility. And, uh, I, uh…"

"I think we should."

"What?"

"Not yet. But eventually."

"Really?" Her eyes light up. "I mean, I, um, really?"

"Yeah." I take her hand. "Or maybe I want an excuse to fuck you every day."

"Since when do you need an excuse?"

"I'll drop by on your lunch break. Take you in the bathroom."

Her eyes go wide.

"Or your office."

She clears her throat.

"You keep doing that and it keeps not working."

"I'm hoping you get the hint."

"You know I don't get hints."

"How about—" She leans in to whisper. "Stop trying to embarrass me with the driver."

"How about I keep doing it?"

She shakes her head.

"You gonna keep blushing?"

"Maybe."

"Then I'm going to keep doing it."

"You're evil."

"I consider that a compliment."

Her gaze shifts to the window. She watches as the car passes our hotel. "You really want kids?"

"I do."

"Since when?" she asks.

"I don't know. Today, maybe."

Her eyes meet mine. "Today?"

"Maybe."

"That's not a long time."

"Are we going to start trying tonight?" I ask.

"Well… no. But, um… I thought, with your mom—"

"I did too." I swallow hard. Shit is still messy with my mom. She dragged her feet for a long time. She's in recovery now, but it feels so tenuous. Like she might slip at any moment.

Our relationship is still messy. But we're getting there. Slowly.

And even if we don't, if she stops trying…

I won't like it. I won't take it well. But I will survive it.

"Oh." She presses her lips together. "Well, um, I'll take that into consideration."

"Will you?"

She nods. "Yes, like with the sex."

"Oh?"

"Mhmm."

"I'm not getting lucky tonight?" I ask.

"You might. You might not." Her smile lights up her hazel eyes.

Fuck, she really is beautiful. And her joy is everything. And this—

God dammit, this thing must be a million pounds. It's burning a hole in my pocket. And I can't even make a stupid joke about how I'm used to carrying something huge.

I can't tip my hand.

The car turns. Slows to a stop. "We're here," the driver says.

"Thanks." I pay the tab and help Quinn out of the cab.

She looks around the waterfront with wide eyes.

I take her hand. Lead her onto the path. There are miles and miles of cement curving around Lake Michigan.

Every inch of it is beautiful, but this spot is my favorite.

The city glows against the starry sky. The moon casts highlights over the massive lake, the metal railing, the two of us.

Fuck, she looks beautiful like this.

I need a better word, but that shit isn't my strong suit.

Quinn is lovely. Radiant. Gorgeous. Perfect.

She's an anxious mess sometimes, she's awkward as all hell, she still can't cook to save her life.

But she's perfect.

Fuck.

I can't fuck this up.

I squeeze her hand.

For a few minutes, we walk in silence.

Then I stop. It's not as seamless as I'd like, but I can't wait for seamless.

I need to do this.

I need her to make this official.

"I've been thinking for a while." I press my hand to the railing.

She turns to the lake. Watches the water rock back and forth.

"This has been a busy year. It's been hard. Everything with my mom, and flying back and forth to Chicago, and all that shit with Chase."

She nods.

"I've had a lot of bad days. But every time I get home and see you, that shit fades away." I turn to face her. "You're the best thing in my life."

Her eyes meet mine.

"I want you in my life for a long time. Forever." I take her hand. Lower myself onto one knee.

Her jaw drops.

I pull the ring box from my pocket and pop it open. "Quinn Thorn, will you marry me?"

Her eyes go wide. "Oh my God. Wes. I… You…"

"That a yes?"

She nods. "Of course."

I slide the ring onto her finger.

She takes my hands. Pulls me onto my feet. "I love you so much."

"I love you too."

She rises to her tiptoes to press her lips to mine.

Everything inside her flows into me.

And everything inside me flows into her.

I kiss her like she's everything I need.

Because she is.

She really fucking is.

———

Want more Inked Hearts?

Sign up for my mailing list for an exclusive extended epilogue of *Losing It*.

Griffin's book, *Accidental Husband*, is coming spring 2019. Until then, keep your Inked Hearts fix going with Brendon and Kaylee's book, *Tempting*, a smoking hot forbidden romance.

Turn the page for a sample.

Tempting

SPECIAL PREVIEW

Chapter One

BRENDON

Get *Tempting* Now

Kaylee plants her palms on the table. Her cheeks spread to her ears. They're pink. Then red. She's laughing so hard her tits are shaking.

Damn, that tight blue dress, the same blue as her glasses.

She looks amazing, like the sweet, innocent angel she is and like the sex goddess I'm desperate to unleash.

But I still hate that scrap of fabric with every fiber of my being.

I hate every ounce of air between us.

Every flint of wood in this table.

Every guy here looking at her the way I am.

Fuck, if I don't get ahold of myself, I'm going to break a few arms. And maybe my hand. And I can't exactly finish Alex's back piece at nine a.m. tomorrow with broken fingers.

Em wraps her arms around Kaylee.

Kaylee laughs, pushing her long blond hair behind her ears and gathering it at one shoulder.

Her eyes flit around the room.

They catch mine.

They scream *I'm about to wish for you to take me to your room.*

Or maybe that's in my head.

Today is the day.

She's no longer a temptation that can get me locked up. Just a temptation that can rip away everything that matters to me.

Em leans in to whisper in her ear. I know my sister. I know exactly what she's saying. *Wish for someone to fuck tonight.*

Not happening.

Not as long as I'm here.

I hate to be a cunt-blocker, really, I do, but there's no way Kaylee is taking home anyone on my watch.

I have no idea how she's managed to stay single this long.

She's beautiful. Smart. Funny. Kind. And innocent... fuck, the way her cheeks are blushing.

The way she's leaning over the table, letting her eyelids fall together, parting her lips...

I could teach her so many things.

I could teach her everything.

But I can't.

She's my sister's best friend.

And as much as Em is a brat, she's all the family I've got.

These two are the most important people in my life.

My cock is going to have to cool it.

It's not getting anywhere near Kaylee.

Tempting

———

I sit on the Kelly green deck chair, the one under the old lamp with the too yellow bulb.

Even though we're in one of the most crowded cities in Southern California, the beach is empty. Still. All the voices and laughter are coming from the house. The roar of the ocean isn't enough to muffle the party.

I should head inside and kick out Emma's friends. Insist on driving Kaylee back to her place. Lecture both of them about drinking too much.

But I'm not in the mood to play Dad today. I'm tired of playing Dad, period. Emma and I never got along, not exactly, but we used to have a rapport. We were a team. A *you're annoying, but not quite as annoying as Mom or Dad* team, but we were still a fucking team.

Now, the majority of my relationship is lecturing her and yelling some equivalent of *go to your room*.

And her yelling back *you're not my dad*.

I force myself to look out at the ocean.

It's beautiful. Dark water. Soft sand. Stars bright enough to shine against the black sky but dulled by light pollution all the same.

None of it distracts me.

None of the eight million things going on in my life distract me.

I need a way to get Kaylee out of my head. I've tried everything—work, play, other women, fucking myself, not fucking myself.

Nothing helps.

I pull out my sketchbook and flick my pen a few times. A few more. My warm up sketch is a messy abstract shape. It means something, I'm sure, but I don't have a clue what that is.

I turn the page. Outline the octopus going on Will's bicep tomorrow afternoon. Attempt to fill in the shading.

The details don't come. The only image in my mind is Kaylee. The brightness in her green eyes, the smile spreading over her pink lips, that coy hip tilt. Like she knows how badly I want my hands on those hips.

Like she's going to roll that dress up her thighs, place her palms on the table, and shoot me a *please, fuck me now* look.

I don't need a tattoo mockup.

I need her naked in my bed.

"Hey." The side door slides open and Kaylee steps outside. Her steps aren't soft the way they normally are.

They're messy. Quick.

Her eyes are brighter than normal.

Bolder.

She plops on the lounge chair, next to me. Her thigh presses against mine. Her fingers skim the edges of my sketchbook.

She leans over my shoulder, pressing her chest against my arm, looking up at me with those doe eyes. "Can I see?"

Not the sketchbook. The shit I have in here, of her, will terrify her. Kaylee is sweet. Innocent. I haven't asked, but I'd bet—I have bet Dean—she's a virgin.

My cock rouses at the thought of being the first inside her. Fuck, my lips, my tongue, my fingers—every part of me wants to be her first.

Not happening.

"You looking for a nautical tattoo?" I shoot back.

Her smile spreads over her cheeks. "Maybe. What do you suggest?"

I drag my fingertips over her shoulder, drawing the

shape that best suits her. It's a bad idea, touching her like this. It's doing shit to me.

And from the way her eyelids are pressing together and her lips are parting with a sigh, I'm pretty sure it's doing shit to her.

Fuck, I need a thousand cold showers.

Even if Kaylee wasn't Em's best friend, she's a sweet girl. Someone who deserves a nice guy. A guy who can give her a normal life. Not an asshole who destroys everything he touches.

Even so, I trace the outline of a would-be tattoo up to the tip of her shoulder. "A mermaid."

"I like it."

"I know. You've seen *The Little Mermaid* a thousand times."

"At least two thousand." She looks up at me. "What do you say? Right now? I'm finally old enough to sign the form."

"Okay." I take her hand and pull her to her feet. "Let's walk to the shop. One topless mermaid."

Her eyes go wide. She stammers, presses her toes together. The plastic of her heels clicks. Her teeth sink into her lip. "I, uh..."

"Hate having your bluff called?"

"No, I just... I need to think about it a little more."

"Bullshit." I can't help but smile. She's adorable flustered.

"No, just regular... uh... that isn't why I came out here."

I arch a brow.

She scoots toward me. It's a tiny movement. Soft. More like the Kaylee I know. The sober one.

"Well, it's my birthday." Her fingers curl around my wrist. "And I want a birthday kiss."

How about a birthday fuck? How about a birthday coming on my face until my lips are numb?

"I only give birthday spankings." My voice is steady even though my heart is pounding against my chest. Fuck, the thought of bending Kaylee over that table and—

"Okay." She presses her lips together. "Let's go. Right here, right now."

"You can handle eighteen?"

She nods.

She can't, but it's tempting anyway...

"Let's go, Brendon." She takes my hand and places it on her hip. Her eyes meet mine. They bore into mine. They demand every thought in my head. Or at least all the ones about stripping her naked. "Or did I call your bluff?"

"Bend over and place your hands on the glass if you want to find out." She *is* calling my bluff. And now I'm calling hers.

Only this is one time—

My sister saves me from my filthy thoughts. She bounces out the door, throws her arms around Kaylee, and pulls her from her seat. "Stop hiding from all the guys at the party."

"Your brother is a guy."

Emma scoffs. Her nose scrunches. It lights up her dark eyes—the same deep brown as mine. She runs her fingers through her violet hair and just barely restrains herself from rolling her eyes.

Kaylee's fingers brush the back of my hand as she turns toward Emma. "Sorry, Em, but it's undeniable. Just look at him."

Emma sticks out her tongue and mouths *gross*. "Mr. Look What a Brooding Bad Boy I Am will be here tomorrow." She grabs Kaylee's hand and pulls her toward the door. "These other guys won't." Emma looks to me. "You don't have to stay and supervise."

"Nice try," I say.

Emma laughs. She blows me a kiss then turns back to her best friend. "Don't wait up."

Kaylee's eyes meet mine. "Did you mean it?"

One part of me did. The rest of me knows better. I play coy. Shrug.

"I'll collect eventually."

"Birthdays only."

"Even so."

I watch her round hips sway as she walks away.

Fuck, that dress...

Fuck me.

How the hell am I going to get this girl out of my head?

Get *Tempting* Now

Author's Note

Thank you for reading *Losing It*. I hope you loved Wes and Quinn's story as much as I did (awkward virgins are so fun, aren't they?), and I hope you look forward to Juliette and Griffin's story, *Accidental Husband*, coming Spring 2019.

If you enjoyed this novel, please help other readers find it by leaving an honest review on Amazon or Goodreads.

Want news about new releases and sales before anyone else? How about exclusive sneak peeks and bonus scenes? Sign up for the Crystal Kaswell mailing list.

If you love to review and want to get books before anyone else, join the Crystal Kaswell ARC team.

Want to talk books? I love hearing from my readers. You can find me on Facebook or join my Facebook group.

You can find more of my books here.

Acknowledgements

My first thanks goes to my husband, for his support when I'm lost in bookland and for generally being the sun in my sky. Sweetheart, you're better than all the broken bad boys in the world.

The second goes to my father, for insisting I go to the best film school in the country, everything else be damned. I wouldn't love movies, writing, or storytelling half as much if not for all our afternoon trips to the bookstore and weekends at the movies. You've always been supportive of my goals, and that means the world to me.

Thanks so much to my amazing audio narrators, Kai Kennicott and Wen Ross. You always bring my characters to life in a way that blows my mind.

A big shout out to all my beta readers. You helped give me the confidence to put out a book a little more heartbreaking than usual. And also to my ARC readers for helping spread the word to everyone else in the world.

A special thanks to my fellow pop-punk addict, Molle, for fangirling over music with me, for talking me through my business decisions, and for reminding me that loving my work matters as much as all the marketing money in the world.

Athena Wright, you are the best author friend a girl could ask for. Thank you for your feedback, for being my chat buddy, and for always being there to give me the perspective I need. And thank you for mocking me when I deserve it and telling me no when I need to hear it.

Thanks so much to my editor Marla, my designers Okay Creations and Tempting Illustrations, and to Wander Aguiar for the amazing cover photo.

As always, my biggest thanks goes to my readers. Thank you for picking up *Losing It*. I hope you'll be back for Juliette and Griffin's book *Accidental Husband*.

Stay In Touch

Sign up for <u>my mailing list</u>.

You can also <u>join my Facebook group</u>, <u>like my page on Facebook</u>, or <u>friend me on Facebook</u>.

Also by Crystal Kaswell

Sinful Serenade

Sing Your Heart Out - Miles

Strum Your Heart Out - Drew

Rock Your Heart Out - Tom

Play Your Heart Out - Pete

Sinful Ever After – series sequel

Dangerous Noise

Dangerous Kiss - Ethan

Dangerous Crush – Kit

Dangerous Rock – Joel

Dangerous Fling – Mal

Dangerous Encore - series sequel

Inked Hearts

Tempting - Brendon

Hooking Up - Walker

Pretend You're Mine - Ryan

Hating You, Loving You - Dean

Breaking the Rules - Hunter

Losing It - Wes

Accidental Husband - Griffin - coming spring 2019

more coming in 2019

Standalones

Broken - Trent & Delilah

Come Undone - A Love Triangle

Dirty Rich

Dirty Deal - Blake

Dirty Boss - Nick

Sign up for the Crystal Kaswell mailing list